People We Love

People We Love

Jenny Harper

Published by Accent Press Ltd 2015

ISBN: 9781783752614

Acknowledgements

In 2012 I happened to spot a feature in one of the newspaper colour supplements about refugees fleeing the Blue Nile state for the border with South Sudan. The article comprised mainly an extraordinary set of photographs by Shannon Jensen of hundreds of pairs of shoes worn by the refugees. The images of these battered and worn-out shoes, mismatched flip-flops and flimsy pumps were extraordinarily powerful and triggered the idea for *People We Love*. Thank you Shannon Jensen.

Some years ago I read about an elderly woman who had been placed in a care home twelve miles from the village in which she had lived all her life. One day, she walked back and climbed in through her former kitchen window. She was in her eighties. This was also an extraordinary story, and I couldn't help but speculate about the strength of the instincts that had driven her to make that walk.

The shoes in the catalogue notes that appear at the beginning of each chapter in *People We Love* fall into four categories. They are based on either real characters from history, or on contemporary stories I have seen or read about. (A few relate to my own family!) A few are completely generic, chosen because the stories they tell fascinated me (the 'concealment shoes' in Chapter One, for example), or they relate to the main characters in my book: Lexie, Patrick, Pavel, Martha and Tom in particular. I hope they give you as much pleasure in the reading as I had in the researching and writing.

One Note requires particular mention. In Chapter Twenty-six I describe handmade gentlemen's shoes that belonged to Edwin Garrett. His widow, Elizabeth, wished them to be enjoyed and appreciated and they were given to the charity *500 miles*, inspired by Olivia Giles. The last few chapters of this book were written in Elizabeth's cliff-top retreat south of Aberdeen and I owe her huge thanks for her generosity in letting me use this facility.

I came across Brian Ashbee's essay, 'Artbollocks', and loved it. It first appeared in the April issue of *Art Quarterly*, 1999, and the full text can be found online.

As usual, thanks are due to all my writing friends and supporters, without whose continued encouragement I might have given up. Particular thanks are due to Eileen Ramsay, Bill Daly and Jane Knights. The team at Accent Press has been terrific, and has done a magnificent job in turning my words into a book, with support all along the line.

Finally, I received special support from my friend Dr Elizabeth Goring, a knowledgeable former museum curator, Mediterranean archaeologist and contemporary jewellery authority whose insight and perceptiveness, not to mention expertise in exhibition curation, proved invaluable. I am deeply indebted.

Note: Hailesbank and The Heartlands

The small market town of Hailesbank is born of my imagination, as are the surrounding villages of Forgie and Stoneyford and the council housing estate known as Summerfield, which together form The Heartlands. I have placed the area, in my mind, to the east of Scotland's capital city, Edinburgh.

The first mention of The Heartlands was made by Agrippus Centorius in AD77, not long after the Romans began their surge north in the hope of conquering this savage land. 'This is a place of great beauty,' wrote Agrippus, 'and its wildness has clutched my heart.' He makes several mentions thereafter of The Heartlands. There are still signs of Roman occupation in Hailesbank, which has great transport links to the south (and England) and the north, especially to Edinburgh, and its proximity to the sea and the (real) coastal town of Musselburgh made it a great place to settle. The Georgians and Victorians began to develop the small village, its clean air and glorious views, rich farming hinterland and great transport proving highly attractive.

The River Hailes flows through the town. There is a Hailes Castle in East Lothian (it has not yet featured in my novels), but it sits on the Tyne.

Hailesbank has a Town Hall and a high street, from which a number of ancient small lanes, or vennels, run down to the river, which once was the lifeblood of the town.

In my novels, characters populate the shops, cafes and pubs in Hailesbank and the pretty adjoining village of Forgie, with Summerfield inhabitants providing another layer of social interaction.

You can meet other inhabitants of the town and area in *Face the Wind and Fly*, *Loving Susie* and *Maximum Exposure* – with more titles to follow!

JH

'SHOES TELL STORIES'

Stories of much-loved babies, who can't even walk; of the tottering steps of little children towards adulthood; of special events in our lives; of dances, and marriages, and mountain climbs and escapes.

Artist Alexa Gordon's latest paintings capture a number of moving life stories.

You are cordially invited to the opening of her exhibition in Hailesbank on Friday 24th January.

RSVP

Chapter One

Catalogue number 15: Child's shoe. 16th-century? 'Concealment shoe'. Found in rafters of agricultural worker's cottage outside Hailesbank. Donors: Eric and Sheila Flint, Forgie. 'Concealment shoes' have been found concealed in wall cavities, chimneys, or among roof rafters of many old houses. They were thought to ward off evil.

When Jamie was alive, Alexa Gordon wore hippy dresses in luminous colours and danced barefoot on the lawn at midnight.

When Jamie was alive, they ate drizzle cake and made scones heaped high with cream and jam.

When Jamie was alive, she had a future.

And then it all changed.

I don't know what you thought you were doing, she said silently to her brother for the hundredth time, getting into that car that night. You might have accepted the risk for yourself. But you had no right at all to ruin everyone else's lives.

She looked down at the bowl in front of her. Breakfast cereal stared back, sodden and limp. She pushed the dish away.

'You must eat, Alexa dear,' her mother Martha said, capturing a stray grey lock that was hanging in front of her face and twisting it round her fingers.

'Don't fuss, Mum,' Lexie answered without thinking.

Martha bit her lip and hunched into herself as she pulled her tired-looking peach candlewick dressing gown closer round her thin frame.

Idiot, Lexie chided herself. *It's the anniversary of Jamie's death. Think before speaking, today of all days.*

The problem was that her mother's tendency to fuss had

1

become an obsession with her wellbeing. It was understandable, but sometimes hard to bear. Lexie looked down at her plate. She had barely touched the cereal.

'It's gone soggy,' she said, trying to be conciliatory. 'If I make toast, will you have some?'

Concern could run both ways.

She saw Martha's mouth twitch at the corners. Whatever else she might be, her mother wasn't stupid.

'A little,' Martha touched her hand lightly. 'If you have time.'

Lexie stood up and cleared her plate from the table. Living at Fernhill again was both strange and stiflingly familiar. She was thirty years old and once believed she could build a career as an artist. Now all she had to remember this by was a tattoo round her thumb and hair the colour of a scarlet ibis, plus a tendency to see everything in terms of how it might be captured on canvas.

Thanks for nothing, Jamie—

'Brown bread okay?'

'Fine. Thank you.'

She cut two slices and pushed them into the toaster. Outside the tall sash window, the garden was blanketed in an early morning mist. In the far corner, by the pergola, she could just see the blossom on the cherry tree, delicate and wraithlike.

'I do appreciate this, Alexa. Your being here, I mean.'

A blackbird took off from one of the branches and a small flurry of petals swirled softly towards the grass. Lexie pursed her lips. How could she fail to know this? Martha's thanks were expressed ten times a day, their utterance a delicate trap. She was all her parents had left and she had to be there for them. This meant, she told herself, that she did *not* regret marching into Patrick Mulgrew's gallery in Edinburgh a year ago and telling him she was withdrawing her exhibition.

Even though it meant the end of their relationship as well.

Her throat swelled with unshed tears and she had to summon all her willpower to push away the hurt she still felt at their separation. Thinking about Patrick wouldn't do any good. Instead, she retrieved the toast and rearranged her face into her

2

customary jaunty smile before she turned round.

'I know you do. Come on, Mum. Let's eat. Then I must get to work. I take it Dad left early?'

She didn't really need to ask. Where her mother was all dependence, Tom Gordon had turned into The Great Provider – strong, uncompromising and utterly resistant to any kind of conversation about his son.

Martha's eyes glazed over.

Some family we've become, Lexie thought. Surely we weren't always like this?

'I'd better go, Mum. Dad's called a special meeting.'

'Please be tolerant, darling. I know he's obsessive about the store, but it's because he wants to show he loves us.'

'I am tolerant. Most of the time, anyway.'

She and her father were two of a kind in many ways. They certainly both threw themselves into work as a diversion.

'Will you be all right? What are you going to do today?'

Martha stood up. Her dressing gown hung off her body in loose, sad folds. Once she'd been a legal secretary – smart, efficient and very organised. Grief was eating her up.

'I'm going,' she said, 'to do some gardening. I think.'

Lexie found the shifts in her mother's character profoundly unsettling. And now she had to prepare to be unsettled all over again, because her walk to work would take her past Patrick Mulgrew's house.

Ten minutes later, Lexie stepped through the front door of Fernhill and pulled it closed. It was eight thirty in the morning and she tried to leave the ache of loss behind her in the gloomy spaces that had once been filled with laughter. She tugged her old tweed jacket closer, glad of its warmth. There was no point in being bitter. It was a waste of time to think about the things that might have been.

Despite the obvious truth of this, there was no way of avoiding Patrick's house. It took seven minutes to cover the distance between Fernhill and The Gables. Seven minutes of separation. For a brief time she and Patrick had both found it amusing that he lived in Hailesbank near her parents while she

3

lived in Edinburgh, near his gallery. They hadn't been together long enough to change that.

Three minutes. She reached the end of James Street and crossed onto Darnley Place. Patrick's continued proximity was a fleabite that itched, she reminded herself, nothing more. She didn't care about him now: she could never have sustained a relationship with Patrick because they were too different. The way she saw it, she put family first and Patrick thought only about profit. Better to find that out sooner rather than at some point in the future, when they might have become knotted together, like roots round a boulder, so that separating would tear at the fabric of life.

Six minutes. Patrick owned a smart art gallery – or, to be more precise two, one in London and one in Edinburgh. People saw him as either discriminating and astute or snobbish and arrogant. Lexie lengthened her stride. She found it impossible to forget Patrick because everything that mattered to her was so tightly entwined with him: ambition, career, and passion. Was that why she'd loved him so much? In the short time they'd been together, he'd taken her heart, her body and her brain – the complete package – and made them all his.

Seven minutes. There it was now, a million pounds' worth of sandstone and lawn, the epitome of everything the man stood for – style, statement and substance. Crow-stepped gables, baronial turrets and an old Scots pine standing sentinel by the gate.

Lexie glanced down at the tattoo round her thumb. 'ARTBOLLOCKS' it read – an indelible statement of belief about art and honesty.

'Why disfigure your beautiful hands like that?' Patrick had once asked, tracing the letters with his long fingers as they'd lain limb to limb, half drugged by ardour.

'So that I never forget,' she'd answered fiercely, 'about pretentiousness.'

He'd lifted her thumb to his lips and kissed each letter, one at a time. Eleven feathery kisses.

'You're very different,' he'd said, 'but I think I might just be in love with you.'

His car wasn't there, she noted, which was a relief. They'd learned politeness this last year, but kept their distance. Too many words had been spoken that could never be unsaid. Still – he didn't know it – but fending off the hurt she felt about their break-up was like rolling back the tide: impossible.

By the time she arrived at the Thompson Memorial Park, the mist was beginning to lift and the park was already alive with its quota of elderly dog-walkers and mums with buggies. She glanced right – a habit she had developed – to catch a glimpse of the river as it flowed past the foot of Fisher's Wynd. She found the water soothing and it worked its magic again this morning because at last she was able to put Patrick firmly out of her mind and focus on Jamie. This was his day, after all, and despite her anger about his death, he'd always be a part of her.

Stay with me, bro.

When she reached Kittle's Lane she turned right, so that she'd pass Cobbles. If Pavel was in the shop already, she'd wave to him.

Lexie adored Cobbles. She loved the jumble of antiques Pavel seemed able to conjure up from nowhere. Each object, however humble, had a story to tell. A stone hot water bottle shivered out a tale of freezing nights in icy beds; a moustache cup in fine porcelain whispered of male vanity; a carpet beater, twisted from rattan into a Celtic knot, hinted at the hard labour that housework once was. Most of all, Lexie loved the vintage clothes that peeked tantalisingly from cubbyholes or begged for attention from serried ranks of hangers on rails at the back of the shop. She was addicted to vintage.

Half way down the lane, she spotted Pavel Skonieczna sashaying out of the shop. He placed his sandwich board on the pavement and stepped back to admire it, his hands wafting up to his mouth with characteristic grace. COBBLES, read the elegant copperplate script, ANTIQUES AND COLLECTIBLES. Lexie smiled. Pavel (always dressed in vintage, always colourful) was the perfect advertisement for his own shop. Today he was smart in green tweed – his favourite suit – teamed with a mustard moleskin waistcoat and brown brogues.

She speeded up. 'Pavel! Hi!'

Shoulders straightened and tweed turned. 'Lexie. Darling. You're early today.'

Lexie grimaced. 'I know. Dad's called a staff meeting before we open.'

Pavel shook his head. 'You shouldn't be working in that place. It's not right for you.'

Spot on, Pavel. Like trying to shove a jelly through a sieve and expecting it to come out whole on the other side.

'I know. But what can I do?'

'Stand up for yourself. You always used to. They use you.'

'It's not that simple.'

She let her parents use her, because she had to. It was the only way she could think of to make things better. It was her way of helping herself as well.

'You're a good daughter.'

Lexie hesitated. Pavel confided recently that his partner Guy had died some years ago and he'd moved to Hailesbank to escape the sad memories. His only family now was a snake of a sister who had disowned him and, because he never talked about it, Lexie guessed how much it hurt him.

Pavel spared her the embarrassment of having to think about what to say.

'Is it about that marketing plan?'

'I expect so.'

She'd spent the last month working with Neil Taylor, the assistant manager at her father's furniture store, on a plan designed to drag the old family business protesting and spluttering into the twenty-first century. Or rather, Neil had been working on it, in his careful, business-like way, and she had been attempting to modernise the store by selecting more stylish stock and updating the layout. At least, that's how she saw her role. Her father was proving resistant to change.

'I'm a bit nervous, Pavel, to tell you the truth.'

'Do you think he'll veto it?'

Lexie shrugged and pulled her jacket across her chest. The sun might be dappling the river already, but it hadn't dropped in on Kittle's Lane yet.

'You know Dad.'

6

Compassion glowed in Pavel's eyes and Lexie looked away. Sympathy was always the hardest part of friendship to accept.

'I must dash,' she said. 'Sorry.'

'Good luck, darling.'

'Thanks!'

The store where Lexie was heading was at the east end of the High Street. It was part of a run of shops built in the mid-nineteenth century when Hailesbank had been at its most prosperous. Her great-grandfather had taken up the first lease, and the sign he'd proudly commissioned to run above the entire shopfront was still there.

GORDON'S FURNITURE EMPORIUM (EST. 1892)

The elaborate letters were painted in pure gold leaf on a forest green background and the whole sign was covered in protective glass so that, a century and a half later, it still announced its presence with undimmed glory.

'The trouble is,' Neil had observed when they'd studied the frontage as part of their research, 'that sign is probably the last smart thing left in the whole place.'

He'd put his finger on the problem. Was there really any need to look further to discover why Gordon's was struggling for survival?

Lexie pushed open the heavy oak door and marched in. A man was standing by the overstuffed chesterfield, the tartan one she particularly disliked. He was around six feet tall and strongly built, with wide shoulders and narrow hips, and he was casually dressed in a rugby shirt and jeans. One of the new guys from the removal firm, probably. She hadn't seen him before.

Or had she? Although he was facing away from her, towards the back of the store, there was something disturbingly familiar about the figure.

'Can I help you?' she said, the nagging in the recesses of her brain making her voice sharper than usual. 'We're not actually open yet.'

He whipped round.

'Christ! Where'd you materialise from? I didn't hear you come in.'

Lexie wasn't breathing. Why wasn't she breathing? It should be simple, shouldn't it? She did it all the time. She'd done it all her life, for heaven's sake.

'Cameron?'

The man stepped forward.

'You haven't changed a bit. Not even the hair, I see.'

Six years was a long time, yet it disappeared in an instant. Lexie's lungs inflated with sweet oxygen before a sense of devastation caught the back of her knees. She was drowning in desire again, just as she always used to be. Shocked by her reaction, she forced herself to look amused – one humiliation by Cameron Forrester was enough for a lifetime.

'Well, well, the wanderer returns. Have your folks killed the fatted calf?'

'Nah. Mum won't buy meat at the supermarket and the butcher's closed since I was last here. She made apple crumble for me. I've missed crumble.'

His grin was just as Alexa remembered it: irrepressible. The smile faded as he scanned her face. He'd changed. Once, he would just have flashed a wink and cracked a joke; now there was something more observant – or was it more calculating? – in the way he was studying her.

'Crumble, huh?'

The words emerged as a croak and she cleared her throat.

Cameron Forrester had been a member of the Hailesbank Hawks until injury had put him out of rugby for good. He still bore the scars: a broken nose that gave his face a lived-in look, and a scar under his chin from where a studded boot sliced it open in a hard-fought league game. 'Badges of honour', he used to say, when Lexie teased him about the nose or ran her fingers along the white seam of the scar.

'You're looking terrific.'

He took another step closer. Instinct made her edge away. How was it possible that he looked so like the Cameron she'd fallen in love with all those years ago?

'Am I?'

Her reserve seemed to fluster him.

'I've been away,' he said needlessly. 'Running activities for

8

children on a cruise ship. Children! Me! Can you imagine?'

'Not really, no.'

Questions scratched at her mind like horsehair. *Does he know about Jamie? Does he know I'm back living in Hailesbank? Is that why he's come?*

'So how are you, Lexie?'

He edged towards her for the third time. She clutched at a high-backed recliner, upholstered in gunmetal and steel blue chenille. The cloth felt coarse and unfriendly under her fingers, but this time she managed to stand her ground.

'Why did you leave, Cameron?'

Why didn't you write?

'I heard about Jamie,' he said. 'I'm so sorry.'

'Thank you.'

The stock response slipped out before she could stop it. It was what she always said whenever anyone offered condolences. Damn him! Using Jamie as a personal shield was unforgivable.

'What a bloody waste,' he blurted out.

People didn't usually say things like that. They tiptoed round the subject, they never trampled right through the heart of it.

'Oops,' he said, seeing her expression, 'Sorry. Me and my mouth. But honestly, it's true, isn't it? Jamie had so much going for him.'

'Can we leave this?'

'Shit. I'm not good at—'

Lexie swung away. She spotted a sagging cushion on a nearby sofa and grabbed it, bashing the middle to plump it up. *What are you good at, Cameron? Apart from breaking hearts.*

'Did you want something? I've got work to do.'

'Just to say hi. And see if you'd meet me for a drink after you're finished here.'

'*Meet* you?'

'Well,' he muttered, dropping his head in a semblance of repentance so that all she could see was a mass of thick, sandy hair. She didn't need to stroke it to remember how it felt.

'I owe you an explanation.'

'I really don't want to hear it.'

9

Liar! She really *did* want to hear it, but six years of hurt got in the way of admitting this.

'No. Fair enough.'

The grin was back, but wry – another new trait. Cameron had never been one for navel-gazing. He was a physical contact man. A cheerful, generous, blunder-in-feet-first-but-in-a-well-meaning-kind-of-way man. The absolute antithesis, now that she thought about it, of Patrick Mulgrew.

'Take your point.'

He ran his hand through his thatch so that it stood momentarily on end before tumbling, in the old way, down across his eyes again. When he turned to go, she was conscious of disappointment. At the door the grin reappeared, spiced this time with mischief.

'It's okay, I can see you need time to get used to me being back. It doesn't have to be today, we can meet up tomorrow. I'll call you.'

Infuriated by his presumption, her spirit returned and she hurled the cushion at him.

'Don't bother! I won't change my—'

But it fell, softly, a yard short and the heavy oak door swung on empty air.

Six years of silence and now he was back. Where did this leave her, for heaven's sake?

Chapter Two

Catalogue number 8: cavalry boots, spurs and leather gaiters. Donor: Janet McMurray, Inverness. 'These were the boots and gaiters my grandfather wore in the Battle of Omdurman in 1898, where he rode alongside Winston Churchill. Short boots with leather gaiters were more comfortable than the full cavalry boot.'

Capital Art in Heriot Row was bright and airy. The walls of the Georgian rooms were painted in Farrow and Ball's Strong White. Not Wimborne White or All White or Slipper Satin or any of the other near-white shades on offer, but Strong White which, in Patrick Mulgrew's opinion, was the exact shade required to set off any work of art he chose to hang on the wall. It was not so bright that the background glare overpowered the work itself, nor so creamy that the colour balance of the painting might be affected. And within these four walls, it was what Patrick said that went.

The floors were stripped floorboards (original, naturally) almost a foot wide and subtly mellowed with age. Discreet wires ran along the ceiling to allow lights to be suspended. They could be slid easily from one position to another to accommodate the changing displays. Above them, the elaborate cornice told of wealth. This had been the home, once, of a rich man.

Capital Art Edinburgh had been Patrick's first venture into art dealing, but his flagship gallery was in London. He spent time in both cities, and was planning to open his third gallery in New York so that he could reach a wider (and even wealthier) clientele. Today he'd felt compelled to be in Edinburgh, because it was the anniversary of Jamie Gordon's death.

He was here, but he was in a bad mood, and Victoria Hunter-Darling was bearing the brunt of his foul temper. Victoria was twenty-three and a year out of St Andrews University, where she'd completed a good degree in History of Art. Now she was embarking on the career of her dreams. Patrick scanned the list of sales and his thick eyebrows knitted alarmingly.

'I thought I left instructions that Lord Whitmuir was not to be allowed to reserve any more paintings until he's settled his outstanding account?'

Victoria shifted from one high-heeled foot to the other. (Patrick demanded style, but had banned anything that might mark the floor, so she spent a great deal of time searching for the perfect shoe).

'He was very insistent.'

'If he's stickered it, it's unavailable for other purchasers,' Patrick explained with what he hoped was patience, 'and he owes us too much money already. There's no way that man is going to remove another square inch of canvas from this gallery until he's paid his bill. Got it?'

Victoria chewed her upper lip and looked devastated.

'What should I do?'

He sighed. 'Take the bloody sticker off and I'll call him.'

Victoria, looking relieved, scurried off.

Patrick liked the comfort of money. The son of an Irish farmer, he'd spent a childhood on the wrong end of grind and poverty. When he'd turned eighteen, he'd been handed ten Irish pounds by his father and told he was on his own. That had been the day that he'd sworn a private but solemn oath that he'd do everything in his power to haul himself out of that life and into a better one.

He gazed around. The large gallery was showing works by a well-known Scottish Colourist. Patrick had used his contacts and his considerable personal charm to coax and wheedle the current owners to put them up for sale. The profits promised to be astronomical – which was why he would not, under any circumstances, allow Lord Whitmuir the slightest leeway. In the small gallery, he was showing the work of a young artist he had been cultivating for three years. Each small exhibition had raised the artist's standing and popularity and, therefore, the prices he was able to command for his work. In the same gallery, he had installed three glass cases to show high-value, hand-crafted jewellery. These were restocked on an ongoing basis and no item was allowed to remain there for more than two months. Unsold pieces were returned to the maker and replacements requested. Jewellers whose work declined in popularity were dropped. There was no room at Capital Art for sentiment.

This was why Alexa Gordon's bombshell a year ago had been so devastating – and why he still refused to forgive himself for crossing the strict boundaries he had set down for himself. Never get involved with employees or artists under contract.

Victoria reappeared.

'I've taken the sticker off.'

She proved the point by extending a pretty finger. Half a red dot adhered to the end.

Patrick muttered, 'Never again,' and marched off to the back door.

Victoria nodded eagerly.

'No, of course not, Patrick. Never again.'

In the modest but immaculately tended garden at the back of the gallery, Patrick was too agitated to sit down on the picturesque bench beside the life-sized sculpture of the woman reading a book. It was a favourite spot for smokers and he'd had many offers for 'Marlayne', but he was too fond of the bronze to sell her – another folly of sentiment. He fumbled briefly in the jacket of his exquisitely cut Italian wool jacket for his cigarettes before remembering that he'd given them up two years ago. There were times when he craved a cigarette, less for the nicotine high than for the blessed distraction of lighting the thing, the ritual of holding it, placing it to his lips, inhaling, tapping off the ash.

He glared at Marlayne. Was it because the figure reminded him a little of Lexie Gordon that he was so attached to it? He'd never confess to anyone (certainly not to Diana Golspie, the woman with whom he currently shared a bed when it suited him) that memories of Lexie still haunted him. He saw her in everything: not just in Marlayne, but also in the frisky gait of the terrier passing his door and in the fresh, clear skin of a baby left asleep in its buggy while its mother wandered the gallery. He saw something of her in every new protégé, only to find each fell short of the standards she'd set. Once he'd glimpsed a girl with hair the exact fuchsia pink of Lexie's and had begun to stride down the street after her, before realising that she was too tall by a foot.

Patrick allowed himself to scan Marlayne's curves. The tilt of the head was similar, and the relaxed way she was holding the book, but the neck was too short and the waist too broad, and the nose altogether too hooked. Lexie's nose turned up a little at the end.

He found he had stretched out a hand and cradled it round the figure's cheek. He snatched it away abruptly and swivelled on his heel.

Enough. He strode back into the gallery.

'Esther Goldwyn's just phoned,' Victoria said. 'She's excited about the piece in today's paper. She wants to talk.'

Patrick grunted. Esther was his latest signing. She was smart and talented, but she was not nearly as talented as Lexie. He hadn't found an artist in a decade with Alexa Gordon's gift for rich, evocative painting.

'Tell her I'm busy, but I'll phone later.'

He perched on the edge of the hand-crafted oak desk and picked up the phone. He was in no mood for compromise. It was a good time to call Lord Whitmuir.

'Who was that?'

As Cameron disappeared, Lexie turned to find Neil Taylor behind her, neat as a button and thin as a pin.

'No-one,' she said, breathless. 'Someone I – an old friend.'

As she took in the look on his face, thoughts of Cameron vanished.

'You've seen Dad.'

Neil was thirty-five – too old to still be an assistant in a

14

place like Gordon's. Once he'd had ambition but now he stayed out of loyalty to her father.

'Aye.'

'And?'

He shrugged.

Lexie clicked her tongue.

'Damn. I hoped we'd done it carefully enough to slip it past him. What's he said?'

'Not a lot.'

She'd always known this would be a difficult day, and it was certainly turning out that way. She stared bleakly at Neil's freckled face and tried to control her frustration. He was capable, organised and full of ideas, and he wasn't being given a chance. If anyone was right to step into Jamie's shoes, it was Neil – but her father wouldn't contemplate the thought. If they were not careful, there would be nothing to step into.

He's so bloody stubborn.

She'd never say it, of course. Instead, she hooked her arm through Neil's and turned him towards the back of the store with a cheerfulness that was far from what she felt.

'Don't worry. Rome wasn't built and all that. Let's try and salvage something, shall we?'

She felt him straighten up. She squeezed his elbow and smiled at him.

'Bet you a quid that Morag Toe-rag says "challenging retail climate" before the end of the meeting.'

'My guess is twice.'

'You're on.'

Lexie's father, Tommy Gordon, had been born into furniture retailing. He represented the third generation of Gordons in Hailesbank, and each one had towed the Emporium like a stately carriage forward to the next. Somewhere in the dusty archives, she knew, there was a faded sepia photograph of the front of the store shortly after it opened. Archibald Gordon, the founder, stood four-square on the pavement in front of the oak doors, stiff in dark suit and starched collar, a full set of moustaches making his thirty-something face look much older. Flanking him was an array of assistants and porters, clerical staff and cleaners, all proud as punch of their grand store.

She watched her father walk across the showroom floor and lower himself into the carver at the head of the mahogany table. The sense of family had always been strong. Once this had been an asset, but now he was beginning to bow under its burdens.

'We've got half an hour before we open and we need to do this quickly.'

It was nine thirty and already he looked worn out. The bags under his eyes were heavy enough for wheels and his skin was stretched taut over his jaw, pulling his lips into a thin line. She knew he couldn't have forgotten what day it was. Had he lain awake all night, thinking about Jamie, just as she had? She scanned the lines on his face, etched like deep furrows in a ploughed field, and felt a rush of protective love.

'We'll need to press on.'

He took out his half-moon reading glasses and looped the cord round his neck, then hooked them onto his nose. His eyebrows poked out over the top like unpruned bushes.

'Neil?'

'I'm expecting a rep from a new supplier from Sheffield.' Neil pushed a catalogue across the table. 'He's not offering anything too radical, but it's a little more contemporary than our current stock. We need to have something for the younger buyers of the new Morrice Homes, the show house opened at the weekend and—'

Tom flicked through the book and pushed it back.

'Not now, Neil. Let's stick with what we know sells.'

Lexie knew she had to show solidarity.

'Neil's right, Dad. There's a whole new market out there and we're not tapping into it.'

There was a doleful voice from her right: Morag Ferguson, the office manager-cum-bookkeeper. Morag, with her frizzy perm and round glasses, was a leftover from another era, a time when jobs were easy-come, easy-go and credit cards were 'flexible friends'. She found double-dip-recession trading deeply uncomfortable.

'We can't take risks. Not in this challenging retail climate.'

Lexie could feel Neil pressing on her foot and faked a sneeze to disguise a bubble of laughter.

'Sorry. Beg pardon.' She needed this laugh.

'I'm afraid I have to go with Morag on this one,' Tom said, oblivious. 'Neil, just replace the stock we sold. After all, if we shifted it once, we can do it again, it's obviously popular.'

'We could sell loads if we had more contemporary stuff to offer,' Lexie persisted, but her father's face had closed down. She gave up and opened her sketchbook. Sometimes she found drawing easier than talking. She drew a frown, then glasses, then her father's face took shape round it. A few squiggles and she captured the sense of hunched shoulders and stress. She could see Morag squinting across at the drawing and flipped the page over quickly. How she viewed her father was private.

'Windows,' Tom said, flicking through the pile of papers in front of him. 'Alexa?'

'It's nearly Easter. Let's do something really Spring-like and colourful, something that'll lift people's spirits, get them excited about coming in.'

'There's no budget,' Morag said in a flash. 'In this challenging—'

'Retail climate,' Lexie interrupted, wrinkling her nose in Neil's direction because he had won their bet, 'I know. But I can do it cheaply. It may not even cost us a penny.'

'Fine. So long,' Tom added with the once-easy smile, 'as there are no bunnies or chicks.' It was a laudable attempt to lighten the discussion. 'Morag, I'm sure we can find something in the budget if we have to. Which brings me to this marketing plan.'

He opened the file she and Neil had spent so much time on.

'Thank you for doing this.'

Lexie's fingers tightened round her pencil. His voice said it all; he didn't want to upset them, but knew he was going to have to.

'I do appreciate all the trouble you've gone to, but we're going to have to put it aside for now. The costs you've shown for setting up a fully functional website are huge. And we'd have to spend a lot on literature.' He flicked the pages again. 'We can't afford the investment right now. Besides, we're a traditional, long-established store and that's what people come to us for.'

But not enough people.

'We can't be certain about our market unless we do a survey, Dad.'

'Even a survey would cost us.' He looked at her above his half-moon spectacles. 'It's not for now, Alexa. Sorry.'

There was exhaustion in his voice. She snapped her sketchbook shut. Something inside her head muttered, *If you don't like my plans, what am I doing here?* This wasn't the time to talk about it. She'd speak to him privately. Later. Soon. If she wasn't going to win this fight, maybe the time had come for her to claim back her own career.

'We'll look through it again and see if we can come up with some cheaper options.'

It wasn't a good compromise – the marketing plan should be coherent and strategic, not a kind of pick-and-mix – but it was the best she could think of for now.

Tom shuffled his papers together.

'Fine. Thank you. We'd better open up.'

'You owe me a quid,' Neil muttered as they headed off.

Lexie grimaced at him and pulled a coin out of her purse.

Morag, jostling past, ducked to peer at it, the flyaway, dried-up ends of her permed hair tickling Alexa's chin.

'What's that for?'

Lexie winked at Neil above Morag's head. Without such tiny pleasures, she'd go insane.

Chapter Three

Catalogue number 13: White clog-style leather slip-on comfort shoe, with leather insoles and shock-absorbing heel. Used by neurosurgeon Alastair Whyte during operations. Donor: Alastair Whyte, Edinburgh. 'During complex, life-saving operations, it's vital that you are thinking only of the task in hand, and are not distracted by discomfort or tiredness,' says Alastair Whyte.

The day went from bad to worse. Lexie's best friend Molly called at lunchtime, just as she was about to pull on her jacket and head up to Cobbles. While Gordon's slid shamefacedly towards oblivion, Molly was hard at work building a hugely successful enterprise at Fleming House, a Georgian mansion at the heart of a large local country estate. She'd only launched herself into the job a year ago, but her enthusiasm and sheer hard graft were paying off in a big way. The house had already become a prime venue for weddings, corporate dinners and country fairs and Molly was working on plans to convert the Home Farm into a top-notch restaurant and conference centre. Perpetually rushing, she sounded breathless now.

'Hi Lexie, have you seen *Scotland Daily*?'

'Haven't had a minute. Why?'

'Oh, nothing. Well, it's just a little article in the arts section.'

Lexie groaned. She knew exactly what Molly was going to say.

'Don't tell me. Patrick's found a new genius.'

Molly was apologetic. 'Something like that. Sorry.'

Patrick had a knack of discovering new talent, usually young painters or photographers just a year or two out of college, and then proceeding to make them into high-value artists. Being chosen for an exhibition at Capital Art was the pinnacle of a young artist's ambition. Lexie knew how he worked because she'd been one of the chosen few.

Molly said into the silence, 'He'll take you back, you know, when you're ready.'

'You're wrong. Patrick never forgives and never forgets.'

'Then hell mend him.'

Lexie couldn't help smiling at her vehemence.

'Thanks, Moll, you're a true pal. And thanks for letting me know.'

Molly knew all about the row, of course, but she knew nothing about the affair with Patrick. Lexie had never told anyone – not even her best friend – about the irresistible tide that had swept her from the safety of single status and into Patrick's arms, and discretion had proved to be its own reward because it had been over almost as soon as it had begun. The last thing she'd needed a year ago was people concerning themselves about her love life. Besides, she was now convinced that Patrick had an affair with every new protégé, so what was there to tell?

'How are you today, Lex?' Molly said, 'do you want to meet?'

Lexie was touched at her concern.

'Maybe later? Are you free this evening?'

'There are no events on, but I'm really busy. As usual.'

Lexie thought of what her evening would be like, alone with her parents. If they could only sit round the table and talk about Jamie, maybe even laugh at good memories shared, it wouldn't be nearly so painful, but they were a long way from that, too many questions were still unanswered.

'I'll call later and see how you're fixed. I'd really appreciate a drink.'

'No probs. Bye, Lexie—'

'Oh, Molly—' Lexie was going to tell her about Cameron, but Molly had already hung up.

Hailesbank was still a relatively unspoiled market town. Once it had been a wealthy place, now it managed to thrive simply because it was within easy commuting distance of Edinburgh. In the centre there were a few fine fifteenth- and sixteenth-century buildings and some grand Georgian houses. The Victorians had added stone-built terraces, arranged like ribs on either side of a spine. A maze of small vennels and wynds lined with workers' cottages meandered from these like arteries down to the vital life-blood of the River Hailes, after which the town was named. Lexie headed down one of these vennels at lunchtime, with a sandwich in one hand and a copy of *Scotland Daily* in the other. The sun was blazing down and, in the first lucky break of the day, her favourite bench was free.

When she could put it off no longer, she opened the newspaper. The story about Patrick was on the arts pages, as expected. 'MULGREW'S MAGIC: A STAR IS BORN'. There was a photograph of him staring at a beaming girl so fresh-faced, despite the heavily-kohled eyes and scarlet lips, that Lexie guessed she was straight out of college. According to the caption, her name was Esther Goldwyn. The picture credit read 'Joey Wilkinson'.

She didn't bother with any more. She closed her eyes and tilted her face to the sun. Joey Wilkinson. Wasn't he the photographer who'd taken her picture last year? She could still see his long, thin face and dark eyes, intense and focused as he'd set up his lights and composed his shot.

'Could you just look at your painting, Lexie? Chin up a little more? That's it, excellent. Patrick, if you could turn your face to the camera ... Perfect.'

And it had been. Except that the pictures had never been used, because before the article had been published, Jamie had died, Lexie had pulled out of the show to come home, and the whole edifice of the career she'd been building had collapsed around her.

Lexie shifted uncomfortably. Now the vintage clothes she was wearing were too hot. They hadn't heard of breathable fabric in the 1950s. Why was Patrick creeping into her mind today of all days? She didn't want to think about him, with his expensive Italian tailoring and all the other expensive trappings he so prized. She particularly didn't want to think about the mad black hair or the clever eyes that had snared her with their quick humour.

'You finished with yer paper, hen?'

She opened her eyes. A man was standing in front of her, gesturing at the newspaper, which had slipped from her fingers onto the bench beside her.

'Sure. I was just going to chuck it away.'

She handed it over and stood up. Who cared about Patrick Mulgrew anyway? Besides, she had someone else to think about: Cameron.

From up on the High Street came the sound of the clock on the town hall striking two – ding, ding – just as it had rung for more than two hundred years, chasing folk back to work. No time to drop in on Pavel now, the 1940s dresses would have to wait.

The twenty-first century office is peculiarly quiet. Business is conducted on the internet and by email, and human contact can be minimal. Even Lexie, to her shame, exchanged a stream of emails every day with Neil, who sat in the room next door – so when the telephone rang in the middle of the afternoon, she guessed who it was before she picked it up.

'Alexa, it's Mum here.'

She had been refining her ideas for the Easter window. She had sourced a chartreuse green sofa that could be returned later and was playing with the idea of purple and scarlet cushions. If she added a riot of hyacinths and crocuses, daffodils and narcissus, the colour scheme would sing. She clicked on a link to Designers Guild and spotted the perfect fabric. Gran Paradiso, Rose. Bouquets of glorious flowers in a deep pink leapt off the fabric. It would be the only item she needed to spend money on, so Morag could lump it, challenging retail climate or not. She had to have drapes for the room set or the whole effect would fall flat.

'Hello, Mum.'

'I thought we might have fish tonight, darling. What do you think?'

From the sublime to the ridiculous.

22

'Didn't Carlotta come round?'

'*Boquerones.*'

'Oh.'

'And *puntillitas.*'

'I see.'

Carlotta had arrived in Hailesbank as an au pair some years ago and her exotic, olive-skinned beauty had set the entire Hailesbank Hawks squad into a lather before she'd settled on the captain, Jonas Wood. Jonas was a bull of a man, a mountain of solid beef. He could scoop Carlotta under his arm and charge for the posts with her as easily as he could tuck away a rugby ball, but his love for her shone like a star in the night sky, unwavering and constant. She'd given up the au pairing when they'd married and taken to cooking instead. Jonas required considerable feeding. Now she ran Besalú, a tapas restaurant in Hailesbank, where her dishes found popular approval. Since Jamie's death she'd become extraordinarily attentive to Lexie's parents and Lexie wondered if it might be because she missed her own family, back in Spain. She loved to shower Martha and Tom with Spanish culinary treats ('just little leftovers') – but her parents were conservative in their tastes and viewed some of the offerings with considerable uncertainty. Lexie wasn't entirely sure what *boquerones* or *puntillita*s were, but she guessed they were under suspicion.

Lexie didn't understand Carlotta's constant gifts, nor did she entirely trust her motives. It wasn't as if she and Carlotta were close, or that Carlotta had been a special friend of Jamie's. At the same time, she had to admit that her visits had brought relief to her mother – many of Martha's friends didn't know how to offer comfort. They were embarrassed about Jamie – not because he was dead but because he was found to have been catastrophically drunk when he'd crashed his car.

Martha was saying, 'So I wondered if you might have time to pop into the fishmonger's? Would you mind terribly?'

'No problem.' *She knows I'll do it, and that even if I do mind, I'll pretend I don't.*

And so the circular dance went on.

Resigned to the inevitable, she texted Molly with a brave

apology.

'Can't make tonite. Soz. 2morro?'

She was itching to tell her about Cameron, but jungle tom-toms beat loud and Molly probably already knew.

Cameron Forrester had taken up residence in Lexie's head and she'd decided that she would evict him before she reached the Thompson Memorial Park. These days her life seemed to be filled with small milestones and targets.

Just get through till five o'clock.

Just get through the night.

Just get through this year.

So now it seemed entirely natural to give herself permission to think about Cameron for ten minutes, on the understanding that at the Park she'd banish him. It was a feeling, rather than thoughts, that filled her; a glorious all-pervading warmth. *Desire.* How strange that she should still find Cameron attractive, even after what he'd done – and how infuriating.

The elaborate gates of the Park were in front of her and for a few steps Lexie struggled with her resolution. She kicked against dismissing Cameron so soon, but she knew that to dwell on his return would be a mistake, and to read anything into his motives, madness. Still … Maybe she could walk the long way, round the *outside* of the Park, so it didn't count? But what would that achieve? She stuck to her resolution, went into the Park, and thought about recipes for trout instead.

Patrick left the gallery early. He hadn't intended to, any more than he'd meant to work in Edinburgh today, but he was impelled towards Hailesbank by the idea that he might see Lexie. Naturally, he didn't admit this to anyone, least of all to himself. Rather, he had decided that he must call his agent in New York and because no-one in Edinburgh was yet aware of his plans for expansion, that this had to be done from the privacy of his home office.

He turned off the dual carriageway onto the slip road to Hailesbank. A deer skipped out from thick bushes to his right. Patrick braked, but managed to avoid swerving. The deer was pretty. It was a young one, pale russet with creamy patches along the ridge of its backbone. He had time to look right into its wide, startled eyes (which reminded him, inevitably, of Lexie), before the fawn skidded to a halt, swayed into an uncertain turn, and fled back into the wood. Patrick slid down into second and picked up speed again, trying to ignore how shaken the near miss had left him.

Everything reminded him of Lexie today. And if he was finding it a day for wallowing in memories, how must she be feeling? He itched to press her number on the Bluetooth connection in the car, the one he'd never managed to delete, but he knew it was impossible. There had been moments over the past year when there might have been the chink of an opportunity to say something, to put things right, but pride had intervened and he'd neglected to seize any of them.

He glanced at the Patek Phillipe on his wrist. The watch was another symbol of success. Patrick liked tangible reminders of how far he had come from his lowly roots.

It was five thirty. He might glimpse Lexie walking home, but he played down the possibility in his mind in an effort to minimise the likely disappointment. She'd be home already; she'd still be at work; her father would have driven her home, so that the family could be together. Still, as he neared the Park, he began to look left and right, right and left, for her distinctive clothing and cropped scarlet hair.

It was one year since Jamie Gordon had wrapped his car round an oak tree on the road to Forgie and slipped into a coma. Just under one year since Lexie had trudged up the steps to the gallery and announced that she couldn't finish her final painting, the one that would pull the exhibition together, and since (despite his repeated attempts at persuasion) she'd told him categorically that she was pulling out.

One year, therefore, since he had lost his temper and driven her away.

Everything he'd said had been right, of course. She *was* thoroughly unprofessional. No artist with a shred of self-respect would pull out of an exhibition so near completion. There were too many things to consider: the investment of time and money in her work; the pre-publicity (which in Alexa's case was substantial); the expectations of all his important customers; the

25

gap it would leave in the gallery's schedule; the loss of her reputation (and, more importantly, of his own).

But being right wasn't enough. Of course he'd supported her publicly ('Alexa Gordon has our deepest sympathies'; 'None of us would feel right about going ahead in the circumstances'; 'We'll reschedule the exhibition for a later date.') But could he have dealt with her better? When, five years into their marriage, Niamh had walked out on him and gone straight into the arms of his brother, Aidan, he'd experienced a sense of loss as deep as any bereavement – compounded by the hurt of betrayal. He'd handled his own hurt by adopting a punishing schedule and he'd presumed that Lexie would do the same. But Lexie was different. She was different from every woman he'd ever known (and certainly from Niamh) and he realised now that he hadn't known her at all. He'd thought her announcement another breach of trust, but others might view it as laudable loyalty to her family. With the benefit of hindsight, would he have behaved differently?

He approached the gate to the park and slowed down. A car behind him tooted impatiently. On the right, there was no-one coming out of the park, but a woman to his left looked round at the sound.

It was Lexie – instantly recognisable from a hundred yards, let alone twenty. He speeded up, his heart thudding. Had she seen him? He didn't want her to think he was stalking her, he wanted only to be able to see her sometimes, unobserved.

Annoyed with himself, he punched a number on short dial. He needed company, any company, except his own.

'Diana?' he said. 'How are you fixed for tonight?'

'Did you remember the fish?' Martha asked as soon as Lexie stepped inside the front door.

Lexie held up a bag. 'Got it.'

She was sure she'd seen Patrick's car just after she'd crossed the road from the Park, but it might have been another Mercedes convertible, she hadn't been able to see the driver's face. In fact, it couldn't have been Patrick, he worked Thursdays in London. For a moment she melted, remembering

26

his fiery belief in her ability. Together they'd soared…

Patrick Mulgrew was skilful, capable, charming, astute and passionate, a workaholic who could turn base metal into gold – but he was also a self-centred bastard who couldn't stand not being in control.

She dropped the carrier onto the kitchen table and draped her jacket on the back of a chair. She was still in her workaday 'uniform', a skirt (today it was a 1950s dirndl in pink cotton with a net underskirt) and a tweed jacket. Her boots were Edwardian, butter-soft milk-chocolate leather with a row of buttons up each side that must be fastened with a special hook. Someone had inhabited these clothes before her and she liked that feeling. It was about style too, of course, and detail, and quality of fabric. Why head for the monolithic high-street stores when you could own something unique for next to nothing? Her hands rested on the jacket. It was one she'd bought from Pavel, who had developed a knack for knowing what she might like. Small pleasures, acquired back in impecunious student days in Edinburgh, had developed into a habit.

'Thank you. I was worried that you'd forget. I should have gone myself.'

'It's no bother, Mum. Really.'

Shadows sketched dark half-moons under her mother's eyes and the skin on her face was taut. What had she been doing all day, to be so exhausted? Probably, Lexie guessed, like all of them, she hadn't slept last night.

'Everything all right?'

'I'm a little tired. Maybe I'll rest before Dad gets home.'

'Okay. Don't worry about supper, I'll see to it.'

'Thank you, darling. You're very good to us.'

Without planning to, Lexie said, 'Cameron Forrester came into the store today.'

Martha's concern was immediate.

'Oh, my dear.'

Having blurted out her news, Lexie discovered she didn't want to talk about it. After Cameron's back injury, he'd never really settled. Perhaps he'd been addicted to adrenalin, because without its buzz, his exuberance had turned to a kind of dullness

27

that she'd challenged and picked apart until he'd started staying over less and less. One day, he'd simply left Hailesbank, without explanation or any proper farewell, just a note, propped up on her easel, together with her spare keys.

'*Lexie,*' it had read. '*Sorry. Got to go. Can't explain. Don't wait for me.*'

She'd read it with disbelief. She'd tried his mobile, but it had been dead. She'd called his uncle, who'd been evasive and embarrassed, and unable or unwilling to answer her questions. '*Got to go.*' Go? Go where? Why? Go with someone, or on his own? She'd looked again at the bold scrawl, untidy but unafraid (so utterly Cameron in character) and had been mystified. Was he running from her? What was it that was so impossible to discuss that it required complete and permanent removal?

She'd taken the note to Molly, who'd been appalled.

'What a scumbag!'

'But he's not, is he, that's the point. I can think of a few men who'd run off and wouldn't even bother with a note, but Cameron's not like that.'

Molly had shrugged.

'But he is. Obviously.'

'But he's not. I know him.'

'Lexie, dear heart, it pains me to point this out, but you clearly don't know him at all.'

The truth of this statement had hurt almost as much as the disappearance itself. Lexie had been forced to accept that she must have misinterpreted the tenderness of his kisses and the way he had hooked her hair delicately behind her ears with fingers so strong that they looked incapable of such gentle intimacy. The way – even though it was infuriating – that he'd said things before he thought and apologised afterwards. The way he'd made her laugh with his madcap antics.

To avoid letting her mother see this in her eyes, she busied herself by extricating the trout from her carrier bag and turning to the fridge.

'It's all right,' she said. 'That was all so long ago. What shall we do with these? I was thinking I should maybe find a new recipe.'

'Don't change the subject. Tell me about Cameron.'

Lexie shut the door of the fridge rather more firmly than she meant to.

'There's nothing to tell. He's back. I have no idea for how long, or why, or what anyone thinks about it.'

'But he came in to the store to see you.'

'I said so, didn't I?'

'He's not planning to start something up again, I hope?'

When Cameron had disappeared, her disbelief had turned to distress. And distress had become a breakdown in confidence so that even painting had become impossible for some time.

After a little, when nothing had changed and Cameron had made no contact, she'd taken a grip of herself, handed in her notice on the studio-cum-bedsit in the barn outside Hailesbank, ('So perfect,' she'd once said to Cameron, 'I could work here for ever') and rented space at an artists' co-operative in Edinburgh, where she'd abandoned her colourful landscapes and begun to paint dark, obsessive pictures full of allegories of danger and death. It had been a crazy, tumultuous time and her parents had been deeply concerned.

To reassure her mother now, Lexie said, 'Don't worry, Mum. I'm not interested.'

She meant it, or at least, told herself she did. She had lost the knack of intimacy. After Cameron had taken off, she'd tried half-heartedly to date one or two other men in Edinburgh. There'd been an excruciating mismatch of spirits with a nerdy computer-game designer who'd thought only of the next new technology and had no sense of history. He'd been surprised when she'd suggested they call it a day, but not unhappy.

Then there was Patrick.

'I don't make a habit of screwing my new protégées,' he whispered hotly in her ear on the first occasion he did exactly that, 'but you, Alexa Gordon, are ravishing.'

Four months of glorious but secret passion had followed. Patrick had a rule that he never got involved with artists under contract, and could not bring himself to make this breach of his rules public. Lexie hadn't been hurt by this, because in the wake of the hurt Cameron had caused, she wanted to be quite sure of her feelings before facing the inevitable inspection of friends and family. She wasn't ready to deal with their hopes or expectations, or their criticisms. If they adored Patrick, her parents would adopt him as one of the family, and that would bring pressure of another kind. If they saw only the man who prided himself on self-control, and missed the tender person she knew to be inside, they might dislike him, and she could not bear that.

Besides, there was something exciting about secrecy. Stolen moments behind closed office doors. Weekends in comfortable but anonymous guest houses in remote parts of the country. Covert glances and the swift locking of fingers – they had been thrilling.

Whispered promises: 'When the exhibition is over, if we still feel the same way…'

It was hard not to think that her affair with Patrick might have developed into the most important relationship in her life if she hadn't withdrawn from the exhibition. Or rather, if Patrick hadn't thrown a tantrum of magnificent order and, instead of supporting her decision, made a melodramatic renouncement of absolute finality.

Since then, there had been nothing. She'd had neither the energy nor the spirit for the endless patience and relentless compromise a new relationship would demand.

Her mother's concern clearly ran deep.

'I just wouldn't want you to be hurt again,' she said emphatically.

Lexie smiled. Smiling was her main job this year, after all.

'I know. I'm all right. Go and rest.'

'Where's he been, anyway?'

'Cameron? A cruise ship, I believe.'

'*What?*'

Lexie laughed out loud at the look on her mother's face.

'Working. Go and lie down. I'll fix the fish in a bit.'

At the door, Martha turned.

'Your father will want it the usual way, you know.'

'Yes.' Lexie's lips were still twitching with amusement. 'I know.'

Chapter Four

Catalogue number 6: Bamboo sandals worn by Robert McAndrew, prisoner of war at Hakozaki, Japan. Fashioned from bamboo, patched and mended with torn strips of cotton. Donor: Alice McAndrew, Hailesbank. 'My father never spoke about his time at Hakozaki, but after his death we discovered these, and our hearts cracked.'

The door on the half-landing was kept closed, because her mother treated this room like some sort of shrine. Nothing could be thrown out, or touched, or moved. It wasn't likely to be, because Tom wouldn't come near it, just as he wouldn't talk about Jamie or his feelings about the accident. He had closed in on himself and, clam-like, pulled his shell tight. Nothing could reach him.

When had she last been in here? Ages ago. Yet Lexie knew she had to go in, today more than any other. Coming to terms with Jamie's death would be a long, slow process, but if they could work out *why* he got in the car that night, surely it would help them to understand?

She stood outside the door, hesitating. She half turned away. She swung back. She raised a hand, dropped it to her side, and finally reached out and rested it on the doorknob. The polished wood felt cold and uninviting, but she ignored this slender defence. Going in would hurt no-one. She turned the handle.

The door opened smoothly. There was no protest, not even a squeak.

Lexie had forgotten how good this room was. It faced south, towards the back of the house and the main part of the garden, and it was above the kitchen, so it benefited from the extra

31

warmth from the old Aga in the winter. The window looked down on the cherry tree, now lit by the late afternoon sun, and the pergola, where she and Jamie had played as children. She stepped inside and closed the door behind her, leaning back so that her hands splayed against the wood.

There they were. Two children, sitting on the floor, legs crossed, concentrating. Lexie could see them as plainly as the pattern on the carpet. They were playing cards.

'Snap,' an eight-year-old Jamie shouted triumphantly, slapping a card down. His hair was thick and brown and he was like a stick, all arms and legs and knobbly knees and elbows, but the competitiveness had been there, even then. Especially then. Jamie could never bear to lose at anything. 'And I'm out.'

Ten-year-old Alexa's hair was so long she was sitting on it, the brown curls unruly. 'That's not fair, you cheated.'

'No, I didn't. How did I cheat?'

'I don't know. You must be hiding some cards. Shove over, you little toad, and let me look.'

The card game descended into rough and tumble (as most games usually did) with Jamie winning, as ever.

They'd had their share of sibling spats. Yet each argument now felt like an opportunity squandered. Lexie moved into the room, walked right through the spot where the children had once played and fought, and perched on the edge of the bed. Jamie's presence was so strong that it was almost overwhelming. She'd hated his aggressiveness at the time, but that will to win had become a powerful tool in Jamie's adult life. Had it been some weird, twisted kind of competitiveness that had killed him?

You stupid idiot. Why didn't you stop and think?

When they'd been children, he'd teased her unmercifully – about the fact that she couldn't climb a rope in the gym and because, even aged nine, she'd refused to conform to fashion. But he'd protected her too. Once, when she'd wandered across a road without looking, he'd sprinted five yards in a second and wrenched her to safety.

'Don't ever do that again!' he'd yelled, furious and shaken. 'Think! You could have been killed!'

A year ago Jamie had climbed into a car, knowing he was drunk, and driven into the dark. It was out of character. What had been so important that it couldn't wait?

It didn't make sense. None of it made sense.

The sun was sinking below the trees and Lexie shivered. Something didn't feel right. This room – neither up nor down – had once been a maid's room. There was a modest fireplace on the far wall. In the recess to the right of the chimney breast stood a chest of drawers and, to the left, a wardrobe.

She realised what was wrong. It should be messy. Jamie had never been tidy. She'd never been in here without seeing clothes strewn on the floor, a jersey here, some socks there. He'd left books and magazines open on the bed or the floor, drawers and doors ajar. She thought he'd probably been unaware of this – he'd quite simply always been more eager to get on, get out, get going than to take the trouble to tidy.

Lexie slammed her fist into the bed. Cameron was right. Jamie's death had been a waste.

A small cloud of dust rose into the still air and a thousand motes drifted lazily back downwards, their progress backlit by the low sun. Lexie watched them abstractedly. Why would you put your life at risk? Why would you inflict such pain those who lived on?

On the floor, something glinted. She bent to pick it up – a small gold butterfly scroll from an earring. Lexie didn't wear gold, only silver, so it had to be her mother's. She'd been in here, she realised, but she would never admit it. She dropped the clip into her pocket. She'd put it on Martha's dressing table, but in a corner behind some pot, so that its discovery would be delayed a day or two and seem natural.

A desire to protect each other had made them all secretive.

Later, she washed the trout and patted them dry with kitchen roll. In the larder, she found potatoes and was staring at them considering the options – boiled, baked, chipped, creamed or grated and fried like rösti – when a noise at the window made her turn round.

Someone was standing outside, trying to slide up the lower

frame.

Lexie froze, hands full of unwashed potatoes. All she could see was the top of a hat, dark green and rigid, shaped in asymmetric circles like terraces in a lawn, the sort of hat her grandmother might have worn in the 1950s. It bobbed and wobbled, while arms clad in something baby-blue wrestled with the frame.

'What the—'

The window shot up, wood scraping on wood. She and Jamie used to do that trick. There was a knack to it, even when the catch was closed. If you wiggled the frame in just such a way, the latch loosened then slipped, and a counter-intuitive shove and heave produced the desired effect.

A thin voice said with satisfaction, 'There. I knew it.'

Now there was no glass between her and the figure, and she was being examined.

'Hello, dear.'

Wisps of hair escaping from the hat were as white and fine as best Brussels lace. The eyes were cloudy, as if age had already drawn a veil of time across them, but creased skin split into a toothless grin. The smile was so genuine, so lacking in artifice, that Lexie found herself starting to smile back.

'Hello, dear,' the woman said again.

And to Lexie's utter astonishment, she started to climb in.

With one leg in and the other still outside, age clearly got the better of intention. There was a high warble.

'Oh bother. I'm stuck.'

Lexie dropped the potatoes onto the table and crossed the kitchen in three strides. Behind her, the potatoes teetered and rocked, then headed inexorably for the edge of the table and rolled off, hitting the floor one by one. Thud. Bump. Thud.

'Here. Take my hand.'

'Thank you, Maud.'

Maud? A second skinny leg hooked over the sill. Bemused, Lexie saw sheepskin slippers, brown and battered with a sad apology of wool round the top. The ankles disappearing into them were bony and veined and completely uncovered, the flesh tinged an alarming blue. There was surprising strength in

34

the grasp on her hand, but Lexie tucked her other one firmly under a bony arm as a wobble threatened to become a totter. The baby-blue fabric might have been soft and fleecy once, but it had been washed to the point of extinction and plump fibres had thinned and flatted. Was it a dressing gown?

The skeletal hand was cold. It was only April, and although the day had been pleasantly warm, the temperature was dropping fast now that the sun was low in the sky. Concerned, Lexie steered the woman to a chair by the Aga.

'Here, sit down. You're frozen.'

'You get used to it, at my age.' Cloudy eyes scanned the room. 'You've moved the dresser.'

'The dresser?'

'By the door.'

Lexie stared across at the door. There was no dresser. There never had been a dresser.

Beside her, there was an explosion of laughter as the woman chortled at some memory.

'Father was terribly cross about it, wasn't he?'

'Sorry?'

'Of course, Mother always got her own way.' Another giggle.

'You've lost me.'

The woman clucked impatiently.

'The dresser, Maud. Don't you remember? She said she'd buy it, and she did.'

'Did she?'

'What have you done to your hair?' Cloudy eyes peered at her. 'It used to be so long and beautiful. I used to brush it for hours, didn't I, when we were little?'

Lexie reached up and touched spikes.

'I cut it short.'

'And dyed it red!' she cackled. 'Like a radish! What's for tea?'

Lexie said gently, 'Who are you? What's your name?'

'Edith Lawrence.'

A hoot of laughter pulled the corner of Lexie's lips into a responsive twitch of amusement. There was a quality in Edith's

35

laughter that was seriously infectious.

'Edith Dorothy Lawrence. You can't have forgotten your own sister's name, surely?'

Sister?

'Well, it's nice to meet you, Edith. I'm Lexie. Lexie Gordon.'

Edith looked puzzled. She tugged the dressing gown tightly round herself with a quick, jerky movement.

'Tell me,' she said, 'how are the children?'

'Children?'

What sideways shuffle had Edith's confused mind performed? What children did she mean? Her own, perhaps? Or Maud's, the person she'd been mistaken for?

'What children?'

Edith's bright veneer slipped, as if the answer had thrown her.

'What's for tea?' she demanded once more.

Had she realised she'd said something irrational? Was the change of subject a strategy she'd learned as a cover? Lexie picked her words carefully.

'If you let me take you home, we'll soon find out.'

Unexpectedly, Edith cackled.

'Silly Maud! Teasing me again. This is my home.'

For some reason, an image of one of her paintings flashed into Lexie's mind – a large, complicated canvas, with shadowy shapes and clown-like creatures twisting in and out of a maze of thorny bushes. 'Labyrinth', she'd called it. Patrick had salivated over its 'hugely evocative darkness'. *We walk in a world of dreams and of nightmares,* she'd written in the notes for the catalogue that was almost ready to go to print, *a world where nothing is what it seems and smiling faces can turn to deathly grinning skulls in the blink of an eye or a twist of the mind.*

Twist of the mind? Lexie looked down at the tattoo round her thumb and turned it so that she could read the whole word. ARTBOLLOCKS. How could she ever have forgotten its message? Now she'd been confronted with a mind where small twists had become lethal kinks, masking emotions whose complexity and fragility could only be guessed at, and she found it both disconcerting and intriguing.

'I thought I heard voices.'

She turned and saw her mother standing in the doorway. These days, Lexie was as guilty as Martha about fussing. She wanted to protect her mother – after all, it was why she'd committed herself to living in Fernhill for a year. Since Jamie's death, little changes in routine unsettled Martha and Edith's arrival could hardly be described as normal.

Concerned, she said, 'Mum, meet Edith Lawrence. She just—' how to describe Edith's entrance? '—decided to pop in.'

She gestured at the window, which was still wide open.

'Through the window.'

'Edith Dorothy Lawrence,' chirped Edith with emphasis, her cheerfulness returned.

'Hello, Edith.' There was a brittle brightness in Martha's voice. 'Nice to meet you.'

Her mother used to be spontaneous and charming, but Jamie's death had changed her, as it had marked all of them. Lexie expected her to be uncertain about how to handle their unexpected visitor, but now she watched, astonished, as her mother walked forward and laid a gentle hand on the old woman's arm to make a connection.

She's found someone to care for again.

The sudden re-emergence of the old Martha was slightly shocking. Now Lexie was the one who felt unsettled and inadequate.

'Alexa, have you offered our guest tea?'

She pulled herself together and leapt to her feet. 'I was just going to put on the kettle.' Never, she thought, assume anything.

Martha's light tone continued. 'Tell me, Edith, what's brought you to see us?'

'They left Margaret to die, you know,' Edith said darkly.

'Did they? That's terrible.'

'We used to have tea together.'

Edith sniffed, her nose in the air. The green hat teetered uncertainly on her head.

'But her table manners were terrible. And she took the best

cake without even asking.'

'Who left her to die?'

'Die? Who's talking about dying? No need for talk like that. Isn't the tea ready yet, Maud? Don't forget the sugar. Such a treat, having sugar. We were never allowed it in the war, you know.'

Lexie was fascinated by the twists and turns in Edith's conversation. She set out three mugs but Edith peered at her accusingly.

'Where's the china? It used to be in the dresser, but of course, if you've got rid of it... You didn't sell the china as well, did you?'

'I didn't sell the china, I promise you,' Lexie soothed. 'Give me a moment and I'll find some cups.'

Wanting to please Edith, she removed the mugs and headed for the dining room. As she passed through the hall, there was the sound of a key in the lock and a shadow fell through the glass in the front door.

'Is it too early,' Tom Gordon said in a determinedly cheerful voice, 'to ask for a glass of wine?'

Lexie kissed his cheek.

'Hi Dad. We've got a visitor. A rather unusual one. She climbed in through the kitchen window.'

'Sorry?'

'She's in the kitchen, having tea. We're not sure what to do with her.'

'Climbed in through the kitchen window? Well, whoever she is, she can just climb right back out again.'

He dropped his briefcase in the hall and shoved open the kitchen door.

'Hello, Father,' Edith said. 'I wondered when you'd get home.'

Later, after the evening had played out its odd course and the local police had returned Edith to her care home, Lexie thought about everything that had happened.

Edith must have come to Fernhill because she knew the place. Something had driven her to walk an astonishing seven

38

miles in carpet slippers and dressing gown from nearby Musselburgh all the way to Hailesbank. The urge that had guided her along the highways and byways must have been immensely powerful.

Lexie switched her bedside light back on and sat up. The lace of her short chemise slid across her pale skin like whipped cream, so fine and frothy it barely existed. It was already midnight and she had to get up early, but she knew she wouldn't be able to sleep until she'd drawn Edith's face. It wasn't difficult – the memory of the puckered features was very much alive. Edith Dorothy Lawrence, she realised, had walked into her world and she was obviously not going to walk out again any time soon. She had to find out what her story was – and she wasn't going to sleep easily again until she did.

As Lexie sketched, two other things occurred to her.

First: she'd left the trout on the worktop, uncovered and uncooked, because after all the turmoil and confusion of events, she and her parents had forgotten all about it.

And second: she hadn't thought about Jamie all evening.

She dropped her pencil and closed her eyes, trying to reach him now – but, irritatingly, it was another man who swam into focus.

Bloody, bloody Cameron Forrester, who had barged through a door this morning and sent her, metaphorically, flying.

She picked up her pencil again and drew, rapidly.

Chapter Five

Catalogue number 16: White men's ballet pumps, canvas. Donor: Pavel Skonieczna, Hailesbank. The material is gathered at the toe and tucked in under a suede sole. The heel is similarly treated, with the sole split so that the shoe is completely flexible.

From the High Street, Besalú looked like a traditional sherry bar, with a dark, polished mahogany counter and a stylish array of bottles – *fino, manzanilla, palo cortado, amontillado* and dark, nutty *oloroso*. Carlotta was engaged in fighting a rearguard action to make sherry fashionable in East Lothian, but it was the tapas that had made Besalú popular. A couple of years ago she had surprised everyone by commissioning and project-managing the building of a large extension into the garden at the back to extend the tapas restaurant, together with a small function room at one side. Both were regularly booked out.

The extension housed twenty tables comfortably, and its entire back wall comprised concertina glass doors. In good weather, these could be folded back so that restaurant, garden and river appeared to meld seamlessly. It was not unusual for the bar on the High Street to be bursting and for all twenty tables in the extension to be occupied, so when Molly had phoned, sounding tired and anxious and wanting to talk, Lexie had booked a table immediately.

Just as well, she thought, surveying the restaurant when she arrived, because only one other table was still empty, and it had a 'Reserved' sign placed conspicuously on its tiled surface. She settled with a jug of Sangria and waited.

Molly was late and Lexie was about to text when she spotted her sleek blonde hair at the door.

'Over here!'

She watched Molly negotiate her way through the crowded restaurant. A couple in the corner leaned across the table in an obvious effort to hear each other above a rowdy group beside them while further along, two children among a family party were behaving impeccably. A waiter in Besalú uniform of yellow shirt and red waistcoat (Carlotta's style was both flamboyant and patriotic) balanced a huge tray of tapas confidently on one hand high above his head, and followed her. Lexie saw him deliver his cargo safely to a crowd of underdressed and overconfident teenagers who were probably celebrating the end of their exams. He proceeded to flirt outrageously with them and their shrills of laughter turned heads.

'Sorry I'm late.'

'No problem. Busy?'

Molly slumped down on her chair and breathed a heavy sigh. 'You could say. I'm trying to cope with running everything as well as masterminding the Home Farm renovation. Is that Sangria?'

'I ordered a jug. Too corny?'

'Inspired. Just fill it up.' Molly slid her glass towards Lexie. 'I can't tell you how good it is to get out.'

Molly's five-year marriage to ambitious lawyer Adam Blair had stumbled to an abrupt and inexplicable end a year ago and they'd separated. Lexie liked Adam, a clever man with a dry sense of humour, and found her friend's refusal to discuss the breakup deeply puzzling. Soon after it had happened, Molly had abandoned her promising career in marketing and landed a new job at Fleming House.

In the middle of all her own woes, Lexie still found time to worry about her. It suited Molly to declare herself on a sabbatical from men and her long hours, combined with the remote location of her apartment, up a winding spiral stair in the old servants' quarters at the back of Fleming House, was a perfect excuse to keep herself hidden away. Still, it wasn't like the gregarious Molly that Lexie had known since primary school.

'What did you want to talk about?'

Molly drank greedily and held her glass out again.

'Are you going to be all right to drive?'

'You kidding? Not a chance. I'll get a cab home and someone'll shunt me back tomorrow to pick up my car.' Molly smoothed already sleek hair. 'Just wanted to offload, really. The renovation's getting me down. It's too much work on top of everything else.'

'What's the problem?'

'No problem, it's just eating time. We're going through the tenders for the fit-out. I suppose everything can move forward again after we've done that.'

'Fit-out?'

'You know, the interior design work, the decor, all the furniture and fittings—'

'Furniture?' Lexie had an idea. 'Hey, Moll, any chance of Gordon's pitching for supplying that?'

'I didn't know you did that kind of thing.'

'We don't. Or rather, we haven't done till now – but why not? We could easily fulfil a contract.'

'Well, it's not my call. You'd have to ask the company we select if you can tender to them. I wouldn't have any say in it, you know that, don't you?'

'Of course.'

It was business, and she had to do her best for Gordon's, so she persisted.

'But will you tell me who you've chosen so that we can approach them?'

'Don't see why not.' She drained her glass and refilled it from the jug. 'Now, business over. Tell me about yesterday. Was it awful?'

In all the confusion of Edith's arrival through the kitchen window, the anniversary of her brother's death had slid into the shadows. Now the high, unbroken voice of a ten-year-old Jamie suddenly rang in Alexa's ears.

Into the valley of death rode the six hundred.

Ludicrous. Why now? Why this poem? It had been his favourite. She could picture him, chin up, hands clasped behind his back, reciting it with relish.

Theirs not to make reply. Theirs not to reason why. Theirs but to do or die...

The valley of death. Jamie had driven into the valley of death. Jolted back two decades, Alexa's head whirled with half-forgotten snippets. Mad, bad and dangerous to know. Who was that again? Not Tennyson. Byron. That was it. Byron. Her brother had never been bad (at least, not in a venal sense, only deliciously, fun-lovingly wicked) but that night he'd certainly been dangerous to know. She pursed her lips. At least he'd been alone. If there'd been someone with him... 'Lexie?'

Molly's hand curled round hers and she focused with difficulty.

'You all right? I'm sorry, I should have been more careful how I asked.'

Molly's hazel eyes were awash.

She's upset too, Lexie thought, moved by the staunchness of Molly's friendship.

'I'm fine, Moll, you mustn't worry.'

These moments with Jamie passed like wraiths and were gone. They didn't disturb her.

'Yesterday was okay, actually. In fact, we couldn't have thought about Jamie less.'

Molly blew her nose. 'What do you mean?'

'It was weird. He'd been lurking all day, as if he was playing hide and seek, waiting for a suitable time to leap out and surprise us, and instead it was someone else who surprised us.'

Molly dabbed at a suspicion of dampness on her cheek then stuffed the handkerchief back into her pocket.

'What in heaven's name are you talking about?'

'Maybe Jamie sent the diversion so that we weren't sad.'

'Jamie sent—?'

Lexie held out her glass.

'Pour me some more Sangria, Moll, but for goodness sake let's get our order in or we'll get too smashed to talk. Then I'll tell you.'

The joy of Besalú was that you could order a few small dishes and they arrived from the kitchen quickly. The secret of Carlotta's success was that no-one ever stopped at those – with every drink the temptation was to order more tapas, and when there were tapas left and glasses were empty, to order more drink. And so the cycle continued and the evening passed and profits swelled. By the time they had polished off the *banderillas* and *tortilla*, the *calamares* and the Manchego with quince arrived. Demolishing the crispy squid with gusto, Lexie finished telling Molly about Edith Dorothy Lawrence and her bizarre visit.

'She sounds,' Molly said, helping herself to a lump of cheese and tearing off some bread to go with it, 'just like my grandmother.'

If she'd been upset at the mention of Jamie, there was no sign of it now.

'She's a lot more confused than your gran.'

'Gran's getting worse. Pass your glass, there's some Sangria left.' Molly topped up their glasses and lifted the jug towards a passing waiter to signify it needed replenishing. She giggled. 'Last week she made a fruit cake and forgot to put any fruit in.'

'Anyone can make mistakes. But Edith Lawrence kept calling me Maud. She thinks I'm her *sister*.'

'*Maud!*' Molly hooted with laughter, then appraised Lexie seriously. 'Suits you.'

'Shut up! It does not. It makes me sound like I'm a hundred. Want to see her?'

'See Edith?'

Lexie bent down to the floor and picked up her bag. She was never without her sketchbook.

'Here.'

She turned the pages until she found her drawings.

'Wow. Is she really that old?'

'She looks about ninety, but I guess she can't be.'

Molly flicked the page. 'You're so bloody talented, Lexie. I don't need to meet the woman, you've shown her to me perfectly.'

She turned another page. 'What's this?'

45

Lexie made a lunge for the book, but Molly wrenched it out of her grasp.

'Lexie?'

'Give it here.'

She'd forgotten about the drawings of Cameron, and although she had been dying to tell Molly about him, she'd intended to do it in her own way. Her sketches, because they captured something of the observer as well as the observed, were too revealing.

'Tell me.' Molly held the sketchbook behind her back, her stare unrelenting.

Lexie scowled. It was impossible to retrieve her drawings without making a scene, so she sat back and crossed her arms defensively – but Molly kept staring and Lexie was the first to cave in.

'He came into the store yesterday.'

Molly's jaw sagged in surprise and she dropped the sketchbook onto the table with a thump.

'Cameron did? Cameron *Forrester*?'

Lexie grabbed the book and stuffed it back in her bag before Molly could appropriate it again.

'You heard.'

'He just appeared?'

'He was there when I got in at nine.'

'He's back in Hailesbank, he came to see you, and *he got up before nine*?' The green in Molly's eyes glittered. 'Why's he back?'

'He didn't say.'

'Really? What *did* he say?'

'Not a lot.'

'So why did he come in?'

'I don't know.'

Molly's face was expressive, but not nearly as eloquent as her silences, which she deployed like missiles, with deadly effect. Lexie finally gave in.

'He did say he wanted to meet me to explain, but…'

'There's a but?'

'I don't want to know. That's the truth of it.'

'Don't you? I do. The bugger runs off and simply abandons my best mate, you bet I want to know.'

'Why? What difference does it make?'

'It makes the difference between me cutting his balls off and stuffing them in a pickle jar and maybe, just maybe, being civil to him.'

Lexie laughed.

'I suppose I would like to know, but the last thing I'm going to do is sit down and listen to lame excuses.'

'What if they're not lame?'

Lexie had been happy when she'd been with Cameron. Their characters were nicely counterbalanced. Where she could easily drift into a dream world of her own, he was naturally gregarious. If she hid too long among her paints and her canvases, he would take her brush out of her hand and lead her to the door, cheerfully ignoring her feeble protests.

'You need to be in the world to understand it,' he'd say, kissing the tip of her nose and wiping a smudge off her cheek with his thumb, 'and if you don't understand it, you'll never be able to paint it.'

When she'd first met him (through Jamie, of course, and the Hawks) she'd thought him blunt to the point of insensitivity. Later she'd decided that his tactlessness was more a painful honesty that had a tendency to burst out before thought caught up with it. Above all, she'd found him outrageously sexy. She still did – that chemistry hadn't changed.

Cameron Forrester had been Lexie's first real love and it wasn't lame excuses she feared – it was that he might tell the truth, and that she wouldn't like it.

She looked away.

'I must go.'

'So you still love him.'

'No,' Lexie shook her head. 'No.'

'Methinks the lady doth prot—'

'Shut up, Moll.'

'—est too much.'

'No, I mean, *really* shut up.' Lexie seized her elbow. '*Look*.'

Molly began to turn to where Lexie was staring.

'Don't turn round, he'll see you.'

'Lexie, you're hurting my elbow. And how the hell can I look if I can't turn—'

'Screaming abdabs, he's seen us.'

'Will you just relax and talk in English?'

Two men in two days. Correction. Two *lovers* in two days.

Molly said, 'Isn't that Patrick Mulgrew? No-one else has a mane of hair like that, surely. Or a suit like that either,' she added admiringly. 'Wow. Gorgeous. I haven't seen Patrick in an age. He's got that girl with him, the one who was in *Scotland Daily*.'

Impeccable Ferragamo loafers, a black merino wool suit and a bronze throat rising out of crisp white cotton. The last time Lexie had seen that combination Patrick had snatched up her contract and ripped it in two, his grey eyes glacial.

'Very well,' he said, 'If you must. But I warn you, you'll find it impossible to succeed without me.'

Unforgivable.

In fact, Patrick wasn't on a date tonight, he was working.

Yesterday, after seeing Lexie, he'd driven right on through Hailesbank to the slip road back onto the dual carriageway, and headed for Diana Golspie's impeccable flat in Edinburgh's Georgian New Town, not a stone's throw from his gallery. When Diana had answered the door, cool and elegant in grey silk, he'd stepped inside, virtually ripped off her clothes, and had urgent, ungentle sex with her on the carpet.

'Something biting you?' she'd inquired mildly when he'd thrust and panted his way to a speedy climax.

Ashamed, he'd buried his face in the sweeping arc of her long neck and had showered it with gentle kisses.

'Sorry. I'm a rat. And you're much too tolerant of me.'

She'd begun to unbutton his shirt.

'I just think,' she'd said, 'that it's a little unfair of you still to have all your clothes on while I lie here naked.'

He'd let her undress him, then carried her to bed and spent the next hour being much more considerate.

'I don't want to know what all that was about,' she'd said

48

eventually, 'but I suppose it's not too much to expect dinner?'

Patrick knew he didn't deserve Diana Golspie, but he also knew that there were another dozen Dianas in the same stable. Women who believed they could tame him. Women who craved his ring on their finger. Women who wanted nothing more than to live at The Gables and play golf with the smart set in Scotland, be seen with him at the opera and the ballet and the best receptions. It was why he never asked a woman to spend the night with him at his house in Hailesbank. It was why (or partly why) he'd never lived with another woman since Niamh's betrayal ten years ago. Cynicism had set in as a means of self-preservation.

It didn't mean he wasn't generous to the women he chose to spend time with, and he had accepted Diana's discreetly phrased demand with good grace.

'Where would you like to go?'

It had cost him a packet, naturally, but that didn't matter. The only thing that mattered, yesterday, was not having to think about Lexie Gordon – and now, here she was. Silly to come to Besalú really, but Esther had been so eager to try it.

He offered his arm to Esther Goldwyn, his not-date, and readjusted his expression. After all, he and Lexie were adults, and they understood each other. Once there might have been something between them, now there wasn't, and that was it.

'I believe that's our table,' he said to Esther. 'Let's go.'

He looked down at her. She was pretty but bland, her face a mere canvas she clearly had to paint liberally in order to add character. Esther's art was deliberately shocking (she stuffed road kill to make decorative lamps and coffee tables and fashioned Ascot-style hats to sit on top of stags' heads) but it had humour too. It wasn't world shattering, but he enjoyed it and believed it would do well in London and the States – while Scotland, home of the stuffed deer head, was likely to accept the work with barely a murmur.

Esther was excited. She had migrated from mere euphoria to a state of unalloyed bliss since he'd signed her and although he'd found it gratifying at first, it had palled. Patrick planned to hand the management of Esther's budding career to Victoria. It could be her first big challenge. Neither girl would be pleased, but both would accept the inevitable and get on with what needed to be accomplished.

When they were a yard from the table where Lexie and her friend were sitting, he stopped.

'Good evening, Lexie.'

Lexie raised her dark chocolate eyes to meet his gaze and he was reminded again of the fawn. What was it he'd said the day they'd rowed? He fumbled in the recesses of his mind and came up with, 'You're completely unprofessional.'

He had a horrible feeling that he'd added, 'You'll never make it without me,' but that couldn't be right, could it? Could shock and anger have unshackled the ties between brain and speech so preposterously?

Lexie didn't speak. Esther, sensing tension, fell silent. He had no idea what to say next and it was left to the girl with Lexie to say, 'Hi. I'm Molly. I'm sure we've met.'

Patrick grabbed at this straw.

'Molly. Of course. Delighted.'

He stuck out his hand to shake hers and produced a smile straight from the rulebook on manners: warm but not too intimate, polite and not too impersonal. He drew Esther forward, introduced her.

'This is Esther Goldwyn, I've signed her for a show. She's extraordinarily talented.'

He saw Lexie's eyebrows lift, but her smile matched his own for courtesy.

'Hi, Esther. I saw the article in the paper. Congratulations on your exhibition. And good luck.'

Patrick said, 'We must get together for a drink.'

Politeness masked the depth of his desire for reconciliation, and when Lexie replied, 'I'm quite busy,' and turned her head away, the rebuff had an almost physical effect on him.

'Of course.'

He bent forwards in a tiny half-bow of acknowledgement. The manners he'd learned, not on an Irish farm but at the feet of his masters in the galleries in London, had become so deeply seated that they were automatic and he was grateful he could summon social grace so easily.

'I quite understand. Well, good to see you.'

A waiter lifted the 'Reserved' sign from the last table and they turned towards it.

Behind him he heard the girl, Molly, hissing, 'Why were you so rude to him? It wasn't his fault that…'

And he thought he heard Lexie say, 'Don't, Moll. Just don't.'

But the noise levels in the restaurant were high now and in any case, he wasn't sure what to make of the words.

Chapter Six

Catalogue number 11: Bride's shoe (left), cream silk, kitten heel. 2007. Donor: Bob Hutchison, Hailesbank. 'We were due to get married in August, but in May, Susie was walking home from work when she was knocked down by a car. Susie nearly died and they were forced to amputate her right leg, but she was determined to walk down the aisle. Four months later, she did.'

'We'll need to do the window by the end of the week,' Neil said, sliding onto the chair by Alexa's desk.

Lexie, absorbed in drawing, didn't look up. 'Don't worry, it's under control. I'm thinking about the next few displays, actually. I thought we might major on bedrooms next.'

It was part of their strategy to keep the window fresh and attractive, even though they both knew that any good impression would be instantly dispelled as soon as anyone entered the cluttered store. Thinking of this, she pulled a face.

'I refuse to construct one of Dad's beloved white fitted units. Something a bit more contemporary, don't you agree? Sticking to the theme of bright, fresh colours?'

Lexie's thoughts turned again to the idea of leaving Gordon's. She'd wanted to do this because she wanted to support her parents in the only ways she could think of, but it wasn't what she was best at. She still hadn't spoken to her father, though, because she could see him struggling in the web of potential failure and knew she couldn't abandon him to disaster. Perhaps if she stayed she could persuade him to adopt a more realistic strategy for survival.

She examined her sketches. Would the display look better

with an ottoman, or might that be too much? She'd spotted one in a catalogue, covered in figured velvet, a chocolate background with vast scarlet poppies.

Neil said, 'I can see you're busy. Just wanted to check you haven't forgotten.'

'No, it's all fine.'

She didn't mean to be rude, she became preoccupied when she was deep into designing.

'See you later, then.'

'Sure.'

But the interruption had derailed her concentration. She abandoned her drawings and stretched. Rain had started driving against the window. She stood up and wandered across the room. In the yard below her, a Pettigrew's lorry was backing into the loading bay. She could hear the beep, beep, beep of its reverse warning signal. The turn into the yard was narrow and sharp but Kev, the Pettigrew's driver, was well used to it.

Beep. Beep. Beep.

Why wasn't he taking the usual line? She watched, astonished, as the rear corner of the truck moved towards the bricks. He'd hit the wall in a minute and it would cost a fortune to rebuild. She wrenched open the door and flew down the stairs.

'*Stop!*'

She could barely hear her own shout above the noise of the engine and there was no chance that Kev would. She battered her hands against the back door of the van in the vain hope that he might notice, but the lorry still kept inching towards disaster. Now she was in real danger of being trapped between the van and the wall. She looked around frantically, but there was nothing she could do except retreat and watch it happen.

The truck stopped abruptly. Alexa's heart was racing. Glancing down she saw that, miraculously, the outer wheel had caught on a low stone buttress. The engine died and she yelled into the sudden silence, alarm making her voice sharp.

'You could've taken the whole wall down, Kev! You should've turned hard over as soon as the cab reached the gatepost.'

It was raining heavily now and Lexie was soaked. Water ran off her hair in a steady stream and dripped down inside the collar of her jacket, but she barely noticed it.

The cab door opened and the driver jumped out.

'Sorry. Couldn't see for the rain.'

'Cameron?'

Cameron Forrester's hair shed water like a duck's feathers. Raindrops glistened on his thick brown thatch, others found their way down his face and onto the shoulders of his tee shirt, but his hair seemed unaffected. He grinned.

'Bit close, eh?'

'What the hell were you doing?' Lexie was rigid with fury.

Cameron spread his hands in a gesture of helplessness.

'Give us a break, Lexie. It's my first day on the job and the weather's crap.'

'On the job? What are you talking about? Where's Kev?'

Another man appeared round the front of the cab.

'Hi Lexie. Ah was trying tae tell him.'

'Joe! So something's normal at least.' Sarcasm was a poor tool but the only one that came to hand. 'Can you please explain what's happening?'

Joe McPhail's bulky belly shook as he moved. Lexie had seen him demolish a lunch that would comfortably feed a family of four, but there was real strength in his arms, a necessary asset for a furniture remover.

'Kev's gone. Buggered off to some fancy job in Edinburgh. Says he'll earn twice as much.'

'I'm just temporary,' Cameron said cheerfully.

'You have no idea how temporary you'd have been if you'd hit that wall.'

'Hey. It was a mistake. Anyway, I didn't hit it.' Cameron seized her elbow. 'You okay? You've gone white.'

'I'm fine. If you're done with demolition, perhaps you could unload.'

She turned and strode back inside. She knew she shouldn't blame Cameron. Kev had been making that tricky turn for years. A new driver, in conditions like these, was bound to find it difficult. She towelled her hair dry and glared at her reflection in the mirror, annoyed at her reaction. Would she have been so angry with another man?

When the van had been unloaded and reloaded, Joe declared it was time for a tea break. This involved his flask and a large paper bag full of doughnuts.

'Dinnae worry aboot me, Lexie. Ah'll just step outside.'

That meant a cigarette. Lexie worried about Joe's health. He was a top candidate for a coronary, but there was no point in saying anything, because Joe would never change.

Cameron didn't move.

'It's stopped raining,' she snapped. 'You can take your break outside with Joe.'

'Sure.'

He still didn't move. Exasperated, Lexie said, 'Don't tell me. You didn't bring anything.'

Cameron grinned. 'I didn't realise it was the form.'

'Where Joe is concerned, breaks involving food and drink are a core clause in the job description. I suppose you'd better come up to my office. I've got a kettle.'

'Brilliant. Thanks. Could I have a biscuit too? I did get up rather early this morning.'

'You're a chancer,' but she laughed.

As the kettle bubbled to a boil, she asked, 'So how did this come about?'

'The job? Someone in the pub told me they were looking for a driver to start right away. Seemed like a good idea, so I went in on Friday and they told me I could start today.'

'Have you got an LGV licence?'

'Yeah. Course.'

'Really?' She looked at him suspiciously.

'Would I lie to you? I had to get one for a job I had for a bit, before I started on the cruise ships. I delivered bread for a large baker's down in Oxfordshire.'

Six years was a long time. There was so much she didn't know about what he'd done or where he'd been.

'I'm a bit rusty, as you maybe noticed.'

He looked so genuinely rueful that she softened. 'Well, there's no damage.'

56

'You won't tell on me to old man Pettigrew?'

'I won't tell.'

Cameron never inhabited one mood for long. He changed instantly from abashed to ecstatic.

'Thanks, Lexie. I'll love you for ever.'

He tossed statements like pancakes, and with as little care. They flipped up and over and lay, flat and pale, in front of her.

Would I lie to you?

I'll love you for ever.

'Kev left in a hurry.'

'I think it probably suits them to slim down the number of staff on their books.'

She sighed. 'Everyone's struggling.'

'Yeah, and if I want to keep this job, I'd better move. Joe'll be wondering where I am. Thanks for the coffee.'

'You forgot your biscuit.'

She held out a packet of digestives.

'You're all right. Thanks. Sitting next to Joe puts you off eating, the consequences are a bit too obvious. I'll wait till lunch and find a sandwich.'

It would have been easy for him to run to seed after the accident, but he hadn't. Lexie tried to stop her mind from hopping to memories of taut skin and firm flesh, of muscles that rippled and fascinated and delighted. She failed dismally. She remembered skin that smelled fresh as mountain air, and hair that was spicy, like eucalyptus. Later, after limbs had entwined and bodies writhed together in youthful ardour, there'd always been that intoxicating odour of fresh sweat and sticky sex.

'Lexie? Hello?'

He had stepped right up to her, so close that she could feel the warmth radiating from him. The scar on his face was as familiar as an old friend. Unthinking, she lifted her hand to stroke the white line and he caught it in his fingers. The touch was shocking. Desire stabbed through her and she swayed towards him.

Cameron's voice was husky.

'I asked for this job specially, you know. To have an excuse to see you.'

57

Common sense rode in like the patron saint of chaperones and from somewhere she found strength and an instinct for self-preservation.

'*Don't*, Cameron. Don't open everything up again. Life's moved on. Everything has changed.'

Everything and nothing. She wrenched her hand free.

'I need to tell you why—'

'You don't need to tell me anything.'

'I was a fool.'

'Were you?'

He caught her again. His kiss tasted of coffee and desire, and resistance was impossible. Lexie discovered that a year of celibacy and sadness had left her parched, and she thirsted for love. She was tired of being the one who carried the burden of keeping everything going. She was tired of thinking only of the feelings of others. She was still young, and she had her own needs.

'I never stopped thinking about you,' Cameron whispered.

'Really?' His lips sought hers again and this time she didn't fight the response.

At last he broke away. 'I'd better go.'

'Yes.' But she pulled him to her again.

'Joe will think I'm seducing you. I'll call. Okay?'

He nudged her away with the old gentleness.

'Yes. Okay.'

'We'll go out on Saturday. No arguments.'

He slipped his hand under her chin and eased her face close to his so that she fell under the spell of his gaze once more.

'I'll take you to dinner.'

She tried to keep it light.

'In that case, I'll steer clear of biscuits all day.'

He laughed and released her.

'Do that. Wouldn't do to have a chubby little Lexie. I'll come round to your place at seven, right?'

And he was gone. Lexie clutched the window frame and looked down to watch him emerge into the yard and climb into the cab. She closed her eyes and leant back against a filing cabinet. It felt cold and unforgiving, but her body burned.

Had she ever told him she loved him? If not, she should have done. He was so sexy. And so much less complicated than Patrick.

Chapter Seven

Catalogue number 4: Black leather boot, low heel, pointed toe, scalloped trim bearing eleven small buttons. Believed to have belonged to pioneering doctor, Sophia Jex Blake. Donor: Alison Munro, Edinburgh. 'Sophia Jex Blake was a difficult and determined woman who tried to break into the all-male preserve of medicine at the University of Edinburgh. She matriculated as a student, but was denied a degree.'

She was eating supper in the kitchen with Tom and Martha when her mobile rang. It was Molly, who sounded cheerful.

'I thought we'd try the new restaurant on the Edinburgh road on Saturday. There's nothing on here, for once.'

Lexie glanced at her parents, mute over their shepherd's pie, mumbled an apology and slid into the hall.

'Sorry, Moll, I can't.'

'Can't?' Molly laughed. 'Don't tell me, the gorgeous Patrick Mulgrew is whisking you out to the opera and some fine dining in our fair capital city.'

'Patrick? Don't be ridiculous. Cameron's taking me to dinner,' Lexie hissed.

'He is not!'

'On Saturday.'

'Jesus, Lexie, *why*? Don't you remember what the bastard did to you?'

'That was years ago.'

'So? Has he told you why he bunked off?'

'Not yet. He was going to, but I stopped him.'

'Why did you do that?'

Lexie felt her face grow bright.

61

'He apologised. Why did you think I was going out with Patrick, for heaven's sake?'

'You saw the way he looked at you the other day.'

'What, like a bit of shit under his shoe?'

'The guy fancies you rotten. I'm jealous.'

'Molly, your judgement is flawed by exhaustion. Get yourself a glass of wine, have a long bath and get to bed.'

'You're really going out with Cameron?'

'Yes.'

There was a short silence, then Molly said soberly, 'Be careful.'

On Saturday morning Lexie took herself into Hailesbank with a dual mission: to find a gift for her father's birthday and to find a new dress for her date with Cameron. Both tasks might prove challenging.

In the Memorial Park a group of small boys was playing football. Ball games were technically prohibited, but everyone ignored the edict because no-one these days thought it made any sense. Why have a public park if you couldn't enjoy it? A football cannoned into the back of her knee and tolerance exploded.

'Ow!'

She whirled round to glare at the boys, but it had only been a small miskick. 'Sorry!' one yelled, his face so like Jamie's at that age that she couldn't be cross.

'No problem. Here.'

She kicked it inexpertly back and it trickled across the dew-damp grass. Lexie stood and watched them for a few minutes. They had such energy. She rubbed a hand tiredly across her temple. A headache threatened. She tried to be cheerful for everyone's sake, but sometimes – when she couldn't sleep – it was hard being jolly. It didn't matter. Dinner with Cameron would restore her flagging spirits.

In Hailesbank, the headache worsened, because she found her father impossible to buy for these days. A year ago she would have bought him some new golf balls or a gadget for scooping them out of the stream. But he hadn't touched his golf clubs since Jamie died. He had no interest in clothing. His car had once been a source of great pride and driving a pleasure, but Jamie's road accident had turned him into an ultra-careful old man, with no interest in anything connected with driving. There was no point in buying a voucher for a weekend away or a meal in a smart restaurant. Tom Gordon's world had shrunk to office and home and, of the two, only the emporium sparked any real animation.

In the bookshop on the High Street, she pulled a book off the shelves at random: *The Boy Who Harnessed the Wind*. Lexie recognised the cover. It was the story of a boy in Malawi who made a turbine out of trash to generate much-needed electricity in his village. Why was this still on the shelves? It had been a top seller a couple of years ago. She remembered it because Jamie had found it inspiring.

Jamie had been a passionate person. He'd spoken for the small things (like this book, for example, or the need for children to be competitive in sport) as well as the big ones: freedom, justice and the right to get hammered on a night out. She smiled, remembering how irritated he'd been at the confines of school, how eager to leave and start living life to the full. He hadn't been academically gifted, but he'd had views, and he'd loved his rugby – so very different from the suave Patrick. She couldn't imagine Patrick getting stuck into mud and scrums.

Lexie shoved the book back onto the shelf and moved away from the biographies. She stared helplessly at the cookery section. They were non-starters. Tom didn't cook.

DIY? Never.

Gardening? That was a slim possibility, but although he saw keeping the garden tidy as an obligation, he seemed to get little pleasure from it.

A novel, perhaps? Not his taste.

She abandoned the shelves, dispirited, and tried to shoulder her way through the Saturday crowds. Sometimes it only took something ridiculously minor to tip the balance of her mood from hard-won equilibrium towards dejection.

'Lexie? Are you all right?'

Carlotta's unmistakeable accent penetrated the hubbub. Lexie stopped at once. Carlotta could be guaranteed to lift her mood – and she was with Jonas, who Lexie adored, in the way you love a cuddly toy.

Carlotta was tiny, five-foot nothing of Mediterranean flamboyance, undimmed by northern chill. She had a knack of harnessing whatever weather was thrown her way and using it in some way to show off her beauty. In snow, she unashamedly wore cashmere hoods trimmed with silver fox fur, the perfect frame for her loveliness. In autumn, she chose terracotta, like the soil of her native land, to echo the colour of the leaves. She inhabited summer as if it was a birthright, stepping prettily in sandals and wrapped lightly in glorious bright cottons. Today, as the first spring flowers turned their faces hopefully towards a tremulous sun, she had ventured into dark rose, with a wool jacket and short, swinging skirt like a tulip just opening to the skies.

'You look so tired, Lexie, I am worried about you.'

The 'rrs' rolled off her tongue in a tripping cadence.

'It's kind of you but, really, I'm fine. I was just wondering what to give Dad for his birthday. He's so difficult.'

'I think he likes music, yes? There is a concert soon at the Usher Hall in Edinburgh. That young violinist, Nicola Benedetti.'

'That sounds great, thanks for the idea.'

Jonas said, 'We were thinking of you on Monday. We didn't want to intrude, but we all raised a pint, down at the club. You know—' He trailed off awkwardly.

Jonas was as reserved as Carlotta was flamboyant. He inhabited his features comfortably, but the rugby had taken its toll, as it had with Cameron. Jonas was all muscle, but when the day came and he stopped training, he was the sort who would turn to fat unless he took good care of himself. None of that mattered, because he was kind and straightforward and these traits made him loveable.

'Thanks, Jonas.'

'Anniversaries are so hard,' Carlotta said. 'I took your mother some little treats to cheer her up.'

64

'Yes. Thank you. You're very kind. It was a difficult day. I know she was glad of your company.'

'No problem.' She looked up at Jonas. 'We must go, *mi cielo*. I have to get things organised for tonight. We have the visitors coming, Lexie, for eating.'

'Not working at Besalú tonight then?'

'Besalú can run itself sometimes. Miguel, he is very capable. Come, Jonas.' She sent a sparkling smile towards Lexie. 'I have nothing to wear. You know how it is.'

Jonas hooked his arm round his wife's shoulders and pulled a face that signalled resignation.

'Guess who'll be sitting for hours in the dress shop while she asks my opinion about a dozen outfits? As if anything I said would make the slightest bit of difference.'

Carlotta laughed her tinkling laugh and pushed at him playfully.

'Oh Jonas! *Cariño!* You know what you think matters to me.'

Jonas looked down at her with a gaze so replete with adoration that Lexie felt a surge of envy. It must be extraordinary to be loved like that.

'Well, don't let me hold you back. Carlotta. Thanks for all your little treats. Mum really appreciates them, and your visits.'

'Oh, you know, it's little to do. Bye, Lexie.'

'See you.'

Lexie had meant to get to Cobbles all week, but events had conspired to get in her way. Pavel had tantalised her with the mention of 1940s dresses, and her date tonight was an excuse for self-indulgence. She pushed her way through the jostling crowds and turned right into Kittle's Yard. In the distance she heard the faint 'ching ching' of the old bell that was set off when Cobbles' door opened. A man stepped out and was swallowed up by the crowds of shoppers. For a moment she thought it was Patrick, but Cobbles was not Patrick's kind of shop. She hoped it was a paying customer. There were days when it must cost Pavel more to keep the shop warm than he took in through the till.

She pushed open the door to the repeat of the 'ching ching'.

'Hello Pavel! It's Lexie!'

Pavel was in the back of the shop. Today he was wearing a pink and cream-striped jacket, with a crimson cravat tucked into a cream silk shirt.

'You're looking very dapper.'

'Thank you, darling, one does try. I'm so glad you're here, sweetheart, I was worried about you.'

'I should have called, sorry. It's been a hell of a week.'

'Was it bad, then? The anniversary?'

'Actually, it was very interesting.'

She picked up a small, pretty bowl – Minton? Spode? – put it down again and started to poke around in Pavel's rummage box, with its familiar 'Everything Under £5' sign. Lexie loved the rummage box. She had been coming in here since she was at school and she'd always dreamed of finding some hidden delight. Sometimes one person's rubbish was another person's treasure. Today she discovered a silver fob watch with a cracked crystal, a policeman's whistle, several pairs of cuff links, a fireman's cap badge, half a dozen old coins, two matched gilt frames for miniature photographs and a nutcracker in carved sandalwood and steel.

'Oh yes?' Pavel's hands fluttered over the box, tidying as she rummaged.

She picked up a pair of cufflinks and examined them.

'To hell with concerts in the Usher Hall.'

'I don't follow, darling.'

'I need to get something for Dad's birthday. Carlotta suggested concert tickets and Dad does still love music, but to be honest, I think that getting him out in the evening would be tricky. I'd much rather get him something with a history – any ideas?'

Pavel always had suggestions.

'I have the perfect thing.'

Cobbles operated a strictly hierarchical system of display. At the front of the shop, spaciously arrayed and beautifully lit, were the more substantial and more valuable pieces – a pair of Hepplewhite-style mahogany dining chairs, a Regency side

66

table, an exquisite Victorian cut crystal and polished brass oil lamp, a selection of good paintings. In the back room, where they were standing, more modest delights lurked. Pavel edged past a stripped pine trunk, round a plaster blackamoor lamp that looked good from a distance but didn't bear closer inspection, reached far into the corner and lifted out a box.

'Rosewood, inlaid with mother of pearl, see? And...' he opened the lid with a flourish, 'it still has its original green silk lining.'

Lexie stroked the polished wood.

'It's beautiful. He can keep his cufflinks and change in there and he'll appreciate the craftsmanship. What are you asking for it?'

Pavel looked at the tag.

'It says seventy-five pounds, but I've had it for ages, darling. I could let you have it for forty?'

'*Pavel*,' Lexie admonished, 'you really mustn't let things go too cheaply. How will you survive?'

'Well sweetie, I like my special things to go to a good home. Anyway,' he added quickly, seeing Alexa's expression, 'that leaves me some profit and it's only taking up space. Promise you.'

'Are you sure?'

'Tell you what—' Pavel perched himself on an old kitchen chair next the till, and crossed his legs, 'Let's agree on forty if you'll brew up a wee cuppa, darling, and tell me what was so interesting about Monday. What do you say?'

She grinned at him. Gossip was meat and drink to Pavel.

'Sounds like a bargain.'

The telling was not to be hurried, because there was a sudden flurry of customers – one man even bought a stamp album and some old coins – and Lexie had to throw away the first cup of tea and make a fresh one by the time things settled down again.

'So.' Pavel lifted his cup and crooked his little finger ostentatiously. 'Do tell Uncle Pavel everything.'

Lexie knew he'd love the story, and he did. When she finished, he observed with a satisfied sigh, 'Edith Dorothy

Lawrence sounds like a real character.'

'She called me Maud and thought I was her sister. It was impossible to follow her conversation. At moments she seemed extremely lucid, then she was off the wall completely.'

'Dementia is cruel.'

'Yes, though she seemed quite happy in her own world, most of the time. You know, she must have been in Fernhill before. She knew how to open the window, and she talked about the kitchen as if she was familiar with it. I'd love to know why she came. I don't think she just wandered randomly. It's such a long way to walk.'

Lexie put down her mug.

'Changing the subject, have you heard? Cameron Forrester's back in Hailesbank.'

A shadow of concern crossed Pavel's face. 'Have you seen him?'

'He came into the store.'

Pavel's bright eyes were shrewd. 'What did he have to say for himself?'

'I'll find out tonight. I'm going to have dinner with him.'

'Oh Lexie, sweetie, do be careful.'

She pursed her lips. Why did everyone try to protect her from Cameron? The past was long gone, and he had changed – besides, so had she.

Pavel pinched his thin lips together, but if he was considering a lecture he abandoned the idea and said instead, 'So you need a dress.' Pavel loved dressing Lexie.

'I'd almost forgotten. That's the main reason I came in.'

'I've got the very thing.' He went to a rail by a curtained-off door at the back of the shop, pushed some dresses aside and produced a hanger with a flourish. 'What do you think?'

'Oh my God!' Style, cut, material – quality lasts. Bewitched, Lexie reached out to touch the soft fabric. 'It's beautiful. Will it fit?'

Pavel's face broke into a gratified smile. 'I *knew* you'd love it. I could absolutely *see* you in it.'

She took the hanger and examined the dress with reverence. Luscious crimson and pink roses, the exact shades of her hair, tumbled carelessly on a black background. It had a boat neck and tight, elbow-length sleeves. She stroked it in awe. The thick cotton was soft and luxurious under her fingers.

'It's perfect. God, I hope I can get into it.'

'Let's see, shall we? You've lost weight this year.'

Lexie stepped into the small, curtained-off area in the corner, pulled off her trousers and sweater and slipped the dress over her head. It fell neatly onto her hips and for a moment she thought it wasn't going to be big enough, but a slight tug and the folds of fabric unfurled and shimmied down her thighs

'What's it like?'

Lexie pulled the curtain aside. 'It's only just big enough.'

Pavel stepped back to scrutinise her. 'You look stunning. *Stunning.*' His hands busied themselves around her, a little tug here, a small tweak there, until everything sat perfectly.

The dress changed how she felt inside, as vintage clothes so often did. Was it because something of the previous owner rubbed off along with the fibres of the fabric, or was that ridiculously fanciful? This dress was special. It seemed to be telling her, through subtle touches on her skin, that she was ready to drink again at the well of affection.

I *love* it,' she said, and smiled properly for the first time in a week.

Chapter Eight

**Catalogue number 12: Gold heeled sandals worn with bridal
lengha choli in traditional Indian wedding ceremony. Donated
by Parveen Robertson, Glasgow.** 'These shoes date from 1953,
when my mother was married in Kolkata, India. They were
worn under a bridal *lengha choli* – a short blouse and skirt,
with a long saree-type scarf (the *lengha*). The *lengha* was deep
red and heavily decorated with gold.' ...

Ready for love? This came as something of a surprise to Lexie,
but she knew that a dress like this couldn't lie. She prepared for
Cameron's arrival in a state of high anticipation. Where would
he take her? If it was to the smart new restaurant over the river,
she'd know he saw the date as important. But he knew she liked
Indian food, so maybe he'd pick one of the three Indian
restaurants in town. Lexie's tastes had changed and grown in
the last four years. Had Cameron's? She realised how little she
knew about what he had become and the flutter in her gut
intensified.

She turned sideways and examined her profile in the mirror.
The cut of the dress was neat, but it could have been made for
her curves. It wasn't revealing, but it was certainly alluring.
Teamed with black-heeled t-bar patent shoes, it was the perfect
outfit for a date – but if Cameron took her to an Indian
restaurant she'd be ridiculously overdressed.

Then the doorbell rang and it was too late to change her
mind. She heard her mother answer it, and all at once she was a
teenager again, all jitters and excitement. Silly. This was
Cameron, for heaven's sake, this wasn't a date with some new
man, whose voice and style and sense of humour were

unfamiliar. She wouldn't have to strain to find commonality, or wonder, through the chit chat, what it might be like to have sex with him. She took a last look in the mirror and eyes the colour of a thrush's wings studied her face. She twisted her head away. Sometimes it was better not to look too closely.

From the landing she could see the top of a straw hat. Her mother, in faded beige chinos and a crumpled tan tee shirt, had been gardening. From the little of her thin body that was visible, Lexie sensed that she was tense with disapproval, but straining to be polite. Martha found ways of conveying what she was feeling without expressing it in words. She listened to the conversation, phrases bandied back and forth laden with unspoken meaning.

'Hello, Cameron. It's been a while.' (Where the hell have you been?)

'Hi Martha. You're looking well.' (A lie, but a laudable one.)

'Alexa said you were back.' (But that's all she said.)

'I've missed Hailesbank.' (Like a sore head?)

At this, Martha abandoned subtlety and became more direct.

'Really? You could have come back sooner. It's been here all the time.'

'Circumstances, I'm afraid. I'm back now, and I couldn't wait to see Lexie.'

Silence followed, which gave Lexie a fair idea of what her mother was thinking. Any minute now she'd say something irretrievable like, 'Don't you dare hurt her again'. She gave a light cough and started down the last flight of stairs to the hall.

Two faces turned upwards in her direction. Her mother's, tired and watchful, cheeks hollowed by grieving – and Cameron's, Jamie's best friend, her one-time lover, and quite possibly her future lover too.

His familiar features broke into an admiring grin. 'You look great.'

Lexie's lips began a soft curl upwards, before she heard him add, 'But you're not going to wear that, are you?'

'I'm sorry?' On the last tread, she faltered.

'Didn't I say? Oops. We're off to the pub at Port Seton.

There's a boules match on the beach, I thought you'd like it. And they do great smoked sausage and chips. You did say we could use your Dad's car, didn't you?'

Lexie tried to hide her dismay. She disliked games, was not a fan of smoked sausage and had not offered transport.

'Jeans would be best, sweetie. And trainers. I'll wait.'

He had forgotten her likes and dislikes. The easy intimacy had been lost across the years. Well, they'd have to reconstruct it. Lexie sensed her mother's displeasure and mustered enthusiasm to counteract it. Tonight she'd go along with his plans.

'It's all right about the car, isn't it?' She appealed to Martha, willing her not to fuss.

'Well, your father's not using it,' Martha said. Her voice was neutral, but Lexie heard the false notes and cringed. Martha would come round, once she saw that Cameron made her happy – because he'd always made her happy, hadn't he, right up till when he left? Give it time.

She turned and ran back upstairs to her room. Jeans didn't feature in her wardrobe. She'd once had the opportunity to buy a pair of Gloria Vanderbilts at a specialist vintage fashion auction in London. It was Patrick who'd spotted the event, a huge affair being mounted in aid of a children's charity, and suggested they go. 'My treat,' he'd insisted when she'd balked at the cost of flying to London just for the auction. The day would live for ever in her mind. She remembered every whirlwind moment, from the pre-dawn start for the airport to the bitter disappointment of being unsuccessful in her bid for the lot she'd set her heart on – early Manolo Blahniks, a sublimely made pair of stilettos in scarlet leather, entwined with wild flowers fashioned from feathers, sequins, ribbons, silk brocade and bits of lace. The bidding had soared immediately, way out of her budget range, and she'd had to duck out.

'It's not the end of the world,' Patrick had teased, seeing her face.

'No,' she'd agreed gamely, but the disappointment had been bitter.

'What about the jeans?'

'One thing I hate.'

She'd come away with only a jacket, not Chanel but just as smart. It was still one of her favourites.

So now: what to wear to fit in with Cameron's plans? She settled on cream linen slacks and a pair of flat pumps, teamed with a Liberty floral print top and cream 1950s bolero. It was a warm evening.

In the middle of the afternoon, the telephone rang at Capital Art. Victoria answered it in her best plummy voice.

'Good afternoon, Capital Art, how may I—?'

She hadn't even finished when a crisp voice broke in, 'Put me on to Patrick, will you?'

Victoria was startled, but remembered her training.

'I'll just check if he's in. Who may I say is calling?'

'Tell him it's the Queen. Tell him anything you want, just put me through.'

She was not accustomed to such directness, but she soldiered on.

'I'll see if he's available. One minute please.'

She put the call on hold before she was interrupted again.

'Patrick? There's a woman on the line asking to speak to you. She wouldn't give her name, said I should tell you it's the Queen. I wasn't sure what to—'

'Sharp voice, slight foreign accent?'

Victoria was surprised.

'Yes, that about describes her, I guess.'

Patrick was in the office to the side of the gallery, but Victoria could hear the groan from the reception desk.

'Would you like me to tell her you're out?' she asked helpfully.

'It's a kind thought, but no, you'd better put her through. It's my sister, Cora.'

In the office next door, Patrick picked up the phone. Cora was, in fact, his step-sister. At thirty-three, she was younger than he was by a decade, the progeny of his mother and her second husband, Theo Spyridis, and she had inherited the best of her father and the worst. The best was his tawny-skinned good looks, the worst his utter fecklessness. She was bright and had spurts of ambition, but also had a tendency to abandon paid work in favour of life in Greece as soon as her bank balance grew – only to realise, when bills mounted unsustainably, that she had to find another job back in Britain. Sometimes she turned to Theo for help in this, sometimes to their mother, Orla. If she got no joy with either, she called Patrick.

There was no preamble. 'I need a job, Pats.'

He hated the abbreviation. 'Have you tried the Job Centre?'

'Don't be ridiculous. I'm not prepared to do any old thing.'

In the past, Cora had been a gofer for a film director and a receptionist at a television studio. She had cooked haute-cuisine meals at an exclusive ski chalet at Zermatt and for a boardroom in the City, run a high-profile account in a public relations agency in London, and organised two Balls and a countrywide treasure hunt for an impecunious conservation society. What she had never done was scrub floors, wait at tables or work in a call centre.

'Haven't any of your contacts got anything for you?'

'Times are hard, darling, in case you hadn't noticed. How's your business going, by the way? Haven't you snagged a rich heiress yet?'

'I could ask the same of you,' Patrick said briskly. He adored his little sister, more than he would ever admit, but she had caught him at a bad time. He was about to fob her off when an idea occurred to him. He had been looking at premises on the High Street in Hailesbank – not for another art gallery, but with the thought that he might open a shop for upmarket handcrafted objects. Top end art was a niche market and a craft shop offered the advantage of turnover. Cash flow is king. Besides, Patrick admired well-made artefacts and Hailesbank was the perfect testing ground for such a venture.

'There might be something—' he began.

She was onto it at once. 'You're a darling. I'll come up tomorrow on the nine forty-five from Heathrow. You can tell me about it then.' And she rang off.

Patrick was left staring at the phone and wondering whether

he should have kept his mouth shut. Still, Cora was more than capable of doing the job, if she liked the idea, and he only wanted someone temporary to get the place up and running.

He replaced the phone, glanced at his watch, and realised it was getting late. He picked up his jacket, checked his appearance in the mirror in his office, and headed for the door.

'I'm going out,' he called to Victoria. 'You're okay to lock up, aren't you?'

Victoria braced her shoulders and straightened her back. It was a new responsibility and showed Patrick's faith in her. 'Sure.'

'Good girl.'

She watched as he ran down the stone steps to the pavement with natural grace, his jacket hooked over his left shoulder with one finger, his mobile clamped to the ear on the other side. Was he going to meet Cora? She wasn't entirely convinced that Cora was his sister. Many women traipsed adoringly after Patrick and she was sure he used a number of euphemisms to describe their status in his life. She wouldn't care how he described her, so long as it wasn't 'good girl'.

Patrick wasn't going to meet Cora. He was taking Diana Golspie to the opening of an exhibition of Etruscan art at the National Museum in Chambers Street. It had been in his diary for weeks. Such receptions were a great place to meet and network, and Diana was the perfect companion: glamorous, knowledgeable and a relaxed conversationalist.

He tried to forget the discussion with Cora as he pushed the buzzer on the door to Diana's flat. The last time he'd been here, he'd treated her appallingly and the memory of it still made him feel guilty. He should not take out his feelings about Lexie on Diana. Even though he made up for it by treating her to an expensive meal, he resolved to make amends all over again by being extra nice to her this evening.

'You're looking sumptuous.'

He didn't have to lie. Diana was a handsome woman; tall, with endless legs and a glorious mane of auburn hair. She was confident and assertive, and she adored being pampered. In short, she was about as different from Lexie Gordon as any woman could be.

'Thank you, darling.' A cloud of Givenchy smothered him as she leaned in for a kiss. 'Time for a drinkie?'

'I could murder a beer.'

'I hope you've not made any appointments for afterwards. I've booked a table at that little place in Gullane.'

'*Gullane?*'

'Well-known golfer's paradise?'

Gullane was down the coast, well on the way to Hailesbank. 'How will you—'

Diana continued as if he hadn't spoken, 'Sir James and Lady Catriona are joining us.'

He had to hand it to her. She was an arch manipulator. Diana knew perfectly well that Patrick never invited women to The Gables, but she also knew he had been courting this wealthy couple for some time with a view to investing in the global expansion of Capital Art, without success. Securing their company at dinner was a coup, but the price – he saw it coming – would be a night in his bed. She had manoeuvred him into a very tight corner.

Diana flicked open a bottle of lager and handed it to him.

'Don't worry, darling, I've put a couple of little things in a bag. You can bring me back in the morning.'

Her fine-featured face was serene – she knew better than to show triumph. Patrick had to admire her balls. In many ways, Diana Golspie was the perfect match for him. He gave in graciously.

'You,' he pulled her close and kissed her with zest, 'are quite some woman.'

At a small pub in the seaside community of Port Seton, Lexie was staring at a piece of smoked sausage. It lay, glossy and brown, across a mountain of chips in a wicker basket lined with greaseproof paper. She could see beads of fat glistening on the paper and felt nauseated.

'Might I have fish instead?'

Cameron laughed. 'Sausage, sweets, that's the speciality in

this pub.'

'It's a fishing port. They land fish here. Surely someone can find a piece of fish somewhere.'

On the next table, a man overheard.

'The fish is fresh from the sea, right enough. Give the lady a break, man!'

Cameron beamed. 'No worries,' he said without rancour. He reached across to Alexa's basket and lifted her sausage.

'Jimmy! Bring the lady a single fish, will you? Ta. Okay, sweets?'

He stuffed the end of the sausage into his mouth and munched on it appreciatively.

The fish, when it came, was meltingly moist and Lexie was appeased. Outside, when they'd finished eating, Cameron pulled her close and kissed her ear.

'Sorry, love. I forget not everyone shares my taste. Okay?'

He was strong and muscular and her body responded to the feel of him just as it used to.

'Perfect,' she whispered, closing her eyes so that the salty smell of him took over her senses.

'So let's wow them at the boules, eh?'

On the beach, Lexie removed her shoes and felt the sand squidge between her toes. A bubble of seawater appeared as her toes disappeared in the warm damp. They were going to play on the firm surface left by the outgoing tide. Beside her, the low sun streaked the water with a flash of orange and gold. She watched it dreamily. Sunsets were notoriously difficult to capture in paint without appearing unreal and Lexie itched to take on the challenge.

'Over here, love. Best of three ends. Let's go!'

Cameron was like an excited puppy, eager to play, and she couldn't help smiling. This was what she needed – this injection of energy into the monotonous drudgery she had allowed her life to become. It was good for her.

'Ready!' she called, smiling and paddling towards him. A wave washed over her feet, altering the pattern of the ripples left by the receding tide yet again. It felt like a new start.

'Happy?'

Cameron glanced across at her as he steered Tom's Volvo down the dual carriageway back towards Hailesbank.

Lexie yawned and stretched. 'Blissfully relaxed.'

'Told you you'd enjoy it.'

'I hate to admit it, but you were right.'

'That last ball you threw was pure genius,' he chuckled, putting on his indicator to signal the turn onto the slip road. 'Landing right on the jack like that. Squashed it right into the sand. Never knew you were so talented at boules.'

'Nor me.'

He was laughing and looking across at her when there was a bang and the car juddered. Cameron slammed on the brakes and Lexie was thrown forward towards the windscreen.

'I'm going to die,' she thought. 'Just like Jamie.'

She heard a scream and realised the sound was coming out of her own mouth. The seatbelt bit into her shoulder and its hard edges dug into the flesh all the way down her torso before she was thrown back. Her head hit the padded cushion of the headrest with a soft thump. Cameron shouted, 'Shit,' the car slewed round and skidded to a halt halfway across the grass verge, the engine cut out and there was silence.

It was eleven o'clock at night, and the sky was a velvety Prussian blue, but this was Scotland and it was May, so it wasn't quite dark. Lexie opened her eyes cautiously. She could see nothing but sky, and trees lit by a gibbous moon.

'What happened?'

'I hit a deer. It just ran out in front of me.' His face was chalky white in the moonlight. 'There was nothing I could do.'

Her heart began to slow as the terror receded. 'I didn't even see it.'

Cameron slumped across the wheel.

'Fucking hell. What's your dad going to say?'

'It wasn't your fault. He'll just be thankful we're all right.'

Headlights swept across the car as a vehicle turned down the slip road. Immediately, Lexie grew anxious.

'Are we clear of the road?'

'I think so. I'd better see what the damage is.'

Cameron got out as the other car pulled in behind them. Lexie opened her door in time to hear a voice say, 'Everything all right? What's happened?'

There was no mistaking that voice. As Lexie's eyes became accustomed to the half-darkness she began to make out Patrick Mulgrew's familiar figure.

Behind his shadowy shape, another materialised. The moon crept out from behind a passing cloud and slid off auburn hair to light a face of classic beauty, and a voice made husky by tobacco smoke said, 'Patrick? What is it, darling?'

Lexie clutched at the door of the car. She was unable to decide what was worse: hitting a deer, or meeting Patrick in this way.

Patrick recognised her at once – it was impossible not to in this light, with the moon seeding her vivid hair with winking diamonds.

'Lexie?'

'Hello, Patrick.'

He was uncomfortably conscious of Diana, coming up at his shoulder. Of all the times to meet her. It took a moment to register that Lexie wasn't driving.

'We hit a deer,' came a voice from the driver's side of the car. 'There was no chance to swerve.'

Patrick remembered the deer he'd just avoided last week and the memory of startled eyes saddened him. Luck, it seemed, had run out for one small fawn.

'A young one? White spots on its back?'

'Didn't have time to see, there was just this almighty thud then we crashed to a stop.'

Lexie began to weep. There was no sound, she didn't even sniff, but Patrick sensed distress and looked over in time to glimpse a streak of silver on her cheek. She reached up and dashed it away with her sleeve, but another chased it, then another. He ached to gather her in his arms and even started to move towards her before two voices cut in.

'Is it dead?' from Diana, with curiosity and, 'We'd better take a look,' from Lexie's companion.

Lexie jerked her head away.

There was no sign of the deer, only a significant dent in the front bonnet of the Volvo.

'Do you think it will survive?' Lexie's voice was thick.

'Probably limped off to die,' her companion said, 'but I'm sure it'll be quick,' he added hastily when Lexie let out a sob.

Patrick wanted to punch the man and carry Lexie to his car. He wanted to cuddle her and care for her and chase all thoughts of the deer away, but these things were impossible. There was a brief discussion about the car and whether it was all right to drive, but the damage was superficial and Patrick could find no excuse for detaining them.

'Will you be all right?' he asked Lexie in a low voice as Diana strode off.

She nodded, her eyes still round with shock.

'Can I call you?' It was the second time he'd asked this, in just a matter of days.

There was a slight hesitation before she shook her head, but she was still staring at him. The moment stretched and stretched, then her eyes flickered to the man she was with and Diana called, 'Coming, darling?'

He was left in impotent frustration watching Lexie climb back into her car.

Chapter Nine

Catalogue number 29: Dr Martens, black leather boots with distinctive yellow stitching around the sole. Donated by Kevin Murieston, Hailesbank. Klaus Märtens boots became popular in Britain among factory workers, postmen and policemen, but by the 1970s had become the favoured footwear of skinheads. They were adopted as a fashion statement by the grunge movement in the 1990s. 'These remind me of my misspent youth,' says Kev...

Alexa couldn't get Edith Lawrence's face out of her head. The old lady hardly seemed capable of forming stratagems, yet somewhere within her muddled brain was a compass that had steered her to Fernhill.

Alexa wanted to find out more, but was concerned that doing so might upset the delicate balance of Edith's mind. But discussions with the staff at Edith's care home were encouraging and her son (sixty-five years old, in London, and not in good health himself) was sufficiently intrigued to give his permission for a return visit to the house.

'You really think she might have a secret?' he wheezed, when Lexie called him to discuss the matter, 'Mother? Well, if the people at Sea View are alright with it, then so am I. Let me know how you get on.'

Lexie arranged to bring Edith back for lunch. She was worried about doing everything herself – handling Edith, driving (which she hated), concentrating on the route and trying to talk all at the same time. What if Edith proved to be upset and needed calming? It would be much better, she decided, if there was someone with her to help – but who? Molly was too busy, Neil would be working, Carlotta ditto. Her father would be at the Emporium and no doubt her mother would be fussing over the lunch preparations. A little reluctantly, thinking he might find it tedious, she asked Cameron.

'No worries,' he agreed cheerfully, 'Sounds interesting.'

'I'm not sure about that. She's very odd.'

'I'm okay with odd.' His grin was easy and she experienced again the sharp jolt of the electricity that so often arced between them. It was only a matter of time, she knew, till they found themselves in bed once more. Time, or timing.

They'd bring Edith to Fernhill in another week.

On the appointed morning, Martha despatched Lexie into town.

'I forgot to buy bread,' she said, her shoulders sagging in the way that was now so dispiritingly familiar. 'Would you? That new baker's...?'

Lexie wanted Edith's visit to go well but she was irritated by this extra duty. Still, she thought, the walk would do her good, and she could say hi to Pavel on her way back.

The bread was still warm, and the delicious smell of it wakened her senses. She turned into Kittle's Lane and there was no sign of the sandwich board on the pavement. She glanced at her watch. It was half past ten and Cobbles was still closed. She couldn't understand it – Pavel always opened up sharp.

'I like to get properly organised before the rush,' he'd explain, with a self-deprecating smile.

They both knew there was never a rush.

She pressed her nose against the window, cupping her hands round her eyes to cut out the sun . He hadn't even switched on the lights. As her eyes became accustomed to the gloom, she made out the Regency console table, then the shield-backed mahogany chairs. She half expected to see Pavel doing some quick polishing or rearranging of the candlesticks on the dining table, but she could see nothing. She pulled out her mobile and dialled the shop. Immediately, she heard the trilling of the telephone from the back room, but there was still no sign of Pavel.

Really worried now, she peered inside again. This time,

84

something moved. Was that a flash of white on the Persian rug? Yes – there! A hand, surely. She rapped on the door frantically. Pavel must have collapsed, she could just make out the shape of his favourite burgundy velvet jacket among the jumble of chair legs and lampstands.

'Pavel!' she shouted, her voice shrill with anxiety, 'Pavel! It's Lexie! Can you hear me?'

The hand moved again, then she saw him struggling to sit, his slender frame creaking as if it needed oiling. She rapped on the glass again.

'Pavel!'

His legs were sticking straight out on the floor in front of him, thin pins encased in black velvet. After what seemed an age, he looked across at her and she saw a glimmer of life come back into his eyes.

'Can you get up?' she called. 'Take your time now.'

He mouthed something at her and started to twist onto his knees. This was sensible. She saw one hand grasping the chair nearest to him and he began to claw his way upwards. When he was three-quarters upright, he placed both hands flat on the striped satin of the seat upholstery and paused, his shoulders drooping, his head hanging down as if its weight was too much to bear. Finally, he straightened and turned. By the time he reached the door, he was smiling bravely, although his face was grey.

'Hello, darling.'

'What happened?' His hands were trembling. 'Come back in, sit down.'

She pulled a chair clear of the table and lowered him onto it, her hands firm under his arms. He was slim to the point of skinniness, but right now he felt like a dead weight.

'Not quite sure, sweetie. Must have fainted.'

She felt his forehead. The temperature seemed normal. 'How are you feeling now?'

'Right as rain.'

She laid her fingers on his pulse and frowned. It was racing unnaturally, the blood pounding through the veins like horses at a gallop.

'Well,' he admitted as her glare intensified, 'maybe a little shaky.'

'Any pains anywhere?'

'No.' He shook his head but a tell-tale hand crept up to his chest.

'Liar.'

'I'm all right. I need to open the shop, darling.'

'You sit right there. I'm going to get you some tea. And I have to get you to the hospital.'

'Don't be ridiculous, Lexie darling.'

'The doctor, then.'

'I'm fine.'

'Pavel, you are quite clearly *not* fine.'

The colour was returning to his face and something of the old glint to his eyes.

'I'm going to open the shop, Lexie.'

'You're an obstinate man.'

'And you're a bully.'

They glared at each other, then Pavel's creased face split into a smile.

'All right, you're not a bully you're a sweetheart. I'll accept the tea, but then I *am* going to open up.'

Lexie, like her father, could be very stubborn. She stood her ground. 'Only if you promise you'll make an appointment with the doctor today.'

'If you insist,' he conceded with a sigh, 'but it was just a little turn, that's all.'

By the time she'd made the tea, he'd shuffled into the back room and was sitting by his desk.

'Can you manage a biscuit? It might be good to eat something.'

'Not yet, sweetie, you're such a fusser. Just the tea.'

His hand was still far from steady, but the tea seemed to revive him.

'Any idea why you fainted? Have you been feeling funny?'

'No, not at all. And I feel so much better now, you have a magic touch with the teapot.'

'You're doing too much. You're in here at all hours, Pavel.

You can't go on like this.'

'I'm *fine.*'

'Isn't there anyone who can come and help out? Your sister?'

'Hanke? You have to be joking. I haven't seen her since my mother's funeral and anyway, she lives in Slough.'

'Then I'm going to help you. You shouldn't be here on your own all the time.'

'You? Lexie, darling, you're working flat out as it is, and besides, there's your demanding mother…'

'She's not demanding,' Lexie jumped to Martha's defence, 'she just needs support. She'll get back to normal soon. We'll all get back to normal soon. We have to.'

'Sweetie, listen to yourself…'

'Anyway, that's irrelevant. I can easily spare some time to help out here. I'd like to.'

She dug her heels in and refused to let Pavel open the shop until he'd agreed a plan, so she won the battle of wills this time.

'Saturday mornings, then. That's all.'

'Saturday mornings,' she agreed. 'I'll open up and manage things until midday. That'll give you a bit of free time. To *relax* in,' she added with a stern glance. 'And just you remember that you have given me your promise that you'll go to the doctor and get a check-up.'

'You are *such* a bossy boots,' Pavel sighed, his hand closing round hers, 'but I do love you.'

Because of Pavel's 'funny turn', she was a few minutes late getting home from Cobbles and Cameron was sitting on the doorstep at Fernhill, waiting for her.

'There's no-one in,' he said, jumping from sitting to standing in one fluid movement.

'Really? Mum must be in the garden. Sorry I'm late, I had a crisis.'

Cameron held up a set of car keys.

'Do you still trust me?'

'It wasn't your fault,' she reiterated for the dozenth time. Whenever she thought of the accident, she thought not of the fawn, nor of Cameron, nor even of her parents (who'd had to be told). It was Patrick Mulgrew her disloyal brain remembered. Correction, not just Patrick: Patrick and a woman, damn it. 'You did well not to turn the car over. Yes, I trust you.'

'Phew. Jonas has lent me his Discovery. Thought a high car might be easier for the old wifie. Should we get going? You can tell me about your crisis on the way.'

'Not much to tell. Pavel collapsed. I found him on the floor at the shop.'

'The old geezer at Cobbles? I didn't know he was even still alive.'

'He's not that old, and this is the first time he's had a problem.'

'Is he okay?'

'I think so. I've made him promise to let me help out at the shop on Saturday mornings. I think he does too much.'

Cameron glanced across at her and shook his head.

'Oh Lexie, Lexie, you're such a sucker. You let people trample all over you.'

'I do not. I just want to help him.'

'You always want to help. Your parents. Pavel.' He reached a T-junction and halted before turning right and accelerating again. 'Don't get all indignant. It's what I love about you, but you do need to think about your own needs.'

There it was again, that phrase dropped so casually into the conversation. *It's what I love about you.* When Pavel said it, she accepted it cheerfully for what it was, but when Cameron said it – well, what did he mean, exactly? Nothing, she suspected, calming herself down because she was determined not to read too much into the words. He said it too easily, it was just his way of talking.

'He's on his own, and he's such a dear. He never complains, but I think he misses his partner Guy terribly. His sister's a complete witch, apparently,'

'You mean she can't cope with her brother being gay.'

Lexie sighed. 'Yes, I expect that's it.' She leant forward and turned on the radio.

Cameron had turned along the winding back road from

Hailesbank to Musselburgh, rather than the busy main road. It was the route she'd have chosen herself, because she hated driving in traffic, but why had *he* come this way? It went past the farm where she'd had her studio years ago, before he disappeared.

It was distracting sitting in the car so close to Cameron. He smelt fresh and soapy and she imagined him stepping out of the shower, his hair damp, drops of water glistening on pink, scrubbed skin. She crossed her legs.

There was the barn, up on the hill. Just an old barn, with four sturdy walls and a roof pierced by huge slanting windows that let in the most wonderful light. Just a barn – yet it had been a perfect studio, the space of her dreams, with its huge workspace and small bedroom and kitchen. She'd been so happy then.

'I thought about you every day,' Cameron said.

'What?'

'When I was away.'

He slowed to take the sharp bend on the road below the barn.

'There's no need to lie to me, Cameron.'

'But it's true.'

'*Damn* that!' she burst out, consumed with a sudden fury. 'How *dare* you?'

Cameron looked startled. 'Okay, maybe I shouldn't have—'

'Shouldn't have what? Shouldn't have disappeared without a single word? Shouldn't have left me wondering what the hell had happened? Shouldn't have left me feeling a bloody failure?'

'You didn't think that, surely?' He looked at her, his sandy eyes suddenly intense.

'Watch the *road*.' Her hand curled convulsively round the thick handle on the door. 'What do you *think* I felt?'

'But I was the one who was a failure.'

'No, you were in control. You were the one who took the decision to go off. How else could I look at it? Whatever happened, I was the one who'd failed to keep you interested enough to stay.'

'No! That wasn't it at all. I didn't—'

'Oh, spare me your excuses now, please.'

Lexie didn't understand her own outburst – her anger had

89

sprung from nowhere. She wanted to mend fences with Cameron, but she needed to understand what had made him leave.

Frustratingly, he did shut up, which annoyed her even more.

There was silence. They crossed the flyover above the A1 and approached the first houses on the outskirts of the old fishing town of Musselburgh. They were nearly there and soon she'd *have* to talk to him.

Cameron broke the silence.

'You look great when you're angry, by the way,' he grinned. 'Your nose goes pink.'

'It does not!' Her hand flew to her nose.

'Does so. Where's this place we're headed to, then?'

'Next left. See the large sign? Turn in there.'

Cameron inched the car expertly into a tight gap in the car park in front of the building. As Lexie struggled into the narrow space between the door and the neighbouring car, a large truck drew up and stopped on the road outside. At the corner, the lights had turned red and a small queue of traffic formed quickly. Engines belched fumes, music throbbed, cars roared past in the other direction. How had Edith Lawrence managed to walk out of this gate and along this road and be challenged by nobody?

'Not much of a sea view, is it?' Cameron said, locking the car.

Lexie eyed the developments along the coastline.

'Maybe Sea View was an accurate description fifty years ago. It is a bit depressing, isn't it?'

'I guess there might have been trees here,' Cameron gestured round the car park, 'and maybe a lawn. Looks as if they tarmacked it over to make parking spaces for visitors.'

'Looking at trees,' Lexie said, 'helps ill people to recover. I read that in a newspaper recently.'

'Well, there's no recovery from old age,' Cameron said with his customary bluntness, 'so I guess it makes no difference to this lot.'

Edith was ready for them, after a fashion.

90

'She's wearing odd shoes,' Cameron hissed as Edith trotted with surprising nimbleness along the corridor towards them, her arm through a carer's.

He was right. On her left foot was a black walking shoe, laced criss-cross and finished in a bow, double-knotted for security; on the right, a navy slip-on with a more pointed toe.

The carer apologised. 'We couldn't find a pair. Edith's a demon for hiding things, aren't you my love?' She gave the old woman an affectionate cuddle.

Edith chortled. 'You have to,' she said with a sly sideways glance. 'People steal things here.'

Cameron grinned at her. 'Like squirrels? Hiding things for a rainy day? What do they do with one odd shoe?'

'I needed to escape,' Edith said with great precision, 'and you need shoes, you know.'

'That's very true. Shoes do it for me when I'm escaping.'

'*Cameron!*' Lexie hissed out of the corner of her mouth.

'Well, come on, slippers are no good for running away, are they? And as for bare feet —I ran away once, when I was six, but my mother knew I'd just hidden in our neighbour's garden and that I'd come back when I was hungry. Isn't that right, Edith? Doesn't do to be hungry, eh?'

'Maudie makes great rice pudding,' Edith said. 'Are we having rice pudding for lunch, Maud?'

Lexie grew weak at the thought of an afternoon of this. 'Maybe. I don't really know.'

'The coat's not hers either,' the carer confided, 'but we couldn't find a name tag on it, so it will do.'

'Where's my bag?' Edith asked, looking around. Her hair had been washed and looked soft and silky, like a baby's hair. It was so fine and thin that the pink scalp was clearly visible.

'Here it is.' The carer turned to Lexie and said under her breath, 'There's no money in it, I'm afraid, just a hankie and some odds and sods.'

'Come on then, gorgeous,' Cameron tucked his arm through Edith's, 'let's go.'

'Where are we going?'

'We're going on an outing, Edith,' Cameron said, 'A special

trip.'

When he switched on the charm, Cameron could be irresistible. Edith went straight into full flirt mode. 'An outing, how delicious. Will we have ice cream?'

'If you want.' He started to move her along the corridor towards the front door. 'And sweeties. What kind of sweeties do you like?'

'Humbugs.'

Cameron laughed. 'Humbugs? *You're* an old humbug, you daft thing.'

Lexie was shocked. You can't say that to her, she wanted to hiss, but Edith just cackled.

'Humbug yourself,' she said.

Chapter Ten

Catalogue number 1: Ladies' court shoe, black patent leather, slightly pointed toe, simple bow embellishment, small heel. Donated by Martha Gordon. This shoe says everything about Martha Gordon's lifestyle as a legal secretary. They are smart, but practical, designed to give comfort throughout a working day, while still being stylish. For Martha Gordon, however, they tell the story of a life she has lost. 'I am no longer the woman who wore these shoes,' she says...

Artists are taught to observe. There are dozens of colours in a peach: russet, gold, pomegranate, butternut, caramel, tan, bisque, copper, terracotta, carrot, burnt almond, ochre, clementine, brioche, honey. The light streams in from the left onto a silver jug, but reflects there, and there. The symmetry of the daisy is mirrored by the spokes of a bicycle wheel.

Lexie knew all this, it had been drummed into her often enough at college – and yet when Edith Lawrence entered Fernhill, she found herself looking at the home she'd grown up in with new eyes.

'Leo's looking tired,' was the first thing Edith said, before they were even inside.

'Leo?'

Bent fingers stroked the front door knocker, a scowling lion's face fashioned from iron, with a heavy ring through its nose. How many times had Lexie come in through this door and forgotten to notice it? It had been there for ever.

'A wire brush, that's what you need. Mother's help used to do it every week, she kept it lovely. *Look* at the rust.' Edith tutted reproachfully.

'We'll clean it tomorrow,' Lexie promised, annoyed at her own inattention. She should have noticed the lion. Martha wasn't up to observing such details of housekeeping at the moment and didn't have the energy to deal with them.

'Roar,' Cameron said, opening his mouth wide and turning his head sideways in a poor imitation of the Metro-Goldwyn-Mayer trade mark. He'd been enjoying Edith ever since they'd left Sea View, and his observations were becoming more and more hilarious. Lexie shot him yet another glance she hoped was withering, and said cheerfully to Edith, 'Do come inside.'

Edith sniffed noisily. 'Ahhh! Roast beef. Is it ready?'

'I'm sure it'll be ready in a minute.'

She threw up a hand dramatically to shield her eyes.

'It's terribly *bright*.'

Lexie looked around at the hall, surprised. It had been redecorated at least twice since they'd lived here, and was currently painted in shades of stone – pale above the dado rail, a fraction darker below it. The space didn't seem unduly bright to her. She tried to picture what it had been like originally, but couldn't.

'Can you remember?' she asked her mother. 'Was it dark before we painted it?'

'I don't recall,' Martha said, coming forward. 'Hello Edith.'

'The stair window made a red patch like a rabbit in the corner when the sun was out,' Edith said, ignoring her and heading for the far corner of the hall, where Tom now kept his neglected golf clubs. She shoved impatiently at the bag. Cameron caught it just before it toppled over. 'See?'

Her finger pointed in triumph at a blood-red patch low on the wall. Lexie looked up. Just at this time of day, and only because the sun was shining, there was indeed a rabbit-shaped patch of scarlet on the deeply-embossed paper – refracted light from the Edwardian stained glass on the stairwell distorted by some small unevenness of the wall.

'It's a miracle,' Cameron said from behind the golf clubs.

Lexie grabbed the bag from him and dumped them back in the corner.

'Edith,' she said, turning her back firmly on Cameron, 'why

94

don't you come into the living room? Maybe you'd like a little sherry?'

But Edith was standing stock still at the bottom of the stairs, staring up. Her mouth had sagged open and her eyes were wide, the pale irises made paler by emotion.

'Oh my,' she whispered, 'oh my.'

'Through here?' Lexie tucked her hand gently under Edith's elbow and tried to turn her towards the living room.

Edith shook her off impatiently.

'Upstairs,' she said, all the brightness leached from her voice. 'It's upstairs.'

'What's upstairs, Edith?'

'I have to go up.'

'That's okay. Here, let me help—'

She started to take Edith's arm, but Cameron shot forward and got there first.

'Let's go together, shall we? I'll take one arm, you can hold on to the banister with the other hand.'

It was an odd procession: the frail ninety-year-old woman with shoes that didn't match; the sturdy man in jeans and trainers; the girl in the vintage pinafore with cropped crimson hair; and tagging behind them all, the sixty-something woman whose face was alight with interest for the first time in a year. Near the top of the first flight, Cameron said, 'Which way, darling?' with such unexpected gentleness that a lump formed in Alexa's throat.

Edith didn't miss a beat. She didn't turn the corner to the second flight, but instead moved unhesitatingly across the landing and reached for the handle on Jamie's door. Lexie, still only half way up the stairs, froze. Behind her, she heard her mother's sharp intake of breath. Edith was fretting with the knob, its smoothness making it hard for her slight hands to grasp, so Cameron reached round and turned it for her. The door swung open and for a moment Edith was silhouetted in the sunshine like some apocalyptic figure. Her feet, in their odd shoes, were planted wide apart to provide a broad base to steady herself, and the coat-that-wasn't-her-coat flared outwards at the hem, then settled as she stilled. Wisps of white hair framed her head like the seeds on a dandelion. One puff and she'd be gone.

Then she was inside, and Lexie flew up the last few stairs in an instant. What did she want in there? Why Jamie's room? And how – dear God – how would her mother react?

By the time Edith reached the fireplace, Cameron, Lexie and Martha were all in the room. Edith made her way to the chimney, unsteadily but with determination and purpose. Cameron's joviality was overtaken by curiosity, while Martha stood by the door, her tension obvious.

The silence was absolute.

Then Edith fell to her knees, Cameron rushed forward to help her and Martha jerked as if released from a trance.

'Just move this, laddie,' Edith said impatiently to Cameron as she tried to shove aside a heavy stoneware vase filled with dried flowers. Lexie noticed it for the first time. When had that been put there? Surely it wasn't something Jamie had ever done? He definitely hadn't been a dried-flowers type of guy.

Cameron lifted the vase and put it well out of the way. By the time he turned back, Edith was kneeling on the slate hearthstone, trying to peer up the chimney.

'It's in here,' she said, her voice quite sure of itself.

'What's in here, Edith?'

'Up there. Up there,' she said impatiently, reaching her arm forward and trying to stick it up inside the chimney.

'Okay. Why don't you move aside, and let me find it? Lexie?'

Lexie responded hastily, pulling a couple of pillows off the bed as she passed. 'Why don't you sit back on these and let Cameron find it?'

Whatever 'it' is.

Edith's body was rigid, but she allowed herself to be guided onto the pillows where she sat, for all the world like a small fairy on a toadstool, supervising proceedings.

'I can't feel anything,' Cameron said after a tense interval.

'There's a loose brick. On the left.'

'Really?' He fumbled around, dislodging a shower of soot. 'Damn.'

Martha said, 'It hasn't been swept in an age, we never use the fire.'

A brick fell onto the hearth with a resounding clatter and split in two. 'Hell,' Cameron cursed. 'Sorry.'

Edith leant forward. 'That's it!' she said, her voice higher than normal, 'go on, laddie, in there. It's in there, behind the bricks.'

Cameron's head had almost disappeared up the chimney. Lexie watched as another small cloud of soot swirled lazily downwards, settling in his hair and on his face. There was a scraping sound, then a grunt. He was leaning as far in as he could.

'Got it!'

He pulled out a small box with a jubilant flourish.

'Here,' Edith demanded, almost rolling off pillows in her eagerness.

Cameron placed the box carefully on her lap. Her face was working energetically, the mouth puckering and crumpling, trailing a fine web of lines and wrinkles in its wake, the nostrils flaring as if she was trying to grab for breath.

Lexie stared down at the box, fighting the impulse to kneel down and rip off the top to see for herself what was inside. It looked innocuous enough, just brown card, smeared with soot and faded with age, but otherwise in good condition.

'What is it, Edith?'

But Edith didn't take off the lid. Instead, she clutched the box messily to her chest, her breathing quickening alarmingly.

Cameron said, 'All right, ducks?' and sat on the floor next to her. His hair was thick with soot and there was a smudge across his cheek, but Lexie had never found him more attractive than she did in this moment of tenderness.

'Would you like me to help?'

He had one arm around Edith, his other hand stroking hers in a gesture so sweet that it caught Lexie's breath. After a few moments, Edith began to relax. Her breathing slowed and her arms unclenched. The box, released, fell to her lap with a soft bump.

'Here. Shall we do it together?'

When she nodded, he lifted the lid. Lexie craned forward, but the contents were obscured from view, covered with crumpled and yellowed tissue paper. Martha grabbed her hand and squeezed tightly. Edith's puckered hands hovered over the paper, trembling. At last she peeled back the tissue.

Nestling inside was a perfectly pink pair of crocheted baby bootees.

Deep in Lexie's throat, a lump formed. She gulped to shift it. Beside her, Martha swayed and her hand gripped Lexie's fingers so tightly that they ached.

'I thought,' Edith said brightly, 'that I'd dreamed it.'

She looked around at the anxious faces peering down at her and explained,

'I do get quite muddled, you know.'

The emotions of earlier – the impatience, the distress – appeared to have vanished and she was beaming. She lifted the bootees out of their protective wrapping and laid them against her cheek.

'They were Charlotte's, you see. Charlotte was my baby.'

Her chin jutted forward.

'Father said I couldn't keep her, but I did. I wouldn't let anyone take her away from me. I didn't care what they said. She was my baby, my first little child.'

'Why did you hide the bootees, Edith?' Cameron voiced what Lexie was afraid to ask.

'She died. My little baby, my sweet thing, my darling died, and Father wouldn't let me keep anything of hers, nothing at all. He said it was shameful and I had disgraced the family, but once Charlotte had gone I didn't care about anything any more.'

She lifted her nose to the ceiling and her voice sharpened.

'I was only sixteen, you see, and the boy had run away. Papa said when she died it was a judgement on me and he threw everything out. But I hid these up the chimney, and I never forgot. No,' she folded the bootees into the palm of her hand and closed her fingers round the fine wool as if to conceal them from sight again, 'I never forgot.'

She opened her hand and the bootees sprang back into shape.

'Then I got muddled, and I thought I'd got it all wrong. But

98

they're *here*,' she crooned, 'and I was right all along. Wasn't I, darling Charlotte?'

'Would you like me to put them back?' Cameron asked, 'or will you keep them?'

'You keep them for me.' She thrust them at him, then looked at the serious faces around her. 'Is lunch ready yet? I'm really very hungry.'

Shoes, Lexie thought as she watched Edith down second helpings of rice pudding, tell stories. Stories of tiny, much-loved babies who can't even walk, of the tottering steps of little children towards adulthood, of special events in our lives, of dances, and marriages and mountain climbs and escapes.

Charlotte's tiny bootees told two tales; of a baby who never found her chance in this world, and of a mother who spent a lifetime secretly mourning her.

She had an idea.

'Edith,' she said, laying down her spoon, her own pudding almost untasted, 'would you let me take your photograph with Charlotte's shoes?'

'Alexa, darling—' Martha began.

'Are you sure that—' Tom said.

Cameron just looked at her, while Edith seemed oblivious. She simply carried on spooning rice into her mouth.

Swept up on a wave of enthusiasm, Lexie ignored them all.

'I have an idea, you see. I want to paint your bootees – Charlotte's bootees. I'd like to tell Charlotte's story. A photograph would really help me. How would you feel about that?'

Edith's bowl was empty. She put her spoon down with obvious reluctance. Lexie waited.

'Charlotte and I,' said Edith with great clarity, 'would love to have our picture taken.'

We can only turn our faces to the future when we have laid the past to rest. The feeling that this was true had been plaguing Lexie for months now and Edith had underscored it emphatically.

She replayed the scene in the bedroom over and over in her mind. Why, when the rest of them were in tears, had Edith begun to smile? Why would you wait half a lifetime to search for a memento of such unbearable sadness, only to beam with contentedness when it was finally in your grasp?

A few days after they'd returned a chirpy Edith to Sea View, the answer finally came to her. Edith had found peace.

The irony was that she had found it in Jamie's room.

Lexie went to Martha, who was mending a hole in one of Tom's sweaters.

'Damn these moths,' Martha said, glancing up as Lexie came into the kitchen. 'We never seem to get rid of them. They've chewed a great hole in your father's favourite alpaca sweater.'

'Can I talk to you, Mummy?' she said, lapsing unconsciously into the childhood appellation.

Martha was surprised. 'Of course. I hope we can always talk.'

'It's time,' Lexie said, swallowing, 'to clear out Jamie's things. Don't you think?'

Martha paused in her darning, one hand high in the air, trailing behind it a long thread of brown wool.

'It's the only way we can move on,' Lexie persisted, 'do you see? We have to face it together. We have to talk about Jamie. We have to *deal* with things.'

Martha resumed her darning, her face intent. She lifted the sweater to the light and examined her work. She said, 'It's so difficult to see the hole when you're working with dark colours.'

'I know it will be hard,' Lexie continued steadily, 'and I know that Daddy will take a little longer to join us, but you and I should make a beginning.'

Martha's hand rose and fell in a jagged rhythm.

'It was Edith who showed me the way,' Lexie continued. 'Didn't you see how tranquil she became after she found Charlotte's shoes? And I thought, that's it. That's it absolutely. We must uncover our own lurking demons, and deal with them. Then we can start to live our lives again.'

In the corner of the room, the clock on the wall ticked remorselessly. Outside the window came the sudden alarm call of a blue tit, a rapid trrr-trrr-trrr that signalled the arrival, in all likelihood, of a cat. Other than these sounds, there was nothing, just the shrillness of Martha's determined silence.

'Well,' Lexie said eventually, 'I'll start to sort things, at least. I'll make three piles: things to be thrown out, things to go to charity shops, things to keep. How does that sound?' She stood up. 'I'm going to start now.'

'Don't expect me to join you,' Martha said.

It was better than a straight 'no'.

Chapter Eleven

Catalogue number 17: Miner's boot. Knee-length leather boot, safety caps attached by studs to toe and sides. Private collection. Boot recovered from Mauricewood Pit, near Edinburgh, after disaster of 5 September 1889: 'Patient labour and diligent search were rewarded yesterday in the recovery of the last seven of the bodies of the unfortunate victims ... One man's identity was established by his widow recognising his tobacco box, his boot and the neck of his shirt.'

Cora Spyridis arrived on the eleven o'clock flight and stood in the middle of the arrivals hall, waiting for her brother. When he finally succeeded in parking his car (no possibility of leaving it for a few minutes to nip in these days, it had to be driven into the official car park and money paid), he spotted her at once, texting furiously and completely oblivious to the admiring glances she was attracting.

'There you are, Pats,' she cried, glancing up from her phone and spying him.

Heads turned as brother and sister embraced. They made a magnificent couple.

'Cora.' He held her at arm's length and studied her. 'Greece agrees with you. What makes you think Scotland will?'

She shrugged. 'Needs must. Anyway, you haven't told me about this job yet. I might be back in London on the next plane.'

He looked at the bags strewn round her feet. 'That's why you've only brought a toothbrush, I suppose.'

'You never know what you might need. I thought I'd better come prepared for anything.'

'Nothing changes.'

How was it the woman he loved was so fundamentally unmaterialistic, while all the other women in his life – Diana, Cora, the legions of beautiful faces that came and went – had to surround themselves with *things*?

Half way to the car park and laden with cases, Patrick stopped short so that Cora almost cannoned into him.

The woman I love. Did I think that?

'What's wrong?' Cora looked alarmed.

'Nothing. Just remembered something.'

Remembered bright hair bejewelled by the moonlight. Remembered eyes like a fawn's, telling him – what, exactly? He grew angry. It wasn't love he felt for Lexie, he told himself, but another emotion entirely. He'd made an overture of peace, dammit, and she'd turned it aside. Comparisons became inevitable. Next to Diana's poise and assurance, what did Lexie have? Not beauty measured by a classical yardstick. Not style – at least, not Diana's effortless elegance. Not tact, or sophistication or—

Yet she had loyalty. Her loyalty to her family had overridden personal ambition, and that must have cost her a great deal.

She had courage.

And she had honesty, which shone like a beacon beside Diana's subtle manipulation.

Damn Lexie Gordon!

She played games with his heart and she didn't even know it.

Cora looked around the living room at The Gables admiringly.

'You certainly keep it beautiful, Patrick.'

'Thanks. I try.'

A gloriously rich abstract by Barbara Rae hung above the marble fireplace. On the wall opposite the window were a painting by Anne Redpath and a large oil by Sir Robin Philipson. Patrick might decide to sell any of the paintings at any time, but he was particularly attached to the Philipson, an intricate and subtle rendition of the interior of a cathedral.

The floor was oak, a herringbone pattern, burnished to a high gloss. There were two Le Corbusier sofas, stark and simple in cream leather and chrome, and the Arne Jacobsen 'egg' chair that had started his passion for design classics some years ago.

Diana, seeing Patrick's home for the first time the other day, had almost drooled, but had complained it 'lacked a woman's touch'. He supposed she meant no flowers, no cushions and no curtains, and his interpretation was that by 'a woman's touch' she'd meant to say 'my touch'. He'd skirted the comment at the time, but now he thought perhaps he could do worse than ask Diana to share his home.

'What's this?' Cora asked, nudging a velour-covered fireside stool with her foot. 'It's seriously out of place, Pats.'

'It's nothing. I just haven't put it away yet.'

'Put it away? Why's it here at all?'

'If you must know, I've got a collection of odds and sods in the back. Mostly rather good antique furniture, actually. I won't lose out.'

'Antiques? Hardly your style, I'd have thought.'

'I buy them from a shop in town. Cobbles. I very much like the owner, an elderly man, half Polish. It's quite simple. He struggles to make a decent living because he has no business sense – but he does have fabulous taste. I buy from him, store things here, sell them on in batches to a London dealer for a good profit. Pavel makes money, I make money, the dealer in London makes money. Win, win, win.'

'Does he know you buy just to sell them on?'

Patrick's shoulders lifted. 'I expect he believes my house is furnished with the stuff, but as I never invite anyone in, how's he ever going to know?'

His sister's gaze was penetrating.

'What?'

'You're an old softie under that hard shell, aren't you?'

Patrick laughed. 'Don't you dare tell anyone.'

He prepared lunch quickly and expertly, chopping fresh herbs into salad leaves with liberal abandon. He roasted pine nuts quickly in a dry pan and sprinkled them on top. The kitchen was simple but high-tech and the cheese was stored in the walk-in larder at a constant ten degrees Celsius so that it was always perfectly ready for eating.

105

'Looks delicious,' Cora smiled, eying the fine array on the cheeseboard.

'I must have had some sixth sense about your arrival,' he grunted, 'because I asked the housekeeper to lay in some extra. Pass the bread, will you?' he asked Cora, and when she handed it to him, put the loaf into the oven until its crust was crisp.

'Wine?'

'Need you ask?'

As it was warm, he set the patio table and they basked in the sun and grazed.

'Not quite Greece,' said Cora, 'but surprisingly pleasant for Scotland. Heard from Aidan at all?'

Where angels fear to tread...

'No,' he said shortly.

'I don't think things are going well between them.'

Patrick reached out and snapped off a faded bloom from the rose bush next to the patio. Something in him surged at these words – probably triumphalism because it certainly wasn't hope. In any case, he didn't want to be sucked into a conversation about his brother.

'Don't you want to know about the job?' he asked.

Cora gave him a hard stare, her brown eyes shrewd.

'I suppose you'll never forgive him. But you can do better than Niamh, you know. I'm surprised you haven't found someone by now.'

Patrick thought of crimson-spiked hair and a loyalty so far beyond his experience that he'd been unable to comprehend it, but what he said was, 'Job, Cora? Or if you prefer, I'm happy to drive you back to the airport.'

'You made a mistake, Pats, that's all. You have to stop beating yourself up about it one day.'

'I'm not into self-flagellation.' He reached into his pocket and pulled out his car keys. 'I think the next plane is in an hour. We could just make it.'

Cora laughed.

'Okay, okay. I've got the message. So tell me about the job.'

The hardest thing was making a start, so Lexie made herself

106

tackle the most challenging tasks first – like putting her hand inside Jamie's underwear drawer and pulling out garments he'd once worn next to his skin. Socks, briefs, vests, all went into a large bin bag. There was a shop in Hailesbank that bought textiles by the kilo.

Downstairs, she heard the doorbell. Its off-key chime had always grated. She was aware of the creak of the door as her mother answered it, and of the low murmur of voices, but her focus was on her task and she bent back to it with scarcely a pause.

One drawer emptied. There, that wasn't so bad. Next, leisurewear. Pyjamas, sloppy jumpers, assorted running gear. She picked up a sweatshirt and laid her cheek on the soft cotton. Had it been washed since he'd last worn it? She thought not, because she was sure she could smell a faint whiff of Jamie's distinctive cologne.

Lexie closed her eyes and let the smell wash over her, musky and powdery, with overtones of orange and cinnamon.

Christmas, five years ago. Downstairs in the front room, with the fire roaring and the lights on the tree twinkling like stars in an evening sky.

'Perfume?'

She could hear his voice now, not so much mocking as lightly amused. 'Perfume? *Moi*? Sis!'

'Give it a try. Dare you! Anyway, I can't take it back, so don't waste it.'

'Christ, must I?'

Then Martha's voice. 'Don't be so ungrateful, Jamie,' and the rustle of cellophane.

'Actually…' sniff, then, grudgingly, 'it's not bad.'

'Thanks. Give me some credit for good taste.'

He'd given her a bear hug and said affectionately, 'Smug cow. I got something for you too. Here.'

He'd tossed her a parcel. The gift-wrapping had hardly been expert, but at least he'd made an effort. 'What is it?'

'If you open it, you might find out.'

The package had been squidgy and soft. 'A scarf? A dishcloth?'

'Just bloody open it,' he'd laughed. As she'd pulled at the cockeyed bow to release the ribbon he'd added, with sudden doubt, 'God, hope you like it. I looked everywhere.'

She'd pulled aside tissue paper and glimpsed brightness: purples and greens, yellows, creams and white, red, mauve, pink, flowers, stems, peacock feather and rooster tails, a riot of pattern and colour and shape.

'What's this?' She'd lifted the fabric up and shaken out soft folds.

'They described it as an artist's smock, but God knows if that's what it is.'

Jamie had looked embarrassed, as if he'd regretted the purchase.

'It's *amazing*.' Lexie had held it up in front of herself and looked down to watch the flowing pleats drop. The fabric had felt washed and well worn, although it wasn't thin or faded.

'The owner thought 1960s.'

'Definitely 1960s.' She'd looked inside the back, but there'd been no label. 'Home made, at a guess, I've never seen sleeves like these.' She'd lifted a soft corner. 'Look, they're like angel's wings. Oh Jamie, you are *clever*.' She'd kissed him delightedly and pulled the smock on over her thin sweater. 'But it's much too good to paint in.'

Lexie still had that smock. It hung on a hanger on the back of her bedroom door. She'd never worn it for painting, but she'd looked at it every day and thought of Jamie and the trouble he'd gone to.

She sniffed the sweatshirt again. Yes, the scent was still there, powdery and spicy. Some girlfriend (picked up and blithely discarded along the way later that spring) had told him she loved it and given him more, and it had become a staple.

Lexie walked over to the window and looked out.

Jamie.

As casual as you like with girls. Easy come, easy go. They'd flocked after him, unsurprisingly, but for years he'd barely seemed to notice them – he'd been too immersed in the physicality of rugby to be serious about anything else in his life. Then there'd been a sweet young girl called Estelle, a slip of a thing whose patent adoration soon became overwhelming. Who was next? Charlotte the Harlot, as he'd wickedly dubbed her in private? 'Curvaceous and voracious, Lex,' he'd confided. But her overpowering sexual appetites had interfered with his training.

He'd never taken these girlfriends seriously: Anne, Jane, Eve, Suzanne, Leanne, Joanne – whoever – a string of beautiful and adoring women he couldn't in truth be bothered with. They'd been out of the door and on their way before they'd realised they'd been rejected. And if ever there'd been one more important than the others, he'd never told her.

Something had changed in the months before he died. Lexie had sensed it in things unsaid more than feelings voiced. He'd had no girl in tow when she met him, for a start – and Jamie had always worn women on his arm like bracelets, or draped around his neck like a chain of office, glittering with diamonds. Thinking back, it occurred to her that he'd stopped admiring passing waitresses and barmaids, stopped making puerile quips about the shape of their bottom or the size of their breasts. Yet he'd been almost high with happiness – or, at least, more relaxed and content than she ever remembered seeing him.

She turned away from the window and resolutely put the sweatshirt into the charity bag. There was no point in keeping it, not now. It would never be worn again in this house, so why not let someone else enjoy it?

Now sorting things was beginning to be a challenge, because Jamie's filing system could hardly be described as logical. She came across a hairbrush, a tie, some belts and an odd cufflink in the next drawer, alongside three crumpled polo shirts and a navy merino sweater.

Lexie could feel Jamie's presence all around, like an itch she longed to scratch. He was laughing at her. Get on with it, sis, just chuck the lot, he was saying. Be done with it. *Be done with me.*

She tried to find a sense of humour from somewhere as she unearthed half a packet of Jaffa cakes from their hiding place among a swamp of crumpled running gear.

That's what I'm bloody well trying to do, you annoying,

inconsiderate bastard.

She wiped a hand across her forehead. The room felt airless, as if the life had been sucked out of it. She tossed the Jaffa cakes into the rubbish bag and crossed to the window, to wrestle with the catch.

'Carlotta has persuaded me that you might be right,' said a voice from the doorway.

Lexie whirled round. Two bright spots burned in the pallid grey of her mother's thin cheeks. She looked uncomfortable, *but she was here.* Carlotta, her glorious thick mane of black hair tumbling onto the thrilling flame-orange of her jumper, almost looked more nervous than Martha. Odd.

'It's good, yes? I say to Martha, it's time. Lexie is right. It's time now.'

A bubble rose in Alexa's throat. 'It's good, Carlotta. Yes. Thank you.' Why was she so distrusting of the woman? They all owed her a great deal.

Carlotta stepped into the room like a skittish foal, fearful of shadows.

'This is Jamie's room, yes?' She looked around, nodding slightly. Her hair bounced and shimmered as she moved and gold glittered from a chain round her neck, perfect against her olive skin. She was so fine-boned she looked like a doll, unrealistically beautiful. 'I have never been in here.' She spread her hands expressively. 'Yes, he is in this room, I can feel him here.' Her gaze fell on Martha and she said firmly, 'But he will always be where he is important, yes? In here,' She folded her hands elegantly across her chest, 'in all our hearts.'

Oh please, Lexie thought, spare me the drama. But Carlotta's words seemed to help Martha, who took a step forward and across the threshold.

'This photo I love.'

Carlotta moved to a black and white photograph of Jamie, aged around fourteen, hanging on the far wall. He was lying in coarse grass and sand, laughing up at the camera, as if he was mocking the photographer. And so he had been, Lexie remembered, because she'd just pushed him over, cross at his teasing. The camera had been in her hand and she'd pressed the

110

shutter. Later, when the image had been developed and Martha had seen how crisp it was, and how perfectly it captured Jamie, she'd insisted on getting an enlargement framed. 'It is so innocent, yes?'

'We were having a family day out,' Martha said, her voice thick. 'I'll never forget that day. It was perfect.'

Not for me, Lexie thought. She remembered it as one of those days when Jamie's teasing had driven her to distraction. Still, it had toughened her for life, made her fight for what she wanted. What had happened to that Lexie, the Lexie who knew where she was going and was utterly determined to get there? She'd been submerged by a sense of duty and a loss of confidence. *Bother* Jamie.

'I will go.' Carlotta edged away from the photograph. 'This is a private time, I think. Martha, you call me and tell me what you think of the *polvorones,* yes?'

'Of course I will.' Martha clutched at Carlotta's hand. 'You're very kind.'

'Is nothing. See you tomorrow. Bye Lexie. No need to come downstairs, I will close the front door, trust me.'

'Goodbye, Carlotta. And thank you.'

Carlotta turned and was gone in a bright streak of tangerine.

Lexie, determined to keep stark emotion at bay as long as possible, said, 'It's hot in here. I thought I'd get some air in, but I can't find the key for the window.'

Martha crossed the room and opened a small carved box. 'Here.'

Sweet fresh air flooded the room and the oppressiveness of Jamie's presence receded.

'Thanks, that's better,' Lexie touched her mother's arm. The contact was light, but it established a connection between them, and that seemed important. 'I've almost finished the chest. I was going to tackle the wardrobe next.'

'I'll give you a hand.'

They worked side by side, wordlessly, except for the odd query.

'Bin or charity shop?'

'Bin.'

Lexie held up Jamie's kilt outfit. 'We should sell this. It's too good to just give away.'

'No. I don't want to profit from any of this.'

Lexie laid it carefully onto the bed. 'You're right.'

She gazed at it thoughtfully. 'How would you feel about letting Pavel have it? It's far too good for a charity shop, and he really could use some extra cash. I'm sure he'd make sure it went to a good home.'

'Why not? A good home—' Martha's voice quavered a little, '—is all I want for his things.'

Lexie drew a long, careful breath. 'We're doing the right thing.'

Martha sank onto the bed and laid her hand on the black Prince Charlie jacket with its silver buttons. The heavy wool weave must be sixty years old at least, but it showed no signs of wear.

'This was your grandfather's jacket.'

'You know I love the idea that something of the wearer stays with the clothes. We can imagine Jamie chatting away to all the people who buy or inherit this stuff—'

Lexie swept an arm in the direction of the bin bags. "Get a move on," he'd tell the lazy kid who should be putting on his socks, "don't just bloody lie there".'

Martha laughed and Lexie's heart twisted inside her chest at the sound.

Martha said, 'That sounds like Jamie. Or, "Mum, this shirt needs cufflinks and I can't find any."' Her laughter faded. 'I'd tell him, "That's because you never put them away in the right place—"'

Lexie let the memory lie between them for a few moments, then she reached into the wardrobe and pulled out Jamie's rugby boots. 'What about these?'

Martha's cheeks were hollow and her eyes puckered at the corners.

'His boots. Oh Alexa, his boots—'

Lexie had run out of strategies for distracting her. The trouble was, she thought, I feel Jamie in all of these things too. He inhabited them, his boots most of all.

Martha clutched the studs to her chest, unheeding of the dirt that caked them. She held them as Edith had cradled the baby bootees.

Charlotte and I would love to have our picture taken.

Shoes tell stories.

Jamie's boots, perhaps more than anything in this room, told his story.

Lexie said, 'Will you let me take some photos of these? Like I did for Edith?'

'Photos?'

'I'd like to draw Jamie's boots. Paint an oil picture.'

Martha's face was grey. Once she'd been a lively, interesting woman, who'd lived for others more than herself. Now she was little more than a shell, her spirit caged by grief. *Bastard*, Lexie raged again, *you made her old before her time.* She wasn't even sure now that she did want to paint Jamie's boots, because surely her work would betray the anger she couldn't help feeling?

'Oh, never mind,' she started to say, just as Martha held the boots out towards her.

Their laces dangled forlornly, still caked with mud from the last game Jamie played.

Chapter Twelve

Catalogue number 10: Clown's shoes. Donated by Frank Dawson, Broxburn. Blue, yellow and red leather brogues with red laces. 'These shoes help me to get into character,' says Frank Dawson (aka 'Booboo'). 'They are just as important as make-up, if not more so.'

'I'm going to paint again, Pavel, but not the same kind of things I was doing before. Nightmarish scenes don't do it for me any more.'

'Darling, what has happened? You look so perfectly *joyous*.'

'I had a revelation.'

'A revelation? Shining lights and angels singing? Ooh, sweetie, do tell.'

'The idea was that you would get some extra rest,' Lexie tutted, 'not hang around here chatting.'

In the elaborate Venetian mirror above his head she caught a glimpse of her own face – clear, pale skin and large brown eyes set off by the ruby-red hair. She ruffled her crop until it stood up and considered her reflection. Pavel was right – there *was* a luminous quality about her appearance today, as if she was reflecting some ethereal radiance. She had been aflame ever since Edith's visit. Her new idea was burning inside her head, scorching her imagination until she knew that soon nothing would stop her from making a start.

She looked at Pavel sternly. 'I can tell you everything another time. This is meant to be your morning off. And by the way, if you'll just give me a spare key, you won't even need to get up on Saturdays.'

Pavel blinked at her, unmoving.

'Honestly. You're meant to be resting. I can do everything for you.'

'Darling, I know you can—'

'Did you go to the doctor for a check-up?'

'I'll phone soon and—'

'You mean you haven't phoned yet?'

'It's been busy,' Pavel pleaded, picking at a fragment of thread on the sleeve of his striped boating jacket and flicking it to the floor. 'I had a fair and two auctions this week. Now do stop nagging me, sweetie, and sit down and tell me about your idea.'

Lexie crossed her arms mutinously, but Pavel outfaced her.

'I'm not moving, Lexie, until you tell me about revelations and transmogrifications.'

They were well matched for stubbornness. Today she allowed Pavel the victory in the battle of wills. She laughed.

'All right, you win. I'll make some tea then, shall I?'

When they were settled, she regaled him with the story of Edith's visit and the discovery of the baby bootees up the chimney in Jamie's room.

'That's so sad!' Pavel produced a large cotton handkerchief and blew his nose delicately. 'Fancy keeping a secret like that all those years.'

'I know. My heart almost stopped in sympathy, but do you know something weird? Edith just sat there and beamed.'

'Oh my God!' Pavel sniffed. He dabbed at a suspicious glint on his cheek with one finger.

The transparency of Pavel's emotions was one of the most endearing things about him.

'She'd kept a lid on her emotions all these years, but as soon as she saw the bootees, instead of crying, she just sat there smiling, as if she was at peace at last. That's when I realised that we have to deal with what happened – Mum and Dad and me – or none of us will be able to move on.'

'Ooh, you are so right.' Pavel pushed his handkerchief back into his pocket and sat up straighter. 'It took me years to come to terms with poor Guy's death, but the day I said to myself, "Pavel, darling, he's not here but you are, so just mop up those

116

tears and get on with it," was the day I started to stop aching.'

He hardly ever talked about Guy, and Lexie was touched.

She confided, 'That's why I started to clear out Jamie's room. I didn't think Mum would help me, but she did, and now I'm certain I was right. It was the first time we'd been able to talk about him. We even laughed a bit.'

'And your father?'

'Oh Dad— Dad's impossible. He's so determined to be strong that he refuses to deal with his emotions. I'm certain that's what's driving him down the wrong path at work, too. He's got his head down, he's in such a deep rut that there's no way he can see over the top. Have you finished your tea? Let me wash the mugs out.'

Pavel snatched his mug away from her.

'Not likely, not till I've heard the rest.'

'And then you'll go away? Take a break, like we agreed? Deal?'

'Deal, Miss Bossyboots.'

'Okay. Well, it was Edith who gave me the idea.'

'About painting again?'

'Yup. Stay with me here, Pavel.' Lexie leant forward. 'Shoes. Wearers. Occasions. Shoes you walk in, dance in, play games in, get married in. They tell stories, right? Something of the wearer stays in them, just like it stays in clothes. Yes?'

'Oh yes, ducky. You and I, we know that.'

'Right. My head was in a whirl after that scene – Edith perched on a pile of cushions like a tiny old leprechaun or something, hugging those woollen bootees to her chest and smiling. Just grinning as if she'd discovered some hidden treasure. The story moved me, but it was the image that haunted me. I couldn't get that picture out of my head, and it came to me that I really wanted to *paint* the bootees. I want to see if I can capture the spirit of baby Charlotte that still lives in those little sherbet-pink bootees. That's the challenge.'

'So if someone stands in front of the painting, they just have to know why you painted them? I love it, Lexie darling, I really love it.'

'I knew you'd get it! Edith got it too, for all she's muddled.

117

Do you know what she said? She said, "Charlotte and I would love to have our photograph taken."'

'Oh, that's so sweet!'

'Isn't it? So I took some photos. Funny, it was only a couple of hours later, but because of her dementia it was like the first time all over again.'

'So you're inspired.'

'It's not just Edith. It feels like a beginning. Seeing the effect of the discovery on Edith prompted me to ask Mum if we could clear out Jamie's room. She wasn't going to let me, then she did. Then she wasn't going to join me, then she did. Carlotta talked her into it.'

'Oh, Carlotta—' he began dismissively.

'I know you're not a fan of Carlotta's, Pavel, but she did persuade Mum to help. And she knew when to leave us to get on with it alone. She was quite tactful and sensitive.'

Pavel lifted his nose to the ceiling. 'If you say so, darling.'

'When Mum found Jamie's rugby boots, they had a profound effect on her, too, just like baby Charlotte's bootees did on Edith. I asked if I could paint them and Mum said yes.'

'What a lovely idea.'

Pavel started to drum his fingers lightly on the desk, deep in thought. He stopped drumming and started to lift his head, then dropped it again and drummed even faster. At first Lexie waited patiently, but the repetitive noise began to get to her and she was about to beg him to stop when he lifted his hand in the air with an elegant flourish and declared, 'I've got some special shoes.'

'Oh, really? That's terrifi—'

'I'd love you to do something like that for me. I'd pay you, of course.'

'Oh, I couldn't possibly—'

'Not only could you possibly, you will accept payment, and a realistic payment at that. This is your profession, Lexie, professionals get paid.'

'I really don't—'

'If you say no, darling,' Pavel said with a poker face, 'I won't tell you my story. And it's a really good one.'

'Your story?'

He sat back and crossed his arms, his mouth pulled into a twist of amusement at his own private joke.

'What story's that, Pavel?' Curiosity was Lexie's weakness, and her strength. She always hungered to *know* – what made the sun orange or the sea blue, or Jamie die? Now she wanted to know what it was that Pavel was hiding from her. She prodded him lightly, conscious of the slightness of his frame. 'Tell me!'

'You'll let me pay you for a painting?'

'Oh good gracious, Pavel, you've worn me down! Yes, I'll let you pay if that's what you want, now *tell!*'

Pavel uncrossed his arms and stood up. He started to walk across the room, his gait still uncertain, Lexie noted with fleeting anxiety.

'Where are you going?'

'I'll be right back. Just you sit there, darling.'

Frustrated, Lexie did as she was told. After a minute, she had a poke around the rummage box. A hat pin emerged, decorated only by a plain black bobble. She tossed it back. In the corner of the box she spotted a card with six bone buttons sewn onto it. She picked up a tiny barrel-shaped tape measure. Pavel had clearly bought a sewing basket and emptied it into the rummage box. Nothing of promise. Where *was* he?

A business card had fallen into the box and was lying under a broken watch and some fine chains, probably not silver. She fished it out, thinking it might be important.

PATRICK MULGREW, it read, DIRECTOR, CAPITAL ART EDINBURGH.

She dropped it onto the desk as if it was burning hot. What was it doing there? There was something scribbled on it. Curiosity got the better of her and she picked it up again. *Sheraton table*, the note read, with a price that made her eyes water. What did it mean? Was it random, had Pavel scribbled it on the first bit of paper to come to hand? She remembered the Sheraton dining table that had sat in the front for so long and disappeared a week or two back. Did Patrick buy it?

In her shoulder bag, her mobile rang and she dropped the card again. So what if he did buy it? He could afford it. She fumbled for her phone, saw Molly's name come up and pressed Accept just in time.

'Hi.'

'Where are you?'

'Cobbles. I'm helping Pavel out on Saturday mornings.'

'*Lexie!*'

'What?'

'You do far too much for other people.'

'So everyone keeps telling me. Actually, I'm planning to do something all for myself, so there.'

'Really? What?'

'Are you still on for dinner?'

Molly had an evening off and Lexie had booked a table at Besalú for Molly, Jonas, Cameron and herself. Carlotta would be busy but might join them for a drink.

'You bet.'

'Then I'll tell you this evening.'

'Shit, have I really got to wait till then?'

The door into the cobbled courtyard at the back of the shop opened and Pavel reappeared.

'Must go, Moll. See you later.'

Pavel was carrying a small carpet bag.

'Clear a space on the desk, darling, there's a sweetheart.'

Lexie picked up the rummage box and dropped it onto a nearby chair.

'Thank you, sweetie.' He placed the bag with great precision onto the desk.

Alexa's curiosity grew. The bag was crafted from an old kilim and its rich, earthy colours glowed enticingly in the light from the desk lamp. 'What is it?'

Pavel loved drama. He stretched out as if to open the bag, then clapped his hands round his chin and said, 'Oh heavens, sweetie, I haven't talked about this for years. Everyone's forgotten.'

'Talked about what?'

'Maybe I shouldn't ... maybe I should just—'

'*What?* Pavel, I swear I'm going to shake you. You can't stop now!'

He stood up straight, took a deep breath, placed one hand theatrically on his chest, and used the other to fan his face.

'You're quite right. Time to reveal.'

He opened the bag. Lexie craned forward, but the holdall was a deep one and she couldn't see what was inside.

'Here.'

He reached in and lifted out a tissue-swathed parcel. 'Open them, darling.'

'No you open them. Go on,' she encouraged, as Pavel hesitated.

Hands a-flutter, he peeled back the tissue to reveal a pair of white canvas ballet shoes.

'Ballet shoes? But they're huge.'

'Thank you, sweetie,' Pavel said, clearly affronted.

'They're yours?'

'Yes, they're mine.'

'I didn't know you were a ballet dancer.'

'I wasn't. Not exactly. Oh dear, my legs are all a-tremble, just remembering it all.'

'Here, sit down.' Lexie guided him onto her seat, then picked up the shoes curiously. They were white canvas and scuffed with wear. She turned them over. The sole was fashioned in two parts to allow the foot to flex. 'You wore these to dance? Where?'

'Have you ever heard of Bad Boys?'

'Bad Boys? They were a glam rock band, weren't they? Didn't they have a hit called "Love Your Blooming Cheek"?'

Pavel's smile had become positively beatific.

'Pavel? Were you in the band? Oh my God, you *were*, weren't you?'

She racked her brains feverishly, trying to remember who'd been in the Bad Boys line-up. She was sure there was no-one called Pavel.

He inclined his torso neatly towards her in a bow of acknowledgement.

'I confess, darling. I didn't call myself Pavel Skonieczna, of course, I was Paul Scotland. And yes, I wore these shoes to prance around the stage, darling, positively prance.' He laughed. 'It must have looked a little pathetic, I suppose, but you see, my absolute hero was Freddie Mercury and I didn't quite have his originality, so I, well, I paid my tribute in my own way.'

'Pavel! You're a rock star! How could I not have known this?'

'It was another era, darling Lexie. But do you know, I would so love to have a painting of these.'

Lexie was thrilled.

'And you shall have it, Pavel. I'll do yours first of all.'

Chapter Thirteen

Catalogue number 20: Running shoe. Modern white trainers. Donated by Ellis Ruthven, Hailesbank. 'Years ago, my wife kicked me out. She called me lazy, a slob, a leech, and so I was. Someone bet me I couldn't run a marathon, and so I did. I began to raise money for charities. Running became a way of life. I discovered a new energy, and a new purpose. After a time, my wife took me back. Over the years, I have raised more than a million pounds for charities.

Cameron had abandoned his jeans in favour of dark chinos and swapped the customary sweatshirt for a pale red pullover in fine wool. It was the first time Lexie had seen him smarten up and she rather liked it. He pulled her close as they strolled through the park towards Besalú and her body melted where it touched his. *I'm ready*, it was telling her. *I'm so ready.*

'Tell me what happened with Molly. I know her marriage failed, but you didn't say why.'

'It happened soon after Jamie died and I feel really bad because I wasn't there for her – well, not enough, anyway. Things were difficult at the time.'

'She must understand that.'

'Yes she does, but still, *I* feel I let her down. She's always been so strong for me. Anyway, she took on this job soon after that. It came with an apartment at the back of the house, so she thought it was perfect. It meant that Adam could still live in the house till they decided what to do with it.'

'In Edinburgh?'

'Yes. She won't talk about it.'

'I thought you girls were as tight as wheel nuts.'

123

'So did I.'

He dropped a kiss on top of her head and she felt herself melting all over again.

Besalú was busy. It always was these days.

'Your missus is doing a fabulous job,' Cameron told Jonas.

'I bought the place because I thought it would stop her getting bored, but I never imagined she'd do all this.' He swept his arm in a semicircle to take in the whole extension. 'I never seem to see her nowadays.'

They ordered Rioja and studied the menu.

'Don't know why I'm bothering,' Lexie said, pushing it away, 'I know what I want. *Calamares* and Manchego with quince jam. I'll eat whatever anyone else orders anyway.'

'Did you hear about Lexie's big idea?' Cameron said. 'Tell them, doll.'

'Where will I start?'

'The old biddy, of course.'

It was the second time Lexie had recounted the tale of Edith's visit and the discovery of the bootees, and her delivery was getting more dramatic.

'—so when she opened the box, what do you think was inside?'

'Drugs?' Jonas suggested, helping a waiter who had arrived to unload the second round of drinks onto the table.

'Jewellery?' Molly asked hopefully.

'A pair of baby bootees,' Cameron chipped in, rather spoiling Alexa's reveal.

Jonas drained his pint and signalled to a waiter. 'Wow.'

'Whose were they?'

'She lost a baby, years and years ago, of course. It was illegitimate and her family practically threw her out. The bootees were all she had left.'

'That's so sad.'

'You'd think so, wouldn't you? But finding them again made Edith very happy. You should have seen her face. Anyway, when I saw Edith sitting there clutching those tiny bootees, I had an urge to paint them.'

124

Molly's pleasure in Lexie's news was immediate.

'That's *fantastic*. You haven't felt up to painting all year.'

'Thanks. Actually, there's more to it than Cameron knows. I started to clear out Jamie's room—'

Molly sucked her breath in sharply.

'—It's all right, Moll, honestly, you don't need to worry about us,' she hastened to reassure her friend. 'It needs to be done, or we'll never start to get over it. And it worked, because Mum came and helped me. And when we found Jamie's rugby boots, I had this urge to paint them as well. Because – don't you see? – they say so much about him. They kind of *are* Jamie.'

Cameron's face split into a wide grin.

'Brilliant idea, Lexie. Love it.'

Molly croaked, 'Perfect.'

Jonas slapped his thick thighs delightedly.

'Brilliant! Maybe we could even auction it for the Club.'

'When I told Pavel Skonieczna about it, guess what? He produced a pair of shoes too. Well, not shoes exactly, ballet pumps. *His* pumps.'

'Pavel was a dancer? Figures, I suppose.'

'Not a ballet dancer, no. A rock musician.'

'*Pavel* was?'

'He was the lead singer in Bad Boys.'

'Bloody hell,' Cameron said. 'They were good.'

Molly leant forward, her emotion of earlier replaced by a keen interest.

'You should make something of that.'

'What do you mean?'

'It's a great story. No-one round here knows that, do they? I didn't know it. Did you?' she appealed to the men, who shook their heads. 'Well, sell the story to the local rag. They'll be thrilled.'

'You think so? Do you know, I have a feeling that Pavel would enjoy a bit of limelight, but I'd have to ask him.'

'Sure. They'll want his photograph, anyway. It might help Cobbles too. Didn't you say the shop was struggling? People might go in just to gawp, but they could end up buying things.'

'Maybe I'll give it a go. Oh, by the way,' Lexie delved into her bag, 'I thought you might like this, Moll. It was on the mantelpiece in Jamie's room. You two were always so close.'

She pulled out a framed photograph. They were sitting on green grass liberally sprinkled with daisies and Jamie's arm was behind Molly's shoulders, two fingers stuck up behind her head in a comic rabbits'-ears gesture. They were looking at the camera and laughing. Lexie remembered the day it was taken, maybe a couple of months before Jamie's death. They'd gone on a picnic – Jamie, Lexie, Adam and Molly – to Tantallon Castle, an imposing ruin perched on the rocks near North Berwick. The day had been perfect, one of those rare spring days when it's more sunny than in the south of France and the wind drops so that you can almost hear the fluttering wings of the skylarks as they tumble over and over through the air high above. Molly had a piece of cake in her hand and her mouth was stuffed with it so that her cheeks appeared full. Jamie had found it extremely funny, Adam (off camera), maybe less so.

Molly burst into tears.

'What?' Lexie cried. 'Don't, Moll. Please don't. I thought you'd be pleased. I can take it back.'

She reached for the photograph, but Molly snatched it away.

'Sorry,' she said, dashing the back of her hand across her face, 'It was just a bit of a shock.'

She studied the photograph again. 'I remember that day. Didn't we have such a good time? But don't you want to keep it?' she asked, but she was still clutching the photograph as if it was glued to her hand.

'We've got plenty of photos of Jamie. It's yours if you want it.'

Molly dropped it quickly into her handbag.

'Thanks, Lexie, I love it. Honestly.'

Cameron kissed Lexie under the old town hall clock , where trysts had been kept for centuries. His kiss tasted of beer and garlic, but she liked it. The flicker of desire he'd awakened on the day he'd reappeared in Hailesbank flared into life.

His hand rummaged under her blouse.

'This feels ridiculously juvenile.'

'Know what you mean.'

It had been a long time since she'd gone to bed with anyone, and making love with Cameron had always been blissful. 'We can't go back to Fernhill. They always want to check I'm in and that I'm safe.'

Her body remembered the feel of him and lust was making her weak. She didn't want to stand here petting like some teenager, but when he withdrew his hand she was maddened by thwarted desire.

'I've moved in with a mate and he's away for a week. We can go there. Can't wait —' kiss, '— to get you back—' kiss, '— shall I tell you what I'm planning to do to you?'

Lexie flushed in the semi darkness.

The flat was small and messy. Lexie eyed the crumb-strewn floor, piles of old newspapers and half-full mugs of cold coffee with dismay.

'Cliff's quite untidy,' Cameron said, noticing. He dumped the mugs into the sink on top of the dirty dishes already heaped in there, grabbed a grubby dishcloth, gave the kitchen table a perfunctory wipe and asked, 'Want a drink?'

She shook her head. The thought of accepting any food or drink in this flat made her queasy. Desire was sinking under unsavoury reality and she was beginning to regret coming.

Cameron turned out the light. The untidiness disappeared and all she could see was the contours of his face illuminated by a shaft of light from the hallway.

'You're very lovely, Lexie,' he said, pulling her close. 'I've always thought so.'

Her insides liquefied and she wondered if it was just lust or if she would fall in love with him again. He took her face between his hands and kissed her sweetly and with such delicacy that she was astonished (as she often used to be) at how a man of such strength could be so gentle. It was a beguiling blend. His scar was a seam of silver in the moonlight. She reached up a hand to touch it and the desire ignited again.

Sensing it, Cameron's quick, fluttering kisses turned more amorous and his tongue slipped between her lips. She pushed her body close to his.

'You must know how I feel about you, Lexie.'

His hands settled on the small of her back and he pulled her close. He loosened her dress and pushed it off her shoulders so that it slipped to her waist.

No! I can't do this!

She pushed him away.

'What? What's wrong?'

Lexie reached for the light switch and blinked as light flooded the room. She reached down quickly to pull her dress up. Maybe it was just the mess, she told herself, but this didn't feel right. And besides, he hadn't even told her yet why he had gone.

'Sorry, Cameron.' She moved away, found her handbag, turned back to see his bewildered stare. 'Maybe another time.'

'Was it something I –'

'No.' She leant towards him and kissed his cheek, moving away quickly before he could clasp her again. 'No, not you. I'll be in touch, OK?'

A vision of Patrick filled her head as she ran down the stairs and out into the night. 'Can I call you?' he'd asked after Cameron had hit the deer, but she had shaken her head. She forced the image away.

Chapter Fourteen

Catalogue number 26: Flying officer's boots, WWII, sole of right boot torn loose from uppers. Donated by Squadron Leader Derek Browning, Forgie. 'We were in an old Gypsy Moth, practising spinning. I stamped hard on the rudder pedal, but the sole of my flying boot jammed between the rudder bar and the side of the cockpit. Talk about panic! I managed to wrench it free just in time...'

Pavel was ecstatic at the idea of his story resurfacing, and the local paper was eager to publish, just as Molly had predicted. For the next few days Lexie found herself in the heart of a whirlwind. A reporter came to do an interview, someone dug out a load of old photos of 'Paul Scotland', and a photographer was sent to take a picture of Pavel, wearing the pumps and camping it up like the old pro he was.

Eric, the young reporter, said, 'What makes the story perfect is the bit about your painting, Lexie.'

He was on the edge of his seat, his enthusiasm bubbling to boiling point.

Lexie was astonished that meeting a member of a half-forgotten rock band from forty years ago caused such excitement in a young man, and even more surprised that he was interested in her project.

'A painting of some old ballet pumps?'

'It adds another dimension. It takes it forward, gives us something else to play with. Could you do us a quick sketch? There might be a small fee, I'll see if I can persuade the editor.'

She dashed off a pastel drawing and they used it as part of the article – a full double page spread, under the headline,

'Hailesbank Antique Shop Owner Is Bad Boy!' The picture they used of Pavel was fantastic; he was wearing a striped blazer and white polo neck, and was pulling up his trousers at the ankles to reveal the white ballet pumps. There were several photos of the band in its heyday, statistics of their albums and hits, quotes from a couple of other members of the band (now in Hawaii and Eastbourne), and Lexie's drawing. It looked striking, considering it was reproduced on newsprint. There was even a photograph of Lexie and Pavel together, with the caption, 'Respected artist Lexie Gordon is to capture Paul's famous pumps in an oil painting.'

Lexie was quoted as saying, 'It's part of a project I'm planning. I believe that not only do shoes retain something of the wearer, they also tell stories. That's what I'm hoping to capture. I'm thinking about paintings of a pair of baby bootees and a pair of rugby boots, but I don't want to say any more about the project at the moment.'

A few days later, shoes started to arrive at Fernhill. Shoes in boxes, shoes in carrier bags, shoes hand delivered, shoes posted, shoes brought by special courier, shoes clean, shoes dirty, shoes in pairs or single, old and new (or nearly new), but shoes with one thing in common: each had some significant meaning to the owner.

'Look at these,' Lexie said, holding up a pair of white leather clogs to show a bemused Martha. She delved into the box and produced a note. 'It says they're surgeon's clogs. Just imagine,' she laid them carefully on the kitchen table, 'what they must have seen.'

'What are you going to do with them all?'

'I've no idea.' Lexie opened another parcel. 'Heavens above! What are these?'

She pulled out an oversized shoe with huge bulbous toe arcs ludicrously high above its heel. It was made from blue, yellow and red leather and had bright scarlet laces.

'Oh, that's a clown's shoe,' Martha said, breaking into a spontaneous smile. She took the shoe from Lexie and turned it round and round, studying it. 'Do you know, I remember going to the circus when I was six years old and seeing a clown wearing shoes just like this. He was constantly falling over the toes. I thought he was so funny, but of course there was pathos too, because it can hurt to be laughed at.' She shook her head. 'That's the appeal of clowns, isn't it? They manipulate extremes of emotions.'

As they examined the parcels, delivered by courier half an hour ago, the doorbell rang again.

'It's the postman,' Martha said, squinting down the garden to the road outside.

'Quite a mailbag today,' he said, 'I was going to leave a note for collection, but seeing as you're in, you can come and fetch them from the van if you like.'

This time there were four sets of baby shoes, accompanied with wads of pictures and copies of birth notes and two pairs of cream satin wedding shoes.

'Not quite so interesting.'

'But special to the people who've sent them. I have a feeling this isn't going to stop for a while.'

'You could be right,' Lexie said, wondering what she might have started.

'You'd better make a note of them all. Whatever you decide to do you'll have to have some way of knowing who they belong to and how to return them.'

'Wow, what a responsibility. And this could turn out quite expensive.'

'But it could be really interesting.'

Lexie raised an eyebrow. Martha, interested in something? She studied her mother and realised she wasn't sitting over breakfast in her old dressing gown, she had dressed. This was progress. Now that she thought about it, something about her mother had altered since they'd begun clearing out Jamie's room.

'You've had your hair cut!' she exclaimed. 'It makes you look years younger.'

Martha patted her hair. 'Oh that,' she said. 'Yesterday. I thought no-one would notice.'

Lexie was ashamed. Deep in all the fuss over Pavel, she'd

missed the changes in Martha. Her mother was wearing make-up again, a touch of shadow on her eyes and a dash of colour on her cheek. And she had mustered enough enthusiasm for the day ahead to get dressed. These were all positive signs.

'Interesting or not, I'll have to think about this carefully. I have a horrible feeling I could get swamped.'

'I'll log everything for you,' Martha said. 'Do let me. It will be good to feel I'm doing something useful again.'

Lexie didn't have to fake appreciation. She smiled gratefully.

'Okay. Thanks. That'd be really helpful.'

She was about to set off for work when a text came in on her mobile.

'It's Carlotta. She says, "Don't leave yet, I have a cake, and something else for you. See you in ten minutes". Bother. I wanted to get going.'

'What kind of cake?'

'She doesn't say.'

'I hope it's one of her almond ones.'

Lexie stood up and started repacking all the shoes. 'You'll need a book to list these in. I might have something upstairs.'

'Don't worry, dear. I'll walk into town and buy one at the stationer's.'

'Are you sure?'

'It'll do me good to get out.'

As this was indisputable, Lexie merely said, 'Leave a column for me to add notes, will you?'

'Of course. Look, here's Carlotta now.'

Today, in a black jersey shift and lime green bolero, Carlotta could hardly have been more simply dressed. It's impossible for her not to look sexy, whatever she wears, Lexie thought with a bead of envy.

'I am so glad you are still here. I have a cake—' Carlotta laid a tin carefully onto the kitchen table, '—and these.'

She opened the carrier bag she was carrying and put a shoebox on the table beside the cake. Alexa's heart sank. She guessed what was coming.

'My wedding shoes,' Carlotta said, opening the box with a

132

flourish.

'They're beautiful,' Lexie examined the soaring heels (Carlotta's attempt to rise towards Jonas's giddy height). She didn't need to lie. They *were* fabulous, with their lace-covered body and crystal-encrusted heels, a pretty pearl-centred flower decorating the peep toes. A small lace detail enhanced the heel at the back, drawing the eye to the ankle. But what could she do with wedding shoes? The story they told was only special to the wearer. 'What do you ... why—?'

'It was the article in the paper. Pavel, he is so charming, but who would have guessed at such a glamorous past? Then I thought, dear Lexie, she will photograph these for me, like in a special way, you know?'

'Carlotta, I can take photos of your shoes, of course, I'd be very happy to, but you know, you could do that yourself.'

'Then I thought, Lexie knows how to do the design, how do you call it?' Carlotta smiled at them both. 'Ah yes, the graphic design. And I thought, I will ask Lexie to make me a book!'

'A *book*?'

That was unexpected. Lexie had been turning over in her mind how she might politely explain to Carlotta that she'd be very busy over the next few weeks painting Pavel's ballet pumps, and Edith's bootees, and Jamie's rugby boots: that she couldn't take on any more at present. But – a book? She was sufficiently intrigued to say, 'What kind of book?'

'You know.' Carlotta waved her hands vaguely. 'A memory book. You can do such things on-line now, but most people do not have artistic ability or training. But you, Lexie, you have the skills to make something very special.'

She delved into her handbag and produced a small bundle of photographs and letters, tied with pink ribbon. 'I have brought the things I would want in mine. Here—' she started to untie the ribbon eagerly, her small, olive-skinned fingers with their scarlet nails fumbling with the knot. '—some photos from the wedding, of course, and from the time we were courting, and our honeymoon. Some lines from a letter written by my grandmother in Spain. She could not come, you see. And maybe a quick drawing – not a big painting, I know you have no time

133

for this – just a pencil drawing of the shoes. And don't tell me—' she went on quickly as she saw Lexie open her mouth, '—that these things take too long, I have seen you draw, Lexie, and you can do this thing in minutes, very beautiful.'

Carlotta might be on to something. She *could* draw quickly, and she did a graphic design module as part of her art course at college. She'd find designing a simple memory book easy – and it might be quite satisfying.

'I would pay, of course,' Carlotta added, perhaps sensing her weakening, 'for your time and skill. And for the cost of the book, naturally.'

'It's not a bad idea, Lexie,' Martha put in.

Lexie swept up the shoes and Carlotta's memorabilia and packed them carefully back into the shoe box. 'I'll think about it.'

'*Fantástico*!' Carlotta clapped her hands. 'There is no hurry, except that I think you will be very busy and as your friend it would be nice to—'

'I'll think about it, Carlotta,' Lexie cut her short, 'and I'll let you know. Now, I really must get to work. Dad'll be thinking I'm bunking off.'

Patrick took Cora to the empty shop on the High Street. Until a year ago it had been a small grocery store, but the advent of a supermarket on the fringes of the town had forced its closure. Patrick did little shopping. He had a housekeeper, Mrs Mackie, who lived a few streets away and who ran his house like clockwork. She not only ensured it was kept clean, she also washed, ironed, baked and shopped, making sure his store cupboard was kept full of all the ingredients he most prized. Sometimes he left special requests ('I really fancy a piece of Vacherin this weekend Mrs M'), but as he seldom entertained, preferring to eat out in Edinburgh or at Zebedee's or Besalú, his demands were modest. He paid her a generous part-time salary and she protected his home better than any mastiff.

It was Mrs M who had told him about the closure of the grocery store.

'Criminal shame, that's what it is.'

134

He'd been trying to concentrate on plans for Esther Goldwyn's exhibitions – she needed a fair bit of mentoring, unlike Lexie, whose paintings soared all by themselves – and had been a little irritated at the interruption.

'Shame? What is?' he'd asked vaguely.

'That mini market closing. On the High Street. Opposite the town hall. You know the one.'

Amazingly, Patrick did know it, and the seed of an idea began to form in his mind. The site was in a prime position and although the High Street was showing all the signs of town-centre failure common to most urban communities in Britain, Hailesbank was fundamentally an affluent place and there were other ways to entice shoppers. There were few who would believe it, but Patrick Mulgrew wasn't entirely focused on making money. He'd seen too much poverty, too many blighted neighbourhoods, back in Ireland not to think about putting something back in to the community – as long as he could do it in his own way.

A craft gallery. And a coffee shop. He'd often thought of adding a coffee shop to Capital Art, because people enjoyed being able to sit and drink coffee with their friends in beautiful surroundings. Coffee would draw people in whether or not they meant to buy, but once in, at least they would see what's on offer and might be tempted. At Capital Art there was no suitable room within the gallery and there was a popular coffee shop across the road. But the site in Hailesbank, would be ideal – and besides, people were more likely to make impulse buys of smaller value items.

'You see what I mean?' he asked Cora as they stood at the centre of the empty space.

She looked around. There were two large windows onto the street, on either side of the door. These were boarded over, but once the boarding was removed, light would flood in. Shelves still clung to the walls, hanging off at dangerous angles here and there where impatient hands had simply swept stock away. The walls hadn't been touched for years (no need, when they were hidden) and in some places a sickly pallid green appeared, in others yellowing cream. The floor was covered with linoleum.

Cora kicked the lino aside.

'The floorboards seem okay,' she said.

Patrick watched her with interest. Although Cora's ability to put her thumb on his tender spots could be bloody irritating, the flipside of this was that he trusted her judgement.

'It's a good space,' she pronounced. 'What's through here?'

They moved through an archway into the adjoining room, which also had a large, boarded-up window.

'Hmm,' Cora said considering, 'You know, you could put a café in here. Tapestries and wall hangings on the wall, display shelves in the far corner, the serving counter here and—' she flung open a door at the rear of the room, '—oh yes, ideal. The kitchen area here. I see there are toilet facilities.'

Patrick didn't allow himself to show it, but he was delighted at Cora's reaction, it matched his own so exactly. He had known his sister a long time, however, and understood how to handle her.

'You don't think the whole thing might be more trouble than it's worth?'

'Rubbish. It could be a gold mine, handled by the right person,' Cora scoffed.

'I'd need to get someone in for a few months who knew what they were doing. Someone I could rely on.'

She shoved at his chest.

'I know what you're doing. You know full well I want the job.'

'Shall I sign the lease then?'

'When can we start?'

'Tomorrow, if the lawyer pulls his finger out. You really think the coffee shop will work?'

They left still talking over ideas.

'I'll need your guidance over Scottish crafts people. I know a few top English ones who'll send stuff. They'll be thrilled.'

'Exhibitions or rolling stock?'

'A mixture of both, obviously. New exhibitions to draw people in, rolling stock to keep turnover up.'

When they reached the end of Kittle's Yard Patrick stopped.

'I'd like to take you to meet Pavel Skonieczna. But you won't say anything about my room full of curios, will you?'

Cora was amused. 'I won't.'

Cobbles looked empty, but Pavel appeared from the gloom at the back at the sound of their arrival. When he saw Patrick, his face broke into a smile.

'Patrick, my boy!'

Patrick didn't shake his hand, he gave him a quick hug instead.

'I hear I'm talking to a rock star. And I never knew.'

Pavel chuckled, clearly delighted. 'You saw the article did you? What fun, darling, isn't it? And I thought my glory days were over.'

The doorbell chinged again and a young couple came in. The youth was skinny and wore a hoodie, the girl wore her hair scraped back in a ponytail.

'Can I help you?' Pavel asked.

They stared at him for a minute, then the girl stuck out a photograph. Pavel saw it was a print of the photo the newspaper had used.

'Will yer sign that for us?' the girl asked. As an afterthought she added, 'Please?'

Pavel signed the photo. The young couple seemed excited. They remembered to thank him, then left.

'Isn't it all a bit of a nuisance?' Patrick asked, concerned.

'Darling, for a sad old man like me, squirrelled away in a dark shop all day long, it's been utter joy. Half the kids at the High School have been in for autographs. I love it. They chatter away, want to know everything about Bad Boys and what it was like being a rock star and did I know so-and-so or thingummyjig. Then there's been the folk of my own generation, the sixty and seventy somethings. Lots of them have vinyl albums they want me to sign and some were even at my concerts. Such fun.'

'But do they buy antiques?'

Pavel gave a little shrug.

'Some do. You'd be surprised.'

Patrick thought they probably didn't. He said, 'This is my

137

sister, Cora Spyridis.'

'Enchanted.' Pavel took Cora's hand and bent over it in a deep bow. 'Where have you been hiding her, Patrick?'

'Cora prefers the heat of the Greek sun to shivering in Scotland, but she has kindly agreed to run a new venture for me, for a few months at any rate.'

'Wonderful.'

'I don't want people to know the connection between us, Pavel. It's important. I don't want to muddy the waters.'

Pavel looked puzzled. 'Muddy the…?'

'Branding. Fine art and craft are very different things. So keep mum, will you?'

'It's a rather fine distinction. Do you think people will be bothered by it?'

'*I'm* bothered.'

'Well, if that's what you want, my lips are sealed.'

Pavel made a zipping sign across his mouth.

'Thank you. But I don't mind *you* knowing. While she tells you all about it, I'll take a look around, if I may?'

A few minutes later he returned.

'What have you got on that pair of Meissen vases?'

'Aha. Spotted them, did you? I had a feeling you'd like them.'

Actually, Patrick hated them, but he'd checked them thoroughly and seen that they were perfect, which was rare with this type of flower-encrusted china because it was so delicate.

'What's the damage Pavel, come on now?'

They commenced a game, the rules of which were well known to both of them. Pavel named a price, Patrick gasped in shock and named a considerably lower one. Pavel reduced his price, Patrick raised his, and so it went on until they agreed.

'Pack them, then, and I'll drop by with the car and pick them up.'

'You've chosen well, you old scoundrel.' Pavel took Patrick's arm and drew him close. 'What do you think about Alexa's new idea?'

'Paintings of shoes? Doesn't sound too exciting.'

'Oh, I think you're wrong there, my boy, quite wrong. I

138

think our Lexie is onto something very special, and I've had an idea.'

He drew Patrick even closer. Cora, growing bored, drifted to the back of the room and studied a bronze Art Deco figurine of a girl dancing. She thought it would look very fine on Patrick's mantelpiece and meant to persuade him to buy it.

Lexie planned to drop in at Cobbles and tell Pavel about Carlotta's idea, but just as she was about to push open the door she spotted Patrick talking to Pavel inside. There was a woman with them. She loomed out of the shadows at the back and laid a proprietorial hand on Patrick's arm. Was it the woman from the other night? She couldn't really see and didn't want to. She turned away quickly. Another encounter was unthinkable.

She had to get to work anyway, she was late already. She shut Patrick out of her mind and thought again about Carlotta's suggestion of a book. She was beginning to get an idea of how to set up the pages, drop in the main images, ghost in others, add in a few lines from the letters – make it look pretty and intriguing, really something to treasure. Carlotta was right: it wouldn't take long for her to draw the shoes. A couple of quick sketches (maybe in pencil, maybe in crayon or pastel) would pull the whole book together and stamp it as 'an Alexa Gordon production'. Each book would be unique and she could present the customer with the original drawing, prettily framed.

Could she make this into a commercial venture? Possibly. It would certainly be fun to make a book for Pavel, even though she wanted to paint him a proper full-sized oil painting, so that she could add real depth and detail. She could make a 'Jamie' book too.

Thanks sis, said his voice in her head.

Shut up, I wasn't talking to you, just about you, she thought, irritated by the intrusion. Jamie had been in her head a great deal in the last couple of weeks, as if disturbing his belongings had roused his spirit.

In her pocket, her mobile buzzed. She hoped it was Cameron, she hadn't heard from him, even though she had left messages. But it wasn't Cameron, just a text from her dentist confirming a check-up.

She pushed open the oak doors and hurried through the store. There was one customer looking at a recliner, but his body language suggested that he wouldn't be buying any time soon. Julie, a twenty-something with a chip on her shoulder on a month's trial from the Job Centre, was the only member of staff visible. Where were the others? Where was Neil? She nodded at Julie, who scowled and returned her attention to a broken nail.

When Lexie was half way to the back stairs, Julie said, 'Eh, I forgot, Neil says you're to go up sharpish.'

Lexie's excitement deflated as guilt set in. She must speak to her father about leaving. She hated the tedium of coming into the office and now that she'd decided to turn back to her art again…

'It's almost a quarter to ten, Lexie.'

Neil was looking pointedly at his watch.

'Sorry. The postie arrived with lots of parcels, then a courier came with more, and to cap it all, Carlotta pitched up too.'

'Couldn't your mother have dealt with the post?'

'Actually no, not this morning. Surely I'm allowed to be late, for once?'

Neil's voice was perfectly level.

'It's just that we have to get the tender in for the furnishings at Fleming House. It's due in at five and we've barely started the work.'

Lexie's eyes widened. 'Oh God, sorry! I'd completely forgotten.'

'Never mind. Come on, we'll need to get started. Morag'll be champing at the bit. Let's gird our loins for battle, eh?'

Neil was right. Morag was in an uncompromising mood.

'We have to be realistic,' she said, patting her frizzy hair and putting on the pinched, self-righteous look that seemed to suck all the joy out of living. *If she says 'challenging retail climate'*, Lexie thought, *I swear I'm going to batter her.*

Morag said, 'It just won't be worth our while unless there's a decent profit in it. We've got enough to do keeping the core business of the store afloat.'

'It'll give us turnover,' Lexie defended her idea, 'and

profile. When people see what we've done, they'll come here to get stuff for their own homes.'

'I very much doubt that. It's a commercial setting, not a domestic one. And turnover isn't profit. It's not even cash flow. In fact, it could make cash flow quite difficult for us.'

Neil chipped in. 'Lexie is right. We don't need to make it a loss leader, but profile would certainly help right now, especially if it changes people's ideas about our image.'

Morag tested their arguments to destruction, but by four o'clock, everything was ready for a final proofread.

'I'll do it,' Morag said. 'I'm good on detail. You go and do something else, I can make any little changes, if necessary.'

Nitpicking bored Lexie.

'Are you sure?'

'Yes. For heaven's sake send that girl Julie home, she's fed up with being in the store all day.'

'Okay, Morag, thanks.'

'It's looking terrific,' Neil said as they descended to the shop. 'If we don't win the tender with that, we'll never win anything.'

Lexie had spent most of the day thinking about shoes. Still, she was eager for the shop's success because that could be a stepping-stone to greater freedom. Now it was just a matter of waiting.

Chapter Fifteen

Catalogue number 9: Platform sandals, 1970s. Cork soles, suede uppers in brown and orange. Platform 3", rising to 4" at heel. Donated by Alice McInnes, Hailesbank. 'I used to commute from Stirling to Glasgow in the 1970s, where I worked as an editor at a large publishing house. I thought these shoes were the height of fashion, and saw nothing wrong with wearing them to work, under my ankle-length floral skirt.'

When Lexie reached Cobbles, Pavel was taking in his sandwich board.

'Darling! How wonderful. Come in for some tea? Or sherry?'

Lexie never drank sherry anywhere else, but she enjoyed these moments of companionship with Pavel. The sherry tasted good when sipped from the delicate cut crystal Edwardian glasses she knew he would never sell.

'Sherry would be perfect. And I have a story to tell you.'

'Ooh, just the thing. It's been a little quiet here today.'

"A little quiet" meant no sales and probably no company, so Lexie was glad she had something to share with him. 'It's about the article. There's been a development.'

He ushered her inside and turned the sign on the door to 'Closed'. They sat in the back of the shop and she watched as Pavel poured pale amber liquid into two glasses.

'Cheers, darling. Chin chin. Now, tell.'

'Shoes,' she started, 'are arriving at Fern House. By the sackful.'

'Darling! How amazing! Shoes? It's not because of that little article about *moi*, is it?'

'Little article? Pavel, it was a double page spread. Anyway, I'm very grateful, because the whole thing has given me an idea for a project.'

She explained about the shoes, and about Carlotta and her suggestion of making a book.

'It's the first time I've felt enthusiastic about my art since I had to abandon my exhibition. I think I'll give her idea a try.'

Pavel stared at her thoughtfully. 'I think you could do better than that, darling.'

'I'd do them really well,' she protested. 'I've got—'

'Of course you would, that's not what I was going to say.' His pause was pure Pavel: theatrical in the extreme. 'I think you could do a whole exhibition.'

'Of shoes?'

'Think about it. Already you have three stories. The tale of Edith's baby – so moving, darling – the funny little memories of Pavel, the old rocker, and Jamie's boots. And now you have more stories coming in.'

'People's wedding shoes?'

'They mean a lot to them. Never forget that. Anyway, those are the shoes for personalised books like the one you will do for Carlotta.'

'I suppose there could be other stories that would merit a painting as well. The paintings would take much longer, maybe a week or two each.'

Lexie's excitement was growing by the minute. She could smell the heady redolence of oil paint and she craved the feeling of a brush between her fingers. There was a place she went to in her head when she was painting that was hers alone, and she missed it with a physical ache.

Pavel persisted. 'So keep going doing the books, but pick the best for the exhibition. The books are your cash cow—'

'—but it's the painting that's really important.' She clapped her hands delightedly. 'Yes!'

Lexie had been on the verge of a big breakthrough before and once again Patrick's furious roar echoed round her head. 'Never offer your work to me again! Your career with Patrick Mulgrew is over.' It had been the worst kind of bullying, at the

144

worst possible time. Shocked and grieving, she'd been able to think of only one thing – being at Fernhill, helping her parents, coming to terms with what happened. Wouldn't it be fantastic if she could show Patrick she could succeed without his help?

Excitement died even as it was ignited. 'It's not going to work. Even if I could get the idea put together in the right way, I'd need someone to mount an exhibition. You can't just stick it in a garage. Come to that, I don't even have a garage.'

Pavel threw out his chest and straightened his shoulders.

'What, Pavel?'

'I can think of a solution.'

'Stop teasing me. *What?*'

'We can have it here, darling.'

'Here?'

Lexie looked around. She'd been coming into Cobbles since she'd been at school, and in all those years it had hardly changed. Everywhere you looked there were treasures – but an exhibition? She shook her head.

'Pavel, you're such a sweetheart, but—'

'Now don't pooh-pooh my suggestion, darling, let me show you something. Come with me.'

He stood up, a little stiffly, and his hands clawed at the edge of the desk.

'Are you all right?'

'It's just when I stand up.'

'Have you seen the doctor yet?'

'I'll call when I get a moment.'

'*Pavel.*'

'I'm fine,' he said impatiently. 'Come.'

A burgundy velvet curtain covered the back door, its heavy lengths puddling on the floor. So far as Lexie could remember, there had always been a curtain here. She was aware vaguely that the door led to Pavel's apartment, but when he drew the curtain back with a flourish, she stepped back in surprise. She'd expected a corridor, maybe stairs. Instead, daylight flooded into a small courtyard. In the centre was a cherry tree, its branches laden with small, green fruit. Under the branches stood a wooden bench, its lilac paint peeling picturesquely, its legs

145

wedged between the lumps and bumps of the cobbled ground. 'Cobbles,' she said aloud as comprehension dawned, wondering that she has never thought before about the name of the shop.

'This is where I have my cup of tea in the morning, darling, if it's warm enough.'

'I'm stunned. I never knew this was here.'

His face split into a triumphant grin.

'It's always been my little secret, but maybe I'm too old for secrets now.'

Lexie followed him across the courtyard to another door. She had no idea what to expect – certainly not the stacks of broken chairs, frayed cardboard boxes bursting with books and papers, pictures stacked against the wall, their frames obviously broken or shabby, assorted dinner services and tea sets that had clearly seen better days, dolls, bears, garden statues, old implements, samplers, vases and lamps that seemed ready to burst into the courtyard.

'Wow.' It was a feeble reaction for such an astonishing sight.

Pavel looked rueful. 'Now the terrible truth is out. I'm such a hoarder, darling.'

He swept his arm in a great arc from one corner of the room to the other.

'It's all in order, of course, I know where every last speck and spot is, but be truthful now, what am I to do with all this rubbish? An old man like me?'

'Not old, Pavel—'

'Once upon a time I meant to turn this into a small fine-art section, but as you can see, sweetie, I never got round to it. Time I had a clear-out.'

'I can't take it all in.'

'There. Two secrets in two weeks. You never guessed I had so many skeletons in my little cupboard now, did you?'

She surveyed the room. There were two large windows into the courtyard, as well as the glass-panelled door. Shabby blackout material hung crookedly from poles across the windows, but if this were taken down, the light would be perfect for a gallery. Visualised without the junk, and there was

146

clear potential.

'It's a beautiful space,' she said,

'I knew you'd love it.'

'But Pavel, I couldn't possibly—'

'What else would I use it for? Nothing. Just rubbish, as you see. I'll get in a dealer, darling, sell the whole lot for best price, get the walls painted. It would be such a relief, sweetie, I can't *tell* you.'

He picked up a walking cane that was propped against the wall and leant on it picturesquely.

'You see? Everything's too old and too dirty for me even to sit down.'

'Pavel—'

'It's small, of course, but big enough for what – a dozen exhibits? Paintings on the walls, the original objects on plinths, perhaps a film projected onto the far wall? The floor's good.'

He hooked back the corner of a threadbare rug with the cane and revealed broad floorboards.

'Just need a polish, or maybe a lime wash. Now,' he let the rug fall back and tapped the floor imperiously with the stick, 'I don't want to hear any more arguments, sweetie, because I've got them all covered. It's what they call win-win, I believe, in modern parlance. You take the room for your exhibition, I get the rubbish cleared *and*—' he paused dramatically, '—I get a lot more people coming through the shop to get to it. And as you so eloquently told me, darling, when you were trying to get me to agree to the newspaper article, increasing the footfall into Cobbles can only be a good thing.'

He stuck his free hand on his hip, challenging her to defy him.

The protest that had been forming on Lexie's lips morphed into a slow smile. Years ago, she'd thought him an unlikely soul-mate, but time had taught her that friendship comes in many guises and what Pavel offered her was beyond price.

She shook her head in disbelief. 'You've floored me. What can I say?'

'Thank you would do nicely.'

She reached for his hand and squeezed it.

'Thank you, Pavel,' she said, leaning in to kiss a pallid cheek, 'Oh, *thank* you!'

It seemed as if Pavel's instinct had been right. More shoes arrived daily and some had remarkable stories attached to them. Early one morning, Lexie threw on a silk kimono and stood in the centre of her bedroom, surrounded by parcels. It seemed that her mother had rediscovered her secretarial skills and organised a stacking system. The log book listed everything in date order of arrival at Fernhill. She perched on the corner of her bed and scanned the items at the top of the list.

> ➢ Baby bootees. Edith Lawrence, Musselburgh.
> ➢ Rugby boots. Jamie Gordon, Hailesbank.
> ➢ Ballet pumps. Pavel Skonieczna, Hailesbank.
> ➢ Clown's shoes. Frank Dawson, Broxburn.
> ➢ White neurosurgeon's clogs. Alastair Whyte, Edinburgh.
> ➢ Bridal shoes. Carlotta Woods, Hailesbank.
> ➢ Baby shoes. Kaylie MacDuff, Hailesbank.
> ➢ 16th-century 'concealment shoe', found in rafters of cottage outside Hailesbank. Eric and Sheila Flint, Forgie.
> ➢ Bridal shoe. Anne Grant, Hailesbank.
> ➢ Edwardian riding boots. Harold Fitch, Melrose.

It ran on, already, to several pages. If she was really going to pull together an exhibition, how would she ever choose from these? She picked a box at random and opened it. Inside was a pair of well-worn trainers. Lexie (who had never seen the point of exercise) was about to close the box again when she spotted a note.

'Of all the shoes I have ever worn,' wrote Ellis Ruthven, a local man, 'these are the most important to me. I wore these trainers for my tenth marathon. It doesn't sound much, but you see, eleven years ago, my wife kicked me out, calling me lazy, a slob, a leech. I had to face some hard truths and found that she was right about everything. To help ease the pain and humiliation of what had happened, I started to run. Soon someone bet me I couldn't run a marathon, and so I did. I began to raise money for charities. Running became a way of life. I discovered not only a new energy, but also a new purpose. After a time, my wife took me back. Over the years, I have raised more than a million pounds.'

Unexpectedly moved, Lexie clutched the letter to her chest. *It's about the stories*, she reminded herself, and placed the letter and the trainers carefully back in their box. *The things that change us*.

As early as she dared, she called Molly, but it went straight to answer. She left a message.

'Hi, Moll, it's me. Lots to tell you, but I guess you're still asleep. Call me back when you can, yes?'

She counted the parcels – forty-one – and checked the list. Forty-one? It was nothing, just an exercise in filing, but a few weeks ago Martha could not have done this – or, at least, she would not have had the inclination. Was Edith Lawrence, with her heartbreaking compulsion to revisit a forgotten past, the most unlikely messenger of deliverance?

Her phone rang, breaking into her thoughts. 'Hi, Moll, thanks for calling back.'

'What's happened? You sounded a bit weird. Are you okay?'

'Weird? Thanks a lot.'

'No, I mean, uptight.'

'Excited, more like. I'm standing here in my bedroom, swamped by shoes.'

'What, you mean, like a shoe mountain? Brilliant, any good ones to spare for me?'

'No, you don't get it. Not new shoes, they're all sorts. Old riding boots, trainers, clogs, good-luck shoes, break-your-heart shoes, everything. Mum's having to log the lot because it's quickly becoming chaos.'

'Why?'

Lexie explained. '...And Carlotta came with her wedding shoes yesterday,' she finished, 'She wants me to make a book for her.'

'A book?'

Lexie ran through this idea too. 'But the best thing is – wait for this – Pavel's got a room at the back of Cobbles he's just using as a store. He's going to clear it and have it painted.'

A lump formed in her throat, but she managed to choke out the news.

'For me, Moll. He's going to let me have an exhibition!'

'That's *brilliant!* Hey Lexie, it's what you deserve. Time to stop doing everything for everyone else and get on with your own life.'

She was about to tell Molly about her plan to leave Gordon's when the Fleming House tender came through, but bit her words back in time. Molly was too closely involved, it wouldn't be right to discuss it.

Chapter Sixteen

Catalogue number 24: Edwardian made-to-measure riding boots. Black leather with brown leather band at the top. Donated by Harold Fitch, Melrose. The brown leather section at the top was pulled up over the knee to protect the riding breeches on dirty roads. When the rider dismounted and entered a house, he would fold down the tops so that mud-spattered boots would not dirty the furniture...

Victoria Hunter-Darling was feeling harassed. It was the opening of the Esther Goldwyn exhibition tonight and Patrick had disappeared. She had called him a dozen times since lunchtime, but he wasn't picking up her calls, Esther was furious because she claimed the labels had been cut on a squint and she hated the font. Besides, their usual caterer was on holiday and whoever was deputising clearly didn't have a clue because they'd sent trays of dessert bites instead of savoury canapés.

'I can't let you move that to there,' she told Esther rather desperately as the girl unplugged a stuffed pheasant table lamp and tried to plug it in at the reception desk.

'Why not?'

'I need the computer on, and it doesn't leave enough room for the other brochures. Plus, we need the price sheets there.'

Esther ignored her.

'The brochures can go on that bit at the back, they're not for tonight anyway. What the hell are you going to do about the labels?'

'I really don't—'

Victoria started to flounder, when there was a loud pop and

one of the spotlights faded into darkness. Worse, three bulbs in the stuffed seagull chandelier centrepiece appeared to have popped too.

'*Shit!*' she said, forgetting to be ladylike. She had visions of a main fuse blowing and the entire gallery being plunged into darkness any moment.

'What the bloody hell is—? Christ, no!' Esther's voice rose an octave. 'We've spent hours getting that bloody spot in the right place and now look at it! And my chandelier! You'll have to get the ladder back up at once.'

Victoria was exasperated. It wasn't Esther who'd spent hours placing the spots, she'd had to do it. Besides, the step-ladder was quite large and now that the exhibits were in place they'd be in danger of knocking over the black-and-white painted wardrobe topped with the stuffed curled-up badger. Esther had insisted on putting too many pieces into the show, she'd always thought that, but the bloody woman was so awfully insistent...

Was there a spare spot? And where was Patrick? There was less than an hour to go till the first customers would appear and the place was still a shambles. There were four exhibits still to be put in place, the rest of the lighting to check, the girl from the caterer had disappeared somewhere instead of setting out the glasses and making sure the white wine was chilling and the red opened , and she really ought to nip down the road to the shop and buy in some crisps and nuts because they couldn't serve double chocolate ganaches and mini strawberry pavlovas, could they?

Just as she felt she was about to crack, the door opened and Patrick walked in with a stunning woman. She was almost as tall as he was, her dark brown hair fell thickly around her shoulders and her skin was smooth and deeply tanned. Victoria was familiar with jealousy and recognised the feeling at once. She longed to appear capable and in control, but Esther's fuming gaze was drilling into her back and this vision of beauty filled her with instant inadequacy. Patrick was known to have a short fuse and she absolutely hated the idea of being at the dynamite end of it. Still, what could she do?

'Patrick!' she croaked. 'Help!'

Losing your temper is only worthwhile if it produces the desired effect. In this situation, it would have been counter-productive. Patrick sized up the situation in an instant and took charge.

'Cora will see to the food, I will sort the lights and the exhibits. You, Victoria, will sit down at the computer with Esther and retype all the labels. Use the template for the mailings and print them out on the self-adhesive labels, then the pair of you can go round together and stick them all on. Straight. Then get out a broom and sweep round to make sure there are no little bits of packaging lurking anywhere. Got it?'

In minutes, ordered efficiency replaced chaos and panic, spotlights were replaced, the badger remained undisturbed and a small colony of seagulls clustered together near the ceiling and holding lightbulbs in their beaks was restored as the eye-catching centrepiece it had always been intended to be.

'My fault,' Cora said apologetically, reappearing with a tote bag filled with snacks purchased from the corner store. 'Sorry. I should never have insisted on getting my hair cut, but it was sorely in need. Where are the bowls to put these in?'

Victoria dived into the store and reappeared with a stack of glass bowls.

'Here,' she said breathlessly, returning to the printer, where the last of the replacement labels had just emerged.

'Everything is fine,' Patrick said calmly, returning the step-ladder to the store. 'We've still got twenty minutes.'

This was nothing. This was situation normal. Things happened, they were sorted.

Only sometimes, they could not be sorted. Burst spotlights could be replaced, but words once spoken couldn't be withdrawn. Lexie, thought Patrick, had become wary of him, and that was something he could not easily fix.

After the madness of the opening was over and Esther had been praised and pampered and expensively fed, along with her sponsors and entire family, Patrick drove Cora back to The Gables.

'Much as I love you—' he told her as they turned off the main road into Hailesbank.

She groaned. 'What's coming?'

'—As I was saying, much as I love you, I'm used to living on my own.'

'Do I get in your way?'

'You move things.'

'Such as?'

'My favourite spatula.'

'You're not still on about that, are you?'

'The scissors.'

'I found a better place to keep them.'

'The anti-static cloth I use to clean the computer screen. You still can't remember where you put that.'

'Jesus, Pats, you are getting crabby in your old age. Do you want me to go back to Kalamata? Is that what you're saying?'

He swung into the driveway at the back of the house. The headlights sprayed across the stone-built garages that once would have housed a coach and horses.

'Of course not. I was thinking you'd be more comfortable in the annexe.'

'The annexe? Where the hell's that? Across the river?'

'Right here.'

'Here? Where?'

'In front of your eyes. I had the rooms above the garages converted a couple of years back, God knows why, I wasn't expecting visitors. I think some architect nobbled me at a reception. I seem to recall he spun me a line about maximising the potential of the property, sweating the assets or some such garbage. I must have had a glass of red wine too many, because he assured me the next day that I'd agreed to his suggestions. Anyway, there it is. There are two bedrooms and the rooms are comfortable. They'd damn well better be, given the price I paid for them.'

Cora looked at him.

'You want to watch it, Pats. You're getting to be really anti-social. How will you ever find a woman if you can't compromise on the little things?'

154

'Who says I want a woman?'

'I do.'

'See? This is exactly what I mean. If you move across here I won't have to have these damn silly conversations.'

'Idiot.'

'What do you think?'

'Are you suggesting I move right now?'

'Don't be ridiculous, it's almost midnight.'

'Then I'll look at it tomorrow. Now will you chill?'

'It will give you more privacy too.'

'Stop trying to justify yourself, Pats.'

'You know you like privacy.'

'Patrick.' He flicked the lights on in the hallway of the main house and she glared at him in the sudden brightness. 'Shut. Up.'

He grinned. 'Thanks for your help tonight, by the way.'

'No problem. Now can I go to bed? I promise I won't move a single thing before breakfast.'

Patrick liked his bedroom better than any other room in the house. He closed the door, tugged off his shoes and socks, sank his feet into the thick carpet and allowed himself to relax. The room was spacious, with one large window overlooking the park and another facing into his garden. There were, therefore, two sets of curtains to draw. He padded across to them and dragged the heavy cream fabric across the dark panes.

Cora was right, he was a private person. He didn't like to talk about his childhood in Ireland and he most certainly didn't want to talk about Niamh.

He dropped onto a winged chair near the garden window. It was upholstered in grey-blue tweed – the exact colour, now he thought of it, of Niamh's eyes. The thought took him back to the day he'd first seen her, perched on a wall at the edge of one of his father's fields, wincing as she'd tried to pull off a walking boot.

He'd watched for some moments as she'd twisted the boot and turned it, but for some reason had seemed unable to pull it free. Perhaps sensing his gaze, she'd looked up and seen him and despite the shyness that had dogged him aged seventeen,

155

he'd been jolted into action.

'Can I help?' he'd called, striding towards her across ploughed, heavy earth.

'I've got a stone in my boot but I can't get it off.' Her smile had taken his breath away. 'As you can see.'

He'd knelt by her side, not caring that the dampness of the soil was seeping into the fabric of his trousers.

'There's a knot,' he'd said, peering at the claggy laces.

'Can you loosen it?'

He had her boot in his hand. He was looking at her ankles, trying to resist following the slender line of the bones as they extended upwards, towards knee and thigh. He wanted to be close to her, like this, for ever.

'I'll try.'

He'd worked at the knot as slowly as he dared, glancing up at her from time to time, seeing the sharp sweep of her cheekbones as the flesh softened towards her delicious lips, and the long fluttering length of her eyelashes as she gazed down at her feet, concerned.

He could delay no longer. 'There.'

He'd eased the boot off – the deliciousness of it! – and she had shaken out a tiny stone.

'Thanks.'

She bent her knee up to her chest in one fluid, supple movement and wriggled her foot back into her boot.

He had never been as close as this to such a pretty girl before. He only knew the girls at school – lumpen, wide-hipped beings, destined to marry rough-handed farmers and breed a new generation for the land.

He was a farmer, but he was not rough-handed. He knew that this was not his destiny. He would leave Ireland, find a vocation, become rich. He would have a beautiful wife. He would have this girl.

He was in love.

Patrick jerked upright. Why in hell's name was he thinking about Niamh, when he'd sworn he would never find a corner for her in his mind again? The humiliation when she'd left him for his brother was long past, he'd more or less got through everything before he met Lexie.

Quirky, generous, stubborn, talented Lexie.

He leapt to his feet. He'd thought that Lexie was different from Niamh – until she, too, betrayed his faith in her. Perhaps he'd been silly to react like that, but surely it had been understandable?

He opened the majestic Georgian wardrobe, took out a box and carried it across to the bed, where he sank down onto the soft white covers, so carefully laundered by Mrs M.. For a minute he stared at it sightlessly. The box was so full of memories, and of regrets, that he was almost afraid to open it.

At last he lifted the lid and set it to one side.

Yes, these were just as he remembered them: objects of great beauty – and a stark reminder of what he had forfeited the day he had lost his temper so badly with Lexie. And yet, she was the one who'd been in the wrong. It should be Lexie who crawled back, begging forgiveness.

For a long time, Patrick sat immobile. He might be the one with right on his side, and common sense dictated that he should sell the damn things, but he couldn't bring himself to do it.

The centre of Hailesbank had held up fairly well in the face of commercial development south of the river. The retail park, supermarket and leisure centre there were popular with the young, aspiring residents who commuted into Edinburgh for work. Lexie preferred to stay loyal to the shops and facilities in the heart of the old town, but there was no denying that its pub, the Duke of Atholl, was tired and shabby. Tonight, Lexie had arranged to meet Cameron in the Crown and Thistle – not only because it was much nicer, but also because she liked to stroll across the river and over the new bridge.

A decade ago, the old coaching inn on the south bank had been seriously run down. The roof needed urgent attention, the garden was filled with unsightly weeds and the bar was a throwback to the 1950s. Then it was bought by a young couple who had halted the slide into disuse, and managed to turn the business around.

It was a lesson, in how things could be done, Lexie thought as the pub came into view. How come they had managed to modernise, yet Gordon's remained frozen in time? And what would it take for Tom to understand this? Lexie stopped in the middle of the bridge, overcome by a strong sense of Jamie's presence. He'd loved the Crown and Thistle. It had been his natural habitat: Jamie and some girlfriend, hanging out on a Saturday night when the match was over and there was a victory to celebrate or a loss to obliterate.

Arms circled round from behind her and hands covered her eyes.

'Guess who?'

Lexie giggled. 'Get off me.'

Cameron turned her around and pulled her towards him.

'You look just like a Liquorice Allsort. Pink and white and good enough to eat,' he said, laughing.

'Silly. Where've you been hiding, Cameron? You haven't been in to Gordon's.'

'Old man Pettigrew put me on other runs. Anyway, you said you'd call me.'

Lexie remembered the circumstances of their last parting and blushed. She'd been ready to sleep with him again – or thought so. Her sudden about-turn must have been humiliating.

'And so I did.' She smiled at him, willing him to put the episode aside.

'Let's get a drink, eh? I'm dead thirsty.' He tucked her arm under his and turned towards the pub.

'I saw the article about Pavel.'

'Wasn't it great? And guess what? People have been sending me shoes. Dozens of them.'

'Really? Why?'

'They seem to want paintings.'

'Weird.'

'I do good paintings,' she said in mock indignation.

'I know you do, lovey, but people want paintings of shoes? Don't you think that's a bit odd?'

'Not really. I think it's sweet. Carlotta wants me to make a book.'

158

He turned his head aside. 'Oh, Carlotta ...'

'She brought in her bridal shoes and a load of letters and ribbons.'

'I should have thought Carlotta would—' He broke off.

'Carlotta would what?'

His shoulders rose dismissively.

'I've forgotten what I was going to say.'

'But that's not all.' Alexa's excitement about the exhibition bubbled to the surface. 'Pavel's offered me a space to hold an exhibition in!'

'Pavel? What space has he got?'

'I never knew about it, but there's a small cobbled courtyard outside the back of the shop – Cobbles, get it? – and there's a good-sized room on the other side. It's full of junk, but he's going to get it cleared and the room done up for me.'

As they reached the pub door, a Land Rover passed, towing a trailer carrying two rams.

'Off to the Royal Highland Show,' Cameron said. 'Nice-looking beasts.'

Before his disappearance, Cameron had worked on his uncle's farm just outside Hailesbank.

'You used to love farming. Don't you want to get back to it?'

'Maybe.'

They sat in the garden, near the river. A family of mallards paddled by, the young almost ready to break free of their mother's protectiveness. Lexie thought of the rams and how Cameron used to arrive at her studio smelling vaguely of hay. Why had he left, years ago, so suddenly and with no explanation. She'd waited weeks for him to explain, yet he hadn't brought the subject up at all. She couldn't wait any longer, she had to know.

'Why did you go away, Cameron? You were happy, weren't you? With the farming? *We* were happy, weren't we? I thought we were.'

Cameron found the antics of the duck riveting.

'Look at that one, arse in the air. What a way to have to get your food.'

'*Cameron.*'

He turned towards her, his mouth twisted into a wry grimace, his manner apologetic.

'I wasn't ready, sweetheart, that's the truth of it. You were so damn possessive that I felt, you know, swamped. I needed to get out, get some space.'

Had she been possessive? Lexie searched her mind for the evidence, but couldn't recall feeling that way. He must be right, of course, otherwise why would he say it?

'Oh. But couldn't we have talked about it? You didn't have to just disappear.'

He took possession of her slender hands and traced the tattoo round her thumb with his fingers.

'You're right. I behaved like a pillock. Of course we should have talked, but I was scared you might persuade me to stay. I was bloody immature, I admit it.' He lifted his gaze to her face. 'All that time I was away, I was thinking, Cameron, you've been a fucking idiot. You had a jewel there and you let her slip through your fingers. When I finally faced it, I came home. Can you forgive me?'

'I don't think—'

He raised one hand and held her under the chin.

'You're a miracle, woman. Look at you. You gave up everything when Jamie was killed, and came home to support your parents. I don't know anyone else who would have done that. But you're bloody talented, Lex. You're going to make a roaring success of this exhibition and I want to be the one who's around to help you. Will you let me?'

She searched the familiar face with its skewed nose and long scar as if she might find the answer to his question there. What did she think the other day? *I'm ready for love.* Had that changed?

'I'm certainly going to need help,' she said.

Chapter Seventeen

Catalogue number 2: Black leather traditional lace-ups by Clark's. Donor, Tom Gordon, Hailesbank. There's nothing remarkable about these shoes, except that they seem to personify the story of Tom Gordon, my father. They are plain, inexpensive, serviceable, worn and a little old-fashioned. They make me choke with pride and admiration for all they stand for: the way my father plugged on doggedly, determined to hold his family together, whatever the personal cost.

Lexie was sitting in the bathroom at Fernhill clad in only an ancient tee shirt and running shorts, applying dye to her hair. She had smeared Vaseline round her hairline to stop the vivid dye colouring her skin, covered her head with a shower cap, and set the alarm on her phone to go off when it was time to rinse the colour off.

She glanced at it. Five minutes to go.

Her mind slipped back to shoes. She thought of shoes from the moment she woke until she put her head on her pillow at night. She had become obsessed with shoes. They paraded in front of her eyes – not filled with slim feet or bony feet or calloused feet, just shoes.

Not just shoes – shoes that told stories.

She had thought about the premise of her exhibition a great deal. She was desperate to make a start, but something was getting in her way. It wasn't the fact that she was still working at Gordon's, although that had to be addressed. It wasn't that she had no studio to paint in, somehow she would overcome that hurdle.

161

No, it was something else, something she had never told anyone. Something she was desperately ashamed of.

Three minutes to go.

When she'd gone to Patrick Mulgrew a year ago and told him she could not finish the painting that was to form the centrepiece of her exhibition, she'd allowed him to think it was because of Jamie's accident – because he was in a coma and, later, because he'd died. That hadn't been the whole truth.

The truth—

Ping. Ping. *Ping.*

The alarm grew insistently louder. Time.

She pulled on protective gloves and dropped the shower cap in the bin. She dipped her head deep into the washbasin and started to pour jugs of lukewarm water over her head, rinsing and re-rinsing until the water ran clear. She squeezed an inch of conditioner onto the palm of her hand, massaged it in and repeated the rinsing process. Finally, she grabbed a towel and patted the water off her short crop.

She raised her head and stared at her reflection in the mirror. Dark eyes stared back at her, the lashes long and thick, the pupils pinpricks in the brightness of the lights. Only she knew the truth concealed behind that stare.

Damn it.

The truth had nagged at her a year ago, when she'd realised she could not complete the last painting. It hadn't been grief that had forced her to stop, it had been the realisation that the work she'd been producing for Patrick had been dishonest.

There, she'd confessed it at last, even if it was only to herself. It had been dishonest because she'd been painting not what was in her heart, but what she thought would appeal to the art world. She'd decided that huge canvases with a dark theme and disturbing images would catch the eye of the critics and attract buyers, so she'd pushed the work further and further in that direction, ignoring the warning voices in her head. *It's not what you're about. It's just artbollocks.* So when Patrick Mulgrew spotted her paintings and offered her a show, she'd been caught in a trap of her own making.

'Lexie?' her mother called through the bathroom door.

'Yes?'

'Everything okay? Supper's nearly ready. Dad'll be home soon.'

Stupid. 'Ready in ten.'

She returned to her room and picked up the hairdryer. She didn't need to blow her short crop dry but she liked the feel of the hot air on her head. Her cut had a little length on top, but the sides and back hugged her head, emphasising the shape of the skull and the length of her neck. It was easy to manage. Once she started painting, she'd forget everything, so the simpler the better.

She slipped on a pair of coloured leggings the exact scarlet of her hair and discarded the dye-stained tee shirt in favour of a lime-green cardigan, buttoned up to the second last hole. She took a moment to examine the effect. Her hair had turned out well, the colour had covered the roots and it had a pleasing sheen.

Her room was now jam-packed with shoes. She had to get a studio, and she had to do it quickly. She'd planned to stay until the work for Fleming House came through, but why? She'd done what she could at Gordon's and the time had come to reclaim her own life – and now that Cameron had come clean and confessed that he had been immature, she felt able to give herself to a more physical relationship with him again.

She smiled. Whatever it was that had come between them that first time in his flat, she'd well and truly got over it now. *I want to be the one who's around to help you. Will you let me,* he'd asked her in the pub. Well, why not? It seemed that Cameron had grown up in the past six years, maybe at last he was ready to commit.

Tom Gordon had won a great deal of respect in the local community for the way in which he'd coped with his son's tragic death.

'Brave feller,' was the general consensus. Others said, 'Dignified. Very dignified.'

Martha and Lexie saw another side of him – his determination to fight grief and adversity could make him

163

impossible to live with. Somewhere along a path littered with emotional obstacles and traps he had managed to lose some of the qualities that used to make him endearing: a sense of humour, spontaneity, empathy. As they sat down to eat, Lexie was all too well aware that she'd have to find the seam of understanding she knew lay somewhere in her father's character if she was to extricate herself from the business without hurting him.

'I've been thinking,' she started as her mother filled bowls with pasta.

'Careful,' Tom grunted, offering her wine.

She held her glass out. 'You know these shoes ...?'

'If you mean the dozens of parcels that seem to arrive here every day, I would say, yes, I know what you're referring to.'

'And my idea of painting some of them?'

Martha chipped in, 'And doing the books, like Carlotta suggested.'

'And the books. Well,' Lexie watched as Tom picked up his fork and started to spear the food, 'Pavel Skonieczna has offered me an exhibition. He's clearing a room specially for me. I'd like to take some time off from Gordon's, Dad.'

Tom's mouth closed round the pasta. He began to chew. He said nothing.

Lexie ploughed on. 'I said I'd do a year to help out. I think I've done what I can. Once the tender comes in from Fleming House, as I'm sure it will, cash flow will begin to improve. Anyway, Neil's more than capable of taking on more responsibility.'

Tom was eating steadily. Martha was toying with her food. Lexie hadn't touched hers.

'I do think you should consider letting Neil take on more, Dad. It's time you and Mum had a holiday, for a start. Give him a bit of rope and see what happens.'

It can't get much worse, she wanted to add, but bit the words back.

Martha said, 'Your father would miss your support at Gordon's.'

'I know. I'm sorry. But I'll still be around to talk to about

164

things and – be honest – I'm not really cut out for a life in retailing, am I?'

Tom's head was down. He was examining a prawn as if it might spring to life again, headless, tailless, legless and without its protective carapace.

Martha said, 'Where would you paint, Lexie? There's nowhere here that's suitable.'

'I'll find somewhere to rent. I've got a bit saved up.'

Tom put down his fork and looked at her levelly.

'Will you come back, do you think?'

Lexie, who had spent twelve months struggling to be unselfish, wanted to weep with love and gratitude. He had acknowledged her request. His longing to establish his succession was painfully evident and conveyed the depth of loss he felt, but he had given his tacit permission to go.

She leapt up and hugged her father ferociously, then tilted her newly re-coloured head to one side and smiled at him.

'Can we take it one day at a time, as we have this last year? I think that's all I can manage, even now.'

Her father's arms stole round her, drawing her close. She could smell the sweet, familiar residue of that morning's aftershave and feel the scratch of the evening's stubbly shadow on his chin. This was how he used to hug her when she was a child and ready for sleep. This was how he'd comforted her when she fell and grazed a knee. This was how – she realised – he had not been able to hug her since Jamie died.

She tightened her arms round him.

It might not seem much, but it was the first sign of emotion he had allowed himself and she treasured the moment.

Esther Goldwyn's exhibition received much critical attention. Inevitably, opinion was divided – some critics saw it as a satirical comment on contemporary art, others as a visionary interpretation of recycling, topped by a delightful tongue-in-cheek humour. Lexie, who couldn't face attending the opening even though she had an invitation, was moved by a reluctant compulsion to read the reviews. Despite herself, she couldn't help feeling a stab of envy. *It should have been me.* She put the thought aside. She'd made her own choices. Jamie's death had been a factor, of course, but it had been the catalyst, not the cause, of her withdrawal.

Would she have faced the truth about her art if the accident hadn't happened? She couldn't be sure about the answer to that.

She put all the papers into the recycling. That was all past. She had a new agenda now – and Molly had offered a way forward. She was going to look at a possible studio somewhere in the grounds of Fleming House.

Although she much preferred walking to driving, Lexie borrowed Tom's car for the visit. If she moved out here, she'd have to invest in a bike.

At the junction on the far side of Hailesbank she signalled right and began to turn, just as a car rounded the corner into her path. She stepped on the brakes and screeched to a halt inches from tar-black metal.

'Oh God, sorry!'

The driver's window slid open. It was Patrick.

'Are you all right?' There was concern rather than anger in the voice.

Lexie sent up a fervent prayer of thanks that she hadn't crashed into this of all the cars in Hailesbank.

'Fine. Thank you.'

'You are meant to let traffic on the main road pass, you know, before turning,' he said in a mild voice.

'I didn't see you.'

'Are you really all right, Lexie?'

She just wanted to be on her way.

'Yes. You?'

'Yes.'

'Then can we both go, do you think?'

His voice stiff, he said, 'Take care then,' and slid his window up.

She completed the turn and tried to think of their disagreements rather than the good times they'd had together, because that way it was easier not to want him. It was now a pleasant drive along the country road, and by the time she'd reached the new sign at the entrance, she'd regained some equanimity.

166

FLEMING HOUSE. WEDDINGS, CONFERENCES, EVENTS.

Molly was certainly getting things licked into shape. Before she'd taken up the job, everything at this country-house estate had been run down but now the approach was delightful. A dozen red deer were grazing peacefully a hundred yards away across the green parkland, their hides gleaming russet in the evening sunshine. Lexie lost sight of them as the drive wound through a stand of birch fluttering in a wisp of a breeze and scattering dappled shadows across her bonnet. Then she picked a path between towering rhododendron bushes, drooping with heavy flowers. After a mile, she left the tarmac for the gravel in front of the main entrance to the Georgian mansion. The idea of a studio here lifted her spirits. She forgot about Patrick and thought only of possibilities.

'Hi!' Molly must have seen the car coming, because she was waiting on the gravel. 'Hey, the hair's looking good!'

'Topped it up yesterday. Where's this building, then?'

Molly laughed. 'You can't wait, can you?'

Lexie leapt out of the car, adrenaline surging. 'When you said, about the outbuilding, I couldn't think where you meant.'

'I don't think I've ever shown you the walled garden. It's been woefully neglected. I don't think anyone's grown so much as a potato there for decades, but if you can stand weeds, it has a charm of its own. Come on, let's walk.'

The house was satisfyingly symmetrical. Steps ran up to the grand entrance, which was framed by four magnificent columns. A wing on each side completed the building. They rounded the corner to the back.

'See those sash and case windows?' Molly gestured to the first floor, 'They run from floor to ceiling of the ballroom. That's where we hold most of the wedding receptions. They look out onto the formal gardens over there.'

They walked past clipped box hedges and careful plantings.

'That's where most of the gardening resource has been focused, obviously. It's very popular for photographs. The walled garden's behind the high wall almost hidden by those sycamores. The greenhouse has been cleaned out and made watertight, so the gardeners have started using it again, but they haven't time to restore the veg patch. You'd be left pretty much in peace, if you want the place.'

'I never knew this was here.'

'We don't bring the public round this way.'

Lexie spotted a door and two windows, and realised that there was a small cottage built into the wall. Molly took a bunch of keys out of her pocket and stopped.

'Here we are.'

The door scuffed along the floor and Molly had to push hard to get it to open. Lexie's first reaction was disappointment, because the hallway was tiny and very dark. Inside she pushed open a door on the left. This room was small and the window looked out into the trees, so would get little natural light. On the other side, a matching door opened on an identical room. In this one there was a stone sink and a wooden dresser, its green paint cracked and faded. Her anticipation was fading into despondency.

'I did warn you it wasn't exactly luxurious, didn't I? But hang on in.'

There was a bathroom, of sorts. It looked as if nothing had been done to the plumbing for fifty years. The toilet had a high cistern and long chain flush and the bath was an ancient roll-top, grimy and clearly beloved by the local spider population. The symmetry of the architecture was maintained by a storage cupboard on the other side of the hallway.

It could all be scrubbed up and made usable, but there was only one thing Lexie cared about – a room in which she could paint. These rooms were too small and too dark. Molly paused in front of the last door.

'Ta-da!' she proclaimed dramatically as she threw it open.

Lexie gasped. The cottage might only have been built for a gardener, but the original architect had clearly insisted on echoes of grandeur from the main house. Three sash and case windows had been let into the walls from floor to ceiling, allowing light to flood in to the room. When she looked more closely at them, she saw that the centre one was not actually a window but a door constructed to resemble the other two windows, and it opened directly onto the huge walled space that

168

had once been Fleming House's kitchen garden.

'Oh. My. God.'

The room was almost as large as all the others put together and its ceiling was higher, arching into the structure of the roof. Lexie walked to the windows and looked out at the garden. Low evening sun was about to dip behind the wall, but for the moment it was bathing the space in gold. The grass had been cut, but beyond that, little had been done. What would once have been nursery beds and vegetable plots had become overgrown with wildflowers – campion and candytuft, thistle and tansy, and a host of other plants she could not even begin to name. The greenhouse Molly had mentioned was way to the left, almost at the far end of the garden. Its elaborate white ironwork supported what seemed like an acre of glass, but it was so far away that she would not be troubled by activity there.

Molly was clasping the bunch of keys to her chest.

'What do you think?'

'I couldn't possibly afford the rent on a place like this!'

'It's a mess.'

'It just needs a good clean. Don't any of the gardeners want to live here?'

'They all live locally. Lady Fleming says we haven't got the resources to do a proper job here at the moment, she'd be delighted for you to have it on a nominal rent for a year, and she'll send a squad of cleaners down for a morning to help make it habitable.'

'I'm gobsmacked. I don't know what to say.'

'Just say yes. I was thinking maybe your dad would let you have a few ex-display bits and bobs from the store, like a bed and a couple of chairs, and a table for the kitchen? There's no cooker, but you could maybe get a plug-in hob and a microwave – or one of the halogen oven things, like big bowls? You'd need a small fridge too, but other than that, not a lot.'

'Wait a minute – are you suggesting I could actually *live* here?'

'Why not? I know what you're like when you start working on something. You never stop. It'd be bloody dangerous for you to even think of cycling back to Fernhill at some unearthly hour.'

Lexie rubbed her hands round her face, trying to take it all in.

'Am I dreaming, Moll?'

'Nope. It can be yours by Monday.'

Lexie clapped her hands in delight. The noise echoed round the empty room like the sound of a starting gun.

Chapter Eighteen

Catalogue number 30: Black leather brogues. Donor, Arthur Donnelly, Edinburgh. 'In October 1986, I was a journalist, attending the meeting in Reykjavik between Reagan and Gorbachev that marked the beginning of the end of the Cold War. I followed the two men into the press conference, my shoes treading where theirs trod. My partner finds my reluctance to part with these shoes overly romantic, but I felt I was walking in a moment in history.'

By the end of July, Lexie was settling into a new rhythm of life. She ate, slept and breathed her work. Early in the morning, she tumbled out of the bed that had been her one extravagant purchase. The bedroom had been cleaned and painted white, and was graced with a threadbare rug from the attic at Fernhill. She liked the fact that it was worn and aged. Many feet had padded across this rug – her ancestors, probably. She liked the idea that she'd brought her past with her, that she hadn't severed all links with her family, even in making the break from home.

She bathed in the roll-top bath, which had been made respectable with the assistance of strong detergents and elbow-grease. She made toast in the kitchen. She loved the kitchen. She'd painted the walls white, spent precious hours sanding the old dresser and giving it a coat of duck-egg emulsion, and she'd hung a new cream-spotted cotton curtain in a matching shade under the wooden counter top to conceal her few kitchen necessities. It was basic, but it worked.

Martha drove over every few days, usually with another

small consignment of shoes, all meticulously catalogued. Lexie had turned the large walk-in cupboard opposite the bathroom into a computer room and her mother was helping out by photographing the shoes and scanning in any letters, old photographs or other sentimental items sent with them.

One morning Lexie was pulling on her old painting clothes when there was the toot of a horn. She peered outside.

'Thought I'd do this while I could,' Cameron said, jumping down from the cab of the Pettigrew's lorry.

'What? What are you talking about?' Lexie laughed, bemused, as Cameron crunched her into his arms and dropped a light kiss on the top of her unbrushed hair.

'I'm leaving Pettigrew's. My uncle wants me back on his farm.'

'Brilliant! Isn't that what you wanted?'

'Sure. Look,' he followed Joe McPhail's bulky form round to the back of the lorry and watched as the roll-door rattled up noisily.

'What's this?'

'Your dad says it's damaged stock.'

'Stop gabbing, man,' Joe called, 'and get on with it.'

The pine table that appeared was small and utilitarian. Lexie recognised it – it had been sitting neglected in the corner of the store for some time – but she didn't mind its plainness, it would be perfect in the kitchen. Four chairs followed.

'Wow. I can sit down to eat!'

A bulky sofa emerged from the van. It was a dull brown, but it looked extremely comfortable.

'Where d'you want this?'

'And these armchairs?'

'Did Dad really say I can have these?'

'No,' Cameron muttered breathessly as he hoisted one end of the sofa into the air and backed towards the cottage door, 'I broke in and nicked them.'

Lexie's throat tightened. He might not voice it, but her father had found his own way of expressing his love.

'Can you put them in the studio, down the far end?'

Cameron and Joe edged the bulky items expertly through the

cottage and dropped them in place. She flopped down on a chair and splayed her arms and legs out in a pastiche of exhaustion, although in truth she felt wired to a new energy source.

'Brilliant!' she sighed.

'I could get you a telly,' Cameron said.

Lexie laughed. A television would introduce the wrong kind of energy. She liked to listen to the radio while she worked, or just enjoy the calm of the garden cottage.

'If you want to watch rugby, Cameron Forrester, you'll have to go down the pub. I can't have a TV in here.'

'I'm off out for a fag,' said Joe. 'You two love birds can have five minutes before we have to get on, eh?'

Lexie smiled at his retreating back. Making love with Cameron seemed so natural now.

'Thanks for doing this, Cam,' she said.

'Self interest,' he grinned as he bent to kiss her.

When she recovered her breath, she said, 'Are you pleased? About the farm, I mean?'

'Sure. My Uncle Hugh can be a grumpy old git, and he wasn't best pleased when I went AWOL that time, but I guess this means he's forgiven me. Anyway,' his eyes became knowing, 'he's got no kids of his own, so I figure he'll leave the place to me one day, if I play my cards right. Maybe time to settle down, eh?' His grin widened.

'Put the lassie down, Cameron, you don't know where she's been,' Joe shouted from outside.

Cameron edged towards the door.

'I'll be round tonight, huh? Fancy something Indian? I can bring a curry.'

'Great. See you later.'

She intended to start work, but not long after Cameron left, Molly appeared, carrying two large hessian bags.

'There was a wedding yesterday, they over-catered. There was loads of chicken casserole and strawberry pavlova left. I've put them in plastic containers, see?'

She opened the bags for Lexie to inspect.

'Yum, I'll put it in the fridge. Look what Cameron arrived with this morning, by the way.'

'It's really looking like home,' Molly said, admiring the new furniture. 'Any more shoes?'

'Are you kidding?' Lexie picked up a sheet that was draped over something by the back wall and revealed a stack of shoeboxes. She opened one at random and handed the box to Molly.

'God, what are these?'

She picked up an old boot, so battered that its sole was hanging half off. 'Yuk.'

'No, listen.' Lexie read the note in the box. 'They're Flying Officer's boots from the second world war. The guy's written, "I was still in training, on an old Gypsy Moth. We were practising spinning, and recovering from the spin. I stamped hard on the rudder pedal, the Moth was spinning to the earth, then I realised that the sole of my flying boot had jammed between the rudder bar and the side of the cockpit. Talk about panic! I managed to wrench it free just in time".'

She dropped her hand and smiled at Molly.

'Does that make you feel differently about them?'

Molly looked at the boot now with interest.

'Wow. I see what you mean. It's a great story. Makes you think about what those poor guys went through.'

'That's it. That's it exactly. It's about the stories of people's lives.'

Lexie dropped the note back into the box and closed it.

'Here's another.'

She lifted out a bundle of tissue paper and folded it back carefully.

'Isn't this gorgeous? Careful –' she handed it to Molly, '– it's very fragile.'

'It's so tiny.'

'It's a child's shoe, from about the sixteenth century. They found it in the rafters of an agricultural worker's cottage outside Hailesbank and they think it was put there either by the builder or the tenant, as a good luck charm. It wasn't unusual, apparently. They call them "concealment shoes".'

Molly handed it back.

'To be honest, I thought you were just off on one of your

arty jags when you started all this, Lex, but now I see where you're coming from.'

'Thanks.' She opened another box and found herself staring at a brilliantly coloured and elaborately sequinned pair of high-heeled shoes. 'It's all about journeys. These were the shoes an Indian woman wore to get married in before she came to live in Scotland. They must have meant a lot to her if she brought them all the way here.'

Molly's visit left Lexie fired up to start work, but no sooner had she set out her paints than she heard the front door open again.

'Dad!'

It was the first time her father had visited. He was dressed for the office.

'Just thought I'd sneak a look at the place that's stolen my daughter away from me.'

'Oh, Dad—'

'Just joking.' He looked around. 'Nicer than I thought.'

'Thanks to your generosity. Thanks for the stuff, Dad.'

'Is it all right?'

She showed him the kitchen and the spacious garden room.

'Nice. Surprisingly nice. Now, sit down on the sofa and close your eyes.'

'What? Why should I?' she said, puzzled but obedient.

'Keep them closed till I tell you.'

She heard the front door open, then the metallic clunk of a car door closing. She was tempted to peek but didn't want to spoil his surprise. There was a heavy thump by her feet and she opened her eyes, startled.

'What are you—? Oh *Dad!*'

It was a heavy cherrywood coffee table that had been in the showroom only for a month and was one of the few pieces of furniture in Gordon's that she really liked.

'It got damaged,' Tom grunted.

'Really?' Lexie was sceptical. 'Where?'

He pointed to a scratch along the side.

'Dad! That can be polished out.'

'Not worth it. Anyway, I'd like you to have something you

really like here, not just unsaleable odds and sods. Okay?'

She threw her arms round his neck and kissed him.

'Okay. Very, very okay.'

When her mother appeared an hour later, she gave up on work completely.

Cameron began to stay for an occasional night. Lexie enjoyed his company, but there could be problems. If he wasn't working the next morning he tended to hang around when she was keen to start painting. One morning he materialised at her side when she had already been at work for an hour or more. She was immersed in a detail of one of Jamie's boots and barely registered his presence.

'That's jolly good.'

She whipped round to find him examining her work. Lexie didn't like her work being looked at until she was ready to show it. She leapt to her feet and stood pointedly in front of her easel.

'I didn't hear you.'

'Is that coffee I can smell?'

'I made a fresh pot half an hour ago.'

Cameron yawned and stretched. He'd pulled on a pair of joggers but was still bare-chested and she could see his muscles ripple under smooth skin.

'Great. Shall I nip out and get the papers?'

Lexie bristled. 'Listen, I'll stop and have a coffee with you, but then I have to get on. Okay?'

'Hey, chill a bit, can't you? I've got a day off. I thought I could take you out for lunch somewhere. We could go down to that pub in Port Seton, there might even be a game of boules going on.'

'Sorry, Cam. I've got to work.'

'What's the big rush? You haven't even got a date for the exhibition yet, have you?'

'We're hoping December. But there's so much to do still. Anyway,' she crossed her arms defensively, 'I'm in the mood for painting.'

He tutted and sighed, and slouched off to the kitchen. Lexie followed him. She hated when they rowed, it brought back all

176

her insecurities.

'Don't be like that, Cam. We can go out another time.'

'Tomorrow? I'm off tomorrow too.'

'You know I can't go out on Saturday mornings, I still help Pavel out in the shop. It's the least I can do for him. I could be free by lunchtime, if you like.'

He sighed heavily and poured two mugs of coffee. He spotted a card on the mantelpiece above the old fireplace.

'What's this? Invitation to the opening of The Maker's Mark. What's that, when it's at home?'

She took the invitation from him and replaced it on the shelf.

'It's a new craft gallery in Hailesbank. The woman who runs it is called Cora Spyridis. I've not come across her before.'

'Why've you been sent an invitation, if you don't know her?'

Lexie shrugged. 'I'm a local artist. She will have made it her business to make sure people like me are invited.'

'I guess so. Are you going?'

'Probably. I expect it'll be a good evening.'

'You didn't tell me about it.'

'I didn't think you'd be interested. You don't usually like galleries or openings. I can meet you afterwards, if you like. We could go to Besalú.'

'When is it?'

'Tonight.'

'*Tonight*? You've kept quiet about it, haven't you?'

'I'd forgotten about it, to be honest.'

'I'll come with you.'

'Really?'

'I'd like to.'

'Okay then. Why not?'

'Where is it?'

'On the corner of the High Street. It's where that convenience store used to be.'

'Want me to pick you up?'

She shook her head.

'Molly's coming. She'll bring me.'

'Right.'

He crossed his arms and placed them in front of him on the table, then lowered his head and used them as a cushion.

'I'm bloody tired. Can't I persuade you to come back to bed?'

'Why would I come back to bed if you're tired?'

An arm snaked out and grabbed her.

'Ow! Ouch! Get off!'

'I think you're a witch. I'm waking up.'

At another time, Cameron feeling interested would be welcome, but not right now. She used the only defence she could think of.

'I'm expecting Mum. She said she'd be here before eleven.'

He groaned. 'What's the time now?'

'Half ten.'

'Shit. I suppose I'd better get going then.'

She tidied the kitchen while he dressed. It was impossible to settle while he was still around and painting was a compulsion. She *had* to paint.

'I'm off then, sweets. See you tonight. Seven?'

'Seven.'

She watched him as he climbed into his car. Everything was finally turning out well for her. She had the studio, she was working towards her own exhibition, she had good friends, and she had Cameron.

But the rhythm of her work had been disturbed. Where the morning had started productively and she'd felt in harmony with her materials, now she felt restless and critical. She applied some paint with a palette knife, stood back and studied it, added some more. It wasn't right. She scraped it off and wiped the blade of the knife down the side of the palette. What a waste.

She studied the painting again.

Don't worry about it, said a voice in her head.

Jamie had followed her here. She hadn't expected otherwise. She'd never be rid of him – nor did she want to be. Still, she *did* worry about her work.

But it was not this painting that was troubling her, and she had the odd sense that Jamie knew this. He was referring to the painting stowed away in the corner: the painting she'd been

178

working on when she'd heard about his accident.

I have to look at it.

At her request, friends at the co-operative in Edinburgh where she'd been renting space had wrapped the canvas in brown paper. She remembered telephoning from the hospital and begging them to destroy it, but none of them would take responsibility for that act.

'We'll cover it for you, if you think it'll upset you. One day you might feel differently.'

The truth is...

She threw her palette knife down on her work table and strode across the room.

The canvas was a big one and there was a lot of brown paper. The paint was still wet when they'd wrapped it and torn strips adhered stubbornly to the canvas when she ripped at it; messy, but unimportant. When most of the paper was off, she turned it right side up, leant it against the wall, then backed away and forced herself to look.

The exhibition had been themed the power of the subconscious. Lexie had visualised a nightmare for the large canvas that was to form the centrepiece. The focal point was a young boy lying on his back, his arms and legs splayed. Blood had stained his clothing and dripped from his blank, staring eyes. He was clearly dead, although there was no indication of what had killed him. Around him, all was grimness and desolation. Women wept, men decayed into skeletons, crows picked at bones. Technically, even though it was unfinished, it was as good as anything Lexie had ever done. It was accomplished, detailed and riddled with allusion and symbolism. It was meant to be evocative, to stir up deep and dark emotions, but all Lexie felt as she looked at it now was a sense of disgust.

Artbollocks! Jamie's teasing voice came into her head.

Shut up! I don't need you to remind me.

She flipped it back to the wall because irritatingly, he was right. She had been breathtakingly cynical. The work wasn't what she knew or believed. It wasn't *her*.

She couldn't think about it now. She'd paint instead. And if

179

painting didn't help to bury the past, she'd turn to the mechanical task of putting together another book or two and let the stories of other people's shoes soothe her.

Chapter Nineteen

Catalogue number 18: Ladies' winklepickers made by Stan Bartholomeu, Battersea, London, 1960. Cream leather with eight-inch point enhanced by black detailing, two-inch slim heel. Donor: Madge Radcliffe, Edinburgh. 'I was a young secretary in London when the craze for winklepickers swept the country. I put in an order and saved up for weeks for these, but truthfully, they were terrible to walk in, you had to pad around like a duck. But I never could bear to part with them.'

The Maker's Mark was a shop transformed. In a little under three months, Cora Spyridis had engaged a cohort of workmen, and directed, bullied, pleaded and cajoled them into getting everything ready for tonight's grand opening.

Patrick, who had an eagle eye for detail, checked everything from the set-up on the computer to the toilets. He saw that Cora was pretending not to watch as he did his round of inspection, but his eyes lit up with amusement when she uttered an anxious, 'Well?' as he emerged from the Ladies.

'I have to say—' he couldn't resist a teasing pause.

She leant towards him, her thick hair swirling round her shoulders as she moved. There was a small vertical crease between her eyebrows.

'—you've done a terrific job.'

She let out her breath as he beamed, and the crease disappeared.

'I can't believe what you've achieved. You may be a pain in the backside, but I have to hand it to you, you're bloody good.'

'I think that's what they call a backhanded compliment.'

'To get the refurbishment done, all the fitting complete, and a forward programme sorted out into next year, that's a huge achievement.'

'Thank you.'

Patrick looked round the gallery. The café wouldn't be open tonight, but the counter space could be used to set out the bubbly. The main exhibition was a series of fabulously sculpted wrought iron and stainless steel pieces by a local artist-blacksmith. Cora had also set up three mini exhibitions, with local makers supplying silver and acrylic jewellery, hand-painted silk scarves and ties, and a series of amusing ceramic sculptures (mostly of overweight 1930s bathing belles). These added colour and variety, while the main exhibition was about the craftsmanship and design quality that was Patrick's vision for The Maker's Mark.

'Sold anything yet?'

She nodded.

'It's a good idea to sell a couple of pieces in advance. Makes people think they're desirable.'

'Which they are.'

'Of course.'

He hesitated.

'Can I see the acceptance list?'

Cora handed it over and he ran his finger quickly down the names. He recognised many of them – Cora had been working hard contacting Capital Art stalwarts who lived in this part of the country, plus some local worthies. They had invited the press (who never bothered to reply unless they were setting up an interview), all the traders in the area, including Carlotta Wood and Pavel Skonieczna, and as many artists and craftsmen as they could trace locally.

His finger stopped at Alexa Gordon. She had accepted. He hadn't seen Lexie since she nearly drove into him a couple of months ago, but he knew where she was and what she was doing, because Pavel kept him informed. ('I haven't seen her work, darling boy, but she's very excited about it, so I think it will be first class.')

'Is Diana coming?' Cora asked.

'I haven't invited her.'

'Sir James and Lady Catriona will be here.'

'And your point is?'

'Just saying.'

Patrick handed the guest list back.

'I'm nipping home for a shower. Want a break?'

'Much as I'd love to relax, I have to be here. Little and Large,' (her nicknames for her two assistants, Jane and Laura), 'are due in shortly, and you can bet your bottom dollar that our star, Henry the Hammer, will be really early, just to check we've set everything up right.'

Patrick scanned the exhibits. There didn't seem to be a right or a wrong way for most of the iron shapes, which were all abstract in form.

'Which you definitely won't have. Still, the man has arms like Thor, he can move them himself.'

'Right. When will you be back?'

'I'll let it get busy first. By the way, the gallery is nothing to do with me, you're working for someone in London who's very shy.'

'What are you talking about?'

'I don't want people to know I'm involved.'

'Why ever not?'

He shrugged. 'It doesn't sit well with Capital Art. Dilutes the brand.'

'Rubbish.'

'I don't think so. Anyway,' he glanced at his watch, 'best get going. Remember – the owner is in London.'

Cora raised her eyes to heaven as he strode out, but she knew there was only so far you could push Patrick Mulgrew, even when he was your brother.

It was a small new gallery in a small town, hardly New York or Paris, but by the time Patrick got back, the place was so full that guests had spilled out onto the pavement.

'Hey, look who's here,' called one man, a county set caricature in pink trousers and navy blazer, complete with two rows of gleaming brass buttons and pale pink open-necked shirt. 'The great Patrick Mulgrew. What brings you here?'

'I do live down the road.'

Patrick jerked his head vaguely in the direction of The Gables. He had chosen a black suit and black V-neck silk tee shirt. Patrick wore designer in the way Lexie wore vintage: their style defined them.

'Been in yet, Malcolm?'

Malcolm raised a glass.

'Had to get some bubbles. But man, it's crazy in there. Beats the openings at Capital Art hands down, ha ha.'

Patrick smiled politely.

'I'm pleased if it's doing well, it's good to see something of quality in Hailesbank. Hope you'll be getting your cheque book out later, you old cheapskate?'

Malcolm laughed and a blonde woman talking to someone nearby turned round.

'You tell him, Patrick. I've got my eye on one of those wrought-iron sculptures. Just what we need as a focal point in the front room.'

'Oh my God,' Malcolm groaned.

Patrick laughed and pushed on through the crowd and into the gallery, where he stopped and spoke to just about everybody. Half way round the room he encountered Pavel.

'How's the new space at the back coming along?' he asked, unheard amid the hubbub of voices except by Pavel. He'd like to cut his interest in Lexie's career stone dead, but he couldn't.

'Getting there. We can't all work at your sister's ferocious pace, you know. Where's all my best stock heading to, then?'

Patrick lifted an eyebrow. 'Beg pardon?'

'Her Nosiness Bessie Brown, my neighbour across the way, came in a couple of days ago and told me there was a removal van outside The Gables and did I know anything about it?'

'And did you?'

Pavel touched the side of his nose.

'Aged but not stupid, dear boy. I never quite saw you as a fan of Meissen and Hepplewhite.'

'I appreciate a great object as much as the next man.'

'And a profit even more.'

Pavel guffawed. He was clearly not in the least offended.

'You don't mind?'

'Mind? Darling boy, who else spends so much in my little shop?'

'I make quite a profit, you know, in London.'

'And I couldn't afford to ship things there. Couldn't be bothered to either. No, no, dear man, it's a chain, we all know that.'

Patrick's mouth twitched in amusement.

'You're a canny operator.'

'I'll take that as a compliment.'

'You should. I don't know anyone who can smell out prize pieces the way you can. Your contact book must be amazing.'

'And not for sharing. Have you seen Lexie yet?'

'Is she coming?' Patrick affected indifference.

'Silly boy. As if I don't know about how you feel…'

Patrick's eyes narrowed and his gaze intensified. Pavel turned to see what had attracted his attention.

Patrick's wealthy patrons, Sir James and Lady Catriona Armstrong, had arrived and escorting them into the gallery was Diana Golspie. Patrick's lips tightened. He hadn't invited Diana. Tagging along with important clients was manipulative, and he didn't like it.

'Excuse me, Pavel.'

His hand rested lightly on Pavel's arm for a moment, before he turned away. He'd have to be charming, so he might as well get the encounter over with. He started to wind his away across the room, but it was jammed full. Too full – Cora had underestimated the interest in The Maker's Mark. He had only closed the gap between himself and Diana by a few feet when someone bumped into him, spilling champagne down his suit. He pulled a handkerchief from his pocket and dabbed at it.

'Oops, sorry mate! My elbow got jogged.'

He recognised the voice and looked up. It was the man who'd been driving, the one who'd hit the deer. In the bright lights of the gallery he was easier to appraise: a rugged look made more interesting by a broken nose, a thatch of sandy hair falling over one eye, muscles bulging under the white tee shirt. In short, powerfully built, outdoorsy, more strength than brains

185

at a guess, but a type he imagined women might find attractive.

'It's not a problem. Let me find you another drink.'

'No worries. They're coming round topping it up. Anyway, there's some left. Here, Lexie—'

He handed the half-full glass to Lexie, who had appeared at his side.

'Here, take this one.' Irritated by the man's lack of courtesy, Patrick switched the glass with his own. 'I haven't had time to have any.'

Lexie's expression was unreadable, but she dipped her head a fraction and raised the glass an inch, as if in acknowledgement. She looked extraordinary tonight, elegant in the way only Lexie could be: art-school rebelliousness had been refined into something unique and even distinguished. Her dress was 1950s-style, pale peppermint and white stripes, nipped in to a wasp waist, the skirt full and flaring, supported by stiff layers of net. The bodice was sculpted to her curves, with a slash neckline that drew attention to her delicate throat. . She wore simple a pearl stud in each ear. Patrick's heart kick started, as it so often seemed to when he was near Lexie Gordon. He stared until he realised he was staring, and forced himself to switch his gaze to the man she was with. God, he was young. How must *he* appear to Lexie, next to this man? He found the comparison unfavourable and brazened it out in conversation.

'So, all sorted with the car?'

'Car? Oh, was it you that night? Thanks for stopping, mate. Yeah, not too much damage, thank God, it was Lexie's dad's car.'

Patrick was acutely conscious of how terrified Lexie must have been. An accident – at night – had uncomfortable echoes of the past.

'You're all right?' he asked her quietly.

Again, her nod of acknowledgement was tiny, but it was there. Sod Muscle Man. Sod his damn pride. He had to tell her how much he still cared.

'Lexie—'

'Patrick. Darling! There you are.'

Diana was sweeping towards them with great purpose. She

186

asserted ownership by putting her arm around him and turning up her face for a kiss.

'I slipped in with James and Cat—' she drew the couple in so that Cameron and Lexie were edged out of the circle. Patrick made a half-hearted attempt to rectify this, but Lexie had started talking to her friend – Molly? – and the opportunity for conversation was lost.

When the crowds thinned and Lexie and her friends had disappeared, Patrick saw that Diana was still there.

'Lovely little gallery,' Diana said, hooking her arm through his again. 'Well darling, shall we go? I'm yearning to sink onto that wonderful sofa of yours.'

Patrick extricated himself from her grasp.

'I don't think so.'

How could he ever have considered she might make a permanent companion? All he could think of was dark eyes and scarlet hair and a relationship he wished he could restore. He looked at Diana as candidly as he could.

'It's my fault,' he started, and watched with a pang of guilt as he saw that she'd guessed what he was about to say. 'My fault, because perhaps I allowed you to believe that our relationship might become something more serious. But it's not what I want, Diana. I'm so sorry.'

She was in control of herself, as she always was.

'We're good together, Patrick. You know we are.'

'We're too well matched,' he countered, smiling, 'two strong people, who both like to be in control. You're clever and cultured and very beautiful. But be truthful, Diana, you don't love me.'

She was about to protest when she stopped abruptly.

'Do you know,' she said, the beginnings of a smile playing about her lips, 'I do believe you're right. But it's a great pity.'

Patrick put his hand gently on either side of her face and turned it first one way, then the other, placing a gentle kiss on each cheek as he did so.

'Good luck, Diana. Thank you for everything. Follow your dreams.'

187

She didn't look round as she left the gallery. He had to admire her.

'Some woman that,' Cora said from behind him, 'but not for you, I think.'

'No,' Patrick agreed, 'not for me.'

'It's about time, Pats. I mean, it's ten years since Niamh—.'

'Stop it, Cora. I know you mean well, but—'

Cora had no fear of Patrick. She ploughed on. 'She was a cow. You know she was. You shouldn't let what she did have such an effect on you.'

Patrick's eyes glinted dangerously, but all he said was, 'Believe me, there's no effect, other than a slight regret at having a brother excised from my life. Enough, Cora. I mean it. I don't criticise the way you choose to live your life, please keep out of mine.'

He turned towards the door. Cora, watching him, shook her head, but the movement was so small that the only evidence was the slightest sway of her hair near where it touched her shoulders.

He walked home alone. It was a balmy evening and he needed the exercise. Besides, the episode with Diana had had an effect on him – and so had Cora's words. Much more than he cared to admit.

The truth was that although the hurt had long since gone, there had been a lasting legacy from Niamh and Aidan's betrayal. He had built walls around his heart and although it wasn't rational to feel that Lexie's rejection had added to his issues with trust, since then he had strengthened his defences.

The High Street was quiet – this was not the part of town for late-night merrymaking. He passed the Duke of Atholl pub, then changed his mind, retraced his steps and went in to the old bar. The place had a small bunch of regulars, some of whom he knew well enough to pass the time with, so he stopped to down a swift pint. He knew he was putting off going home. There were some feelings no defences could keep out and he had become acutely aware of the emptiness at the core of his life.

He had a sudden vision of himself as a sad, lonely drunk,

and put down the glass on the counter.

The rain had started. He speeded up. It wasn't far to The Gables if he cut up Kittle's Lane. He crossed the High Street. Somewhere, a blue light was flashing. He could see the light glinting off the windows of the baker's and the bank, and half wondered what had happened, while thinking about the success of the opening. Rounding the corner of the Lane, he saw an ambulance outside Cobbles. A small crowd had gathered and there was a sense of urgent activity. Someone was being lifted on a stretcher into the back of the vehicle. Gripped by sudden anxiety, Patrick quickened his pace, but as he arrived, the doors closed and the ambulance began to move off.

'What is it?' he asked, 'what's happened?'

A stout woman in tweed skirt and twin set shook her head. He recognised her as the woman who lived opposite the shop – she was Pavel's 'Her Nosiness Bessie Brown'.

'No' looking good,' Bessie said in a broad brogue. 'The wee man's been taken poorly. It wis me wha' called the paramedics,' she added with a hint of pride. 'Ah wis jist closin' the curtains at ma windae when I spied him clutching at his chest, like, and fallin'. I called the service at once and they came right quick, but ah fear it wis too late.'

'Pavel? Was it Pavel?' Patrick asked, distressed.

'Aye. Oor wee rock star.'

She sighed heavily as the crowd joined in with anecdotes and reminiscences.

'Is he dead?'

'All but.'

Patrick shoved his way through the crowd and into the gloom. Pavel – dead? If it hadn't been for Diana gatecrashing the opening, if it hadn't been for Cora's little homily, if he hadn't gone into the pub, if he hadn't waited for a pint…

He strode home. At least he was still under the limit. He would drive to the Infirmary and see if there was anything he could do.

The sun had set on this evening, but it was a little to the
apples this corner of the room, and there was a reflection
heard been a clear heat was flagged. He would wake the
of many of the numbers of the bank, and on this, the
suggested with his impersonal office manner after the close
of the opening. Inquiring the corner of the bank he saw an
expression on the corner. A sun removed had gathered and
there was a smile of almost startling harmony on. Then, he
at a calculating probe of the voices to print by a short
smile. Parsek quite felt in ones an arm in reach so, but
turned to the numbers chair to him well.

"What is it?" he asked evenly impatiently.

"I am human as raised that we had the money and were
the same purpose as had passed who have it on his story
been here there. For Sophie it is a home I

R. No thing good, I know and the mood too no. He was
down with lawas body to me the ruler who the
apartment of the ruled out in an orderly way which closed
to the author in the woman who see it time in the of the
just then and still. I said the worried expression so I
some time and it, but all that it was too late

"I. We thought I am try know I

"You did was told

"My little enough to the protection of a sick and also his
old entrance.

"No, I am I

"Then

"R. Paths stowed his way through the crowd each told the
change. For I am told with high body in the same and to the
the morning. Jeb made across the fronts the measure of his
"but I gone another part of the bank. I don't come out.

He stands home. At last a he was such as who made the
wound three traffic between, and let. Maybe it was also for the
evening."

Chapter Twenty

Catalogue number 28: Undertaker's shoes. British-made Loakes, Oxford-style, black, highly polished leather. Donor, Ian Draper, Draper and Son, Funeral Directors, Hailesbank. 'My father wore shoes like these throughout his lifelong career as a funeral director. Every pair of shoes he had was polished daily. My father was a great respecter of the dead.'

Lexie was lying awake, staring at the ceiling in her small bedroom. It was only five thirty, but already it was starting to grow light. Outside, she heard the rustle and flutter of the sparrows and blue tits in the bushes and trees that surrounded her home. Their sweet trilling songs told of breakfast procured, of busy home-making and affection and the joy of being alive.

She wanted to get up and work, but her mind drifted back to last night, to the opening of The Maker's Mark, and to Patrick.

It was a beautiful little gallery. She was thrilled for Harry Buchanan, the blacksmith whose work was featured. He was showing ten pieces, none of them cheap, and nine were already sold. The supporting makers had done well, too. She'd seen red dots everywhere.

Cora Spyridis, who had supervised the renovation and put together the gallery's summer programme, was an enigma. Lexie knew most people in the area and certainly most people involved in the creative arts, but she'd never come across Cora before. She'd made a point of spending some time talking to her and had found her charming – full of energy and drive, and remarkably knowledgeable – but Cora had confirmed she was not the owner of the gallery.

'The owner is from London,' she had said in a lightly

accented voice, 'and no, he could not be at the opening tonight, but is delighted everything is going so well.'

The guests at the opening read like a *Who's Who* of East Lothian. She knew many of them – art critics, local gentry and a sprinkling of titled guests, as well as quite a few excited craftspeople and shopkeepers from High Street in Hailesbank.

She should not have been surprised that Patrick had been there. After all, he was one of Hailesbank's wealthier residents – and without question the most knowledgeable about art – but stupidly, she'd neglected to prepare herself for meeting him. She'd been with Cameron while Patrick was with some *über* tall natural redhead whose dark copper locks clashed quite horribly with Alexa's bottle scarlet and made her feel cheap.

Sometimes Lexie wondered if Patrick still desired her. There had been a current of connection between them, she was sure she hadn't imagined it.

But lust was one thing, love another entirely.

There was a loud rat-a-tat-tat at her front door. Lexie sat up, startled. What the hell? The knock came again, more insistently. Who could it be, at this time? She flung herself out of bed and pushed the curtain aside a fraction, peering sideways to try to see who it was.

There was another knock, then a low voice.

'Lexie? It's Patrick. Are you awake?'

Lexie shrugged on an old silk robe She hurried to the front door, which rasped along the stone floor as she hauled it open.

'I am now, for God's sake. What the hell do you think…?'

She stopped. She had never seen Patrick like this. His suit looked as if he had curled up under a hedge and slept in it; his hair, usually carefully brushed so that it tumbled in a well-tended waterfall onto his collar, was wild and unkempt; and his chin was heavily shadowed. He had clearly not been home.

'Do you think we might have some coffee?'

She opened the door and allowed him to come in. She had seen Patrick intense, lecherous, funny, masterful, randy, efficient, cool, angry, disappointed, ecstatic, but never soberly serious in quite this way, and it alarmed her.

She opened the kitchen door and ushered him towards the

table. Outside, the sun was starting to rise above the trees. It was the time of day the room was at its best, because the light fell in a shaft on the few treasured possessions she kept on the dresser – a plate and jug she'd thrown at art college, a bronze bust of a friend she'd modelled in second year, a clock of her grandmother's, a small silver cup Jamie had won at tennis before he'd taken up rugby. She filled the kettle and switched it on as Patrick sank into a chair and rubbed his knuckles into his eyes, like a tired child.

'Sit down, Alexa.'

She noticed the formal form of her name with mounting alarm. She was clenching her hands round the back of a chair for support. The knuckles were white, bone pressing through the thin area of flesh.

'What? Tell me, Patrick.'

He reached across the table and took her hand.

'My darling, it's Pavel.'

She barely noticed the endearment, she only heard the name, Pavel.

'He's dead. I'm so sorry. He had a heart attack last night. It was very sudden, and he didn't suffer for long.'

'Pavel? But he was at the opening. He was in great form. I spoke to him. *You* spoke to him. I saw you.'

'Yes. He was in great form.'

Behind her, the kettle bubbled and steamed. Dazed, she pulled her hand away and began to stand.

'Your coffee. I must…'

'Forget the damn coffee.'

Lexie started to tremble. The kitchen was cool and she was wearing only thin silk.

'Sit down, sweetheart. It's a shock, a terrible shock. On second thoughts—' he got up, 'I'll make the coffee, you need a hot drink.'

She watched him as he found his way expertly around her kitchen. Coffee appeared in front of her, black and strong, just as she liked it. How did he know that? The power of logical thought had deserted her. All she could think was, *Pavel is dead and I shall never see him again*. Somewhere outside she heard a bird sing. The world was coming to life, as it did every day – only not Pavel's world.

Patrick sat again, and this time took both her hands.

'I happened to walk by Kittle's Lane on my way home and I saw the ambulance, but he was already in it and it shot off to the Infirmary before I could check what was happening. Thank God I hadn't drunk much. I was able to run home and pick up my car and follow him.'

'Did you see him? Was he still alive?'

'Yes, he was still alive. We even managed a few words, but he had another heart attack, a major episode. They tried resuscitation, but it didn't – they couldn't – he died, I'm afraid. All I could think was, "I must tell Lexie".'

She didn't think this odd. She didn't think about it at all, she was only grateful that he had thought to come, in person, to break this terrible news. She wanted to sip her coffee but she didn't want to move her hands from the place they felt so safe – inside Patrick's strong grasp. She didn't realise she was weeping until he offered her a square of white cotton, and then the sobs came, great juddering howls as she felt the pity of it and the loss began to register.

'He was so dear to me.'

'I know.'

His arms came around her and she buried her face into his shirt, feeling utter safety in his embrace.

'He was such a support. He wouldn't go to the doctor, I tried to make him.'

Eventually, she was all sobbed out.

'The coffee's cold,' she snuffled, taking a sip.

'I'll make more.'

'No.' She refused to relinquish the mug. 'It's fine. I'll drink it. I like cold coffee.'

'Do you know what his last words to me were?'

She shook her head.

'Tell Lexie to take the sherry glasses.'

'Oh Christ.'

Tears began to well again.

'I'll never drink sherry again without thinking of him.'

194

She made a small sound, she wasn't sure whether it was a laugh or a sob.

'Actually, I'm not that keen on sherry. I only drank it to please him.'

Unexpectedly, Patrick grinned.

'I think he knew that. It was his last little joke.'

He stayed with her for an hour.

'Why did you come?' she asked him when she'd dressed. Now that everything was sinking in, his arrival struck her as odd.

'I think Pavel wanted me to.'

Lexie frowned. She couldn't see how he could know this, if they had had so little time to talk. She was about to debate the assertion, when something struck her.

'Oh, shit.'

'What?'

She had pulled on old leggings and a baggy sweater, and her eyes felt puffy and scratchy, but how she looked was the last thing on her mind – she was thinking about her exhibition. She was on the point of telling him about the room at the back of Cobbles that Pavel had been preparing for her, when she stopped herself. This was Patrick Mulgrew, after all. 'Patrick never forgives,' she'd once said to Molly, and she had to remind herself that this man was multi-faceted. Maybe he was being considerate now, but this was the same Patrick who had shouted in a rage that she was not professional, that she would never be successful without his support. But she had found her true path, and with it had come a gritty determination to prove him wrong, and she would not falter. Anyway, Pavel had promised her, the room was all but ready, and hopefully their agreement would be honoured?

Feeling more positive, she kept her thoughts to herself.

'Nothing. Does his family know?'

'I don't think so, not yet. I'll have to trace his sister's number. You have a key to Cobbles, don't you?'

'Yes. I was covering for him on Saturdays.'

Lexie's lips began to tremble again. She was helping Pavel,

he was meant to get through this. Death was not in the plan.

'He said his sister despised him.'

'Still. Families are complicated things.'

His voice became very gentle.

'Death is a complicated thing, Lexie, you of all people know that.'

The pieces of her life rose before her like a cloud of shredded paper caught by the breeze. They swirled and descended, and formed a jumbled pattern – life with Patrick, the accident, the row, life after Patrick, but not necessarily in that order. She became confused and the distress returned. She stood up.

'I think you should go now. Look at you…'

She couldn't go on, because she did look at him and, disconcertingly, found this unkempt, concerned, slightly vulnerable Patrick desperately attractive.

He rubbed his chin.

'I must look a sight. I hope you don't mind my coming.''

Lexie shook her head dumbly. She couldn't find the right words to tell him how much she appreciated what he had done because there was too much baggage between them.

'I'll find the key for you,' she managed to mutter.

The day that began with tragedy, continued with disappointment. Shortly after eleven, Neil called from the Emporium.

'We didn't get it.'

Preoccupied with Pavel's death, Lexie didn't focus on what he was saying at first. 'What?'

'The tender for Fleming House. The Home Farm fit-out.'

'*What?* How come?'

'No idea. I just got a letter from the interior-design company, saying we had been unsuccessful. Want me to read it?'

Lexie swallowed hard. The day was shot already, this distraction was almost welcome.

'No, I'll come in.'

Julie slouched out of the big oak doors under the GORDON'S FURNITURE EMPORIUM sign as Lexie approached. Rain started to splash noisily onto the pavement in big globules that threatened to soak hair and clothing and footwear.

'Hey, Julie, where are you off to?'

The girl swung round, her expression sulky.

'Told him I wouldnae hang around another minute in there. Place is like a fuckin' funeral parlour.'

'You're leaving?'

'S'right.'

She pulled up her collar and hunched her back against the torrent.

'You should stick it out. The job might become permanent, then you'd get off benefits, have some spending money.'

Julie looked at her incredulously.

'You're joking me. On what I was bein' paid? You dinnae need an assistant in there, anyway, what you need is a fuckin' bomb.'

She stamped through a puddle, sending a spray of water down Alexa's shins.

'Bye then,' Lexie called after the retreating back.

There was no answer.

'Show me,' she said to Neil as soon as she got inside.

He handed her the letter, which she read aloud.

'Dear Mr Gordon, blah blah blah, sorry to inform you blah blah, your tender has in this instance been unsuccessful. If you would like feedback on your bid, please call me on… '

All that planning and research – and hope – for nothing. There would be no cash flow fillip. Worse, there would be no boost to reputation, no interested chatter – 'Who supplied these terrific tables? Really? I didn't know they did anything as stylish as this' – no further enquiries, no altered image. She realised that she'd been banking on this work coming in for Gordon's – foolishly, perhaps, she'd expected their keen pricing, rock-solid delivery guarantees and excellent sourcing to land the contract.

'I don't understand. Our prices couldn't have been beaten. Everything was first class.'

'I'll phone the woman and try to find out why we were unsuccessful.'

'Morag will be relieved, she never supported us on this. Outside her comfort zone.'

'Tom, too, I expect.'

'I don't think so.' Lexie was quick to defend her father. 'Dad saw the point.'

'Maybe.'

Neil picked up the phone, checked the number on the letter and started to dial. 'You go on.'

It was not a comfortable meeting.

'We lost on price,' Neil's mouth was set into a grim line.

'Price? How's that possible? We cut our costs to the bone.' Tom's bushy eyebrows twitched. He took off his glasses and peered at Neil. 'Are you sure?'

Neil produced a document, which Lexie recognised instantly as their tender. He passed round three copies. Puzzled, she opened hers and examined the costings.

'This doesn't look right.'

'It's not.'

'But – I don't understand.'

'These are not the figures we agreed. They've been changed.'

'Changed?' Tom's normally level voice sharpened. 'By whom?'

Neil said, 'Lexie?'

'Not me. I just dropped in all the text you gave me and made sure the formatting was right. Then I passed it to Morag to print and bind.'

All attention swung to Morag, who looked defiant, her eyes round as currants in grey dough. Her face reddened and her frizzy hair quivered with righteous indignation. She warbled, 'There was no profit, the way we had it. I only changed them a little bit. In this challeng—'

'Don't you *dare*,' Neil cut in, his voice icy. 'Just don't you dare.'

Morag squeaked to a halt, her self-defence punctured.

Lexie stared at her, appalled.

'We were *trying*,' Neil hissed between clenched teeth, 'to rescue this establishment. We were *trying* to win a key bit of business. We are on the verge of bankruptcy and this was *important*. Now, because of you, Morag Ferguson, we've lost'

Tom cut in. 'Thank you, Neil. Morag, please will you leave us?'

The bookkeeper picked up her papers and stalked off. Lexie's emotions were ratcheted out to breaking point. They could never have assumed they would get the contract, but to lose it in this way was infuriating. Did this make a difference to her painting? Would she have to stop working for the exhibition and come back to Gordon's? The thought was unbearable, but she looked at her father and the stress he was under made her want to weep for the second time that day.

'She's the *bookkeeper*, for heaven's sake,' Neil hissed. 'She should not be making policy.'

'Morag knows, more than anyone, how difficult things are for this business.'

'But she should not have tampered with our strategy for setting it right. She has to go.'

'She's been here for years. She shouldn't have changed the figures, but she did it with the best of intentions.'

'Either she goes or I go.'

Tom looked shocked. 'I don't like blackmail, Neil.'

'It's not meant like that. I just can't work with her any more. I don't trust her, and I don't think you should either.'

Lexie, torn in two, watched them bat the arguments to and fro. Gordon's couldn't be allowed to fail, there had been too much disaster in her family – but she was appalled by the thought of giving up on her career for a second time to attempt yet another salvage operation.

'Neil's right, Dad,' she said at last. 'Tampering with figures, however you look at it, is dishonest. You need to regroup and I don't think you can go forward with Morag as part of your team.'

As Tom hesitated, Morag solved one problem by reappearing and sticking an envelope into his hands.

'My resignation,' she said in a quavering voice, and left.

Tom, Lexie and Neil looked at each other in silence. At length Neil said, 'Well. Two fewer staff on the payroll in one day can't be bad, in the circumstances.'

Lexie wandered along the High Street. She called Cameron, who was on a quad bike somewhere in a field, where the signal was terrible.

'Pavel's what?'

'He died last night.'

She had to half shout and she grew uncomfortable. Passers-by were staring at her. It didn't seem right to be shouting this news.

'He's dead? What happened?'

'Heart attack.'

'Oh Lord. Hey, doesn't that leave you up shit creek?'

'It wasn't quite my first reaction to the news but yes, you're right.'

'What'll you do?'

Cameron wasn't smart, like Patrick, and he didn't do subtlety, but he was pretty good at hugs.

'Right now, I don't know. Can I see you?'

'Love to, sweetie, but when I finish here I've got that darts match down the pub. Remember I told you? You can come if you like.'

'I'll think about it.'

Crowds, banter and noise were the last thing she felt like. She dialled Molly's number.

'Hey.'

'Hey.'

'You sound really down.'

'Are you busy?'

'We've got a Midsummer Ball on tonight, it's mental here. What is it?'

She couldn't bear talking about Pavel on the phone, not again.

'Nothing. Tomorrow maybe, when you get up?'

'I'll buzz you, OK? Listen, got to go, there's another call

coming in, I've been waiting for it. See you tomorrow, chin up.'

'Bye then.'

But Molly had rung off already. Lexie stared at her phone. All the energy had seeped out of her. She was drained by carrying burdens.

Chapter Twenty-one

Catalogue number 32: embroidered Chinese shoes, three inches long. Donor, Alice Redmond, London. 'My great grandparents were missionaries in China and brought these shoes back to London. Foot binding was a sign of beauty and wealth, as the barbaric practice of breaking toes to shorten the foot meant that women were unable to walk more than a few yards. Working was thus impossible. Over time, some poor country girls were also subjected to the practice, in the hope that they might catch a wealthy husband.'

In the Western world, black is the traditional colour of mourning. It has been so for a long time, maybe not for ever, but probably since the Romans began to don dark togas to mark their respect for the dead. But Lexie, who had gone back to Fernhill on the night before Pavel's funeral, needing company, scanned her eclectic wardrobe and remembered how Pavel had loved bright colours – his mustard moleskin waistcoat, his burgundy velvet smoking jacket, his favourite candy-striped blazer.

Black wouldn't do. Black was for seduction, for evenings under the stars with a lover, or for dancing the night away in a ballroom scattered with shards of silver light.

'This one, darling girl,' she could hear his voice as he pulled a dress off his rack for her, a little affected but full of warmth. Or, 'This could have been made for you, Lexie.'

Loss stabbed at her. The funeral would be hard, the first she'd had to attend since Jamie's. Her parents wouldn't come. They didn't know Pavel well and their grief for their son was still too raw. But she had to go. It was unthinkable not to go.

She reached out and grabbed a handful of tissues from the box on her dressing table, stuffed them into her clutch bag. She would wear the last dress she bought from him, the one intended for her date with Cameron. It slipped over her head and across her hips, the vivid scarlet roses scrunching up and growing deformed, then reshaping as the dress settled into place.

She missed Pavel dreadfully, hated walking past Cobbles and seeing the sign on the door turned to 'Closed'. Anger surged through her, briefly – why hadn't he gone to the doctor, as she'd pressed him to? His death was so *unnecessary*. She pursed her lips at the familiar feelings. After all, surely Jamie hadn't needed to die either....

Enough. Roaming down cul-de-sacs in a maze would get her nowhere. Time to go.

Cameron had borrowed his uncle's car for the drive to the crematorium in Edinburgh. Lexie was grateful for the company.

'I'm glad you were off today, I really appreciate this.'

He shifted into fifth gear and laid a hand briefly on her thigh.

'No problem. Couldn't have you going on your own. What's the form?'

'There's a short service, then tea and cake at some hotel nearby.'

'Not back to Hailesbank?'

'Apparently not. Pavel's sister has come up from Slough and didn't want the extra travel out to Hailesbank.'

'It's only half an hour.'

'Half an hour too far, apparently.'

Cameron lapsed into silence as he negotiated the roundabout that connected the A1 to the city bypass. Safely back on the dual carriageway, he said, 'Will there be a good turnout?'

Lexie thought of Pavel, hidden away in his small shop, surrounded by his marvellous collection of antiques but essentially alone for long hours.

'I doubt it.'

But she was wrong. As they walked from the car park to the waiting area, she realised that there was a sizeable throng.

Patrick, inevitably, was the first person she saw. It was impossible to miss him – he was so tall he'd stand out in any crowd, not to mention his flowing hair and the way he carried himself. Lexie looked for the tall woman she had come to associate him with, but he seemed to be alone. There was Bessie Brown from across the road, with some of her cronies, all dressed for the occasion, dark as a coven of witches. She recognised a handful of shopkeepers from Hailesbank and the young reporter who'd written the piece on Pavel for the newspaper. There was a large group she found hard to place, but decided they must be dealers from the antiques trade. But most surprisingly of all, there was a sizable group of teenagers. Lexie was puzzled, then realised they must be new fans, kids who'd only discovered Pavel in the last couple of months. They'd made a connection with Pavel, they'd warmed to him, and wanted to pay a tribute.

The knot in her throat started to swell uncomfortably. How was she going to get through this?

From the back of the crowd in the waiting room, Patrick watched Lexie, scowling. She was with that rugger-bugger type again. He couldn't be right for her. He was an oaf. He had no manners. He couldn't understand Lexie, surely? He couldn't be equipped to appreciate the subtleties of thought that directed her hand and eye, nor the skills she possessed.

The man – Cameron? – laid his arm across Alexa's shoulders. She turned her face up towards him and Patrick could see the anguish painted there. Driven by some deep protective instinct, he started to move towards her, but a crowd of kids dived towards each other to huddle over someone's phone, blocking his path. When he looked up again, Lexie and Cameron had been swamped by the throng.

He felt a touch on his arm. 'Is everything ready?'

It was Pavel's sister, Hanke. She was about as unlike Pavel as might be imagined – completely round, with curranty eyes, her hair scraped back from her face and pulled into a bun at the back of her head. She was wearing a black dress that hung like a tent from her shoulders and fell over heavy breasts and even wider hips – hips that wobbled as she walked and settled a moment after she stopped, like a jelly carried from the kitchen and thumped down onto the dining table. She was also, as Patrick had already discovered, as oblivious to beauty and elegance as her brother had been sensitive to such qualities. It seemed that Pavel's instructions for his funeral had been well laid out, and that they involved some organising because Hanke, following the notes, had called Patrick.

'Do we have to do this? It seems so tasteless,' she'd asked, explaining his wishes.

Patrick had struggled not to laugh at the directions.

'We must,' he managed to say solemnly. 'It's almost legally binding.'

And good on you, Pavel, old darling, he'd thought, amused. Trust you to have the last laugh.

Now he simply said equably, 'Yes. All set up.'

'We'd better go in then. Get this over with.'

He followed the jelly body and her jelly children into the chapel and thought that it was no wonder that Pavel and his sister had not got on.

Lexie cried all the way through the short service. She cried for Pavel and for Jamie, she wept for her own mistakes and for all the wrongs of the world. Beside her, Cameron sat stolidly, sang lustily, and offered her a grubby hankie when her own tissues were completely sodden. As they got up to leave, a guitar riff rang through the chapel. It was almost deafeningly loud. The crowds, already shuffling along the pews and filing down the aisles, stopped moving. There was another riff. It was unmistakeable. Some people were starting to smile. Then the voice of the young Paul Scotland rang out, high-pitched but true.

'Baby boy, naughty boy, give it to me straight. Baby boy, naughty boy, I love your blooming cheek.'

Cameron started to laugh. Lexie, disbelieving at first, giggled. Everyone was laughing. Some of the youngsters had switched on their phones and were filming. Soon clips would be on You Tube and tweeted round the world, and Pavel

Skonieczna's funeral would become legendary.

Pavel, Lexie thought, thank you. Thank you for this. But I'm going to miss you so much.

The wake was a sorry affair, with tea and sparsely filled sandwiches that curled at the edges. Lexie didn't feel Pavel here, he had been obliterated by his thin-lipped, doughy-faced blob of a sister. She tried to talk to her. She was desperate to know what was going to happen with Cobbles, and particularly with the room that was being prepared for her exhibition, but when she raised the subject, tentatively, Hanke shrugged her bulky shoulders and said something about lawyers and wills. It was impossible to push it. She had to rely on her belief that Pavel would have taken care of everything.

'Let's go,' she whispered to Cameron after they'd downed some grey tea and chatted politely to strangers. She couldn't see Patrick anywhere. He had probably made his escape already. She hadn't had any contact with him since he'd come to tell her about Pavel's death. If she lived to be a hundred she'd never understand that man.

'Want me to drop you back at the cottage?' Cameron asked.

Lexie shook her head.

'No. Fernhill please. I'll go back to the cottage tomorrow. I want to clear some more stuff out of Jamie's room.'

'Oh. Okay. Need any help?'

'No. Thanks. I'd rather be on my own.'

He didn't argue. For all his usual crassness, Cameron could sometimes show amazing sensitivity.

'You know,' he said as they approached Hailesbank, 'I've been thinking.'

'Careful,' Lexie said, on automatic. She was thinking about Patrick Mulgrew again, and puzzling about why he'd slipped away from the funeral without coming to talk to her.

'No, seriously.'

She glanced across at him. He was looking ahead, concentrating on the road, but there was none of the usual amusement in his expression.

'What is it?' she asked, concerned.

'Well, that guy. And Jamie. I mean, life's short, isn't it. You never know what's round the corner.'

'True.'

'Sometimes I think I've ballsed everything up. You know. Messed my life up.'

Lexie gazed at him, nonplussed by the direction the conversation had taken. 'Oh?'

'Well, we're not getting any younger, are we?'

'That's true.'

'*Wanker!*'

'What?'

'Not you,' Cameron grinned, 'that guy in front, cut right in on me. Stupid bugger.'

'Oh. I wasn't looking at the road. You were saying?'

'What was I saying? Oh yeah. Well, I mean, perhaps I've wasted too much time already. You know.'

They pulled up outside Fernhill.

'You're sounding very serious.'

'Yeah well. Death and all that. It kind of gets you, doesn't it?'

He didn't phrase things elegantly, but in his own way Cameron had gone right to the heart of everything.

'Yes,' she agreed. 'Death kind of gets you.'

She waited for a few minutes, but he didn't go on and she was not sure what he was getting at, so she said, 'Well. I'd better go. Thanks for coming today. I do appreciate it.'

'You're all right.' He started to chuckle. 'It was worth it anyway. When that track blasted through the chapel – Bad Boys at their best. Wicked! Good on Pavel, eh?'

It cheered Lexie up.

'Yes. Good on Pavel.'

Martha had gone out. Tom was at the Emporium. Lexie had Fernhill all to herself. She made a mug of tea and wandered round the house, clutching it. This was her home, and yet it wasn't her home any longer. She had moved out for the second time, trying to re-establish her career. Yet the ties that bound her were still here, reaching out for her, sucking her in. She touched the oak banister, polished with age. She and Jamie used to slide down this, provoking Martha's alarm.

'You'll fall! It's so dangerous!'

The house had seen so much. Edith's secret had been walled up in the chimney bricks for more than half a century. Had there been other secrets? More shame? She reminded herself that there had been laughter, too, and love. When Jamie was alive, she'd worn luminous dresses and danced on the lawn at midnight. They'd had parties, wonderful, noisy parties. They'd grown up, made friends, fallen out with them, made up again.

It was time to move on. Properly, this time. The cottage was just a start. She'd stay there until after the exhibition, then see how the finances went. Maybe she'd get an offer from another gallery. Perhaps she could apply for a grant, get by for a year on that. There were possibilities. Pavel would not want her to descend into depression.

She drained her tea, rinsed the mug and placed it on the draining board by the sink. Even though she had moved out, she still had a duty towards her parents – that hadn't changed. She worried about Gordon's, she had to tackle Tom again about letting Neil take over. Martha showed signs of getting through the worst of the grief, and Lexie was sure that all the work she was doing (the scanning, the filing, the project management) was helping to restore her mother's sense of self. There was still a lot to clear in Jamie's room. She had neglected that in her selfish urge to paint. Today was the ideal opportunity to get stuck in, because she wouldn't be able to settle in the cottage.

Jamie's room felt odd now. He inhabited it less than he had done. All his clothes had gone and most of his personal items. There were some big objects – his exercise bike, for example. That could go to a charity shop, along with the bags that had already been sorted. What was left? Just the books. It shouldn't take long – and Martha, in her organised way, had collected half a dozen empty cardboard boxes at the supermarket to make their removal easier.

She started top left. Jamie had missed out on Martha's passion for order – there was no apparent logic to the arrangement of the books on the shelves. John Grisham sat alongside Dickens, but she spotted more titles by those authors further along, next to Larsson and Tolkien. A childhood set of the Narnia books sat beside *War and Peace* and *Kane and Abel*.

She came across *The Boy Who Harnessed the Wind* and smiled. She loved Jamie's eclectic taste. The book fell open at a page marked by an envelope. The passage didn't seem to be particularly exciting. Scanning the page idly, she drew the card out of its envelope and looked at it. It was a Valentine's card, the image was a little girl holding a string. High above her floated a vast red heart balloon. The words 'Guess Who?' were printed inside. There was no signature, just an odd squiggle. Lexie looked at it, puzzled. It was like a question mark, but upside down. Why write it upside down?

She gave up speculating (after all, who knew about Jamie and his many loves?), shoved the card back into the envelope, stuck it into her pocket and straightened up.

There, nothing left to be done. Just the books and bags to deliver to the charity shops, and Cameron would help her with that.

Lexie stuck to her work routine. It was all she could do, until she heard something about Cobbles. There was no other option but to carry on. Her work was good, the concept was original and honest and moving, and she had something to prove. Besides, she wanted to do it for Pavel. Pavel had wanted this.

The light was beginning to change. She no longer wakened with the dawn at five thirty. She couldn't paint until eleven at night, because it was getting dark before nine. It was pointless working in artificial light, so the time available became more and more squeezed. She made the most of it. She got up as the first streak of daylight appeared through the trees, made coffee, and started painting. She worked (ignoring all complaints from Cameron) until she couldn't trust her eyes any longer. Then, and only then, would she consider putting her brushes aside and turning her attention to him. If he was playing darts, or had an early start, or was shattered, she moved from her easel to her computer, to complete more orders for books.

The shoes kept coming. Every other day Martha arrived with

more boxes. Once a week, a pair of shoes arrived that really stood out for her and she put them aside for consideration for the exhibition. There was a single bridal shoe, for example, that reduced her to tears. The donor was a man called Bob Hutchison, who lived in Hailesbank. 'We were due to get married in the August,' he wrote, 'but in the May, Susie was walking home from work when she was knocked down by a car. She was on the pavement, it was broad daylight, and the weather was fine. The car didn't stop. Susie nearly died, and they were forced to amputate her right leg. She was determined to walk down the aisle – and four months later, she did just that.'

It's about the stories.

She put the shoe with the pile for the exhibition and Martha photographed it, made notes, and scanned the letter onto the computer.

There had been no sign of Patrick since the funeral. She'd heard nothing about Cobbles and didn't even know who to ask.

'Tell Lexie to take the sherry glasses,' he'd said. Pavel's last words, he'd said. But there was no sign of the glasses. Presumably they were still locked in the shop, and she no longer had a key. Not that she would think of going in there anyway.

Lexie sat on her stool, paintbrush in hand, lost in memories. There'd be no more excited phone calls. ('I've got the most sublime handbag in, Alexa darling, you must drop by'.) No more little chats over tea or sherry. No more wondering what colourful outfit he'd picked today. No more todays.

Grief erupted again. It was so bloody final. *Death kind of gets you.* She jabbed angrily at the painting, a pair of Indian wedding shoes, so gloriously colourful she couldn't resist choosing them, but the golds and purples sucked her in and soon she was at peace again, absorbed by her work. Her work was her salvation. This was what she'd been missing this last year. At least she was getting one thing back under control.

Chapter Twenty-two

Catalogue number 3: Rugby boots. Tough leather studded boots, worn by Jamie Gordon, lock for The Hailesbank Hawks. Donor, the Gordon family, Hailesbank. Jamie Gordon was a man like many other young men. He loved to play sport, see his friends, work hard, enjoy life to the full. He played a pivotal role in the rugby team he was passionate about, just as he was pivotal in so many people's lives. Sadly, Jamie lost his life in a car accident, aged 28. The boots embody his energy, spirit and talent.

Patrick was sitting in Business Class on a flight from Edinburgh to New York. Beside him sat a very excited Victoria Hunter-Darling. He'd been tempted to put Victoria into Economy, but felt this was being mean. Now he was regretting it, because she was like an excited child, bobbing up and down every few minutes to look at the views, fiddling with the entertainment system to see if there was anything better than the channel she was currently watching, squealing with pleasure when complementary skin care products appeared, or free drinks, or a good meal.

He closed down his laptop, switched the entertainment system to a music channel, stuck on the headset and settled back, eyes closed. Victoria subsided.

The visit to New York was going to be short – just three days. There'd be little time for sightseeing, but he'd managed to get tickets for *La Bohème* at the Met.. Victoria was beside herself at this. Not that she was an opera lover (she had never been to the opera, she told him), but because she would have a chance to dress up. Maybe he'd give her some free time, it would be a shame not to see anything of the great metropolis on a first visit, but he had an agenda. There would be a day with a realtor, trying to pin down possible premises for his gallery. The cost made him shudder, but he remembered the calculations he'd made on the profit side and was confident the risk would pay off. The venture was exciting. He'd be interviewing for a local gallery director (there were some very interesting résumés) and he was going to meet with two artists whose work he hoped to showcase in the first few months.

In particular, he was looking forward to meeting Domenica Martinez again. He'd first met this distinguished Mexican-born artist when he'd been in his twenties. She'd been in her forties then, and the guest artist at the gallery where he'd been working in London. He remembered her vividly: tall and upright, her stance proud and confident, thick dark hair that flowed in unruly waves down to her waist, and eyes of the most astonishing blue. He'd always admired her work, which had matured over the years. The colour and intense vividness he'd been so struck by was still there, but the imagery had become more subtle, more abstract and, in his opinion, even more powerful. She was very sought after now. If he could persuade her to open his new gallery…

Patrick drifted into sleep. What seemed like moments later, the cabin crew woke him with the news that the plane would shortly be landing at Newark. He glanced at Victoria. She looked as if she had been too excited to sleep. She'd suffer for that later.

Patrick adored New York. He loved the vibrancy of the city, the 'can-do' attitude of its citizens, the sense of confidence about the place. He'd first come here, as Victoria was doing now, as part of his on-the-job training with Armando Ardizzone, the gallery director in London who'd showed such faith in him twenty years ago. They'd stayed at the Waldorf, and he had stayed there ever since. The cost was worth it because of the feeling of success it gave him. He loved the sumptuousness of the place, its rich Art Deco magnificence, the respect people showed him when he told them where he was staying, and the convenience of its location, slap bang in the

214

middle of Park Avenue.

'Wow!' Victoria said, for the third time, when they walked into the third empty shell of a showroom. She was showing no signs of suffering (yet) from jet lag. It would come.

He liked this space. It was a good shape. There were three large rooms, offering potential for one, two or three exhibitions concurrently – or the opportunity of installing a coffee corner, an idea he still liked.

When Victoria finally flagged, he sent her back to the Waldorf and spent the evening in a piano bar on Seventh. This was less to listen to the music than to sit in a space where he might avoid thinking about Lexie. He should not be thinking about Lexie. One of the reasons he had come to New York was to get her out of his mind. Work, he told himself, was the answer. It had been work that had saved him after Niamh had left, so surely it could achieve the same miracle now?

Yet he was filled with a sense of despondency which he couldn't shake off. He remembered Lexie in a hundred different poses. He couldn't rid himself of the memory of the first time he'd made love to her – a scorching hot and utterly inappropriate grapple in her room in the modest flat she'd shared with two other artists in Broughton Street in Edinburgh. The flat had been above a wine bar and the chatter of late-night drinkers had floated up on a wave of cigarette smoke through the open window. That particular mixture of sound and smell always reminded him of that moment.

'I don't make a habit of screwing my new protégées,' he'd whispered, 'but you, Alexa Gordon, are ravishing.'

And, my God, she had been. It hadn't just been her slender limbs that had attracted him, nor the graceful sweep of her neck from her shoulders to the crazy red hair. It had been the marriage of these physical attributes with the fearless way she'd challenged established beliefs – and dug her heels in thereafter. The tattoo on her thumb said it all: 'Artbollocks.' He'd smiled wryly the first time he'd seen it, recognising an artbollocks tendency of his own. Now he thought of it every time he teetered on the edge of pomposity about the work he showed, and chose his words more carefully.

215

This was the extent of her influence on him. It reached far beyond sexual attraction, beyond his heart, even. She engaged his brain. The combination, in his experience, was unique and powerful.

When he was so tired that he thought he might fall asleep in the cab back to the hotel, he paid his bill and left. He believed in adjusting at once to local time (especially when the visit was so short), but he had reached his limit.

Victoria wasn't involved in the interviewing, since the appointment of a senior member of staff could not involve a junior. He spent a useful morning vetting applicants, and by the time his young assistant rejoined him for a meeting with the upcoming installation artist, Matte Ruutu, his mood had become expansive – and he still felt upbeat later, as he dressed for the opera.

'You look stunning,' he told Victoria, who had donned her best dress, an ankle-length, clinging creation in pastel chiffon.

She looked thrilled at the compliment.

'I'm so excited,' she said, over and over again as the taxi sped to the Lincoln Center.

Afterwards – after Victoria had oohed and aahed and sighed and wept through *La Bohème* – they visited The View for cocktails and the buffet. Despite himself, Patrick couldn't help showing New York off. He enjoyed Victoria's delight at everything. It so exactly mirrored his own all those years ago that it refreshed his pleasure. Back at the Waldorf, he realised – too late – that she had misread him.

'Thank you for bringing me, Patrick,' she smiled as he paused at her door. Before he saw it coming, she had pushed herself into his arms and was kissing him with every appearance of passion.

He disengaged himself as firmly and as quickly as he could.

'I'm flattered,' he said gently, 'at your interest. But this isn't what I had in mind.'

She blushed a vivid scarlet and took a step back.

'Oh! I'm sorry! I thought—'

In an effort to lessen her embarrassment, he added, 'You're

extraordinarily pretty, Victoria, and a good worker. It's just that I'm not available.'

'You don't need to explain.'

She was biting her lip and her face was still pink.

'I don't want you to think you're unattractive, because—'

'You don't need to explain,' she repeated. 'Really. Listen, can we just forget this?'

'It's forgotten. I'll see you in the morning. Actually,' he seized on a thought, 'why don't you have a lie in, then take a look round town? Go shopping.'

'Is that OK?' she said doubtfully. 'What about the meeting with Domenica Martinez?'

'I'd like to see her on my own. Do you mind? She's an old friend.'

'If you're sure.'

He could see she was torn between her duties and shopping.

'Listen, Bloomingdale's is just up the road, Saks isn't far away. And Tiffany's. Go do a Holly Golightly. Just don't blame me if you wreck your credit card.'

'Well, okay then. If you're sure. Thanks. I'll see you at lunchtime.'

'We'll finish by looking at the last two properties before we head for the airport. OK?'

'OK. Thanks.'

He didn't really know why he was sending her off shopping. After all, what was the point in bringing her all this way just to do what she could do back home? But he didn't want to feel he had to watch every word or worry about awkwardness. In any case, he would need to put all his charm into the meeting with Domenica if he was to secure her agreement to show at his new gallery.

Domenica Martinez lived in a loft apartment in Dumbo, right on the waterfront. Patrick saw the appeal the moment he stepped in the door. Industrial-sized windows ran the length of the old warehouse, hurling light across the room onto the white walls at the far side. The floor was oak and gleaming. A space with white sofas at the far end, a compact, very contemporary

217

kitchen in the middle, a dining table and heavy burr-elm chairs, the edges left rough and misshapen, the wood in its natural state. It was simple, clean and classy – but where did she paint?

She noted both the appreciation and his puzzlement.

'Come in, Mr Mulgrew. You are welcome.'

She was just as he remembered her; tall, striking, and utterly confident in her own skin. The eyes were the same sizzling blue. She still wore her hair loose and long, and if it weren't for the grey and the fine lines that radiated from the corners of her eyes and threaded her upper lip she could still be taken for thirty. She was slim but had good muscle tone and she moved with purpose. Her body radiated energy. She was wearing grey joggers and a white tee shirt. Her feet were bare. It was not an outfit designed to woo him. Of course, Patrick thought, Domenica Martinez was queen in her domain, she could exhibit wherever she liked – it was he who had to do the wooing.

He remembered his manners.

'Ms Martinez.'

He took her hand and lifted it to his lips, bowing slightly.

'Forgive me. How could I let the majesty of your apartment eclipse the beauty of its owner?'

Her laugh came right from the belly.

'Wow. Only an Englishman could say something like that.'

'Irishman,' he corrected automatically.

'Pardon me. Was it courtesy or flattery?'

'An apology. I was being very rude.'

Again the laugh. 'Come in. I know what you're going to ask.'

'You do?'

'You want to know where I paint.'

'Is it that obvious?'

'Let's just say you're not the first.'

She led the way to the back of the building. Perhaps other residents might use the space as a bedroom, but he saw at once how ideally suited it was to painting. The light came in from above, through high, angled windows so that it lost all its hard edges and diffused softly and evenly. Patrick had seen many studios, but this had a special atmosphere. There were many

218

large canvases stacked against the walls, another on the easel. They displayed vivid sequences of colours, shapes and textures that spoke of heat, and the sea, and boats, or perhaps of a lake, but at any rate of life-giving water.

'Like it?'

'Who wouldn't?'

'What does it say to you?'

He thought about this for a moment, then laughed.

'That's funny?'

'No,' he shook his head, 'not at all. I was just thinking about a friend of mine, an artist. She has a tattoo round her thumb. You know what it says?'

'Tell me.'

'Artbollocks. You know what I mean?'

She threw back her head and laughed.

'That old essay in *Art Review*? Of course I know it.'

'Making utterly banal work seem important by couching it in inflated language. I try to avoid it, but sometimes, when you see something that goes right to your heart through all your senses, it's hard to find words to describe the impact that don't sound pretentious.'

Domenica laid her hand on his arm.

'She sounds like an interesting person. I think I'd appreciate her.'

'I'm sure you would.'

'At any rate, what you've said is reaction enough for me.'

Her gaze drilled through him. 'I think we could work together, Mr Mulgrew.'

'Was it a test?'

She laughed. 'Sort of. I dislike pretension.'

He sank into one of the white sofas, giddy with the long hours of travel, the change of time, the viewings, the interviews, handling Victoria. Domenica poured him a Manhattan ('What else, for heaven's sake?'), then another, and they talked about art and the state of the market, about mutual acquaintances, about pet hates.

'Tell me about your artist,' she said at length.

'I'm sorry?'

They had covered a lot of ground and he had forgotten his explanation of earlier.

'The one with the tattoo.'

'Lexie? Nothing to tell.'

'What kind of artist is she?'

He didn't take it at face value and describe her as 'representational', 'surrealist' or 'avant garde' or attach any other labels. Instead he said, 'Thoughtful. Skilled. Bloody ungrateful.'

Domenica crowed with laughter.

'Obstreperous *and* ungrateful. Yet you still admire her.'

Patrick stood up and paced across to the huge windows.

'Not at all. She's very immature. In any case, we fell out, so how I see her is immaterial.'

The back of his neck prickled. He turned. Domenica was standing very close to him and he had the odd impression that she could drill right into him, like a geologist, and draw up a core that would reveal every layer of his innermost feelings, through time. It was an uncomfortable sensation, because there was a lot of emotion buried deep in that core and he'd like to keep it that way.

Domenica said softly, 'So. She means a lot to you.'

'No.' He turned to the window again, but the lie pained him and he had a sudden need to confess to this woman.

'I didn't understand her, at a time when she needed understanding, and now she rejects me. I said things I should not have said, but I can't tell her that. I was angry because she let me down.'

It was the truth, but it wasn't the real reason for his anger. That went deeper. Images of Niamh flickered through his head: Niamh at nineteen, laughing at a dog that had followed them along Ballymastocker Bay in Donegal and wouldn't leave them alone. Her hair was dark as the soil of County Kildare, her eyes grey like the Galway seas in winter. She was beautiful, and innocent and loving.

Niamh had said, 'Would you look at him, Patrick. Those eyes would melt ice cream, so they would. Can we keep him?'

She was like a puppy herself, all eagerness and energy.

'In a one-room flat in Dublin? I don't think so.'

He saw Niamh at twenty-two, in her wedding gown, like an Irish princess straight from the pages of a fairy tale. He couldn't remember the detail of the gown, only that it shimmered in some subtle way, falling in soft folds round her slender body. The innocence of three years earlier had morphed into a glorious awareness of her own attractiveness. She knew she was beautiful and she basked in the delight of knowing that everyone was looking at her (especially Aidan, as it turned out). Patrick believed, because she told him so, over and over again, adoringly, that she had packaged all this gorgeousness into a white-ribboned, flower-bedecked bundle just for his benefit.

But somewhere down the years Niamh changed. She didn't like life in London, where they moved shortly after the wedding. Her attempts to set up a business as an interior designer, then as a shopping consultant, then as a boutique owner, all toppled into oblivion. She became restless and dissatisfied.

Another image, the most persistent: Niamh in bed with Aidan, her grey eyes wide with shock as he barged in, home unexpectedly to change for a dressy dinner. Nothing that followed that moment of discovery – the loss, pain, humiliation, betrayal – had left him yet.

Betrayal. It was a word that had lodged in his psyche and remained there, festering, for ten years. Deception, falseness, a breach of trust. First Niamh, then – the way he saw it – Lexie.

Lexie was not the cause of his anger, she was collateral damage, but the effect was the same.

Domenica was saying, 'What did she do that was so terrible?'

Patrick shook his head to clear the painful memories.

'She pulled out of an exhibition at very short notice. I told her she'd never succeed without my help. She took it badly.'

Domenica was not the sort to let easy explanations slide by.

'Why did she pull out?'

Patrick watched a small crowd gather far below, on the sidewalk. Something had attracted their attention – a street performer, perhaps, or someone offering freebies in some

221

marketing promotion. There was always something going on in New York.

'Her brother had an accident. She wanted to be with her parents.'

'What happened to him?'

'He died.'

She sucked in her breath. Patrick thought about Jamie Gordon, a young man he had never met but whose death had changed the course of his life.

'Can't you put things right? Go to her. Apologise.'

'It's not as easy as that.'

'Apologising is never easy where the wrong has been great.'

At Domenica's suggestion, Patrick took the ferry back across the river, rather than summoning a cab.

'You'll find it cleansing,' she said.

He did it to please her, not because he was convinced. For years he had been driven by the need to succeed. He had goals, targets and objectives, and no time to waste. If a plane was quicker than the train, he flew. He didn't consider public transport – if he couldn't drive, he took a cab. Still, there was time enough on this occasion to indulge her suggestion.

It was seventy-seven degrees and sunny, but as soon as they started across the river, he felt a stiff breeze. He closed his eyes and lifted his face to the wind. Around him passengers chattered. He heard German and Dutch, the strong twang of English spoken by an excited family from Australia. Two African American women with baby buggies and obviously local, discussed night feeds and nappies and honked with laughter about sex (or rather, the current suspension of congress).

'I told him straight,' one said, 'he ain't gonna come near me again, not after what I've been through.'

'Macie,' shrieked the other, 'that ain't never gonna last. Darnell ain't no monk.'

'Anyway,' Macie continued, 'I cain't do it with Jailyn lookin' on.'

'Jailyn's three months old, she ain't doin' no lookin'.'

222

Patrick felt a surge of empathy with Darnell.

People-watching was not one of Patrick's pastimes, but today he had the leisure to indulge. On the other side of the ferry, a young father stood with his arm round the shoulders of his son. They looked Hispanic: black hair, dark brown eyes, lean. At a guess, the man was around forty – Patrick's age – the boy maybe ten or eleven.

The boy looked up at his father's face and said something. The father laughed, his teeth gleaming white as he gathered the boy closer and hugged him.

His father had never been like that. Liam Mulgrew had been embittered by his lot. Widowed when Aidan was born, he'd found working the land and raising his two young sons too huge a role and he'd performed no aspect of it well. Patrick didn't hate his father, he merely felt no connection to him. As a role model he was worse than useless. Patrick had never considered the possibility of parenthood – but now, watching the man scrapping playfully with the boy, a pang shot through him.

The ferry neared the far shore. Patrick didn't want to leave it. He was tempted to sit on it for another journey – two, if need be – but his cell phone buzzed and he found himself disembarking with the other passengers.

Cora's voice was as clear as if she were in nearby Wall Street and not three thousand miles away.

'Hi Pats, how's the Big Apple?'

'Juicy. How's business?'

'Don't you ever think about anything else?'

A seagull squawked in indignation at the theft of a crust of bread by a predatory male and he grinned at the scene. When had he last been on a boat, taken a walk, observed nature?

'Actually, I do.'

'Well you'll be pleased to know business is great. Everything's in place for the next show, which is just as well because there's precious little left to sell from this one.'

'Where are you? Are you at the gallery?'

'I locked up half an hour ago. Listen, I walked up Kittle's Lane on the way home – there's a For Sale sign up outside Cobbles. I thought you'd like to know.'

Patrick whistled.

'That's quick.'

'I've heard that the sister's desperate to get the estate tied up. Do you want to buy it?'

'Buy Cobbles? Why would I do that? Are you looking for a hobby?'

'Don't be so patronising. Now that you mention my plans, I'm giving you advance warning that I want to get back to Greece. It's getting bloody cold here. No, I just thought you might have a sentimental attachment to the place.'

If he bought Cobbles, Lexie could still have her exhibition – if she'd agree. But even if he apologised surely they had gone past the tipping point?

He said, 'It would be nice if someone took the whole place over, stock and all, but it won't be me. Anyway, thanks for telling me.'

'OK. Have you found a gallery there yet?'

'We're looking at a couple more spaces before we fly back, but there won't be a problem – and I think Domenica Martinez will agree to show.'

'That *is* good news. Safe home then.'

'Bye, Cora.'

Did she mean it about going back to Greece? It would leave another void in his life.

He turned to find a taxi. In front of him, the young boy yelped with laughter at some joke shared. His father hugged him close and they weaved an uneven dance along the pavement.

On a sudden impulse, Patrick said, 'Stop right here, will you?'

The cab driver, unfazed by the strange request, pulled up abruptly. Around them, horns blared and cars swerved. Patrick tossed him a fistful of notes.

'Keep the change.'

'Have a good day.'

He was normally irritated by the vacuous phrase.

'Do you know, I believe I will.'

He was at the side of Central Park. There were parks in

224

Edinburgh and in London. He lived beside a park, for heaven's sake – but he had never walked in it, any more than he had walked in Hyde Park, or Regent's Park, or Holyrood Park or the Meadows. Ahead of him was woodland, its green shade enticing. He picked a path and wandered along it. When he reached open grass, he had to resist the urge to take off his shoes and socks and pad across it barefoot. Instead, he settled on a bench and relaxed in the sunshine as the world revolved around him – mothers with buggies, fit young men on bikes, fit *old* men on bikes, kids on skateboards and on roller blades. Couples walking dogs. Fashionable women carrying ludicrously small pooches in smart handbags. Joggers. He was astonished at all this leisure activity. When had he last connected with the world in any way other than through work?

Time slowed and his senses became more acute. He felt the warmth of the sun on his face and smelled freshly cut grass, and was astonished at how calming he found these sensations. There was a dimension to life he knew nothing about. In fact – Patrick's eyes snapped open – why did he work so relentlessly to better himself, to build a business? What was his life for?

His cell phone buzzed.

'Patrick Mulgrew.'

It was Domenica's warm voice.

'Hi, how was it?'

A butterfly landed on his hand and he watched the lazy flap of its wings. He had to try again with Lexie. He'd go to her and apologise, and whether that changed anything or not, he would still make his own private atonement for his angry outburst last year. He'd find a way of making sure she could have her exhibition, even though she would never know of his involvement.

He laughed.

'The ferry? It was life-changing.'

Chapter Twenty-three

Catalogue number 7: Custom made orthopaedic sandals, green leather, built up sole on left foot. Donor, Angela Brown, Edinburgh. 'After years of wearing hideous old lady boots, I saved up enough money to visit a specialist shop in London to order these sandals. Imagine my joy! For the first time in my life I could wear pretty shoes!'

Lexie's momentum had gone. It was impossible to maintain any drive now that the For Sale sign was up at Cobbles.

'Don't worry about it,' Cameron murmured, nuzzling her neck as he lay entwined around her. His nakedness was arousing and, with all sense of artistic purpose gone, Lexie was tempted. She shoved him onto his back and rolled over to look down at him.

'I do love it when you're masterful,' he murmured, grinning broadly.

Wide-eyed with mock exasperation, she reached down and squeezed him just above his knee, where she knew he was sensitive. He jerked, yelped and fought loose. Lexie, no match for his strength, found herself helpless and under his weight. She squirmed, he smirked. His arousal was inescapable and she yielded happily.

Afterwards, he said, 'Not bad, for a beginner.'

'Who are you calling a beginner?' she asked indignantly.

He cradled her face in his hand and stroked her cheek gently. 'Just a joke.'

He kissed the tip of her nose.

'I'll be thirty next week,' he said thoughtfully.

'So I'm a cradle snatcher,' Lexie giggled. She was almost

thirty-one.

'I could get used to this.'

'What? Sex?'

'Waking up next to you. Getting domestic.'

'Domestic!' Lexie yelped with laughter. 'Since when have you done so much as made me a coffee? Domestic for you is dropping by the takeaway and bringing back a pizza.'

'I can make coffee.'

'Prove it,' she challenged. A coffee right now would be blissful.

He rolled onto his back, put his hands behind his head and stared at the ceiling.

'Think I'll throw a party.'

Lexie sighed and flopped onto her pillow.

'I was thinking about Besalú. There's a function room at the side.'

'Sure.'

'You'll help, won't you? And Molly? Carlotta'll play ball, I know she will.'

He rolled out his plans while she listened, the need for coffee put to one side. She had grown used to Cameron being around. Like all men, he had good points and bad. Despite his claims on domesticity he was no help around the cottage, but he was lively and gregarious and she enjoyed riding his social energy. And although he liked to present himself as tough, she had seen his tender side – the image of Cameron cradling Edith Lawrence in his arms as she'd opened the box with the baby bootees would never leave her.

Such unexpected switches between sensitivity and – well, OK, boorishness – intrigued her, but there were enough signs of empathy to make her believe she could build on them. He had never understood her art, but what did it matter, after all, when he was so sexy? Love takes many forms and the chemistry between them was still exhilarating.

'Course I'll help,' she said, smoothing her hand over his chest and across the flat expanse of his belly so that he snaked round her again, groaning. She loved the power she had to excite him.

An hour or so later, Cameron's battered Corsa disappeared round the corner of the main house just as Molly was arriving.

'Hi, haven't seen you in an age,' said Lexie, delighted. 'Silly, when you're so close.'

'I've been swamped.' She held up a plate and peered at it. 'They served petit fours at the dinner last night. Cheesecake bites, marzipan thingies, mini Florentines, weensy strawberry tarts. Have you got time for a coffee?'

'You're wicked,' Lexie opened the door wider to admit her.

Molly followed her into the kitchen. 'Cameron off to work today, is he?'

'Yup. He doesn't start till ten.'

'He's here a lot.'

'What, he shouldn't be? He doesn't pay rent?'

'Whoah, why so touchy? That's not what I meant.'

Lexie filled the kettle and turned on the power. 'Oh?'

'It was just an observation.'

'You don't like Cameron much, do you?'

'I didn't say that. I just don't want you to get hurt again, that's all. Has he told you why he left yet?'

'Yeah.'

'Well? Are you going to share in information?'

It wasn't so awful, was it? Lexie said, a little hesitantly, 'He felt he was in too deep and wasn't ready to commit.'

'And he is now?'

'I think so, yes.'

She was sure that Cameron had changed. He told her where he was going, he was around more, he was thinking of settling down, he'd said as much this morning. Lexie picked up a Florentine and rammed it into her mouth. It was chocolatey and sweet and the nuts crunched pleasingly. She ate another, even though it wasn't nine yet and she didn't usually eat much chocolate.

'Here's your coffee. Did you come over to criticise or was there another reason?'

'Actually, I came over to see you, and to bring you some goodies,' Molly said, her voice rising. She started to stand. 'Listen, I'll just go.'

229

Instantly contrite, Lexie shot a hand out and pushed her back down again.

'Sorry, Moll. Don't know why I'm so crotchety this morning. It's lovely to see you, honestly. Here, have one of these.'

Molly reached for a tart.

'Have you seen Patrick recently?' she asked.

'No. Why?'

'Just wondered.'

'Will you please stop trying to match make? Firstly, I'm perfectly happy with Cameron and secondly, whatever you seem to think, Patrick isn't in the least bit interested in me.'

'No. Sure.'

A banana-shaped piece of marzipan found its way into Molly's mouth.

'And thirdly,' Lexie added with great firmness, 'I'm not in the least interested in him.'

'Right.'

They sat in scratchy silence while Lexie wondered what had prompted Molly's choice of conversation. To underline her commitment to her relationship with Cameron, she said, 'Cameron's thirty next week. He's going to have a birthday party at Besalú.'

'In the function room? Should be good.'

'He wants me to organise it.'

Molly gave a derisive hoot.

'Hah! He's got a nerve.'

'Oh Moll, don't say that,' Lexie pleaded, defensive of Cameron and craving her friend's approval. 'Be happy for me.'

Molly's mouth puckered, then she smiled.

'I am. If you are.' She put her hand on Lexie's arm. 'I guess you should be the one to decide if he's changed. So tell me about this party.'

'I was hoping you'd give me a hand. You're the party supremo around here.'

Molly groaned.

'I know, I know, you're busy. But you're always busy and anyway, I'll do the work. Just give me some ideas.'

'Well,' Molly said reluctant before professionalism kicked in, just as Lexie had hoped it would. 'He was born in the 1980s, wasn't he? So let's start with that as a theme.'

They devised a playlist.

'"Should I Stay or Should I Go?"'

'Not bad. How about, "Come on Eileen."?'

'Good one.' Lexie racked her brains. 'I know! "The Birdie Song."'

'Are you out of your mind?'

'No listen, stick it in later on, everyone'll be up dancing, guaranteed.'

'It's a price to high to pay. Wait, wait, wait.' Molly beamed in triumph. 'Got it. "Super Trouper".'

'Oh yeah, unbeatable. 1980s, 1980s. That was Chris de Burgh, wasn't it? "Lady in Red"?'

Molly groaned. 'Oh, spare us. What about "Wake Me Up Before You Go Go".'

Lexie smiled admiringly. 'You're good at this. Culture Club?'

'Sometimes I worry about you. How about "Fairytale of New York"?'

'It's not Christmas,' Lexie protested.

'Even so, it's a great song.'

'If you like trading insults.'

They sipped their coffee companionably.

'It's ages since we had a party,' Lexie said. 'I think it's a great idea. You will be there, won't you?'

'Course. If I'm invited.'

'I'm inviting you.'

Molly stood and rinsed her mug at the sink. 'I'd better get back. Who'll get the music together?'

'Cameron,' Lexie said, 'right up his street.'

'Make sure he puts in the tracks we want, not just goth rock or heavy metal.'

'I will so. Listen, thanks for the treats. And thanks for coming across.'

'You're okay?' Molly stared at her meaningfully.

'Yeah.' Lexie looked away and busied herself by tidying up.

231

'Your folks?'

'Fine.'

'Lex?'

Lexie's face twisted.

'Oh Moll, I dunno. Mum's found a mission – helping me – but Dad's...' She sighed. 'I worry about Dad. I used to see him every day, now I hardly ever see him. I don't think he talks to Mum. About Jamie, I mean, or about the business come to that. I don't think he talks to anyone.'

'Is he still worried about Gordon's?'

'Of course. Neil phoned yesterday. He's got hold of that girl Julie and sweet-talked her into coming back to help out.'

'I thought she was a plague to all customers.'

'There's a lot more to do now that I've gone and Morag's gone, so he's been able to offer her more money and more interesting jobs, and at least she knows the basics already. He says it's working okay. The problem isn't Julie, it's Dad. He won't listen and he won't change.'

'He's had a lot to cope with. You all have.'

'I feel bad. Neil's having to carry everything.'

'You've got a life too, Lex.'

'I don't like doing my own thing at the expense of others.'

'Listen, you've spent a year helping others. It's your turn now.'

'Yes,' Lexie sighed, 'that's what I told myself. But look where it's got me. No exhibition to work towards any more and meanwhile Dad's business is still in a mess.'

When Martha arrived she said, 'Can I come home for supper tonight? Cameron's out and I'd like to see Dad.'

Martha was delighted. 'Of course. We'd love it.'

'I'll get us a treat.'

'You don't have to, I don't mind cooking.'

'No honestly, I'd like to.'

'Well that would be nice. I must say, Carlotta's cooking seems to be getting more and more adventurous. It was *mollejas de cuello* yesterday.'

'Which is?'

232

'Sweetbreads. Specifically, the thymus gland.'

Lexie wrinkled her nose. 'Put like that—'

'Yes. Some haddock would be lovely, darling, you know how your father likes it.'

On the way home, she called in to see Carlotta at Besalú. The kitchen was filled with the aroma of onion and garlic, seared beef and gorgeous, unidentifiable spices. The stainless steel surfaces were scrubbed and shiny and a series of large containers was arrayed neatly along the far wall. Carlotta was wearing a pristine white chef's jacket and her thick dark hair was pulled back in a tight ponytail. She was threading pickled vegetables onto wooden skewers.

She looked up.

'Hola, Lexie. Forgive me for not stopping but I must get on. Pablo the chef is sick, we are short staffed.'

'Can I help?'

'Thank you, but – wait. Yes. If you mean it?' She stood aside and went to the sink to wash her hands. 'Will you make more of these?'

'Sure. What do I do?'

'Wash your hands and take a jacket. There's one on the hook by the door. Then just copy what I have done. Brilliant. Thank you, Lexie.'

Lexie surveyed the skewers. It didn't look too difficult. She picked a gherkin from the first bowl and jammed it down the skewer, then a slice of pickled carrot. The next item was an anchovy wrapped around an olive. This was a little trickier. She picked an anchovy out of the bowl gingerly, rolled it round a plump green olive, slid it onto the skewer. A square of roasted red pepper, another green olive, a final gherkin. She surveyed the final result with satisfaction. It was balanced, decorative, colourful – but it had taken ages.

'This OK?'

Carlotta was stirring a huge pot of some kind of spicy beef stew. Lexie, who fed herself far too often on quick snacks, sniffed appreciatively.

'Sure. Perfect. Now do another hundred.'

Lexie grimaced. 'Crikey. I'll have to speed up.'

She bent in concentration over the pickles and soon had a dozen skewers completed. She was so completely into her rhythm that she'd almost forgotten why she'd dropped by.

Carlotta was making a sauce. Lexie halted in her skewering and watched as her knife flew through garlic and rehydrated dried peppers, chopping the ingredients coarsely. She removed and binned the coarsest bits of stem from a large bunch of fresh coriander, and threw all the other ingredients into a huge food processor. She pressed a button and the motor started, noisily. Ground cumin, salt. The ingredients began to meld and become a thick, sludgy red. Carlotta opened the lid of the processor and started to drizzle in oil, then threw in a handful of breadcrumbs and added a cupful of stock. The sauce grew in volume as she repeated the process again and again.

Carlotta dipped a spoon in the sauce and held it out to Lexie. 'Want to try?'

Rich red sauce coated the tip of the spoon. Lexie put it into her mouth with all the avidity of a child licking the cake mixer.

'Wow. That's fantastic. What's this called?' The sauce was an explosion of tastes and sensations – peppery, spicy, sweet, a blast of Mediterranean sunshine.

'Mojo sauce. It's Cuban, originally. They add in sour oranges there. You can put in anything you want, basically.' Carlotta poured the sauce into a large bowl. 'It's not enough, I must make more, that will never last us. How are the *banderillas*?'

'Oh!' Lexie had been dreaming. She set about her task with renewed vigour. Gherkin, carrot, onion, anchovy and olive, pepper...

'What did you want to tell me, Lexie?' Carlotta asked as she deftly rubbed the skin off half a dozen cloves of garlic and threw them onto a chopping board

'Tell you?'

'You do not often visit me in my kitchen.'

Lexie looked up, laughing. 'Perhaps I should come more. I'm quite enjoying this. I wanted to talk about Cameron's party next week.'

'Party?'

'Hasn't he been in touch? About his thirtieth? He said he'd arranged to have it in the function room. Next Friday.'

Carlotta's face was unreadable.

'Really? I guess he must have booked it with Tracy. She's in charge of reservations and bookings.'

'You didn't know about it?'

Carlotta flung her ingredients into the blender and started the motor again, so that Lexie missed her reply.

'Sorry?' she said when the speed was turned down. 'I didn't catch what you said.'

Carlotta turned to her and shrugged expressively.

'I didn't know, but it makes no difference. What did you want to ask about?'

'I was wondering about, you know, decoration, the disco, the menu, all that stuff. Cameron's enlisted my help – and Molly's, of course. We thought we'd have a 1980s theme.'

Carlotta's laugh had an edge to it.

'You mean he has got you to do all his work.'

'We're happy to do it.'

'Of course.' She turned her back and switched the processor back on.

Lexie resumed her task of threading the skewers. When the blender stopped she said, 'He's changed, you know. He's matured while he's been away.'

'Really?' Carlotta poured the sauce into the large bowl and rinsed the blender in the sink, her movements abrupt.

Lexie had set up a production line. She skewered ten gherkins, then ten carrots, lining the wooden sticks up neatly in front of her. She rolled ten anchovies around ten olives. 'He's much more settled. You know,' she started threading on the anchovied olives, 'he's been dropping hints. I think he wants to settle down.'

'Settle down?'

Carlotta was scrubbing furiously at an invisible stain on the polished steel surface.

'I was wondering whether he'd say something at his party. Cameron can be a bit embarrassing sometimes.' Lexie laughed. 'You know, like letting drop that you like being kissed on the inside of your thighs.'

'You do?'

'It was just an example,' said Lexie, who did.

Carlotta snorted.

It was the turn of the peppers to join the massed ranks of skewers. They were oiled and squidgy. 'I hope he's not thinking of proposing. Publicly, I mean. That would be the ultimate mortification.'

'Would you accept?' Carlotta asked, her voice sharp. She had finished scrubbing and was raking in one of the huge fridges.

For a ridiculous moment Lexie thought of Patrick's straight nose and perfect features, balanced and symmetrical and so unlike Cameron's scarred face. How had she fallen out so utterly with Patrick? They'd both been overwrought. She blinked the image away. Cameron was nothing to do with Patrick. That brief chapter in her life had been firmly closed and now she was trying to make good another.

'I wouldn't like to be put in a position where I had to make a public declaration. I guess I'd want to think about it. But you know, maybe it's time.'

Carlotta heaved out a huge block of Manchego cheese and dropped it onto the worktop with a heavy thud. 'I would say, very strongly,' she said, agitation making her accent all the more pronounced, 'that you should not consider a long-term relationship with Cameron Forrester, at all.' She placed heavy emphasis on the last two words.

A piece of pepper slithered through Lexie's fingers and she scrabbled to pick it up off the worktop.

'I beg your pardon?'

'He is, how do you say it, a man with an eye for the girls.'

'A paedophile?' Lexie said, aghast.

'No, no, not that. A—' she searched for the word, '—a womaniser. He is unreliable. He is not good husband material. I say this in a spirit of friendship.'

Lexie gave up on the pepper and leant heavily on the counter.

'A womaniser? What makes you say that?'

Carlotta pursed her lips. Her words sounded forced.

'I cannot say, but I know this to be true. Dear Lexie, please make sure he does not propose. Promise me this at least.'

'Well, I'm not sure how I can do that,' Lexie said, her voice tart.

'Discourage him. I beg you.'

Lexie abandoned the skewers and marched across to the sink.

'I'd better go.'

'I hope I have not offended you? I mean only the best.'

'I'm sure you do.'

There was a sick feeling somewhere deep in her stomach. She could disregard Carlotta's words – surely she *should* take no notice of them? – but now they had been spoken, they could not be seized back.

'I'd better go. We can talk about the party some other time. I can see you're busy.'

Carlotta didn't try to dissuade her, she merely watched sadly as Lexie washed her hands and picked up her shopping.

'I'm off home anyway. I have my own cooking to do.'

It came out more sharply than she had intended, but Carlotta stayed silent, her head merely bobbing in acknowledgement.

'Bye then.'

'Bye.'

As Lexie reached the door, Carlotta said, 'I mean it, Lexie. Think, please.'

Lexie marched out. It was all right for Carlotta, she had her ever-adoring Jonas. Not every man could be so perfect.

Chapter Twenty-four

Catalogue number 14: Church's loafers in black crocodile skin. Donor: Patrick Mulgrew, Hailesbank. 'I believe in comfort, but style and quality are also paramount and these shoes are worth every penny. It takes up to eight weeks to make a pair of Church's, and there can be as many as 250 separate manual operations in their manufacture, so you can appreciate where the money goes.'

Lexie browned a batch of cold sliced potato in a frying pan with a little oil and a handful of crushed rosemary. She was enjoying being back at Fernhill, secure in the knowledge that she was not enslaved at Gordon's any longer, and that she could return to her own private space again this evening. Martha, crisp in a white cotton blouse and pin-striped apron, was sitting at the kitchen table, slicing the next batch of potatoes for Lexie – a production line. They were bonding as a team in more than one way.

'I popped in on Edith Lawrence today,' Martha said, assessing quantities with a practised eye.

Immediately, Lexie was ashamed of herself. Edith's story had been her inspiration, yet she hadn't visited the old woman since the discovery of the bootees. She had become selfish.

She jabbed at a piece of potato that was sticking in the pan.

'How is she?'

'Delightful. I've discovered that if you take her back to her childhood she can be quite lucid. We were talking about Fernhill and her memories of it. Do you know, there used to be some outbuildings at the back, where we park the cars? Edith's father let them to a local farmer's wife and she ran a dairy there.'

'No, really?'

'Fernhill Dairy.'

Martha finished slicing potato and stood up to clear away the waste.

'They sold milk and cream and butter until after the First World War. Then the woman announced she'd had enough of cows and milk. She was off to work in the canteen at the East Fortune air base, where it'd be a damn sight warmer.'

'Does she talk about Charlotte at all?'

'I haven't raised it with her. I'm afraid of how she might react. I'd rather stick to happier lines of conversation. Did you know she worked at the air base herself? Just for the last couple of years of the second war, when she'd turned eighteen. She was some sort of filing clerk. Will you go and see her? I'm sure she'd like that.'

Lexie flipped the last slices of potato.

'I should, shouldn't I? Oh, hi Dad. Didn't hear you come in – what's wrong?'

Tom Gordon replaced the look of despair with one of forced cheerfulness, went straight to the fridge and pulled out a can of beer, then sat down heavily at the table. The can stood in front of him, condensation running slowly down its side and puddling into a ring on the table. Martha lifted it, pulled the ring, fetched a glass from the cupboard and poured the beer, while Lexie, concern growing, dried the lake with kitchen roll.

'Dad?'

Tom was staring at the beer, but he didn't seem to see it. As the froth subsided, it remained untouched.

Martha touched Tom's shoulder. 'Tom?'

He jumped.

'What?'

'Your beer?'

She gestured to the glass.

'Oh. Yes. Thank you.'

He gripped the glass but it remained on the table.

Martha pulled out a chair and sat down next to him.

'Perhaps you'd like to tell us what's up, rather than leave us guessing at the worst?'

He picked up the glass with obvious effort and took a long pull at the beer.

'Just tired,' he said, his smile forced.

'Dad,' Lexie reproached, her concern unabated.

'Really. It's been a long day. It's lovely to see you, Alexa, by the way. Martha, your colleague Fiona from your old office came in today. She was asking after you.'

Lexie recognised evasive tactics, but her mother was sidetracked and the conversation drifted into chit-chat as her father's tension eased. Lexie suspected work-induced stress and wondered what new disaster had befallen Gordon's. She determined to call Neil in the morning. Loyalty, the familiar that had sat on her shoulder for the past year, sank its claws into her flesh. *I should be there, helping him.* What had begun as an antidote to grief had set like glue and she was stuck.

She said, 'I'll come back to Gordon's.'

Tom and Martha's heads turned in uncanny unison as they both stared at her in astonishment.

Tom's response, 'It's not necessary,' chimed with Martha's, 'You can't, you've got your own work.'

Lexie picked on the latter.

'Come on, Mum. You know and I know that there's not much point carrying on. I've been kidding myself. I've got nowhere to show my paintings.'

'We'll find somewhere. Don't give up. You owe it to everyone who's sent you shoes. They're all so excited. And what about Pavel? He wouldn't have wanted you to give up.'

'There's nothing you can do at Gordon's, love,' her father said. 'I mean it. You've sacrificed enough for us already. Besides,' he added, laying a protective hand over Martha's, 'look at how good it's been for your mother. She's so much like her old self again.'

The opposing claims on her ripped Lexie in two. Help her father – or provide an escape route for her mother? Give up on the show idea and disappoint so many people – or paint, which was what she longed to do? The desire to prove herself to Patrick was ever-present.

'I just want to know you're all right, Dad.'

'I'll be all right,' Tom said, 'if you'd just stop tantalising me with the smell of those bloody chips and feed me.'

'Mr Mulgrew?'

Victoria, still jet-lagged, had gone home early, full of apologies but heavy-eyed with lack of sleep. Another girl, Sophie, was keeping an eye on the gallery. Perhaps she was busy with a customer because this call had come straight through to Patrick.

'Who is this?' he asked, more weary than he cared to admit.

'You don't know me, my name is Frederick Hampton. I'm a curator at the Victoria and Albert Museum in London.'

Patrick, who focused on fine art, seldom visited the V&A, but he admired the museum. 'How can I help you, Mr Hampton?'

'Freddie, please. Last year I spotted you at an auction in London. The small museum I was with at that time bid unsuccessfully for an item that was up for sale. The bidding went beyond our budget, I'm afraid, and I had to drop out. The lot went to a telephone bidder. I discovered later that the person behind that bid was you.'

'Oh yes?' Patrick feigned indifference, but he knew at once which auction Freddie Hampton was talking about.

'As I said, I'm now at the V&A, and I'm putting together a big exhibition, very prestigious. It will attract a lot of attention and draw international audiences.'

He paused, perhaps hopeful that Patrick would anticipate his request, but Patrick didn't help him out.

At length Freddie said, 'I was very much hoping that you would lend us the item. I'm sure you're aware that it represents a pivotal period in that particular maker's career.'

Patrick thought of the box buried deep in his wardrobe. He had a very good idea of how important it was and he knew that he was about to be very selfish, but the fact was that he could not bear to let it out of his possession. Somewhere deep inside he still hoped that he could present it to the person he'd bought it for.

242

'I'm sorry, Freddie.' He paused, 'It's no longer mine to give.'

'Oh.' The young curator sounded crestfallen. 'Would you be able to give me any details of the current owner? I'd really like to pursue—'

'No. I'm sorry. It has—' he searched for an appropriate word, '—dropped out of sight.'

When Freddie had rung off, Patrick scratched at the stubble sprouting from his chin, a reminder that it was time to head home and catch up on sleep. On his computer, an email announced its arrival with a melodic tinkle. He clawed at the mouse, the screen refreshed, and he saw it was from Domenica.

<So good to meet you, Patrick. Hope you found a gallery just right for your American dream? Just to confirm I'm happy to show for you, so long as we can agree the date and terms. Best regards. Domenica. PS You can tell me I'm an old busybody, but sometimes the direct approach is best.>

Patrick smiled. Domenica was a wise old bird.

Cameron's birthday party was in full swing and he was sweating. His scar was white against the hot flush of his face and his hair was matting into damp clumps. He stripped off the sweater Lexie had given him this morning to reveal a tee shirt bearing the legend 'Brilliantly disguised as a grown up'.

'From my uncle,' he grinned as Lexie grimaced, 'Great, isn't it?'

He pulled her close and rubbed his damp cheek across her face. 'Feel the sweat, babe.'

'Yuk, you're gross!'

She pushed him away but he laughed and jerked her back.

'And you look good enough to eat.'

Lexie was wearing crimson spandex tights with orange legwarmers and a tiger-skin top. Scarlet plastic hoop earrings swung from her ears and she had tied a leopard-skin bandana round her forehead. Entering into the spirit of a period theme came easily to her, but the only item she had been able to persuade Cameron to wear was a pair of late-eighties hi-top trainers, which he had embraced with enthusiasm.

'You are brilliant, d'you know that?' he mouthed into her ear. 'I think I'm in love.'

She took these words lightly, because he was clearly more than half way to being very drunk.

'Cupboard love,' she bawled, 'just because I organised all this for you.'

He laughed. 'You know me too well, babe,' he said, and started to attack the gifts piled on a table next to the dance floor, ripping off the bright wrapping paper with more gusto than finesse.

'Careful,' Lexie said, rescuing a gift card, 'or you'll not know who they're from.'

He squinted at the card.

'Boxed set of "The Killing". Brilliant. From Ange and Mick. Cheers.'

He raised the box to a couple hooked round each other in the corner of the room.

'Not killing each other tonight yet, I see.'

There were guffaws. Ange and Mick were known for their rather public rows.

Cameron seized another parcel, clearly a bottle.

'From Big Al. Thanks mate. I might even share it with you.'

Carlotta appeared from the kitchen in a sleeveless scarlet shift and black pumps. She looked cool and unruffled, despite having just produced a birthday meal for twenty as well as overseeing the demands of a full restaurant.

'Was everything all right?' she asked.

Molly, coming up behind Lexie, dumped a gift-wrapped parcel on the table.

'Brilliant, thanks, you've gone to a lot of trouble.'

'It's no trouble. Really.'

'Wish I could say the same about Cameron,' Lexie grinned, 'He's been a bloody nightmare this last week.'

'Why? What's he done?'

'Oh you know, driving us mad,' Lexie said indulgently. 'Forever adding new people to the guest list. Dreaming up yet another impossible idea for the decorations. Wouldn't make a decision about the menu, that sort of thing.'

'Hah, so like a man. It's better you two did the organising, I think.'

'Definitely.'

'Where's Jonas, Carlotta?' Molly asked.

Carlotta peered around the dimly-lit room.

'He is not here?'

'Nope. He did say he was coming.'

'Yes, I expected him. This is strange. Maybe I should call him, something might have happened.'

She pulled out a phone, but the deadbeat voice of Mick Jones began to grind out and the opportunity for any kind of sane conversation was lost.

Lexie leaned back against a table and closed her eyes, giving herself over to the music. She didn't want to think about Jonas, or about anything else in particular. It had been an exhausting week.

A hand grabbed her and her eyes snapped open. Cameron was tugging at her arm and grinning.

'Come on Lex. First dance.'

'Go, girl,' Molly shouted, shoving her as she stumbled forward.

They shuffled and gyrated in the centre of the floor as everyone started to clap rhythmically, whistling and cat calling.

Cameron swayed against Lexie so that she was forced to match his weight with her own in order to keep him upright.

'You're a great girl, Lexie. Great,' he slurred.

'Sure.'

'Been fantastic, getting back together, eh?'

'Yeah, fab.'

He draped his arms round her neck and hooked her so close that his alcohol-laden breath puffed hotly across her face.

'Don' know wha' I'd do without you. Tell you wha', Lexie, let's tell everyone – let's tell them that we –'

The music crashed to a halt. The silence that ensued was like treacle, sticky and uncomfortable. Cameron whirled round, his eyes slightly unfocused.

'Wha' the –?'

Lexie steadied him with her shoulder as he threatened to topple. Someone threw a switch and the dimness blazed into light. She blinked, half blinded.

A chorus of voices rose as people began to recover from their surprise.

'What's happening?'

'Is it the strippogram?' Someone said with an accompanying belly laugh.

'Hey, what do you think you're—?'

Jonas Wood was standing right next to them in the centre of the dance floor. His feet were planted wide apart. Aggression leached from every pore.

'Jonas?' Lexie said. 'Is something—?'

He glared at her, his usually placid features crumpled into a scowl so ferocious that she caught her breath.

'Wrong? Is something wrong, Lexie, is that what you were going to say?'

She laid a placatory hand on his arm, but he shook it off with a gesture of impatience. He was holding a box. Not gift-wrapped like the others piled on the table next to the dance floor. Just a shoe box.

He snatched off the lid and pulled out a pair of scarlet stiletto sandals.

'I heard you were looking for good stories,' he growled, his face scrunched into a pug-like snarl so unlike his usual amiable expression that Lexie was shocked.

'I'm sorry? I don't…'

Jonas shoved the sandals into her hands and she looked down at them in bewilderment. They were stylish: the leather was soft, the heels were high. On the right woman, they'd look stunning.

Carlotta was pushing her way through the crowd.

'Jonas? *Mi cielo*?'

Jonas ignored his wife.

'You just photograph these, Lexie. They tell a story all right. The story of a lying, cheating bitch who's slept with half the town.'

246

Carlotta cried out and clapped her hands over her mouth.

'No! It's not true!'

She clawed at his arm but he thrust her away with such violence that she spun round and fell to the floor. Lexie stared at Jonas, appalled. She'd never have believed he could be so rough with his adored Carlotta.

'Including the guy who *used* to be my best friend.'

The silence now was absolute. Lexie looked down at Carlotta, still sprawling on the floor, her head hanging down, her shoulders heaving. She looked at Cameron. Jonas's best friend.

She began to laugh.

'Don't be ridiculous,' she said. 'Cameron wouldn't … Cam?'

She appealed to him, expecting the refutation of the accusation to be immediate.

Cameron's mouth was hanging open.

'I didn'… she asked me … it wasn' my fault,' he stuttered through a haze of alcohol.

'Maybe years ago,' Lexie stammered, 'before the two of you got married.'

Jonas's laugh was so completely devoid of humour that it raised the hairs on her neck.

'Oh yes. That too. That's why Cameron ran away.'

Lexie caught her breath.

'And since he came back.'

'No!'

He was lying. He must be, although she couldn't understand why. Cameron wouldn't have slept with Carlotta in the last few months, not when she was becoming so close to him?

'Cameron?' she repeated again, demanding a denial. 'Tell him. Tell him you didn't … you haven't—'

Cameron's eyes were not quite focused. His gaze slid from Jonas to where Carlotta lay on the floor, and then to Lexie.

'Oh, fuck it,' he mumbled, and lurched towards the door. 'Fuck everything.'

His party guests watched his retreating back in shocked silence.

Chapter Twenty-five

Catalogue number 19: Pink baby bootees, hand knitted. Small bleached area on one toe. Donor: Edith Dorothy Lawrence, Musselburgh. 'These bootees are the only memento I have left of my little baby, Charlotte, who died at only six weeks. Charlotte was illegitimate. The boy ran away. I refused to give my baby up but my father punished me when she died by forcing me to destroy everything that belonged to her. I hid these up the chimney in a wee box.'

Patrick had a dinner in London, so stayed over and flew back early the next morning. It was a week now since he had returned from New York and at least once every hour he thought of Lexie and how he might frame his apology. Would it be enough to prise her from that man Cameron's grip?

Patrick exuded confidence in every aspect of his life but was deeply insecure over personal relationships – a fact that would come as a considerable surprise to many. Didn't he always have a beautiful woman on his arm? Didn't they queue up for his attention?

He was brutal when it came to self-assessment. Wealth buys anything, he told himself with painful honesty. It certainly buys women. Yet it hadn't been enough for Niamh – measured against Aidan, he had been found wanting. And Lexie wasn't interested in money. He was a decade older than she was, and though he dressed well, drove a smart car and owned a large house, what could he offer when set against the raw sexuality of the young man she had chosen?

So he delayed engineering a meeting. He'd do it even though he risked the mortification of yet another rejection, but the thing had to be right. Patrick, who would make a decision on the purchase of a valuable painting or the career of a young artist he found promising in a split second, procrastinated.

He picked up his car at the airport, but rather than going straight to the gallery, he decided to head home to shower and shave. He nosed his car into the drive at The Gables and was about to go upstairs when he heard voices in the living room. Puzzled, he hovered by the door. It was not Mrs Mackie's day and Cora usually enjoyed the peace of the annexe. One of the voices, however, definitely was Cora's, but he didn't recognise the other.

He threw open the door.

Niamh Mulgrew was tall and slender, and still as beautiful at thirty-nine as she had been at seventeen. On this overcast day her eyes were pale gunmetal, the exact shade of the sky. Her hair showed the odd hint of grey, but was still for the most part black, perhaps a little less lustrous than it had once been, but enviable nonetheless. Her skin had taken the worst hit from the passage of time – the translucent softness of her youth had coarsened and a spray of fine lines criss-crossed the smoothness round the eyes. But it was the lips that Patrick noticed first. Niamh's mouth had grown thinner, as though years of unhappiness had caused them to tighten and harden. Fine wrinkles marred the upper lip and her lipstick was too dark, he thought, for her colouring.

'Hello Patrick,' Niamh said, rising to greet him.

Her accent was still Irish. He grappled with this fact through the shock. Of course it was – she had lived in Ireland all the years they had been apart. The encounter was like taking a step back in time; he had moved on, changed his life, become urbane and cosmopolitan, while she had moved back to Dublin, to the environment she'd grown up in, to live with Aidan.

And what had she been doing all this time? Patrick realised he knew nothing of the two of them. Over the years he had done the metaphorical equivalent of sticking his fingers in his ears and singing 'la, la, la' any time either of their names has been mentioned, so he had no idea whether she worked, or if they had children – whether they had married, even. When he'd parted with Niamh, he'd sworn that he would never speak to her again. Yet here she was, standing in his house, greeting him with a look of such obvious apprehension that he could not find it in himself to turn his back and sweep out. The grand gesture would seem merely juvenile.

'Hello, Niamh.'

Out of the corner of his eye he spied Cora's relief that there was not to be a fight. Not yet, at any rate, not a simple childish throwing of toys out of the pram.

'I'll leave you two together,' she murmured, 'Time I was at work anyway.'

She touched his shoulder as she slid past and he was grateful for the small show of support. Once she had gone, and the door had swung closed, he turned to face his ex-wife.

A small smile played on Niamh's face and he tried to read it. He was disturbed by its familiarity because while the shell was similar, the substance had changed. Once she had been all innocence and vivacity, now there was something wary about her expression and the gusto had turned to a slightly distressing air of defeat.

'Well,' he said, 'what brings you here? Something happened to my dear brother? Nothing good, I hope,' he couldn't help adding with a childish flare of spite.

'You're looking terrific, Patrick,' Niamh's voice was muted. 'I thought you might have aged more. Actually, I thought you'd be married again, but Cora tells me you're still single.'

When Patrick said nothing, she went on, 'Might I beg a coffee? I'm very—' her voice limped to a halt, but she drew a deep breath and carried on, '—tired. You must be too. I hear you're just back from London.'

Manners kicked in. What harm could it do to offer her coffee?

'Of course. Why don't you come into the kitchen? We can talk there.'

He could see Niamh eying the luxury beechwood cabinets, the cream marble counter tops and the opalescent pendent lights. Was she weighing the differences in their lives? Yet for all he knew, she might live in a palace.

251

'This is lovely.'

He grunted and filled the cafetière from the instant hot water tap.

'Hungry?'

'Not really, no. Thanks.'

She sipped coffee and continued to stare around.

'You've done well, Patrick. I always knew you would. Remember the little flat we had in Dublin when we first got married? We could hardly walk round the bed and the two-ring stove was tucked into a corner behind the sofa.'

Patrick's defences sprang into action. He wasn't about to get drawn into a game of 'do you remember?' because that could be a precursor to the reawakening of all sorts of emotions he needed to keep firmly in check.

'Are you just passing by, Niamh? Visiting Edinburgh? You're lucky to catch me here, I'm away a lot.'

She flashed a shrewd look at him – whatever else she might be, Niamh had never been stupid.

'Okay. Straight down the middle, I see. You never were one for finesse, were you?'

She set down the fine porcelain cup Patrick had passed to her and drew a breath.

'Aidan is dying. He has a lymphoma that started in the neck and has spread through his body.'

She waited. Patrick sipped his coffee and watched her carefully, but he said nothing. Inwardly he was cursing his spiteful remark of earlier – what must she have thought of him? – but he couldn't unsay it now.

'He would never ask you, but I know how much it would mean to him if you'd come and see him before he dies.'

Patrick set his cup down.

'I'm sorry to hear he's ill.'

'Are you, Patrick?' Her grey eyes filled with scepticism. 'You sound so cold. You never used to be cold, you were funny and spirited.'

'It's just conceivable that things happened to change that.'

Niamh bit her lip.

'Do you ever think about me, Patrick? I've often wondered

about that. I've spent a great deal of time thinking about you.'

'Niamh—'

He stood up and lifted his coffee cup into the sink.

'I phoned and wrote I don't know how many times. Did you ever read my letters?'

'No.'

'I thought not.'

'What good would it have done? Hey?'

He rounded on her, suddenly aggressive.

'Saying sorry couldn't undo what happened.'

'If you knew how much I regretted what happened … I hoped that perhaps you could find it in your heart to forgive me.'

He stared her down and under his gaze she became defiant.

'I was bored. You were out all the time. I didn't want to be in London, I hated it, but your damn ambition was so enormous you didn't even notice. And when Aidan came along, with his bloody Mulgrew charm, it was all too easy to—'

Her voice tailed off.

'It didn't mean much. I never meant for you to find out. Aidan would have been gone in another week and we'd have got back to normal—'

Patrick's voice was sharp as the blade of a razor, the cut just as smooth.

'And if I'd never found out, it would all have been all right? Is that what you thought? Or perhaps you would have thought that after fucking my brother, further adulterous adventures would be less heinous, maybe more easily forgiven? Is that it, Niamh?'

'You're as stubborn as ever. I hoped we could—'

'Could what? You didn't come here hoping we could be friends, surely?'

There was a long silence. He was vaguely aware of Cora walking from the annexe down the path at the side of the house. Somewhere further away, the siren of an ambulance blared. Whatever he said to her, Patrick was finding Niamh's nearness unsettling. He didn't need to play games to recollect what she had once meant to him, or feel again the unbridled passion of

253

first love and remember the unwavering belief that its flames could never be extinguished. He recalled the wonder of exploration and the discovery of sweet, secret places that sprang to life as his touch gave pleasure. It was heady and dangerous. For a precarious moment he teetered on the verge. For years he had suppressed the need to be loved and now it was treacherously near the surface.

Niamh said quietly, 'It was a mistake. One horrible, stupid, youthful mistake, that's all. Can you not accept that? Can you not recognise your own part in it all?'

'*My* part?'

Niamh stood and walked across to the doors to the patio. The rain had started and heavy drops rolled down the panes, gathering pace and momentum on the way. She raised her hands and pressed them flat against the cold glass, then leaned forward until her forehead rested on it. Patrick's heart twisted. She never used to be still. Her shoulders never drooped like that, she'd been the one with all the energy.

'Do you have children?'

The question came from nowhere.

She turned.

'Children? No. Our relationship was never like that. It never—' she stopped and pursed her lips as if unsure whether to say anything. 'I never felt right with Aidan. We didn't get together until after the divorce, you know. In my heart I hoped you would take me back.'

She looked away. Her cheekbones were still prominent, and if the lips were thinner than they once had been, this didn't affect her beauty.

Her revelation unbalanced him. For ten years he had imagined a grand passion: Niamh and Aidan, Aidan and Niamh, the names almost merged into a new word inside his bruised mind. Only passion could justify such a betrayal, wasn't that right?

'He was never quite the same man after … Aidan once glittered and shone, much as you did, although he never had your depth. Anyway,' she closed her eyes briefly, 'I was left with the lesser of the Mulgrew brothers.'

254

'You stayed with him.'

'Stayed? Yes. I stayed. I saw it as a kind of punishment. Penance, if you like.'

'You haven't been happy?'

Astonishment pumped through his veins.

Niamh spread her hands, palms upwards, and her shoulders rose an inch or two.

It was not what he had thought. At another time, the revelation would have given him profound satisfaction, but now he just saw three lives wasted.

'I imagined you crowing, the pair of you. Giggling together about how you had deceived me. I thought Aidan ... he was always a competitive little sod.'

'It was never like that. But tell me about yourself, Patrick. You've never remarried?'

For ten years he had swallowed handfuls of anger and hurt to sustain his bitterness. Now Niamh was puncturing the pride that had been his only salve. What would he have left? He shook his head.

'But there's someone special?'

A procession of beautiful women paraded in front of Patrick's eyes: all the Dianas and Arabellas and Josephines of the world of culture and wealth who had made themselves willingly available to him. He was about to deny it, wanting her to understand how deep her injury had gone, when Lexie's crimson crop shoved its way into his head. He couldn't betray Lexie by denying her.

'There was someone,' he admitted, 'but I lost her.'

Niamh was exhausted. She had been nursing Aidan at home, but her mother had come for a few days. Shaken by everything she'd said, Patrick persuaded her to stay for a couple of days.

'You need rest,' he told her.

'There'll be plenty of time for rest.'

'How long has he got?'

She shrugged.

'A month? A few months? It's impossible to say. Will you visit him?'

The habit of years was impossible to shed in hours.

'I don't know,' he said honestly.

'If I stay a couple of days, will you give me your answer then?'

'Yes.'

While she slept or sat in the sunshine, strolled in the Memorial Park or visited Cora at The Maker's Mark, he kept himself busy, still unable to process his emotions. He checked over everything that had happened in his absence. He approved the invitation list to the next opening and initialled the proofs for the catalogue, which was due to go off to print. He finalised an agreement with Lord Whitmuir about staged payments for the Colourist painting. He lunched with Diana, who was so gracious about their separation that he almost regretted parting with her.

It was easy keeping busy at work, but sleep eluded him. On the second night, after hours of restlessness, he abandoned the attempt and went downstairs to make tea. It was three o'clock and to his surprise he saw a thread of light under the living room door. He pushed it open.

Niamh was sitting on the sofa, her knees pulled up to her chest, her head sunk onto them. He watched her for a moment. In the stillness of the night, she looked again like the girl he'd once loved.

'Niamh? Are you all right?'

Startled, she raised her head. Her eyes were sunk in great hollows, her face pinched and drawn.

'I have to get back to him.'

'Of course.'

Patrick perched himself on the end of the sofa and on impulse reached for her hand. It lay in his, cold at first, then growing warmer in his grasp.

'You've given me a lot to think about.'

The tentative smile was back, as if she wasn't sure about what he was going to say.

'When it happened—' Self-awareness came at a price. Patrick took a deep breath. '—I couldn't see beyond my pride. I felt deeply betrayed, but more than anything, I felt a failure.

No—' he stopped Niamh, '—don't say anything, let me finish. I couldn't stomach the thought of Aidan getting something that was so utterly precious to me. There was no possibility of compromise. The betrayal was final. If I'd been able to step back from it all, just for a time, before I closed all the doors to reconciliation, I guess our lives might have been very different. I'm sorry, Niamh.'

There. He'd said the words he'd never thought he would utter.

Her hand curled round his and he felt a gentle squeeze.

'My temper,' he said, 'seems to be my downfall.'

'It was understandable. The provocation was great.'

'I should have learned from it. I didn't allow myself to learn.'

She raised an eyebrow.

'Last year, I met someone I thought I could love. We argued, and I said some unforgiveable things.'

'What happened?'

He shrugged. 'It's no surprise. We haven't been able to talk since. I know I must apologise, but she's with someone else now and I think it's too late.'

'You'll never know unless you try.'

Patrick looked at the woman he used to love. She was not the monster he had imagined all these years and for the first time he recognised that it had been his neglect that had driven her to his brother. However deep her betrayal, the outcome need not have been so catastrophic. The passage of time had softened everything. He had moved on, and now he must finally learn the lesson he'd refused to study.

'Will you come to Dublin, Patrick? Say goodbye to Aidan?'

He gathered her in his arms. She felt thin and vulnerable.

'I'll come,' he said.

Chapter Twenty-six

Catalogue number 33: Hand-made English shoes, donor Elizabeth Garrett, Aberdeen. 'My husband loved expensive shoes and, when he died, I wished I could find someone to share this liking – not easy, as many charity shops won't stock shoes. Then Olivia Giles suggested a solution. Her charity *500 Miles* changes people's lives in Malawi and Zambia by providing artificial limbs and limb supports, including legs and feet. People often can't afford to buy solid enough footwear to protect the plastic feet and so *500 Miles* frequently provides shoes along with the orthopedic devices. Edwin's shoes were perfect!'

The BBC made a film about *500 Miles* and Elizabeth was thrilled when she identified on screen one pair of Edwin's shoes, proudly worn by a middle-aged man to whom they had given new life. 'He probably appreciated the shoes more than my husband ever did,' Elizabeth says.

So now Lexie knew the truth about why Cameron had fled from Hailesbank six years ago. The knowledge drove her emotions along a scale from shock, through disbelief, to a certainty in her own mind that he was seeing Carlotta.

Carlotta – with her Spanish sultriness and thick dark hair her *cielo mio's* and her easy acceptance of poor Jonas's adoration as some kind of birthright! And he hadn't just been having a torrid affair with her six years ago, when he'd been, self-confessedly, 'immature' – but now as well. *Now!* When he had made his smoothly muscled body hers once more and declared admiration and adoration at every turn. As for Carlotta, with her little gifts of food for Martha and Tom and her apparent concern for Lexie...

Lexie turned over again and closed her eyes. But sleep didn't come, how could it when her mind was so full? Her eyes snapped open and although they felt dry and itchy, they refused to close for refreshment.

When the morning finally arrived Lexie rose and made coffee. She considered calling Jonas and asking to meet, because she fancied some kind of mutual grouching session across the red stilettos, which were sitting right now on the kitchen table.

She wouldn't call him, of course. He had enough to think about, like his future and the fate of his marriage. He'd have to decide whether to forgive Carlotta's infidelity – because it wasn't the act that caused the hurt, but the thought of whispered intimacies. And it was about the acceptance of one's own failings, because surely there must be shortcomings or else why turn to someone else?

It was impossible to paint, so she walked instead. She pulled on a pair of comfortable old boots and set off along the path by the river. It was September and the air was distinctly cool. After fifteen minutes, the path disappeared into a copse, and the thin light was filtered through the dying leaves so that it was like walking in twilight. This shadowy, murmuring place smelled of dampness and decay. Rotted-down leaves from last year still lay heaped in ditches and holes, a kick from a toe sprayed the paper-dry covering of leaves left and right to reveal the sodden mulch below. And now the rot was starting all over again.

Deep in one of her pockets, Lexie's mobile buzzed. She felt its vibration rather than heard its tone, and extricated it with difficulty. The screen said 'Cameron'. She pressed the divert button. She didn't want to talk to Cameron. She'd had enough of excuses, she needed to think about what she had lost – or (she tried to make herself think positively) what she had gained.

She was following the river. It wasn't a private path, and it was Sunday, so on a number of occasions she passed other walkers. She lost track of time. She was aware of her phone ringing on a number of occasions, but she didn't need to talk to

Cameron, because she could already hear his voice in her head, muttering his excuses.

You were so damn possessive that I felt, you know, swamped.

Of course we should have talked, but I was scared you might persuade me to stay. I was bloody immature, I admit it.

Sometimes she stopped and rested for a while on some path-side boulder, wondering whether she would forgive Cameron. She thought not, but nothing was clear to her.

At one point she was overcome by drowsiness and curled up under a tree, where the sleep that had eluded her last night overtook her at last. When she woke, the wind had risen and she realised with a jolt that she could smell salt air. She must have walked for miles.

A lone walker appeared on the horizon.

'Excuse me!' she called, 'Can you tell me where I am?'

His look of surprise became an intent stare, and seemed to be focused somewhere near her right cheekbone. She brushed at it with her hand. Was there a smear of earth? Maybe a leaf had stuck to it when she'd used the grass as her pillow?

'Are you all right?' he asked, clearly concerned.

'Fine.'

'You look a little – are you sure you're all right? Do you need some water?'

She was wearing a wafer-thin floral dress that had seen fifty years' of washing, a pair of butter-soft Victorian boots that must by now be caked with mud, and her beloved tweed jacket. It was not normal hiking gear.

'I'm okay. Really,' she said earnestly, to reassure him. 'I'm just not sure where this path emerges.'

'Oh, I see. You're near Aberlady. Does that help?'

'Aberlady!'

She'd walked almost nine miles. She was tired, and hungry, and she had no money.

'Where've you come from?'

Lexie gestured vaguely back along the path. 'Back there.' She gathered herself. 'I live on the Fleming House estate, near Hailesbank.'

'It's a good long walk.'

She could see a faint shadow on his chin. It wasn't so much stubble, more a mixture of Van Dyke brown with a touch of Ivory Black, painted on with a very dry brush. His cheekbones were high and gave his face a fine structure, and his skin was weathered by sun and wind, as if he was close friends with nature. He had honest eyes.

Honest eyes.

Lexie smiled. All she had thought about for fourteen hours had been deception, and now she'd been reminded that honesty did exist – if she could read character at all.

'What time is it?'

He glanced down at his watch. His arms, exposed beneath the short sleeves of a polo shirt, were pleasingly brown.

'Five o'clock.'

'Five o'clock!'

How had Edith walked so far, at her age, and in carpet slippers? Lexie crumpled at the thought and must have staggered a little, because she became aware of his hand under her arm, strong and steadying.

'Here. Sit down for a minute.' He guided her to a rock by the path, lowered her onto it, and fished out a flask from his backpack. 'Have some tea. I couldn't finish it. I don't have any germs, well not dangerous ones anyway.'

Lexie accepted the tea and sipped.

'Can I offer you a lift home?'

'A lift?'

'I have a car up there –' he gestured to the right somewhere, '– and Hailesbank isn't far out of my way. You don't have to say yes, it's just an offer.'

Lexie contemplated her slim legs, which looked oddly white as they disappeared into the boots. Sitting down had made her realise how tired she was. She rubbed her hand through her crimson crop. Her hair felt dry and undernourished, but her scalp was damp with her exertion. She was a mess.

'A lift,' she said, weak with gratitude, 'would be fantastic.'

Steve dropped her at Fleming House.

'I know that place, it's a mile down the drive,' he insisted when Lexie told him to drop her off on the road, 'and you're exhausted.'

'I think I should call you Raphael. Not just an angel, my archangel. Now that I've stopped walking I can feel a hell of a blister on my heel.'

'I'm not surprised,' Steve laughed, 'those boots were hardly made for walking.'

Lights were on in the ballroom in the big house. She could see the twinkle and glitter of the cut crystal drops on the three huge chandeliers that hung along the centre of the high ceiling. There was some kind of function on and she recalled Molly complaining that she wouldn't be free till eight. She longed to talk to her friend, but she knew she'd have to wait, so she ran a bath, then foraged for something to eat. She worried about Cameron coming to the door because she knew she shouldn't forgive him. Molly and Pavel had known this, her mother had known it, she'd been the only one who couldn't accept it. The truth was that she still feared that his presence could weaken her.

When he didn't come, she was cross that he cared so little for her – but she wouldn't check her phone for messages, because she didn't want to hear what he had to say.

She was a seething whirlpool of contradictions.

She waited till almost eight then threw on her tweed jacket again, this time over a red skirt that matched her hair, and walked across to wait for Molly.

There was a wooden seat outside the entrance to Molly's apartment. In the morning, it faced the sun but by evening this spot was shady, and in any case, it was almost dark. If archangel Steve had not given her a lift, she'd still be walking.

She settled back and waited. Just as she was beginning to shiver, the crunch, crunch, crunch of feet on the gravel alerted her to Molly's arrival.

'Hi!'

Molly was startled. 'Oh! Hi! What are you doing there?'

Lexie stood. 'Waylaying you.'

Molly was tired. Lexie could see it in the droop of her shoulders and hear it in her voice.

'I need to talk, Moll,' she pleaded.

She thought Molly was going to put her off because she closed her eyes briefly and rubbed a hand across her forehead.

'I know you're shattered. So am I. But I need to talk. Please. I won't stay long.'

Molly twisted the heavy iron ring set in the old oak door and the latch grated upwards. She said, 'OK. But I must eat.'

'I've eaten. And I don't need a drink.'

Molly managed a smile at this. 'Still topped up to the brim from last night? Me too.'

Lexie was about to deny it – it was exhaustion that was warning her away from alcohol, nothing else – but she hadn't the energy to waste words.

'It's about Cameron,' she said, as they were still winding their way up the dark staircase.

'No, really? You do surprise me,' Molly said, opening the door to her flat and flicking on a light. 'Come in, you silly thing, and give me a minute while I change.'

She flung her black tailored jacket onto a chair and kicked off her heels.

'Make yourself a cuppa if you want.'

'Can I get you some food?'

'Not sure what there is. I'll do something in a minute.'

She padded across the room in stockinged feet and disappeared through the door to her bedroom. The room was chilly so Lexie walked to the fireplace to switch on the electric heater. The photo she'd given Molly for her birthday sat above it on the mantelpiece. She lifted it down. There was Jamie, just as she remembered him best, being funny and a little cheeky, his handsome face alight with laughter. And Molly, before she and Adam had split up, her whole pose relaxed.

A shadow fell across the photograph and Lexie whipped round. Molly's blonde hair was damp from the shower, but the exhaustion seemed to have lifted and she looked more comfortable in jeans and a tee shirt.

'Hi. Feeling better?'

'Much better.'

Molly took the photo gently out of Lexie's hands and placed

264

it back on the mantelpiece.

'Molly – what happened with you and Adam? You've never really talked about it. I always thought you guys were solid.'

Molly turned away.

'I've got to eat something or I'll die. I can't remember whether I've had anything today or not. After last night…'

Lexie heard her open the fridge and followed her into the kitchen. All she could see was the back of Molly's head as she rummaged.

'Damn. I was sure I had some chicken something or other squirrelled away. I guess cheese toast will have to do. I'm too tired to cook even pasta.'

All friendships had boundaries and Lexie knew that Molly was warning her off the topic of Adam Blair.

'Give me that.' She reached out her hand for the cheese. 'You cut the bread and I'll slice the cheese for you.'

Molly moved the conversation into the expected groove.

'So, have you heard from Cameron Forrester today then?'

Lexie laid the slicer flat along the top of the block and pulled it smoothly towards her. A wafer-thin slice curled outwards and she peeled it away and laid it on a plate.

'He's called a few times. I haven't spoken to him.'

Molly picked up the cheese and placed it on top of the bread. Lexie carved another slice and handed it to her.

'What do you want me to say?' Molly asked.

'I don't know, Moll, that's the truth of it. I'm still stunned. I suppose it makes sense of a lot of things, but I can't believe he's done it again. That's what really hurts.'

'Do you want to dissect it all forensically, or do you want advice?' Molly slid the bread and cheese under the grill and watched it as bubbles began to form on the golden surface.

'There's too much to handle. I feel ground down by it all. I thought by giving up the exhibition last year I could really help Mum and Dad, but that doesn't seem to have worked. I thought we'd learn what the hell happened to Jamie that night, and that if we did it would help us come to terms with his death, but that hasn't happened. When Cameron came back, I thought we could start again, and look where that's got me.'

'There's your painting,' Molly pointed out, pulling the cheese toast out from under the grill and sliding it onto a plate.

What Lexie really wanted was someone to help her wallow in her misery, and she was annoyed at this observation.

'I can't paint, I'm too wound up,' she said, 'and in case you haven't remembered, there's nowhere to show my work now that Pavel's died.' Realising that this sounded as if all she cared about was her exhibition and not that Pavel was dead, she added hastily, 'I really miss him.'

Molly finished her toast and pushed the plate away. She reached for an apple.

'Have you thought about The Maker's Mark?'

'Sorry?'

'The Maker's Mark. That new gallery in Hailesbank.'

'What about it?'

'You could go in and ask them if they could show your work.'

'Don't be ridiculous, it's a craft gallery, not an art gallery. They wouldn't be interested in my stuff.'

'No need to snap at me, it was just an idea.'

'Well thanks, but can we stick to the subject, do you think?'

'Which is?'

'Cameron, of course.'

'Oh, Cameron.'

'Yes, oh Cameron. What am I going to do?'

'You mean you don't know?'

'Molly!'

'Or you do know, but you just won't admit it.'

'What do you mean?'

'I'm not going to say it, Lex, you need to say it yourself.'

'You think I should ditch him, don't you?'

Molly picked up a sharp knife and cut the apple in half, then in quarters. She scooped out the core in each piece, and bit one in half.

Lexie stood up and started to pace round the room.

'I know you're right,' she said furiously, 'but it's not that easy.'

Molly finished chewing and picked up another segment.

266

'I need to know *why*, Moll.'

'Why what?'

'Why Cameron slept with – you *know* why!'

'You've always been too curious for your own good.'

'Maybe. Maybe knowing helps healing. Like it would be good to know why Jamie drove that night, when he was so drunk.'

Molly stopped chewing. She said, 'I'm really tired.'

Lexie looked at her. 'Are *you* all right? You look grey.'

Molly stood up. 'Will you go now? Please?'

Concern overtook selfishness. 'You're not ill, are you?'

'Just exhausted.'

Molly's face was drained of all colour and her eyelids were drooping. For the first time, Lexie noticed fine lines on her face and wished she could find a way of making her talk about Adam. Bottling up bitterness wasn't healthy.

'Of course I'll go. Thanks for listening. We can talk again when you're feeling brighter.'

Nothing, Lexie thought as she pattered down the winding staircase to the garden, was simple any more.

Chapter Twenty-seven

Catalogue number 23: Man's tartan satin slippers, 18th century. Allegedly worn by Bonnie Prince Charlie during his stay in Edinburgh before his push to Derby in 1745. Donor: John Barbour, Musselburgh. Mr John Barbour, a keen collector of Stuart memorabilia, asserts that these shoes were handed down through his own family line, having originally been taken by a maid from the bedroom of Charles Edward Stuart after his departure from the Palace of Holyrood House.

The leaves were turning brown.

Lexie noticed it as she pulled on her coat and boots and headed into Hailesbank.

Patrick, returning from Dublin after an emotional reunion with his brother, noticed it.

Cora, walking home from The Maker's Mark the long way, through the Thompson Memorial Park, saw the change as the wind snatched at the branches of a large sycamore and whirled an armful of leaves skywards before letting them settle across the damp grass. She shivered and pulled her coat more tightly round herself. It was autumn. It was time to go back to Greece.

'Excuse me?'

Cora stopped and turned. A woman was staring at her. She had crimson hair and was oddly dressed, in a black and red floral mini-skirt and platform-heeled boots that had gone out with the 1970s. A beautifully-cut black velvet coat fell to mid-calf length and a thick knitted scarf in many colours was wound round and round her neck like the brass neck hoops of the Padaung tribeswomen. She had seen the woman before.

'Yes?'

The woman stepped closer and held out her hand.

'You're Cora Spyridis, aren't you? We met at your gallery opening. I'm Alexa Gordon.'

Cora shook the hand.

'Hello.'

'I'd like a quick word. Do you mind?'

Cora glanced around. There was nowhere to sit, nowhere that would be sheltered or warm, at any rate.

'Of course – but do you mind if we walk?'

They strolled together, passing the exit gate so that they could do another circuit round the park.

'It's getting jolly cold, isn't it?'

'Too cold for me.'

'How are things at the gallery? You seem to be doing really well.'

'Thanks, people seem to like it.'

'I'm an artist, by the way,' Lexie said.

'Really?' Cora grew apprehensive. She'd heard this kind of introduction many times and could guess what would follow. She tried to prepare herself.

'What do you do? What kind of work?'

She imagined either hand knitting (the scarf pointed to this), or some kind of textile design, perhaps – the outfit was a giveaway.

'I'm a painter.'

'Where did you train?'

'Edinburgh College of Art. Then I did a Masters at St Martin's in London.'

'Really? Where have you shown?'

There was a short silence, during which Cora began to feel that despite the pedigree her suspicions were well founded – the girl was not good enough. An eccentric, perhaps, with a small talent, but not a high flyer.

'I'll be honest with you,' Alexa said at last. 'I was signed for a show at Capital Art in Edinburgh, but I had to pull out at the last minute.'

'Capital Art?' Cora was shocked. 'You mean Patrick Mulgrew's gallery?'

270

'That's right. Yes. You see, my brother had an accident and died. I couldn't go ahead, it just wouldn't have felt right.'

Patrick had never told her of this. 'No of course not, I see. When was this?'

'A year ago. Just over a year.'

'I'm sorry about your brother.'

'Thanks.'

'So are you continuing with your exhibition there?'

'No. That's just it.' Lexie looked sideways at Cora, her eyes a darker brown than usual. 'I couldn't. We had a bit of a disagreement, I'm afraid, and I can't go back.'

'Disagreement? About what?'

'I don't really feel I should talk about it,' Lexie said. 'Anyway, the work I was doing then—' she hesitated, '—well, I'm not doing it any more. I'm working on something really different.' She started to get excited. 'It's about shoes.'

'Shoes?'

'Shoes tell stories, you see. It started with these baby bootees up one of the chimneys in my parents' house, then my brother's rugby boots, then – and this is where it started to really take off – a pair of ballet shoes that belonged to Pavel Skonieczna. You know – the man who used to run Cobbles Antiques, till he died recently.'

'Oh yes?'

'Yes. The local newspaper got interested – they ran a big article about him. Did you see it?'

'I know who you mean.'

'Pavel was a real sweetie. He was so encouraging. He was even converting a room at the back of his shop for me to show my paintings in. Then he died.'

'I see.'

Lexie stopped and picked up a leaf.

'Isn't it beautiful? Look at that red.'

She spread it out gently so that she could admire all the shades of russet and ruby, and the gold in its points and spines. She straightened and turned to Cora.

'I was wondering if you might think about showing my work at The Maker's Mark? I know you're really a craft gallery, but

271

I'd say this is a bit of a hybrid. I mean, there'll be shoes and boots and all sorts there, as well as the paintings. And—' she rushed on eagerly, seeing that Cora was about to speak, '—there'll be a lot of interest locally, I'm sure of it. I think you'd do very well. Make a lot of sales, I mean.'

'I don't really—'

'Don't say no. Not yet anyway. Please? Think about it. Let me come in and see you and tell you more about what I'm doing – or you could come and see me? I'm working in a cottage in the grounds of Fleming House.'

'I'm not sure—' Cora was always on the lookout for genuine new talent and there was a lot about this girl that intrigued her, but why hadn't Patrick ever talked about her? And why wouldn't she talk to Patrick?

'Listen,' she said hastily, seeing that Lexie was about to plead again, 'I will think about it, I promise. I don't know when we'd have a gap in our schedules, and I'd have to see your work and discuss it much more fully, you understand that, don't you?'

'Yes, oh yes, but thank you!'

'I haven't promised anything,' Cora warned, alarmed at Lexie's effusiveness.

'I know. I do know, honestly, but I think you'll like it. I'm sure you will.'

'Come in and see me then.'

'When? Tomorrow?'

Cora smiled. 'Tomorrow. Why not?'

Cora changed out of her work clothes and slipped into a pair of soft black trousers and a fine merino sweater, then headed across the garden to the main house.

'How was Aidan?'

'Very poorly. Will you go and see him?'

'Niamh has already persuaded me. I'm going in a couple of days. I'm glad you saw him, Patrick. Was it very difficult?'

'Not as bad as I'd expected. It's hard to wish someone dead when they're already dying. Drink?'

'Please.'

He poured two glasses of wine and offered her one.

'It's time for me to go home, Patrick.'

'Home?'

'Greece. Where I live.'

'Aren't you happy here?'

'Actually, yes, I am happy. But I need to get home. Now that I've managed to save a little, I'll manage through the winter at least. It's too cold for me here.'

'Isn't the annexe warm enough? I could get you some extra heaters.'

'It's very comfortable. But you can't step outside without being blown over, and soon it'll get worse. You know I hate it. I've done what you asked me to, haven't I?'

He flashed her a wry grin.

'Better than I expected, if you must know. You've done a great job.'

'Talking of the gallery, I met a woman in the park. She wants me to host an exhibition for her.'

'Oh?'

'Her name's Alexa Gordon. She said she was going to show at your gallery a year ago, but it didn't work out.'

'Did she say why?'

'She told me her brother died and she had to withdraw. I inferred that you'd had a disagreement over it, so that she felt she couldn't go back. She asked if I would host an exhibition for her at The Maker's Mark. Obviously she doesn't know you own The Mark too.'

'What did you say?'

'I said she should come in and see me in the morning. But I don't think it'll be right for us.'

Patrick refilled his glass and offered Cora a top-up.

'I don't know about that,' he said.

Lexie gathered together her sketch books, Charlotte's original bootees and her notes for the exhibition. She wrapped her 'Charlotte' painting in swathes of bubble wrap. It was the first painting, and the one she was most pleased with. She'd take everything with her tomorrow.

She tried to sleep, but instead spent ages considering the problem of Jonas's bombshell. She needed to know more about what had happened and as she saw it, there were three options.

One, she could talk to Cameron.

Two, she could discuss the matter with Jonas.

Or three, she could confront Carlotta.

She rejected the possibility of talking to Cameron and shied away from seeing Jonas, so it had to be Carlotta. This decided, she fell asleep.

The meeting at The Maker's Mark went well – better, in fact, than she'd expected. Cora Spyridis liked her ideas.

'I can't give you a response now,' she said as Lexie was leaving, her portfolio under her arm, 'I'll need to talk to the owner. Besides, our schedule is already made up for the next few months.'

'I understand.'

Lexie tried not to make her expression too earnest, 'but you do like the concept? The shoes? And my work?'

'Yes. I do. That story about the bride with one leg is so inspiring and the bamboo sandals from the Japanese prisoner of war camp are amazing. It's different and it's stimulating – and your paintings are exceptional. I'd buy "Charlotte" myself if I could afford it.'

'Great! You'll let me know?'

'As soon as I can,' Cora promised.

Lexie walked back to Fernhill to have a coffee with her mother. She passed The Gables on the way and had to make an effort not to turn her head to see whether Patrick was there. He wouldn't be; he'd be at work. She bit her lip in a moment of secret triumph. Wait till he heard she'd managed to get her exhibition staged at another gallery! Assuming Cora Spyridis said yes, of course.

She opened the door at Fernhill and called hello. There was a smell of cooking. Surely Carlotta hadn't been round with one of her little offerings – but she wouldn't have the gall, would she?

'Just making a shepherd's pie,' Martha called back, 'Are you staying for lunch?'

Lexie placed her painting carefully in the hall and stacked the portfolio up against it. She swung her heavy bag off her shoulder and dropped it gently to the carpet.

'Hi Mum. Smells fantastic. I could be tempted, but there's something I have to do. I'll need to make a phone call. Give me a minute?'

'Of course. By the way, there's three more boxes up in Jamie's old room. I haven't had time to open them. Why don't you go and have a look?'

'Thanks. I will.'

It felt strange being back here. It had been Jamie's room once, but it didn't really feel like that any more. There was nothing of his left in here now, not even the faint aroma of the aftershave that she used to fancy hung in the air. She opened the boxes, which contained two pairs of wedding shoes and some kiddies' first trainers. The usual. Martha could catalogue them and she'd put together a quick book as soon as she could – but if the exhibition went ahead, that would have to take precedence.

She sat on the bed. Time to call Carlotta. She dialled and waited. For a minute she thought Carlotta wouldn't pick up, and she was just about to put the phone down when she heard her voice.

'Lexie?'

Taken by surprise, she was struck dumb.

'Yes, hello, Lexie? Wrong number perhaps?'

'No, don't go. Listen, Carlotta, I'd like to meet. Okay?'

'If you want to beat me up, then no.'

'I'm not going to beat you up, I just want to talk. Where can we meet? It won't take long, honestly.'

'Jonas is ... well, he is out. Can you come round here in an hour? I have to get to the restaurant after that.'

'Fine. Thanks. See you then.'

She returned to the kitchen.

'Just coffee, Mum, thanks, though it smells delicious. The shoes are nothing special, could you do the usual, please? Catalogue and photograph? Would you mind?'

'No problem.'

'How's Dad?'

'I wish he'd stop worrying.'

'He needs to hand everything over. Neil should be running that place. He could take you away for a holiday.'

Martha sighed.

'That would be so nice. Venice appeals. Or somewhere even warmer. South Africa, maybe.'

'A safari?'

'I've always wanted to go on a safari,' Martha said, her voice regretful.

'It's not too late. Talk to him.'

'Oh darling, it's no use talking to your father. He's so determined to be strong for us, and to carry on the business even if there's no Jamie left to inherit it now.'

'I wish he could let go. Of everything. His grief, the business. This house, even.'

'Fernhill? You want us to sell Fernhill? I never thought I'd hear you say that.'

'Maybe it's time. *Things* aren't what's important in life, Mum. If I've learned anything over the past year, it's that.'

Chapter Twenty-eight

Catalogue number 5: Ballet shoes, pale pink silk. Used in the December performance of George Balanchine's The Nutcracker in New York, in 1960. Donor: Jessica Kowalski, New York. Jessica, a ballerina with the New York Ballet, heard of this project through a relative in Hailesbank and kindly sent these shoes. 'Ballet shoes, almost more than any other shoes, tell of great beauty and great suffering,' she writes.

Carlotta lived in one of the newish houses on an estate to the south of Hailesbank. It was modest and a little boxy, with a neat square of grass in the front and a slightly bigger patch at the back, surrounded by flowerbeds. She had furnished the place in her own style – Lexie imagined Jonas willingly ceding to her taste. The floors throughout living room, kitchen, hall and cloakroom were tiled and adorned with Spanish rugs. The walls were painted in warm terracotta, muted kingfisher and cream, and elaborate ceramic tiles and photographs framed in dark oak decorated the walls.

Carlotta opened the door. 'Hello. Come in.'

She stood back to let Lexie enter and the two women eyed each other warily.

'No *boquerones* this week, then?' Lexie said.

Carlotta flushed. 'I have been busy. It is a rather strange week.'

'No kidding.'

'Listen, Lexie, I don't know what you think I can—'

'It's all right. I'm not going to kill you. I'd just like a few answers.'

They went into the sitting room.

277

'Would you care to tell me what happened?'

Carlotta winced. She sank onto a sofa. Her thick hair looked unbrushed and she was wearing leggings and a tee shirt instead of her usual glamorous clothing. She looked so tired that Lexie almost felt sorry for her.

'The shoes aren't important. Jonas, he just grabbed them, he tells me, because he knew you were going to be at the party and he wanted to "tell a story", as he puts it. I did have an affair with Cameron, Lexie, it's true. I'm sorry. I did try to warn you, remember? He is very sexy, that man, but not good as a partner.'

'Six years ago – I can understand. We were an item, but not committed to each other. But *now*? For heaven's sake, Carlotta, why? Why do that to Jonas? Why do it to me, come to that?'

'It was for "one last time", Lexie, I swear. He was going to ask you to marry him.'

'But only after shagging you.'

'I tried to say no, honestly, but—'

'Don't tell me he raped you.'

'No. No, not that. I just – you know how he is. I did try to warn you.'

She shrugged and spread her hands wide.

'Anyway, he managed to leave his wallet here. I think it fell out of his pocket, you know, onto the floor. Jonas found it and, well, he put the two and the two together and made a big story.'

'Has Jonas left you?'

Carlotta was startled. Her face crumpled.

'He needs some time apart, he says. Oh Lexie, Lexie, I have made such a big, big mistake.'

Lexie frowned. She had remembered something.

'Just a minute. He said, "Carlotta slept with half the town." Those were his words, weren't they? Did you? Did you Carlotta?'

She remembered the Valentine's card she'd found on the bookshelf in Jamie's room, with its cryptic upside-down squiggle and suddenly remembered that it was how the Spanish wrote their question marks.

'You slept with Jamie too, didn't you? You had an affair

with my brother! My God!' she clapped her hands to her mouth at a sudden realisation, 'that's why you've been bringing all those little dishes of food to Mum and Dad all year! It's blood money, isn't it? You feel guilty!'

'No, Lexie, stop, I—'

'It was you he was going to see that night, wasn't it? He'd drunk too much and you phoned him, maybe you found a convenient little slot when Jonas was away somewhere, and you phoned him. Didn't you?'

She was almost shouting now, her promise to be calm forgotten.

'It was you!'

Carlotta leapt to her feet and backed away. 'No! No, Lexie, you are wrong. It's not true what Jonas said. I did not sleep with half the town, only with Cameron.'

Lexie was breathing hard. She only half heard Carlotta's words because the hammering inside her head was scrambling all sense and logic.

Carlotta said it again. 'I – did – not – have – an – affair – with – Jamie.'

Lexie searched Carlotta's face for signs of falsehood, but she saw none. Yet Jamie had been happier in the months before his death than she'd ever seen him, no longer randomly flirtatious, no longer appearing with a string of adoring blondes. He'd been having an affair – something he could not admit to in public. He must have been.

'But someone did,' she said. 'That's what happened. I'm sure of it. Someone was having an affair with my brother.'

The visit to Edith Lawrence was long overdue and it provided Lexie with a welcome distraction.

'Hello dear,' Edith said with a broad smile. No-one had helped her with her teeth this morning, so her smile was all gums.

'Hello Edith.' Lexie sat on a sofa beside the old woman and took her hand. 'Remember me?'

'How are the children?'

'The children?'

'Would you like some tea? Hello dear—' she caught at the skirt of a passing carer, '—we'd like tea, please, in china cups.'

Ingrained etiquette served as a cover for blankness and Lexie registered Edith's confusion with disappointment. She was eager to tell Edith about her work on Charlotte's bootees.

'How are you, Edith? Are you well? Did you have a nice lunch?'

'Lunch?'

The hour just gone could not be retrieved. Lexie decided to venture further into the past.

'Tell me about the conservatory at Fernhill.'

Edith's face lit up.

'It was very grand. It had a high, high ceiling held up by wrought iron girders and there was a vine growing up one side. It curled all the way to the roof and half over the top.'

Her frail hands rippled upwards and outwards.

'A vine? Did you make wine?'

'Oh no.' Edith pursed her mouth in a prim gesture. 'Father would never have allowed that.'

They talked of Fernhill some more, and of Edith's large family. What had happened to her brothers and sisters? Lexie assumed they have all died or were in care. Edith, true to form, didn't seem upset by this – she lived either in the present or the distant past, and both were happy places.

She risked mentioning Charlotte.

'Remember coming to Fernhill, Edith? Remember what we found?'

Edith looked baffled. Lexie opened her bag and pulled out the stiff envelope into which she had placed a photograph of her painting, 'Charlotte'.

'Here. Look at this. It's the painting I did. Remember you said it would be all right?'

Edith squinted at the photograph, gave a polite smile, muttered, 'Very nice,' and handed it back.

Lexie tried again.

'Remember how you walked to Fernhill and climbed through the window? Then you came back and we found the box with Charlotte's bootees up the chimney?'

At once Edith's face lit up and she beamed.

'There was that lovely boy there, wasn't there? So handsome, dear. He reminded me of my Albert.'

Lexie tried to hide the hurt. Edith had remembered Cameron, but forgotten her.

Bloody, bloody Cameron Forrester.

Lexie parked Tom's car at Fernhill and picked up her bike. It was a cold day, but crisp and clear, and in the few miles between Hailesbank and Fleming House she recovered her equilibrium. Cameron had left twenty-three messages on her mobile and she hadn't listened to any of them. She couldn't even be bothered to check how many texts there were, she just deleted them unread. She didn't know how she'd react if Cameron appeared on her doorstep, but she was cross because he hadn't.

At the back of Fleming House, the door to Molly's apartment was ajar. Lexie propped the bike up against the wall and unwound her bag from her shoulders.

'Hi!' she called, as she started to run up the spiral stairs. 'It's me!'

Molly opened the door. 'Hi.'

Lexie was puzzled by the lack of welcome. 'Are you going to let me in then?'

'If you want to chew over the bloody red stilettos again, I'm not sure I have the energy.'

'I've been to see Carlotta.'

'Oh. Oh God, I suppose you'd better come in.'

'What the hell's eating you these days?'

'Just bushed. I seem to work all the hours. I need to get an assistant, but Her Ladyship's cracking down on costs.'

'She's going to regret it if you fall to bits. What will she do if you go off sick? There was a girl at the art college who went on to do graphic design for a big agency. She got so stressed that she came down with shingles and was off sick for a month.'

'Yes, well,' Molly was crotchety. 'I don't think it'll come to that.'

'What are you doing here, anyway?' Lexie looked at her

watch. 'It's only four.'

'There's nothing on tonight and she told me to go get some rest. See?' She smiled briefly at Lexie. 'She does care about my health.'

'Oh sorry, Moll. Were you lying down?' Lexie was stricken. 'And I'm interrupting.'

'You're all right. What was it, anyway? How did it go with the woman at The Maker's Mark?'

'Brilliant. She promised she'll let me know in a few days, but she loved the idea, and she adored "Charlotte".'

'That's good.'

'I'm not counting chickens. Well, I am, actually. Anyway, like I said, I went to see Carlotta.' She glanced at Molly. 'Sorry, Moll, I won't bore you, I promise I won't, but I really needed to know what was going on so that I can deal with it.'

'And knowing what happened would help?'

'Yes. Like it would with Jamie. Actually,' Lexie unfastened her bag and started to rummage around, 'it helped a lot more than I expected, because now I know why Jamie was driving that night.'

'You do?' Molly sounded startled.

'When Jonas said that Carlotta had slept with half the town, I thought, that's it! She must have been having an affair with Jamie! Look,' she pulled out an envelope, 'I found this in Jamie's room, tucked into a book. It's a Valentine's card.' She pulled the card out of the envelope and turned it towards Molly. 'See the squiggle? It's how the Spanish write their question marks. I reckoned it must have been from Carlotta.'

Molly went white. She clutched at the edge of the table, sank her head onto her forearms and started to moan.

'What's wrong? What is it?' Lexie dropped the card onto the table and curled a sympathetic arm round her, but Molly lashed out sideways with such force that Lexie toppled over and lay sprawled on the floor.

'Ow!' She sat up, rubbing her elbow where it had hit one of the chair legs.

'Oh God!' Molly lifted her face at the sound of the crash. She pulled a handkerchief from the pocket of her jeans and blew her nose noisily. 'Sorry! I didn't mean to…'

Lexie scrambled to her feet, bewildered. 'What's going on?'

Molly wiped her eyes and took a series of deep breaths. She reached across the table to where Lexie had dropped the card and envelope, her hands trembling noticeably. She turned the envelope over and stared at it.

'I suppose you had to know sometime.'

'Know? Know what?'

Molly handed her the envelope. Focused on the contents, Lexie had never thought to examine the outside. She looked at the address: Mr Jamie Gordon, Fernhill, Hailesbank, East Lothian.

The handwriting was Molly's.

'I don't understand. What about the Spanish question mark?'

Molly buried her face in her hands.

'The question mark was a joke.'

The words were muffled.

'Carlotta made a play for Jamie one night and he had to fend her off. She didn't know about us, you see.'

She glared at Lexie as if to defy judgement, and said more steadily, 'We were in love. We loved each other. How else can I put it? We found such joy with each other, such simple, unadulterated passion. Silly word. Unadulterated. Of course I was committing adultery.'

She smiled wanly.

'I'd never have started seeing him if things hadn't become so difficult with Adam. He changed. I don't know where the man I fell in love with went to. Jamie offered me everything I wanted but was no longer getting from Adam.'

Lexie whispered, 'Oh my God.'

'It's a relief to tell you, because no-one ever knew. Adam didn't know. At least, in the end he guessed I was having an affair, he just didn't know who with.'

'Christ.'

'I was going to leave Adam. Jamie and I had it all planned. We'd buy a little house in Hailesbank so that he could carry on at Gordon's, and I'd commute into Edinburgh every day. We needed to find the right time to tell people. I wanted to make it as easy as possible for Adam, so that it didn't affect his work, so that we could sort out the house, all those stupid, practical things. I didn't hate Adam. I never hated him and I didn't want to hurt him. It was just that we'd grown apart.'

'What happened, Moll? What happened that night? Why did everything change?'

Molly sniffed, but found enough self-control to carry on.

'I think Adam had become suspicious that I was seeing someone else. Jamie and I tried to be so careful, but something had alerted him, I don't know what. It wasn't a receipt or a note in my diary or anything tangible, maybe it was just some small change in my behaviour, like dressing with more care or getting my hair done more. That night, he confronted me. I was so shocked I guess I didn't do a good enough job of denying it. Adam was incandescent. I thought he was going to hit me.'

'*Adam?* Adam was going to hit you?'

'You wouldn't ever have imagined it, would you?'

Again the wry smile.

'Quiet, civilised Adam, pillar of the Edinburgh legal establishment. But he just lost it, he became a different person completely. I was scared. Then his phone rang and he saw it was some urgent call from his office he'd been waiting for and he stopped to take it. I grabbed my bag and ran for the door. He was torn between carrying on with the call and abandoning it to stop me escaping. Business won.'

She grimaced.

'Business always wins with Adam.'

'You got out?'

'I dashed out the door and called Jamie. We were so careful, I never used his main mobile, he'd got another one just for me to call, and I used another phone so Adam wouldn't accidentally find any record of calls or texts to Jamie.'

She started to shake uncontrollably.

'I'd never have phoned him, Lexie, if I'd had the slightest idea of how he'd react. I didn't know he'd had too much to drink. I was frightened – and I felt guilty, because I knew I'd wronged Adam, everything had moved on in way I never intended it to. Suddenly I was in a situation I didn't know how to control and I was in a mess. I'd got my bag, with the spare phone in a zipped pocket buried under a load of tampons, but my car keys weren't in it, so I couldn't just drive off. I was frightened that Adam would come rushing out at any minute and run after me and I needed time and space to think about what to do. Jamie was brilliant. He just said, "I'm coming. I'm coming. You're not to worry. I'll be there in twenty minutes. I'm going to look after you."'

The shaking had become a violent shivering. Lexie's mouth was dry, she could barely swallow. She wanted to stuff her fingers in her ears, but Jamie's voice started whispering inside her skull.

Hear her out.

'But he never came.'

Lexie imagined Molly cowering somewhere in the street, hiding from Adam and waiting for a lover who never came. Perhaps dialling his special mobile again and again, growing more and more desperate as the hours went on. Not knowing until Lexie phoned her early the next morning, distraught by the news of Jamie's accident.

Lexie tried to recall how Molly had reacted that awful morning, but she couldn't remember. She'd been too distraught herself, too bound up in the news that Jamie was in a coma to think about others. Aghast, she said, 'Oh my God, Molly. How awful. How truly, truly awful.'

'I'm so, so sorry. If it hadn't been for me, Jamie would still be alive. If I hadn't called him—'

Lexie said, 'You've lived with this for a whole year and you've never said a word?'

'I'm *so* sorry.'

The confession became a wail.

'You can't imagine how guilty I feel. I watched you all suffering, I watched Jamie *die*, for God's sake, and I couldn't say anything. I couldn't let your last memory of Jamie be the knowledge that he'd been scheming and lying and plotting to break up my marriage.'

'But that's not what it was like. Was it?'

'No! But what would you have thought if I'd barged in while

he was lying there and moved the focus onto myself? While he couldn't even tell you about how he felt? I couldn't do it, Lexie, don't you see? I just couldn't do it.'

'So you had to suffer alone. Oh Molly!'

There was a long silence. Outside a car drove onto the gravel and there were voices – the gardeners, perhaps. A bird called to another with a song that was achingly sweet. Overhead, the distant growl of an aeroplane passed into the ether.

'I can't ever forgive myself, Lex. I don't expect you to forgive me.'

'Forgive you?' Lexie was astonished. 'You silly cow, don't you see? It's a relief.'

'A relief?'

'Now I know what happened, it's not just some awful, endless mystery. And I know that Jamie had found real happiness with you. I'd guessed, in a way, that he must have fallen in love, because he was so relaxed in those last months. I just wish you'd both been able to tell us earlier.'

'Do you think I haven't thought that a hundred times? The "if only" game is endless.'

Lexie reached out and laid her hand over Molly's.

'It's okay, Moll. We can't change what happened, but it's going to get better now, for all of us. I promise.'

She couldn't hear Jamie's voice in her head, but there was a caress on her cheek, so faint that it was barely there.

Jamie's farewell.

Chapter Twenty-nine

Catalogue number 34: leather shoes, notable not for the shoe itself, but for the repair. Donor: James Andrews, Guildford. 'Spare a thought in your work for the craftsmanship of the shoemaker and shoe repairer. My grandfather submitted this pair of shoes for a Gold Medal competition for shoe repairs in 1934. You can see how exquisite his work is. The winner, however, topped him with an ornamental repair involving an astonishing 38,947 brass nails!'

The effects of Molly's confession were immediate – it was as if someone had eased the tight lacing on a corset that had prevented breathing almost completely, and then let out the laces a fraction more, so that a small gasp was feasible. In time, with more laces loosened, it might be possible to breathe normally.

Lexie and Molly went together to tell Tom and Martha and, although it was difficult, they were not nearly as judgemental as Molly had feared. Tom merely nodded, but he took her hand.

'We'd have welcomed you, lass,' he said, 'If Jamie loved you, that'd have been good enough for us.'

Molly could barely hold back her tears at his generosity.

Martha, in tears herself, hugged Molly tightly.

'You should have told us, Molly. You should have told us.'

Lexie said, 'She couldn't Mum, not then. And later – it was too late.'

'I know.'

Martha released Molly and cupped the girl's damp face in her hands.

'I respect your sensitivity, Molly, just as I respect your

honesty now.'

The next night Lexie was lying in her bed at the cottage, unable to sleep. She remembered the painting she'd been working on when Jamie's accident had happened. It was still standing in the garden room, its face to the wall.

She climbed out of bed and pulled on a sweater. It was October now and the nights were cold. When she flicked the switch the light was reflected in thirty panes of glass, bright and unforgiving. There would be no hiding from the truth here.

She pulled at the corner of the huge canvas and dragged it into the middle of the room. It wasn't easy to turn it, but eventually she managed. She propped it against the sofa and stood back.

Face the truth. It wasn't Jamie's voice she heard, Jamie's voice had faded, as if he has found peace at last. It was her own. *Face the truth – because otherwise how can you move forward?*

She examined the painting again.

The sense of desolation was overwhelming. It was certainly evocative (as it was meant to be) but the disgust Lexie had begun to feel after Jamie's accident roared back towards her. It was so, so wrong.

At last she understood why she'd felt compelled to withdraw from the exhibition. It had been more than the dishonesty of the work – it had been an irrational but overpowering feeling that somehow the fraudulence and the darkness of her subject matter had combined to *cause* Jamie's death. She had foreshadowed the accident in some way that had actually made it happen.

Lexie spread her hands and laughed.

How ridiculous. How *stupid.*

She hadn't caused Jamie's death. Someone else had started a trail of actions that had led to that, it hadn't been her at all.

She kicked at the canvas, once, twice. A dent appeared, then a tear. She ripped at it with her hands, overtaken by frenzy. When it was well beyond repair, she smiled at the wreckage with satisfaction. There. Another barrier had been removed. Perhaps tomorrow she would paint.

But it wasn't that simple. Lexie slept soundly but not for nearly long enough, and when she woke she knew she had to move aside another stone in the bumpy road she was travelling.

It was still only six thirty. If she reached Cameron's cottage on the farm early enough, she'd be sure to catch him. She had to exorcise the ghost of their relationship.

She shoved Carlotta's red stilettos into her bag and mounted her bike.

It was three miles to Cameron's uncle's farm, but the road was a pretty one. As she cycled, the dawn was breaking. A watery sun began to appear above the treetops so that leaves and branches were shown in spiky silhouette against its light. Birds flitted in and out of the hedgerows and the countryside asserted its right to live again as it emerged from its night time shroud. In the distance, Lexie heard a tractor fire up its engine and prayed that it wasn't Cameron, off to work already.

She raced down a steep hill, the wind ruffling her short hair. On either side of her, the hedges of a mile back had become drystone walls. It wasn't far now. She rounded a sharp bend in the road and saw the sign, 'Threipstone Farm', a hundred yards further along. The tractor was emerging. She peered up at the cab, but it wasn't Cameron, it was a man she didn't recognise. She acknowledged him with a wave, waited until he had turned into the road, and swung her bicycle onto the rough track up to the farm.

She'd only been here once, when she'd helped Cameron move some of his belongings, but she knew it was the third cottage in the block. She leaned her bike against a whitewashed wall and padded across the rough cobbles. There was an old Belfast sink under the window. Someone, at some time, had filled it with earth and planted it with something pretty, but now it had become overgrown and filled with weeds. Lexie couldn't imagine Cameron tending it. She looked at it with pity, but there was nothing she could do to alleviate its suffering.

Six fifty. The sun had inched higher, but a low mist hung over the valley, lending the whole countryside an ethereal air.

She was worried about disturbing the workers who lived in the cottages on either side, but there was no other way of doing this. She lifted her hand and knocked.

No response.

She knocked again.

Just as she was raising her hand for the third time, there was a muttering and a clanking. A key turned and the door jerked open.

'What? I did my extra hours yester— Oh. It's you.'

Cameron was standing there bare-chested, faded navy jogger bottoms sliding from his waist across the muscles of his abdomen down onto the bones of his hips. Lexie caught her breath at the sight, but there was no way she was to be distracted. She pulled the red shoes out of her bag and held them aloft.

'Tell me,' she said, 'about these.'

He glanced quickly back over his shoulder, then stepped outside, pulling the door behind him so that it was barely open. His arms were covered in tiny goose bumps.

'You could put some clothes on.'

'I'm fine.'

He grabbed at her arm and hissed, 'Lexie, what the fuck are you doing here? Didn't you get my messages? You never replied. I texted you loads of times, for Christ's sake.'

'No need to swear,' Lexie said. 'I didn't look at your texts. I wasn't going to bother with any of your excuses, to be honest, but then I thought, why not hear what the bastard's got to say for himself? So how about it, Cameron? How about telling me exactly what happened with Carlotta Wood and what it was you got from her that you didn't get from me?'

'Shh.' Cameron looked around apprehensively. 'Someone'll hear you.'

'You could ask me in.'

'Nah, we're all right here. Just keep your voice down, will you?'

Lexie glared at him, and waited.

'It wasn't my fault,' Cameron said. 'That's what I was trying to tell you, babes, if you'd only listened.'

His voice was placatory, almost wheedling.

'Not your fault. She seduced you, I suppose, and you could do nothing about it.'

'That's it, more or less, yeah. Well, it was two things, to begin with. You were so busy with your painting that you'd never come out with me anywhere. Remember? Back when you were in that studio at that farm. It got really boring, going to bloody parties on my own. I tried, babes. How many times did I plead with you to come with me to the pub, huh?'

'So it's my fault.'

'No – well not entirely. Like I told you, I wasn't very mature back then. So when you were busy all the time and Carlotta began to show an interest – well, what was I to do? You must admit she's one sexy —'

'So it's Carlotta's fault?'

'Yeah. That's it!' He shook his head in sorrow. 'She never could keep her hands to herself, that one. Jonas has got a tiger by the tail.'

'Right.'

Lexie found she was clutching the shoes so tightly that her hand was getting sore.

'So – let me get this straight. I was busy and boring and Carlotta was coming on to you so strongly that you were completely helpless.'

'You make it sound…'

'So what made you go away? What *really* made you go away, Cameron?'

He shrugged. 'I felt trapped between the pair of you, to be honest. I really cared for you, babes, but you were always busy, nose into acrylics…'

'Oils.'

'Oils, then. Whatever. And Carlotta was all over me like a rash and wanting me to "commit". I just couldn't hack it, so I thought the best thing to do was just to go.'

Whatever Lexie had imagined, it wasn't this. Not a quick fling, but a real ding-dong affair. She swallowed and pressed on.

'So what made you decide to come back?'

'Well, you know. Carlotta got married to Jonas and I heard you were still single, so I thought I'd try my luck.'

'Very romantic.'

'I care about you babes. Honest. Plus I was carved to bits when I heard about Jamie, you know? I loved that guy.'

'It took you a year to come back.'

'I couldn't get away from the ship. Two-year contract. Anyway, we were in the Caribbean and it would've cost a fortune to get back under my own steam.'

Lexie crossed her arms. The shoes dangled from one hand and dug into her side, but she was barely aware of this.

'So you decided you'd have another crack at me. Why, exactly? Did you think I might still be so completely under your spell that I'd simply lie down and open my legs for you?'

She regretted this observation as soon as she'd uttered it, because it was painfully close to what had happened.

Cameron grinned. 'Hey, beautiful, I –'

'Stop. Don't you dare! Don't you dare say anything. Except,' she added quickly, 'to explain why you went round to Carlotta on your birthday? Why you fucked her when you were just about to ask me to marry you?'

'Yeah, well. Big mistake. It was supposed to be, like, a birthday pressie, you know? Thirtieth special? Jonas wasn't getting back till later and you were busy putting up the'

'—decorations for *your* bloody party!'

'So I reckoned we'd get a quickie in. Last time before I settled down and all that. That's all it was, honest to God, I swear it.'

'You are unbelievable. I don't believe I've ever met a man with such an appalling moral compass.'

He spread his hands.

'Got it off my chest now, babes. Learned my lesson. Honest.'

'Cameron? What's going on?'

Cameron whirled round as Lexie stared at the cottage. Standing in the doorway, clad only in an old check shirt of Cameron's, was Julie, the girl from the Job Centre.

'I can explain, babes,' Cameron said quickly, 'it's not what you think.'

Lexie's anger exploded.

'Not what I think? You bastard, Cameron Forrester. You

utter, utter bastard!'

Her arms unfolded and became windmills, flailing round and round, the stilettos whirling in a scarlet streak as the sharp heels struck his bare skin again and again. He cowered away from her and put his arms up to shield his head and face as she battered at him unrelentingly.

In the doorway, Julie screeched, 'It's not what you think? What else is it then, you fucking snake! Spent the whole bloody night fucking me, didn't you?'

Doors were opening, someone started clapping, and a voice called, 'Told you it couldn't last, Cam!'

Lexie stood back, panting with the exertion, and looked around. An audience had gathered – Julie, three men, a couple of women and the whole of a herd of cows that someone was ushering towards the milking parlour.

She said softly, 'Don't *babes* me, Cameron. Not ever again.'

Ignoring the applauding crowd, she tossed the shoes onto the ground, strode across to her bicycle, pushed it onto the track and started pedalling.

It was seven thirty and the sun had risen above the steeple of the old church in Hailesbank. It felt gloriously warm on her face as she turned back up the road.

Liberation takes many forms.

Chapter Thirty

Catalogue number 21: Brown low-heeled slip-ons with distinctive brass buckle. Donor: Susan Merry, Edinburgh. 'When my daughter was four, she went to a ballet class on Saturday mornings. The corridor outside was a real bottleneck and she used to panic if she couldn't find me afterwards. One day she said, "Mummy, please will you always wear those shoes with the buckle so that I know you're there?" It's much easier for little children to look at ground level than five feet in the air!'

'What did you think of Alexa Gordon's work?' Patrick asked casually as a waiter poured perfectly chilled Pouilly-Fuissé into two glasses. He lifted his glass towards Cora in a toast.

She chinked his glass gently.

'Cheers. Nice place, by the way.'

They were in a small restaurant in Thistle Street in Edinburgh. The room had an air of luxury, with deep gold carpets, crisp white tablecloths and soft lighting.

'I like it,' Patrick said, in a voice that showed that his mind was more on other things than his surroundings, 'and it's handy for the gallery.'

'Ah yes, the gallery.' Cora sipped her wine appreciatively. She'd miss Patrick's generosity when she went back to Greece.

'You haven't answered my question.'

'About Alexa Gordon? I liked her work. I liked her too, very much, as it happens. I can't imagine why you fell out with her, Patrick, I found her most accommodating. She had some brilliant ideas, very innovative and engaging. But not really right for The Maker's Mark, I don't think.'

'Really? Why not?'

'Honestly Patrick, you must know the answer to that. The Mark is a craft gallery, for makers of objects, not for fine artists. The whole point was to provide quick turnover because of the lower prices.'

'And you'd have to price Lexie's work more highly?'

'Oh much more, yes. Her painting is exquisite, first class, we're talking thousands. The gallery isn't big enough for more than a dozen or so of the oils, the rest of the show will be pastel sketches—'

'—which could be very much cheaper.'

'Yes,' Cora was doubtful, 'I suppose so. But the whole exhibition would involve a number of elements – the shoes themselves would be displayed and there'd have to be small storyboards explaining what's special about them. Some have stories that are very personal to the owner, others have some sort of historic connection that makes them interesting in their own right.'

'Such as?'

'A pair of boots that belonged to Sophia Jex Blake, for example. She was one of the first women doctors, and she trained right here, in Edinburgh. Or a pair of eighteenth-century tartan silk slippers that allegedly belonged to Bonnie Prince Charlie.'

'That's quite something.'

'Sure. But they're not saleable.'

'Point taken.' Patrick scanned the menu. 'What do you fancy? I think I'll just have the Dover Sole.'

Cora pushed her menu away from her.

'Fine. Me too.'

Patrick signalled to the waiter and ordered.

'Those shoes seem to fall into the historic category. What about the personal stories? Give me a for instance.'

'There's a left wedding shoe.'

'Just the left?'

'The bride was knocked down by a car a few months before the wedding and lost her right leg. But she was determined to walk down the aisle, and she did, on a prosthetic leg.'

'Presumably she had a shoe on the end of the prosthesis too?'

'Don't be so literal, Patrick, it's the left shoe that tells the story.'

'Just kidding. It's touching. I like it.'

'There's a pair of trainers.'

'Trainers? What's so interesting about them?'

'The guy was thrown out by his wife for being an utter slob. He started running marathons and raised a million for charity.'

'So they're some kind of symbol of rehabilitation?'

'And forgiveness, yes. The wife took him back.'

Patrick topped up their wine.

'You're getting me interested. I can't think of any other situation in which a pair of trainers would catch my attention.'

'I'm telling you Pats—'

'Patrick.'

'—Patrick, it's not the right show for The Maker's Mark. You should put it on in Capital Art.'

Cora was looking particularly lovely tonight. She had caught her thick hair up in some kind of chignon and she was wearing a silky gold dress in what Patrick believed was known as the Greek style – picturesquely draped from shoulder to waist and falling in soft folds from there. It suited her. Patrick, surveying his sister across the table in the restaurant, couldn't think why some man hadn't claimed her for his own years ago.

It seemed they hadn't done too well in the Mulgrew family. Aidan had never been happy and now he was dying. Cora flitted around the Peloponnese like some exotic bird, while he blundered round Britain enjoying (if that was the word for it) a string of relationships that never provided him with what he needed.

But what was it he needed?

Twice, in his life, he'd thought he had found it. With Niamh, the handsome, grey-eyed witch, who had held him in her thrall for more than a decade and might be doing so still if she had not decided to cast her nets wider.

And with Lexie, who was the absolute antithesis of the kind

of look he normally considered beautiful, but who had captivated him nevertheless. He remembered Lexie at the auction in London, ablaze with excitement about the vintage treasures in front of her.

'A *Chanel*,' she'd almost squeaked when she'd spotted what looked to him like a rather plain jacket.

And, 'Look!' (in an awed whisper), 'Patrick, look, it's a Balenciaga!'

It had meant nothing to him, everything to her. Her eyes had grown brighter and brighter as she'd spotted a Dior, a Mary Quant, a Fortúny. His instincts had been to buy her the lot – it was what most of the women he dated would have craved – but it had never been the right tack for proudly independent Lexie.

And then she'd spotted the Manolo Blahniks and had seemed to stop breathing. Her hands had stilled and her eyes had widened, flecks of gold in the iris glinting in a spotlight.

'I've got to bid for those, Patrick. *Look* at them.'

The estimate had been much higher than she could afford. He'd drawn breath, started to speak, stopped himself. What could he say? She wouldn't accept his help. Yet something inside him that he could not identify had been twisting and digging at his guts. He had to do something.

Cora was saying, 'Patrick? I said, you should put Alexa's show on at Capital Art.'

Patrick sat back and combed his hair with his hands. It fell softly back into place. Cora was right – but he couldn't show Lexie in Capital Art. It was impossible because she would never accept an offer from him. At the same time, he was reluctant to see her drift off to some other gallery and give them the right to make her a star.

He said, 'I can't.'

'And she's not right for me either.'

The sole arrived and they picked it apart delicately, separating skin from flesh and flesh from bone with practised ease.

Cora lifted a forkful of meltingly soft white fish to her mouth and swallowed.

'This is good.'

'Perfectly cooked.'

'Well chosen.'

'Thanks. Enjoy.'

They ate in silence, and when Cora had finished, Patrick laid down his knife and fork and surprised himself by saying, 'I want to show Lexie in The Maker's Mark.'

'That sounds very like an order.'

He was a fool. It made no commercial sense. He wouldn't be able to mark her work up as much as he could at Capital Art and, from what Cora had described, the gallery was too small to show the exhibition to best advantage. And Lexie would be hopping mad if she found out.

Yet it was what he wanted to do, more than anything he'd wanted to do for years – not just because he knew how brilliant she was, and certainly not because he wanted to antagonise her, but because he longed to play an intimate part in unwrapping her brilliance – even if she never knew.

Cora was exasperated.

'Show who you want to, Patrick. I'm going back to Greece.'

He shook his head.

'I'd like you to manage this show. I can't trust it to anyone else.'

She leaned towards him.

'I'm going home, Patrick.'

'Can you last through the winter on what you've earned here?'

'Just about.'

'Is "just about" good enough?'

'It's good enough in a warm climate. I've got friends I need to see. A lover, even.'

'A lover? You didn't tell me.'

'I didn't feel the need.'

He surveyed her silently, then reverted to his argument.

'I want you to show Lexie in January. Then you can go home.'

'No. Sorry. Anyway, the show in January is already booked.'

'It can be postponed.' Patrick would not admit defeat. 'Your

299

roof.'

Cora stared at him.

'It needs some major work, you said.'

'It can wait another year.'

'You can do it this year.'

'If I stay and do what you want, you mean.'

'That's about it, yes.'

She threw her serviette down on the table.

'You're an appalling man, do you know that? Self-centred, arrogant, manipulative.'

'So I'm told,' Patrick said calmly. He tossed another maggot in with the bait. 'The roof *and* the new extension you were talking about.'

Cora's eyes narrowed.

'Why does this mean so much to you?'

'She's good.'

'Show her at Capital Art then.'

'I can't. And I don't want her to know I'm the owner of The Maker's Mark either.'

'My God, you're in love with her!'

Patrick averted his eyes. He watched a waiter who was deep in conversation with a couple at a nearby table. He clicked his fingers as the man straightened up.

'I'd like the menu.'

He didn't want dessert. He never ate dessert.

'What did you argue about, Patrick? Why did she pull out of her show last year?'

'She wouldn't finish the last painting.'

'She was contracted, presumably.'

'And how would I have looked forcing her to stick to her contract when her brother was dying? How would that have affected Capital Art's reputation?'

'These are the things that are important to you? How you look? Your reputation?'

'A gallery is nothing without its reputation, Cora.'

'You let her off, then. But I bet you were angry.'

'Wouldn't you be?'

'I like to think I would be understanding, in the

300

circumstances.'

This pricked Patrick's defiance.

Cora sat back.

'I've never seen you like this. You really care about this girl, don't you? If this means so much to you, why don't you just talk to her? It'd make things a whole lot simpler.'

'I mean to.' He remembered his promise to Domenica, and the determination he'd felt when he returned from America. 'In my own time.'

'Well, I won't do your exhibition. I am not to be bribed or bullied.'

Patrick was at a loss. He didn't know how to persuade her to do what he wanted because he'd never been in this situation. He had always bought what he needed, by paying higher wages, or by outbidding his competitors, or he had achieved his ends by deploying his charm.

He looked at Cora and said, 'Please.'

Cora's astonishment showed.

'Oh my God. He must be desperate. This is the first time he's said please in forty years.'

'I'm asking you, Cora.' He bit his lip again. 'No – I'm begging you. Stay and help me with this one.'

She shook her head slowly and Patrick thought she was about to refuse.

'Maybe. On one condition.'

There was a gleam of hope. 'Which is?'

'Fly me back to Greece for Christmas.'

Patrick groaned. 'Don't tell me. There's a gift-wrapped shag waiting for you there.'

The couple at the next table looked over, grinning.

'Something like that. Deal?'

'Deal.'

Chapter Thirty-one

Catalogue number 22: Dunlop 'Green Flash' plimsolls, white canvas with herringbone pattern rubber soles. Donor David Devlin, Forgie. 'We all remember those cheap and cheerful gym shoes. But they only became "cool" when Fred Perry wore a souped-up pair, the more stylish Green Flash trainers, when he won Wimbledon on three occasions. I had to beg my mother to buy these, rather than a cheapo pair from Woollies.'

Once, Patrick had appeared at this cottage and held her in his arms. He'd come to tell her of Pavel's death. It had been early morning and she'd barely been awake.

Lexie was sure this had happened, she could remember the feeling of safety she'd experienced as he'd cradled her, yet when she tried to fill in the detail, it vanished.

She was standing by the French windows that opened onto the walled garden. Today there was nothing to be seen of the rough grassy space that could never be called a lawn, nor of the thistles and campion that normally colonised the far borders, because everything was under a thick blanket of snow.

She was cradling a mug of coffee. She lifted it to her mouth and took a sip. The sun had just risen above the trees and was hitting the pristine whiteness of the snow so that it shimmered. She wished for a moment that she might capture the haunting loveliness of this view, but others did that kind of thing much better than she ever could.

She had seen Patrick a few times since that day. Once at Besalú (but with a couple of men, not with a woman) and once in the cheesemonger's in the High Street.

'My housekeeper's on holiday,' he'd told her by way of

explanation, his conversation polite but friendly, just like any normal acquaintance, so neutral that she could not imagine there had been any kind of intimate past between them.

In the weeks since the showdown with Cameron, Lexie had spent a considerable amount of time on her own, but not unhappily. Things had begun to settle. A new bond of intimacy had restored the old friendship with Molly – Jamie tethered them with a thread that could never be broken. The old anger at the injustice of his early death had passed into sad acceptance.

As for her relationship with Cameron, she missed it only because she missed the thrill of making love to him. His body, she thought from time to time with pangs of real regret, seemed uniquely fashioned to fit with hers. But she'd mistaken carnality for love, with horrible consequences.

She saw her parents. Martha still came with shoes and lists and love. Molly scurried over with food. Occasionally, she ventured into Hailesbank to meet with Cora Spyridis. There was a considerable amount to do in terms of planning. Still, much could be done via email and a regular stream of correspondence passed between them.

There were only two rooms in The Maker's Mark, and neither was particularly big.

< "Charlotte" has to go on the wall opposite the door, > Cora emailed. < It's the key to everything. >
< Agreed. What about the other two main oils? >
< "Pavel" opposite the door in the back room, "Jamie" on the side where you enter? >
< Why? Why not "Jamie" in the best place. More impact. >
< You'd think so, wouldn't you? But honestly, the lighting is better on the other side, everything works to focus the eyes on the main painting there. >

And so they batted ideas backwards and forwards, to and fro. It was a tricky exhibition to plan because there were so many elements: labels describing the stories, pastel drawings, the shoes themselves and, of course, the paintings. These had to form the centrepiece of the show, so it went without saying that they had to be strategically displayed. And although some of the shoes would be displayed on plinths, Lexie wanted others to give the impression of a journey, of marching, or climbing or dancing, or whatever told their story best.

< I want the paintings to be surrounded by shoes, > emailed Lexie. < They'll have to be propped on thin nails hammered into the wall so that they are invisible. > wall. Anyway, the paintings are what we're here to sell, so they must be shown to best possible advantage, and that means on a clean wall with no distracting clutter. >
< It's all one thing. You can't separate the paintings from the shoes, or the drawings, or the stories. >

They devised an arrangement of plinths of different heights that would draw the eye in from the main door to where "Charlotte" was going to hang. Each plinth would have a pair of shoes on the top, with its own pastel sketch mounted on board and secured to the stand behind. A neat label explaining each story would be fixed to one side.
< I like the idea they'll have to work a bit to find everything out, > Lexie emailed, < and that they'll get a first impression without being told too much about it. It'll be fun to see how different their impression is from the story. >
< True. Those trainers, for example... ;-) >

In the second room, the one where there was usually a coffee counter, Lexie wheedled and cajoled and worked everything out technically so that in the end she got her way. One whole wall would comprise an ascending trail of shoes, from a pair of Edwardian riding boots at the bottom, following a pair of World War I flying boots and a miner's shoe salvaged from a pit disaster in West Lothian in 1889. Onwards and upwards they wound, like so many shoes ascending a mountain path, slanting from bottom right to three feet up the wall at the far left, then turning and following the next shoes upward to the right, four times in all until the pathway of shoes reached the ceiling.

It was a miracle of design. Lexie understood perspective

perfectly, and as the shoes went higher and higher, she chose smaller and smaller ones, so that they would seem to disappear to the summit.

< How can we fix them? >
< We'll make a series of small perspex shelves that can be pinned to the wall. They're not very heavy. >
< This sounds great! >
< How will we identify them?>

Lexie emailed a sketch.

< I'll work this up into a proper drawing and add numbers. We can print off twenty or thirty copies and laminate them. The notes can be on the back. People can just pick one up and use it as a key. >
< Brilliant. You are brilliant. Glad we're working on this! >

Lexie returned her mug to the kitchen, where she rinsed it and turned it upside down to drain. There was no time to waste.

Painting had absorbed her ever since Cora Spyridis had given her the news that The Maker's Mark would be delighted to host her exhibition. She had reclaimed the joy of working as one with brush and palette knife and paint, absorbed to the point of living almost entirely in a world of her own making. The cottage had become not just her home, or her studio, but also a personal universe where meaning was distilled into colour and form and brushstroke with such passion that at the end of each day she was drained of every ounce of energy.

She'd settle again in a minute. The exhibition was next week and although she had promised to do it first, she'd left Pavel's ballet shoes till last. Circumstances, after all, had changed. She wanted to spend time with Pavel. She wanted to remember his fluttering hands and his self-parodying voice, and the respect he'd had for beautiful objects with a past he'd loved to guess at.

She turned her easel to the light and stood back.

Who would ever have guessed the frail, rather stooped old man had such a glorious, colourful history? She smiled, remembering the delight with which he'd accepted the interest of the local schoolchildren and middle-aged rockers. He had adored being the centre of attention once again. The painting of his shoes had to capture this exuberance.

She lifted her brush, then stood quite still, lost in thought.

What *had* Patrick's connection with Pavel been?

Sit down, sweetheart.

Had Patrick really said that? Surely she wasn't remembering correctly? He'd been kind, nothing more.

She lifted her brush again. It was her exhibition she had to think about now. No point in thinking about Patrick.

Lexie worked on, driven by a passion that burned deep inside her. She didn't think about lunch. She didn't break for tea. Only when the light failed did she stop, defeated by conditions. There were other jobs that could still be done – the display plan to finalise and the notes to review.

It was almost midnight before she fell into bed, but even then she couldn't rest. She wanted to look at her slides again, to check the images against her notes. She took the disk out of its sleeve and pushed it into her laptop. As the computer whirred, her mouth lifted at one corner and she shook her head almost imperceptibly so that hair the scarlet of a ladybird's back glinted in the soft light of the lamp by the bed. She was becoming obsessive about everything, just as Molly had predicted.

The new work represented a shift in tone and style. She was afraid of this, but there was no ignoring it. But was her judgement reliable? After everything that had happened, was it even possible to be objective? Still, she had to try, because it was no longer a case of, How will visitors to my exhibition react to this? but, Does my work do the story justice? She believed this with a passion.

'My exhibition.' The words buzzed thrillingly in her head as she bent towards the screen. A small pulse throbbed in the creamy flesh of her neck, just below the sharp angle of the jaw. My exhibition. She couldn't wait for the opening. She'd invite Patrick Mulgrew, just to show him she'd done it all herself.

He'd never believe it – after all, hadn't he told her what he thought of her and her abilities?

It had to be good. More than that: it had to be perfect.

Now she was ready. Her concentration was absolute, her mind focused.

She clicked Play.

Three minutes later she let out her breath, confident that the work was everything she'd aimed for. It was creative and evocative. It was original, and it was moving.

Yet something wasn't quite right. Something was missing.

She pushed her fingers through the spiky cherry-red hair, absorbed in thought.

What was missing? What?

One o'clock already. She yawned, rubbed slender fingers across her temples, and stretched, too tired to think it through. Perhaps what she needed to do would come to her overnight. She ejected the DVD and switched off her laptop, then pushed back the duvet and crawled underneath it. Thinking exhausted her. Everything that had happened had unravelled the thread of her energy down to the last inch.

But sleep wouldn't come, and the feeling of unease would not go away.

There'd be standing room only at The Maker's Mark tonight. Cora, mindful of the first opening, where people had spilled onto the street because she'd underestimated the interest in the new gallery, had refined the guest list so that it was much more targeted to serious buyers. For that reason, she'd suggested to Alexa that she had a mini private viewing for her family and closest friends in the afternoon.

They worked all morning to get the display right. At last, surveying the wall of shoes, Cora felt satisfied.

'You were right and I was wrong,' she admitted. 'It's working really well.'

'So long as no-one jostles too near and they start tumbling off.' Lexie was getting nervous about everything.

'No problem. We can put a couple of posts on either side with silk cord stretched across to keep people clear.'

'Brilliant.' Lexie dusted her hands together and patted down her skirt. 'My folks will be here soon, I'd better freshen up.'

'Who's coming?'

'Mum and Dad, Molly, Edith Lawrence – she's being brought by a carer – and Jonas Wood. He was a really close friend of Jamie's. Oh, and I invited Hanke too. She's Pavel's sister? But I don't think she'll come.'

Cameron should have been invited because he'd been there at the beginning, when they'd found Edith's baby's bootees, but she was damned if she'd offer him a special viewing. He could come with the rest of the general public if he was interested, which he probably wouldn't be. Nor had she specifically invited Carlotta. She wasn't sure of how things stood between Jonas and Carlotta and didn't want to guess it wrongly.

'Right. I'll get the girls to make sure there's coffee and tea. They've bought in a few cakes from the bakery too.'

'I really appreciate this, Cora.'

Lexie had grown to like and respect this tall, half Greek woman. They'd forged a working relationship that had smoothed away difficulties and produced something that was both practicable and – did she dare claim it? – special.

Chapter Thirty-two

Catalogue number 27: Chelsea boots, black leather, well worn. Donor: Frank Partridge, Liverpool. 'I was a teenager in the 1960s when The Beatles started to play in The Cavern. We used to save up all our money to go and listen to them. I also saved up enough for these boots – they were incredibly trendy!'

Martha and Tom arrived first. Tom admired the display in the large room, stood for a few minutes in front of "Charlotte" then wandered into the side room. Lexie followed him nervously. It would be the first time he'd seen "Jamie".

He stood with his hands clasped behind his back and looked at "Pavel". He walked across to where the mountain path climbed up the wall, picked up the information sheet and studied it carefully. He turned it over, read the notes, looked up at the wall again, scanned the notes. Lexie's apprehension grew. Soon he'd turn round and see –

Tom turned.

The notes on the mountain path fell to the floor and she saw his hands spasm and clench. "Jamie" was a complex painting. The rugby boots were jumbled together, as if tossed carelessly down, their laces still caked with mud, signs of the last game he'd played all too evident on the leather. Behind them a complex arrangement of objects merged, ghost-like, to form a background of depth and subtlety. Jamie's face was perhaps the most easily discerned. He was laughing out of the canvas, just as he'd laughed at the camera in the photo at Tantallon.

Tantallon Castle was there – or, at least, a recognisable

portion of its ruined walls. She hadn't included Molly, but a faint pattern of peonies was a copy of the fabric of Molly's favourite dress. It was a clue that only anyone who knew her well would understand. The lion knocker on the front door at Fernhill featured. In the top corner was part of a toy train Jamie had loved when he'd been a boy.

Lexie held her breath. From the other room she could hear Jonas talking to her mother, but in here she was alone with Tom.

There was a strangled noise, a guttural, wrenching choke of a sob. She stared at her father's back, anguished.

She had made him weep.

Lexie crossed the room in two bounds and wrapped her arms round him.

'I didn't mean to upset you. I'm so sorry, Dad. It was meant to be a tribute. You know? Bring him to life in our memories. I'm so, so sorry.'

She felt her father's arm close around her and his head resting on the top of hers. He was shaking.

A moment later, she became aware that Martha had joined them.

'Good,' she said, her voice kind, but firm.

Lexie looked up. Martha was smiling, although her eyes were bright with tears.

'Very good. At last we have found your grief for your son, Tom.'

Tom's clasp loosened and Lexie straightened up.

'All these months you've controlled it, but it's better out — isn't it?'

Martha's back was very straight. How far she'd come, Lexie thought, in these past weeks, from the clingy, broken woman she'd been last year. She looked at her father. He had taken his glasses off and his cheeks were wet. Martha produced a hankie and Tom blew his nose, loudly, but he straightened up and managed a smile. He held out his hand to his wife.

'We made a good thing, didn't we?'

'Two,' Martha said, taking his hand and circling Lexie with her other arm. 'We made two good things, darling, and we still

312

have a precious one right here.'

Everyone reacted differently. Edith Lawrence arrived with a young male carer from Sea View. She was flirting with him. She peered at the shoes on the plinths and the lad read her the notes.

'Ooh, that's nice,' Lexie heard her say. And, 'Winklepickers? My Arthur used to wear winklepickers.'

Lexie crossed the gallery and took her hand.

'Hello, Edith, it's me, Lexie.'

'Hello dear.'

She led her gently towards "Charlotte". She wasn't certain that Edith remembered who she was, but she was better equipped to show her the painting than anyone.

'What do you think? Do you recognise them?'

Edith spied the bootees on the plinth before she saw the painting.

'Those are my Charlotte's baby shoes,' she said, 'I recognise that little white bit at the toe where I dropped a wee splash of bleach.'

'Yes, that's right, they're Charlotte's bootees.'

Edith swung round and looked at her accusingly.

'Where did you get these from? They're mine!'

'I know they are, Edith. You gave them to me, remember? You asked if I would paint them. And I have. Look.'

She put her arm round Edith and turned her to face the painting. Edith looked up at it. She was wearing the green terraced hat she'd been wearing the day she'd climbed in the kitchen window at Fernhill. Today it was secured by a hat pin, but the hair beneath it was so wispy that Lexie couldn't imagine how it was holding.

'What's that?'

'That's my painting of Charlotte's bootees.'

She didn't see it. Her brain couldn't connect the small knitted objects with the flat canvas. She shook her head. 'Don't know what it is.'

Lexie didn't push her. Edith swivelled back to the bootees.

'They're mine. They were my baby's.'

'I know. You said we could borrow them.'

But Edith's mind was set in a groove.

'They're mine,' she repeated, and reached out a hand and took them.

Lexie froze. The bootees were a pivotal part of the exhibition. The canvas didn't make sense without them – yet how could she take them back from Edith? They were hers, and she was so deeply emotionally attached to them that it would be wrong to take them from her. What could she do?

She looked for Cora, but she was nowhere nearby. One of the two assistants was eying her with alarm but seemed incapable of offering any suggestions. The bootees were scrunched up in Edith's claw-like hand.

'Why don't you hold them for a while, Edith?'

It was Martha's voice. Lexie turned with relief.

'Don't worry,' Martha mouthed at her over her shoulder.

The days of Martha's dependency were clearly over. If anyone was in charge of the Gordon family these days, it was her mother.

Pavel's sister was standing in the doorway, almost filling it from post to hinge. Lexie, shocked, crossed the room to welcome her.

'Hanke,' she said, extending her hand in greeting, 'how wonderful that you've come.'

'I had some loose ends to tie up anyway.'

Hanke's small black eyes swivelled from side to side as she tried to take everything in.

'Let me show you round.'

'Anywhere to dump this?'

Hanke swung a heavy bag off her shoulders and held it out.

'I'm sure there is. Hold on a moment.'

They stored the bag under the desk.

She explained the exhibition to Hanke. Nothing. No reaction. Lexie soldiered on, though she would rather have had any response – even a negative one – than this mask of indifference. When they reached "Pavel", Hanke stopped.

'That's a good one,' she said.

'That's "Pavel". That's your brother's shoes.'

'I know that. I used to mend them for him.'

314

'Really?'

Hanke turned to her.

'I don't know what he told you,' she said, 'but we weren't always at loggerheads. 'How much is it?' She leaned towards the label. 'How much? Good heavens, I can't possibly afford that.'

'I'll do you a pastel for free,' Lexie offered at once, 'like these –'

She drew Hanke away to look at the other exhibits.

As Hanke was about to leave she told Lexie, 'I've got something for you. Where's my bag?'

She rooted around in the back and brought out a large plastic box. Lexie glimpsed rolls of newspaper inside.

'For me?'

'Pavel wanted you to have them.'

Lexie opened the lid and unwrapped one of the bundles.

'The sherry glasses,' she laughed. 'He actually did leave them to me.'

'I wish we hadn't fallen out,' Hanke said a little wistfully. 'He was a good brother once.'

Jonas arrived, with Carlotta, who came over to her at once.

'He is back.'

She smiled across the gallery at her husband, who was examining a pair of sandals that had once been worn by an inmate in a Japanese prisoner of war camp.

'We have talked about everything. We are friends again.'

'I'm delighted.'

It was true – she didn't like to think of Jonas's trusting love being so horribly trampled on.

'Jonas has always wanted children and I have been so selfish. I wanted to make the restaurant successful.'

Carlotta flashed a smile that was both repentant and triumphant, or at least, that was how Lexie read it.

'I tell him, *mi cielo*, this is your time now. Besalú can look after itself.'

'So you're going to have a baby?'

'Yes, of course, a baby. A whole family of babies.'

Lexie wondered for a horrible moment if Carlotta was already pregnant. Her baby could be Cameron's! Carlotta saw her face and at once guessed her thoughts.

'You need not worry, Lexie, I am not yet pregnant.'

She gave Jonas a little wave.

'But it's wonderful fun making a baby, *si*?'

Molly was coming in as Jonas and Carlotta left. Lexie witnessed Molly's awkwardness and loved her for her loyalty.

'Christ,' Molly said in a stage whisper that bounced off the walls and returned magnified so that everyone heard, 'I didn't think she'd have the gall to come. You haven't asked Cameron, have you? Because I don't think I could be civil to him.'

'No, I haven't. And I think even Cameron will have the grace not to come, at least not while I'm here.'

Molly snorted. She looked around. She had seen some of the work at the cottage, but never all the drawings and paintings. She let out a low whistle.

'Wow, Lex, is that "Charlotte"?'

'Yes. And Edith's still here, let me find her.'

Molly hadn't seen "Jamie". Protective and apprehensive, Lexie hovered by her side as she made her way round the exhibition.

There was a touch on her elbow and her mother said, 'Alexa, Edith is leaving.'

Lexie, her head spinning, had to detach herself from Molly to watch as the carer helped Edith into the car. So many emotions, so much stress and excitement. As Edith waved a cheerful goodbye out of the car window, her heart lurched.

The bootees!

'Worried about something?' Martha asked her.

'Edith's just left and –'

'– gave me these before she went.' Martha held up the pink bootees.

'Mum! How did you –? You're a miracle worker.'

'You just need a little tact,' Martha said, replacing the bootees on their special plinth. 'Here, you can do this better than I can.'

316

'I'll get one of the girls to secure them properly so that no-one else can snatch them.'

In the small room, Molly was standing in front of 'Jamie'. Her face was ashen as she scanned every detail of the painting – the mud on the laces, Jamie's laughing face, the pretty pattern of her own favourite dress.

Tom was standing next to her. She turned to him and said something in a low voice. Tom put his arm around her shoulders and pulled her close.

Martha took Lexie's hand.

'You see,' she said softly, 'how your work has the power to heal?'

In the evening, there was barely room to move. Lexie met and greeted and talked to so many people that her jaw ached and her cheeks were sore from smiling. Everyone was full of praise and all the oil paintings were sold before the private view was over.

Patrick approached her half way through the evening and she realised that he was attractive in a way that Cameron never had been. Memories from their past flooded in – Patrick waking her before dawn to tell her they were off to London for an auction; Patrick laughing as she tried to feed him the last prawn in the tandoori; Patrick's eyes burning with desire as he bent his head to kiss her for the very first time.

I don't make a habit of screwing my new protégées, but you, Alexa Gordon, are ravishing.

'Hello, Lexie.'

'Hi.'

He wouldn't like it. Most likely he'd laugh at it. Patrick liked sophistication. Sophistication sold. *I do not care what he thinks.*

'What do you think?'

'This is the most honest thing you've done, Lexie. Its honesty connects with people's hearts.'

Was he being patronising or did he really mean it? In the hours after the opening, she returned to his words time and again. *Its honesty connects with people's hearts.* Was *he* being honest? She'd love to think so.

317

Well, whatever. At least she'd done it. She'd put on a show – a very successful show – without the assistance of the grand Patrick Mulgrew.

Chapter Thirty-three

Catalogue number 31: Ladies' two-tone golf shoes c 1936, brown leather with cream uppers and 'kiltie' flap. Donor: Marion Brown, Perth. 'My mother was at school with the famous Scottish golfer Jessie Valentine (then Jessie Anderson) and played golf with her a few times when we were young. Jessie went on to be three times British Ladies Amateur Champion, six times Scottish Ladies Amateur Champion and was selected seven times for the British Curtis Cup team. Mum went on to be a housewife! Jessie once lent Mum her old shoes because she had forgotten hers – and she "forgot" to give them back.'

Exhaustion set in, the kind of deep tiredness that dragged everything down. Lexie moved like an automaton. She had to force herself to get out of bed the next morning, but a bath revived her. In the garden room, she looked at her easel and wondered how she'd ever had the energy to finish the exhibition.

Molly bounced over from her apartment.

'Must fly, Lexie, sorry! Did you see all the comments in the book?'

Lexie shook her head. She hadn't dared look at the Comments book.

'All heaping praise on your little crimson head. Are you okay? You're a funny colour.'

'Just shattered.'

'It's no wonder. Yesterday must be a blur. You were there all day, doing the last bits of the set up, taking your folks round,

Edith, Hanke whatshername, me— What do you think about Jonas and Carlotta, by the way?'

'Great,' Lexie said without enthusiasm.

'You don't sound convinced.'

'Are you?'

'Hm. I think it's great Jonas is prepared to forgive her. I guess Carlotta's realised what side her bread's buttered on. I think she got a bit of a shock when Jonas left.'

'So she blooming well should. Poor man. I can't bear to think of what she's done to him. He worshipped that woman.'

'Perhaps that kind of love isn't really healthy. Maybe they'll start again in a more balanced way. It must be hard to be worshipped like that, a bit oppressive.'

Lexie started to stand.

'I'll put on coffee.'

'No, you sit there, you look bushed. I'll do it.'

As Molly filled the kettle, Lexie remembered all the *boquerones* and *empanadillas*, all the *tortillas* and *puntillitas* that Carlotta had cooked and carried all the way to Fernhill. She'd made the effort to go and talk to Martha many times over the past year, where others – closer friends – had not known how to deal with Jamie's death.

'I guess she's not all bad,' she said as Molly poured coffee.

'Aren't you having any?'

She had only laid out one mug.

'Got to go, sorry.'

'Oh.'

Lexie's face must have shown her disappointment because Molly came round the table to hug her.

'You're terrific, Lex. You just need to take it easy for a few days. Listen, I'll come back at lunch time if I can, okay?'

'Okay.'

Now that the purpose that had driven her for months had been fulfilled, Lexie felt directionless, and it was this as much as anything, she supposed, that had drained her energy.

Outside, a car stopped and a door slammed. Two doors. The thought of visitors made her realise how depleted she felt. She had no stamina for another conversation.

'Hello?'

With any other visitor she might have been able to pretend she wasn't here, but Martha used her key to open the front door so there was no hiding.

'Hi.'

'These are for you.'

She could hardly see her mother behind a vast bouquet of flowers, a fantastic arrangement of winter blooms – huge green chrysanthemums, white tulips, hypericum berries and baby's breath, tied with a green ribbon.

'Wow.'

Reinvigorated by their loveliness, Lexie got up to find something to put the flowers in. She only had one little vase and it clearly wouldn't do. She pulled aside the curtain that hung under the worktop and found an aluminium bucket.

'I think they'll have to go in here. Who are they from?'

'The flowers are from us, darling,' Martha said, finding scissors and starting to snip the stems. The scent from the lilies was heady. 'I wanted to give them to you at the gallery yesterday, but I knew it'd all be a bit hectic. We thought we'd bring them over together.'

'Together?'

Lexie glanced towards the door. Tom Gordon was standing there, smiling gently. His hair was ruffled and he was wearing terracotta corduroys and an alpaca sweater in rusts and greys instead of his usual business suit.

'Dad! I didn't see you there.' Lexie looked at him with concern. 'Is everything all right? Are you okay? Why aren't you at work? I hope it's not because of yesterday—'

'Come here, Alexa.'

Tom pulled her to him and hugged her fiercely.

'Everything's fine, love. More than fine. Your mother and I have made a few decisions, that's all. Sit down and we'll tell you.'

'My God, this sounds serious.'

'All good, we think, and all down to you.'

Lexie found two more mugs and poured coffee.

'I'm curious.'

Tom and Martha looked at each other. Lexie's heart tugged as she caught that look, it was so full of tenderness. It seemed that her parents had recaptured a love that had been tested almost to destruction over the past eighteen months. Tom took Martha's hand.

'We sat up most of the night,' he started. 'Talking.'

'Your painting set it all off.' Tom let out his breath in a soft whistle. 'It got me in the gut.' He held up a warning hand as Lexie was about to interrupt. 'No, it was exactly what I needed, love. Like your mother said, it set my grief free.'

Martha said, 'He'd been trying to be very strong, but he did it at the expense of his health.'

'So that was the first thing. We were able to talk about Jamie, together. We'd started a little bit – bringing Molly Keir round started us talking – but even so, it wasn't until I saw the painting that the ropes tied round my chest seemed to burst open and I was able to breathe again.'

'That's exactly how I felt,' Lexie cried, 'after I found out about Jamie and Molly! I was so relieved to know the reason he'd died, and so pleased to discover he'd been in love with my best friend, it seemed to loosen everything.'

'Exactly. Well…'

Again Tom and Martha looked at each other. Tom said, 'There've been a few things you've been saying that perhaps we ignored. But now we're going to follow your advice.'

'*My* advice?'

'On two things.'

'*Two* things?'

'Don't look so alarmed. The first thing is, I'm going in to the store today to tell Neil I'm going to make him general manager. I'll stay as non-executive chairman, but he'll be completely in charge of operations.'

'Wow, really? That's fantastic news. You won't regret it, Dad, I'm sure you won't.'

'I'm sure now, too. I'm too old a dog to learn new tricks, that's the truth of it. I could see what you and Neil were getting at with all your ideas, I just couldn't face the thought of the kind of changes that I'd need to make to put them in place. Now

322

it's Neil's responsibility.'

'And I'm sure he'll do you proud,' Martha said, her smile peeling back the years from her face.

Lexie said, 'What's the second thing? You'll have loads more time, won't you? Let me guess – you're going on a cruise.'

'A cruise? Cruises are for old folk. Not a cruise, no, but a big holiday.'

'A safari to start with,' Martha said, her excitement evident, 'then who knows? India perhaps? We could be old hippies, recapture our lost youth.'

'Christ,' muttered Lexie, grinning.

'But that's not the second thing,' Tom said.

'It isn't?'

He shook his head. 'No, it's a side effect of the first.'

'Right. I can see that.'

Martha said, 'You suggested it, actually.'

'What did I suggest?'

'That we sell Fernhill.'

Lexie's eyes opened wide.

'Don't look so startled, darling. It makes sense. What would the two of us do, rattling round in that huge barn of a place? We can buy somewhere much more suitable.'

'Our rest-of-our-lives house. No stairs for when we get frail.'

'Stop it,' Lexie said, 'That's years away.'

'Anyway,' Tom said, 'it's my pension. There hasn't been a huge amount squirrelled away in recent years. If I'm really going to stop working, Fernhill will provide the capital we need to enjoy life a bit before we're past it.'

'You're not upset are you, darling?' Martha asked, anxious. 'It's your childhood home and I know how much you love it.'

'I'm most certainly not upset,' Lexie said firmly, although a corner of her actually was. 'I think it's a brilliant idea. Now, tell me more about your travel plans.'

Lexie heard another email pop into her inbox with a melodic 'ping'. Emails had been pouring in all morning. Sooner or later she'd have to tackle them, but she couldn't face it yet. It had just dawned on her that her life was about to change again. Her parents were selling Fernhill, her work for the exhibition was finished, and she wouldn't be able to stay in this cottage for ever.

She wandered into the garden room. It was such a good space. She'd love to be able to stay here. Perhaps if she talked to Lady Fleming about paying some kind of proper rent? Now that she was going to make some money from the sale of the paintings, she'd be able to afford it.

But what was she going to do next? She couldn't live on the proceeds of one exhibition for long and besides, she was buzzing with ideas. It would be fantastic to do a bigger version of this exhibition, and a full catalogue, she'd only used around twenty percent of the shoes that had been sent to her. If she developed the project, she could apply for a grant.

She heard another email pop in. Stop procrastinating Lexie, she told herself, promotion is just a different kind of work and it has to be done.

She went into the small study and settled at the computer.

< Wonderful work, Lexie, well done! Myra >

< Amazing. I was moved to tears. Jenny x >

< When you've got a moment, pop by and we'll do a mop-up. Cora >

< Best exhibition I've seen all year. Okay, so it's only January ;-) Fred M. >

She counted ninety-four emails to be dealt with and started winging back responses. It was gratifying to see how many people had enjoyed the exhibition and taken the trouble to reply. Another email popped in from Cora, so she prioritised it.

< We can finalise the gallery accounts before I go away – that's not for another two weeks. Didn't last night go well? >

Surely this email wasn't meant for her? She had nothing to do with the gallery accounts. Lexie read it over again, puzzled. Email was a chancy communication tool. She'd been in touch with Cora so much recently, she suspected she had just keyed in her name on autopilot and pressed 'send' without checking.

What should she do? Let Cora know she had misdirected it, or just delete it? At least, she thought, her lips curling with amusement, it wasn't rude about her. She was on the point of deleting it when she spotted a postscript.

< Okay, okay, I admit it, Patrick – you were right to make me stay on to do this exhibition. The girl's a star. >

Patrick had been manipulating her behind the scenes all the time.

She picked up her mobile and called Cora.

'Hi, Lexie. Wasn't last night wonderful? There've been so many messages of congratulations. We've sold all the oil paintings and I haven't even had time to count the number of pastel drawings we've sold yet. There are orders for lots more as well. Lexie?' Cora paused at last. 'Are you there?'

Lexie drew a deep breath.

'Thanks for telling me that you've been working with Patrick Mulgrew,' she said, her voice tight.

'Patrick? How did you? I'm sorry, I'm not sure what you… '

'Oh come on, Cora. I don't know how it happened, but you sent me an email clearly intended for Patrick. I don't know what hold he's got over you, but I know he made you stay here and curate my exhibition.'

There was a pause.

'Patrick's been involved, yes,' Cora said at last. 'Is that so terrible?'

'Yes!' Lexie screeched. 'Yes it is! You knew I'd fallen out with him, I told you that.'

'But arguments should be resolved, don't you think?'

'Not behind my back like this. I'd never have gone ahead if I'd known. Don't you get it, Cora? I needed to do this on my own. I didn't want some behind-the-scenes manoeuvring by Patrick Mulgrew. It was important to me to achieve this success by myself.'

There was a sigh.

'I did suggest that might be the case, but you know Patrick. He does things his own way.'

'So why did he do it? What hold has he got over you? Is he your lover?'

Lexie knew this was downright rude, but she was past being tactful.

'My lover?'

There was genuine amusement in Cora's laugh.

'No. He's my brother. And he's the owner of The Maker's Mark.'

Lexie turned the phone off, stunned. She ran over in her mind everything she had ever heard about the gallery since it opened, but couldn't recall ever hearing a hint of Patrick's involvement. She'd spoken to Cora at the opening and remembered her saying the owner was in London. A stretch of the truth at best, a lie at worst.

Her mobile rang. It was Cora. She let it go to voice mail.

She started pacing round the garden room.

Patrick! And she thought she'd done it all herself. It was unbelievable. Should she have known? How could she have known?

She was sunk so deep in her rage that it took some time for her to realise that someone was knocking on the door. Not just knocking, hammering. She wasn't thinking about visitors, she didn't even realise that her feet were moving towards the door, she just wanted the noise to stop.

'Lexie.'

Patrick was standing there, a little out of breath but otherwise shockingly normal, not at all like the demon she'd been imagining for the past hour. She was too angry to be civil. She started to slam the door, but he was too quick for her. His arm shot out.

'Listen, Lexie, Cora called and told me. I don't know how it happened. Please let me come in and talk about it.'

She swivelled away from him and marched back into the house.

'I don't want to talk.'

She was like a sulky child. She did want to talk, but even

more than that she wanted to kick and scream and shout.

He followed her and tried to catch her arm. She shook him off.

'What were you thinking, Patrick? Were you trying to patronise me?'

She glared at him, rubbed her hands furiously across her scalp so that the crimson hair stood on end.

'You were being your usual bloody-minded, controlling self, weren't you? You just had to have things your way, even if I never found out. In fact—'

She whirled round and jabbed at his chest with her finger.

'—it would have been a whole lot better if I'd never found out, wouldn't it? Because then you'd have had the secret satisfaction of knowing what you'd done and knowing I didn't know and bloody *gloating* behind that supercilious smile every time you saw me.'

She came to a halt at last.

Patrick said, 'Can we talk? Without yelling, perhaps? Will you let me tell you why I did it?'

'No! Go away! I don't want to hear.'

She fell silent at last, panting with the exertion of finding the words to express her fury. She anticipated argument and was mustering her strength for another outburst, but he was just standing there, looking at her.

At last he spoke.

'Supercilious?' His voice caught. 'Is that what you really think of me?'

And he turned and walked away.

Lexie stared after him, shaken. He sounded genuinely hurt.

Chapter Thirty-four

Catalogue number 25: One brown brogue, one black lace-up in plain leather. Donated by Robin Harper, Edinburgh. 'When I was elected to the Scottish Parliament in 1999, my presence was in constant demand. One day I dressed in the dark for an early engagement, not wanting to disturb my wife. It wasn't until I was on the platform addressing an audience of pensioners that someone pointed out to me that I had put on mismatched shoes. They were kind enough not to brief the Press!'

'Lexie? I'm going to need your help. Please? Just for a couple of weeks. I'll pay your salary.'

Neil's voice was excited.

'I meant to call you,' Lexie said, trying to snap out of her exhaustion. 'I'm so pleased Dad's done it at last – for you and for him. I'm delighted they're getting away, and I'm thrilled he's handed over to you. You so deserve it.'

'Thanks. Will you come and help?'

'I don't think I have the strength right now.'

It had been a week since the flare-up with Patrick. Lexie had calmed down enough to be able to go in to see Cora, negotiate some neutral territory with her, and discuss the business she needed to discuss. She'd kept on top of emails, visited her parents at Fernhill to talk about everything that had to be done, and seen Molly several times. Each action had taken its toll. She was extremely tempted to take up Martha and Tom's offer of an all-expenses paid holiday. Only her stubborn independence stood in the way of accepting.

'I really need your help, Lexie, no-one else can do it. It's just taking forward all the things we talked about, but it needs to be done quickly. I want everything in place by the time your folks get back from their safari, and I want the sales ledger to be reflecting the new look. Please? It's not just for me, it's for the future of Gordon's.'

Lexie groaned.

'That's blackmail.'

'There's a month to turn this place around. I need to do something with all this old stock, either return it or send it off to a clearance warehouse. We need to get the decorators in – but you'll have to give them instructions – and we need to order up a whole load of new stock. The grand opening is four weeks from today.'

Lexie whistled, her excitement rising.

'That's ambitious.'

'I need you to do some designs and plans so that we can start the whole process next week. Julie will...'

'Julie? Is she really the best person to help you take Gordon's forward?'

'She's good. Now that she's getting to grips with everything, she's very willing.'

'Well, that I can believe.'

'Actually,' Neil sounded shy. 'We've started going out together.'

Lexie started to laugh, but she choked the noise off quickly. 'Really? Have you?'

'She's a vulnerable person. Everyone's always put her down. I think it was lack of confidence that used to make her surly. Now that she's being given some responsibility she's beginning to shine.'

'Well, good luck with that, Neil.'

'Thanks. Are you going to come in? Please?'

Lexie sighed heavily. A couple of weeks at Gordon's would be very strange after the intensity of working for the exhibition, but on the other hand, it would keep her busy while she considered what to do next. And the money would come in handy.

'Okay. I'll be there in the morning. You can brief me then,' she said

'I'm sorry about the mix up with the emails, Patrick, really I am. I don't know how it happened. I was very tired. I must have keyed in Lexie's address without thinking,' said Cora.

'Mistakes happen.'

They were in the departure hall at Edinburgh airport. Cora's bags were lined up beside them as they stood in the check-in queue. It was ten months since she'd descended the escalator into the arrivals hall, although in some ways it felt like years.

'How much shopping have you done since you flew in, for God's sake?' Patrick eyed the bags. 'I either paid you too much or gave you too much time off.'

Cora shrugged. 'It's mostly foodstuffs. Things I can't get in Kalamata.'

'Like?'

'You know. Baked beans. Brown sauce. Tinned haggis.'

'Christ. You eat that stuff?'

'You'd be surprised how much you crave it when you know you can't get it.'

'I'll have to believe you, I suppose.'

The queue in front of them moved forward and they shuffled along.

'Will he meet you?'

'Who?'

'This man. Your lover.'

Patrick realised how very little he knew about his sister's life. In that sense they were alike – they liked private matters to be kept private.

'My lover will meet me, yes.'

'Will you bring him over sometime? You can stay as long as you like.'

'I don't think so. It's not really like that, but thanks for the offer.'

They'd reached the head of the queue. It took a few minutes for Cora to check her bags through and negotiate the price of the excess, then they turned for the stairs.

'You can leave me now, if you like. I know how busy you

are, you don't have to wait.'

'I've got time for a coffee.'

The best Patrick could say about the coffee was that it was drinkable. He watched the black liquid eddy and swirl as he stirred in some sugar.

'You have no idea how much I appreciate everything you've done, Cora. I didn't think I would, but you've exceeded expectations by a long mile.'

'Praise indeed. Thank you.' Cora blew on her coffee. 'I've enjoyed the challenge. Challenges. And the successes.'

'There've been a few, haven't there?'

'I'd like to think so.'

They sat in silence until the coffee was finished.

'Is there anything you can do to show her how you feel?' Cora said, after a while.

'Tell who? What?'

'Don't be an ass, Pats, you know exactly—'

'Patrick.'

'You're Pats when you're being an idiot. As I was saying, don't be a fool, *Pats*, you know who I mean. You're in love with Lexie, aren't you? It's plain as day.'

'Oh God, is it?'

'Don't worry, no-one else would notice, but I'm your sister, and I've seen you through quite a few relationships. You don't look at her as you looked at Diana, for example. You don't speak to her in the same way. You treat her more like you used to treat Niamh, in the old days.'

'Shit. I thought my secret was safe.'

'I'm not going to tell anyone. That's your job. Tell Lexie, for a start.'

'I can't. She won't listen. She thinks I'm the devil incarnate.'

'I wouldn't say that. One of the minor fiends, perhaps.'

'Bitch,' Patrick said amiably.

'So, to get back to my original question, is there anything you can do to *show* her how you feel?'

'I don't get it.'

Cora sighed. 'Men can be so obtuse when it comes to

relationships. If she won't listen, find another way. But whatever you do, make sure you really put yourself on the line. Be absolutely honest about how you feel. It's going to take that to win her round.'

Patrick said nothing for a very long time. At last he looked at his watch.

'I've got to go. Shall I walk you to security or are you okay on your own?'

'Don't be ridiculous, Patrick, I'm not a child. Go.'

He stood up.

'I'll see you sometime, then.'

'Sure.'

'Bye, Cora.'

He bent and kissed her cheek, and then strode off.

Cora watched him go. She pressed a speed dial number labelled 'Nikos', and said, 'Yassas, Anna.'

'Cora? When will you get here?'

'I'll see you at the airport at nine tonight. Can't wait to see you, my darling.'

'Nor me. Love you.'

'You too. See you later, bye.'

'Bye.'

She cut the call and cradled the phone in her hand. There were some secrets she didn't care to share with either of her brothers.

There was a day of embarrassment during which Julie clearly had no idea how to relate to Lexie. As soon as they found themselves giggling over something ridiculously minor and silly, though, they agreed with relief that the past was the past and they were not going to talk about it any more.

'Well shot of him, anyway,' Julie said, 'he was hot as hell but not a keeper, that one.'

'Are *you* a keeper?' Lexie asked pointedly.

Julie flashed a sideways glance at Lexie, unexpectedly coy.

'Neil's a good guy. Just because he's a bit older than me doesn't mean I don't fancy him, you know? I've been messed up all my life, me, but Neil treats me like a princess.'

'He's much too nice to just play around with. Understand me?'

'I don't plan to hurt him.' Julie twirled her ponytail. 'Him and me, we're solid. I'm goin' to get him to propose to me before the year's out, you'll see. He wants kids, an' so do I. An' I can help out here.'

'OK. Let's get on with it then.'

The market research had been done a year ago but nothing had changed. They knew the demographic they were aiming at, which styles and colourways they wanted and the price range they needed to focus on. Lexie took charge of the renovations, Neil did all the ordering and paperwork, and Julie went out stuffing flyers through letterboxes around the new developments in the area, as well as the smaller flats and cottages. Joe McPhail from Pettigrew's volunteered to deliver the flyers for the bigger houses further afield.

When Gordon's Furniture Emporium reopened four weeks later, the place had been transformed. The green and gold lettering on the outside of the store was perhaps the only original thing that remained, and that was only because Lexie couldn't bear to see this last piece of family history go.

Gone were the old-fashioned, over-stuffed recliners, the velour chesterfields and faux-leather chairs. In the bedroom department, rows of divans so tightly packed it was almost impossible to move between them had been exchanged for spacious room sets. There was an emphasis on simplicity and style. Lexie's 'rooms' used chic tones of aubergine or cool shades of peppermint. Smart contemporary prints provided accents here and there. And in a marketing masterstroke , she had agreed a contract with Neil to supply some of her pastel prints of shoes, ready framed, for sale.

Lexie sweet-talked a television newsreader who lived in Hailesbank to come and cut the ribbon, and there was a free glass of bubbly or a soft drink for everyone who walked in the door.

Tom and Martha flew back from South Africa on the morning of the opening.

'Will you be too tired to come?' Lexie, phoning to check they were safe, enquired anxiously.

'Not a bit. There's no jet lag when you fly to South Africa, that's the great thing,' Martha said. 'Well, one of the great things. The elephants at—'

'Have to stop you there, Mum,' Lexie laughed. 'Too much to do. I'll catch up tomorrow, I'm dying to hear about it. Meantime, put on your best bib and tucker, get Dad back into his suit, and make sure you're here by six.'

It was the second time in a matter of weeks that Lexie had moved her father to tears.

'I can't believe it,' he said, looking around. 'I just can't believe it's the same place. Look at it! Where's that chenille recliner that used to be here?'

'All dealt with, Tom,' Neil said firmly. 'And there've been loads of orders already. Now, Tom, Martha, if you'll just come this way, I'll introduce you to our star guest, Louise.'

Martha hooked her arm through Lexie's as they followed Neil and Tom through the store.

'He'll get used to it,' she whispered conspiratorially. 'After the first two weeks away he became so relaxed it was like being with the Tom Gordon I fell in love with.'

Tom was in animated conversation with a striking brunette who looked familiar.

'Louise Brennen,' Lexie said, 'from the telly, you know.'

'Your father looks happy, doesn't he?' Martha leaned close again. 'I've already booked another holiday. We're off to South America this time, but I haven't told him yet.'

'What about Fernhill?'

'Sold already.'

'*Sold!*'

Lexie was thunderstruck.

'We put it with an agent before we went. It was snapped up right away, it wasn't even advertised. All we have to do is pack up and get out.'

'Good God.'

'You don't mind, do you?'

'No, of course not. I'll just have to drop by and make sure I grab anything of mine. Is there anything else you'd like to tell me? Have you bought somewhere else already? Going on a world tour, perhaps?'

'We're going to put everything into storage and start looking when we're tired of travelling. Is that all right?'

'Sounds exhausting.'

Martha looked serious.

'We're not running away, darling. We're not hiding any more. You do know that, don't you? You've done that for us. Jamie will always live in our hearts, but it's a tiny bit less awful every day.'

'I know, Mum. I feel the same.'

A waitress passed with a tray of Prosecco. Lexie reached out and grabbed two glasses.

'Cheers, Mum. Here's to the future.'

Chapter Thirty-five

Catalogue number 35: Prince Charming – if the shoe fits ...
'Glass' shoe, fashioned from clear plastic. **Donor, Antonia Fullerton, Edinburgh.** 'The only surviving shoe from a pantomime production of Cinderella, 1935, Edinburgh. I played Cinders, the glorious Robert Harknett played the Prince. The shoes were specially made by a local cobbler, but they were murder to wear.'

'I've had a word with Lady Fleming. She's happy to talk to you about renting the cottage on a more formal basis,' Molly said, flicking one of Lexie's paintbrushes up and down her forearm in a desultory way, painting an imaginary line from wrist to elbow and from elbow to wrist in an endless motion.

They were sitting in the garden room at the cottage. Molly was wearing jeans and an old fleece with battered Uggs for warmth. Lexie sported thick woolly socks, purple leggings and a shapeless, multicoloured sweater, which fell baggily half way down her thighs. Her hair was in need of a colour refresh and her skin was pale. Outside, the glorious brilliance of the snow had disappeared, leaving only a few small patches where it had been out of the sun. The estate gardeners had not yet attended to this end of the walled garden, so the flowerbeds were full of yellowing leaves , pallid knots and dead stems. It was the end of February.

Lexie had been watching Molly's aimless actions for five minutes, but she could contain her irritation no longer. She leapt out of her chair, snatched the brush out of Molly's hand, and tossed it back onto her brush tray.

'Will you *stop* doing that!'

'Sor-*ry*.'

Lexie flopped back down onto the chair and swung her legs over its bulky arm.

Molly sat bolt upright. Her mouth twisted to one side. She clasped her hands, twiddled her thumbs, and looked at Lexie pointedly.

Lexie glared at her then started to laugh.

'No, it's me who's sorry,' she said. 'I'm like a bear with a sore head.'

'Is it too early to drink?'

Lexie considered the question.

'Well, you can look at it two ways – it's only four o'clock, so yes, it's too early. On the other hand, the sun is well over the yardarm as my granny used to say, so it's definitely okay to down something that'll see us to supper time. White or red?'

'Don't mind. Either.'

Lexie disappeared into the kitchen and came back with a bottle of Medoc and two glasses.

'I don't do this when I'm on my own,' she said. 'Honestly.'

'Nor me.'

They surveyed each other across full glasses.

'This isn't a good habit, is it?' Molly said.

'You've got to have some pleasures in life.'

'Don't you want the cottage?'

'Yes I do. No, no I don't. Honestly, Moll, I don't know. The trouble is I don't know what I want to do next. I suppose I need to find another gallery to show the exhibition if I'm to do it on a bigger scale – in London, ideally.'

'So what's stopping you?'

'I don't know.' She wriggled restlessly. 'The exhibition was great, I just can't decide what to do next.'

Molly said, laughing, 'Maybe you need a different kind of excitement. Like a new man in your life.'

'Ha ha. Anyway, look who's talking.'

Molly went quiet.

Lexie looked at her more sharply and said, 'It's okay to move on, Moll. You can't change what happened, and I won't think any the less of you for looking for love.'

'It's not that easy.'

'Who said it would be easy? Just maybe try dipping your toe in the water again.'

Molly drank deeply and they lapsed into silence again. Eventually, Molly said,

'Have you seen the way Patrick Mulgrew looks at you? He's really interested. I'm astonished you two didn't get together ages ago.'

Lexie flushed.

'Lex? Are you hiding something from me?'

'No, nothing. Anyway,' she tried to divert Molly, 'I was furious about him helping me, you know I was.'

'Sure. But I haven't worked out why.'

'Really? You know I was determined to do everything by myself after he was so awful to me about the last exhibition.'

'Okay, so he lost his temper, but you've never given him a chance since then, have you? You want me to move on – why don't you move on yourself? Talk to him. For goodness' sake, you said to me once, "Patrick never forgives and never forgets". Don't you think you were wrong?'

Lexie was about to argue when she remembered how Patrick had come to tell her about Pavel's death.

My darling, it's Pavel.

He'd held her in his arms and she'd felt safe. And he'd shown his faith in her art – hadn't he found a way of making sure her exhibition went ahead? If it hadn't been for Cora's slip she would never have known of his involvement.

'I wouldn't know where to start,' she said in a small voice.

Outside, darkness had fallen. The only light came from a scented candle that Lexie had lit an hour ago and placed in the centre of the cherrywood coffee table. Fig and vanilla, the label said. Lexie couldn't make up her mind if she loved the smell or loathed it. Right now, it was overpoweringly cloying. Across the table, it was no longer possible to see the colour of Molly's eyes, all she could see was the flickering flame of the candle shining back at her.

'Tell you what,' Molly said, 'I'll think about finding another man if you'll make it up with Patrick. Deal?'

'That's blackmail.'

'Sometimes you have to be ruthless to be successful. Deal?'

'Do you seriously mean you won't if I don't?'

'Yup. Deal?'

Lexie sighed. 'Where's this going to lead us, Molly?'

'Deal?'

'You're so bloody persistent. I suppose so.'

They leaned forward and chinked glasses across the flame.

'Ow,' Lexie said, snatching her hand away from the heat, 'that hurt.'

Molly grinned. 'No gain without pain.'

Lexie composed herself to call Patrick. Three times she lifted the phone and started to dial. Each time, she cut the call before it even started, mainly because she had no idea what to say. Anyway, wasn't it up to him to get in touch first?

A couple of days after her conversation with Molly, her mobile rang.

'Hello?'

'Is that Alexa Gordon? My name is Anthony Spartan and I'm calling from The Spartan Gallery in London.'

A London gallery? Calling her?

'What can I do for you, Mr Spartan?'

'I happened to be in Edinburgh visiting my brother a couple of weeks ago. He dragged me kicking and protesting to a little place in Hailesbank to see an exhibition he swore I'd like.'

'The Maker's Mark?'

'There was an exhibition called "In My Shoes". Your work.'

'What did you think of it?'

Anthony Spartan laughed. 'I wouldn't be calling if I didn't like it. I wanted to talk about the possibility of a follow-on exhibition. How do you feel about that?'

How did she feel? It was what she had dreamed of. Twenty minutes later, she rang off, her head spinning.

She had barely had time to recover from the surprise, when her mobile rang again. This time it was a gallery in Manchester. The owner had had reports from a friend who'd seen the exhibition and she was also interested. Lexie was stunned.

She settled down with Martha's shoe notes and set to work to expand them. Starting with her mother was an easy choice.

1: Ladies' court shoe, black patent leather, slightly pointed toe, simple bow embellishment, slim 6-inch heel. Donated by Martha Gordon. Shoes tell stories. This shoe says everything about Martha Gordon's lifestyle as a legal secretary. They are smart, but practical, designed to give comfort throughout a working day, while still being stylish. Martha Gordon left her job after her son was killed in an accident. For her, they tell the story of a life she has lost.

The next one was obvious, too. Her father.

2: Black leather traditional lace-ups by Clark's. Donor, Tom Gordon, Hailesbank. There's nothing remarkable about these shoes, except that they personify the story of Tom Gordon, my father. They are plain, inexpensive, serviceable, worn and a little old-fashioned. They make me choke with pride and admiration for all they stand for: the way my father plugged on doggedly, determined to hold his family together, whatever the personal cost.

While she was in family mode, she might as well carry on with Jamie's boots.

3: Rugby boots. Tough leather studded boots, worn by Jamie Gordon, lock for the Hailesbank Hawks. Donor, the Gordon family, Hailesbank. Jamie Gordon was a man like many other young men. He loved to play sport, see his friends, work hard, enjoy life to the full. He played a pivotal role in the rugby team he was passionate about, just as he was pivotal in so many people's lives. Sadly, Jamie lost his life in a car accident, aged just 28. The boots seem to embody his energy, spirit and talent.

Here Lexie stopped.
Something was missing – but what?

The nagging feeling had hung around her for weeks. Now the answer came to her. She had told Jamie's story and her parent's stories, but what was *her* story? What shoes would she choose to tell the tale of her own journey through life?

Maybe I'm too young. I haven't travelled far enough to have a story.

No, that's a cop out. Concentrate.

What about the old plimsolls she used to live in as a student, the ones she'd worn week in, week out when she'd been learning her craft? Not good enough – she was hardly the same person who wore those plimsolls.

So what else?

After a while she abandoned the exercise in disgust. She hadn't got enough of a story, that was the truth of it. Yet if she hadn't got a story, who was she?

Patrick stared at the computer screen and swore in frustration. He wasn't used to struggling with this kind of task because it was one he would normally delegate – but this was one job he had to do himself.

Victoria popped her head round his office door.

'Problem? Anything I can do to help?'

Patrick toggled to a spreadsheet screen, feeling like a furtive skiving employee rather than the boss.

'No thanks, Victoria. I'm fine.'

Victoria smiled, but didn't go away. She shifted from one foot to another as if she wanted to say something but didn't have the courage.

'Something on your mind?'

'I wondered – would you mind if I left sharp at five today?'

She was embarrassed and pleased at the same time.

'Only I'm going to a concert tonight with Alec and I need to get home and change first.'

Patrick grinned. 'New boyfriend?'

'Quite new, yes.'

'Off you go then.'

'Sure?'

'*Sure.* Scarper.'

Victoria scuttled off. The brief episode in New York, he was relieved to see, had been put aside.

He returned to the challenge in hand. How the hell did Lexie put together these book things so effortlessly? She could do a whole layout in an hour, she'd told him once. His plan was so simple, surely he should be able to do the job in minutes?

The trouble was that the main picture – a Manolo Blahnik stiletto – was decorated with ribbons and buttons, and flowers. He had photographed it against a white sheet, but there still seemed to be a shadow around the image. He fussed with filters and effects and something called transparency, but he could still see crumples in the sheet behind it.

Was this a good idea? He was tempted to forget it. After all, he'd bought the damn things for her, surely all he needed to do was hand them over?

It had been an icy March and a four-in-the-morning start – pure hell normally, pure magic that day. Just watching Lexie's face as he'd told her where they were going had been worth it, and it got better as her excitement had mounted and she'd viewed the auction lots for the first time. He'd known a dozen dealers at the auction, including a specialist from Cardiff who'd owed him a favour.

'Fran,' he'd said urgently as Lexie was on the other side of the auction room working her way through the catalogue, 'I need your help.'

'I'll do what I can.'

'I need you to bid for Lot 165 – but you mustn't come in until after my companion has dropped out.'

As predicted, the bidding had been fast and competitive, but it had been Fran's paddle that had gone up as the hammer had come down.

Patrick clicked the mouse yet again and the image turned dark purple. *Hopeless*. Sighing, he accepted the inevitability of imperfection and used the best picture he had. If folds and wrinkles could be seen, maybe she would think they were part of the design. Anyway, at least the book was beginning to take shape.

He'd planned to give the shoes to Lexie after her exhibition opened but, a few days after the auction, Jamie Gordon's car had hit a tree so they'd stayed in the box in the bottom of his wardrobe, peered at occasionally and sought after by the V&A, but otherwise mostly forgotten.

Now they would be his peace offering, a token of his love – but they mustn't be just something he could buy because he was wealthy. They had to tell a story. Wasn't that what Lexie's exhibition was about? It was the story that would win her, not the shoes.

He laboured on, but it was another couple of hours before he pressed the 'send' button, and the book finally shot down the line to the printer.

Open yourself to her, Cora had said, be honest. It's going to take that to win her.

When it came back, so long as the quality was acceptable, he'd take the book round to Lexie.

Lexie opened the door to the garden where a brave sun drilled through the cloud and promised a rare winter treat – warmth.

She returned to the kitchen and picked up one of her chairs. She'd sit on the small paved area outside and think. She couldn't decide about the offers for a follow-up exhibition and longed to discuss them with Molly, but that was out of the question because Molly wanted her to discuss such matters with Patrick. Half an hour of early spring warmth and a hot coffee might bring the answer.

She closed her eyes. Last night she'd seen Cameron for the first time in weeks. He'd had his arm round a new girl, a pneumatic brunette with silver hoop earrings and aubergine lipstick. She hadn't been jealous, quite the contrary – she was grateful that Cameron had been able to switch his attentions so speedily.

In the distance there was the sound of a car on gravel and the slam of a door. The gardeners must be arriving to start clearing the winter debris. She had perhaps just a few more minutes of peace.

The idea that shoes tell stories was what she'd based her whole life on for the past months – but still she had no idea what her own story was and the failure to pin it down irked her.

There was one image she couldn't get out of her mind – white 1950s sandals lying entangled with highly polished, hand-made Church's lace-ups. Her own shoes and Patrick's, dropped beside the bed one scorching hot evening in her room in Edinburgh. She could hear the chatter of late-night drinkers spilling onto the pavement from the wine bar underneath the flat. Patrick's naked body beside her, and the overwhelming sense of joy that permeated her whole being.

There was a heavy thump inside the cottage. Lexie's eyes snapped open.

Why did we ever fall out? How could I have been so stupid?

She got up reluctantly to investigate the cause of the noise. In any case, the sun had disappeared again.

Someone had posted a parcel through her letterbox, carefully wrapped in thick cream paper and secured with a crimson ribbon. It must have been hand-delivered. She picked it up, slipped a finger inside the cream gift tag and teased it open.

'Lexie,' it said, 'please read me.'

She tugged at the ribbon and the bow loosened at once. The parcel had been wrapped with great care and a thick wad of tissue protected the contents. Intrigued, she folded it back to reveal a book. It was upside down, so that all she could see was a plain red cover.

She turned it over and gasped.

LEXIE'S SHOES read the title. And the picture, crisp in every glorious, tiny detail, from the scarlet of the towering stilettos to the flowers fashioned from feathers, sequins and silk brocade, showed the Manolo Blahniks she'd once tried to buy.

She ran her fingers over the image, pausing at the artful ribbon details, stopping at the exquisitely arranged scraps of lace. She read the title again.

LEXIE'S SHOES?

Her hands trembling, she opened the book. On the first page all that appeared was a tiny portion of the tip of one shoe, and one single word, LEXIE.

She turned to the next page.

The shoe had crept further into view, but there were no

words.

Mystified, she leafed through the book, turning to the next page, then the next, faster and faster. Each page was completely blank, except for the steady journey of the shoe, which tiptoed further and further onto each page.

She was almost at the end. Finally, one whole, glorious shoe was visible – but still there was nothing else. No words, nothing.

She turned the last page.

There were six words. That was all.

MY LIFE IS EMPTY WITHOUT YOU.

Lexie laid the book on the kitchen table and looked out.

Patrick was leaning against his car and staring at the cottage. She had never seen him looking so anxious. Her heart pounded, she couldn't stop looking at his face. Why was he just standing there? At last she realised that he was holding something … a cardboard box … and on the top of the box was a pair of perfect red stilettos. The Manolo Blahniks!

How had he come by them? Did it matter? The only things that mattered were that he was here and that he had made the beautiful red stilettos relate the story of his love.

Catalogue number 37: Prince Charming – if the shoe fits...

Lexie opened the door of the cottage and walked into the sunshine.

THE END

Face the Wind and Fly

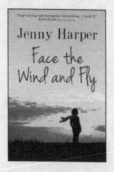

She builds wind farms, he detests them. Can they ever generate love?

After fifteen happy years of marriage, Kate Courtenay discovers that her charismatic novelist husband is spending more and more of his time with a young fan. She throws herself into her work, a controversial wind farm that's stirring up tempers in the local community. Sparks fly when she goes head to head against its most outspoken opponent, local gardener Ibsen Brown – a man with a past of his own. But a scheme for a local community garden brings the sparring-partners together, producing the sort of electricity that threatens to short-circuit the whole system.

Loving Susie

She thought she knew her husband, but he's been keeping a secret ... about her.

Scottish politician Susie Wallace is under pressure. She risks censure from her Party for her passionate and outspoken views on arts funding. A charity she's involved with runs into difficulties. And a certain journalist seems to have it in for her.

Susie stumbles across some information that rocks her world but not, apparently, her husband's – Archie has been in on this particular secret for thirty years. Now Susie wonders if she can trust him at all. Soon, unemployed son Jonathan and successful daughter Mannie begin to feel the fallout too, fracturing the family and leaving Susie increasingly isolated.

Troubled by mounting pressure from her family, her Party and the Press, Susie goes into hiding. The Party needs her back for a crucial vote, but more importantly, Archie knows he needs to find his wife quickly if they are to rebuild their relationship and reunite the family.

Maximum Exposure

She's a professional photographer – but is she ready to expose her heart?

Adorable but scatterbrained newspaper photographer Daisy Irvine becomes the key to the survival of *The Hailesbank Herald* when her boss drops dead right in front of her. And while big egos and petty jealousies hinder the struggle to save the paper, Daisy starts another campaign – to win back her ex, Jack Hedderwick.

Ben Gillies, returning after a long absence, sees childhood friend Daisy in a whole new light. He'd like to win her love, but discovers that she's a whole lot better at taking photographs than making decisions, particularly when she's blinded by the past.

When tragedy strikes Daisy's family, loyalty drives her home. But it's time to grow up and Daisy must choose between independence and love.

Sand in My Shoes

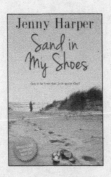

A trip to France awakens the past in this heartwarming and tear-jerking short summer read from the author of *People We Love*.

Headteacher Nicola Arnott prides herself on her independence. Long widowed, she has successfully juggled motherhood and career, coping by burying her emotions somewhere deep inside herself. A cancer scare shakes her out of her careful approach to life and she finds herself thinking wistfully of her first love, a young French medical student.

As her anxiety about her impending hospital tests grows, she decides to revisit the sleepy French town she remembers from her teenage years – and is astonished to meet up with Luc again. The old chemistry is still there – but so is something far more precious: a deep and enduring friendship.

Can it turn into true love?

Jenny Harper

Face the Wind and Fly
Loving Susie
Maximum Exposure
People We Love

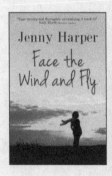

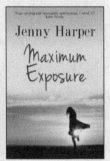

Kate Glanville

A Perfect Home

Claire appears to have it all - the kind of life you read about in magazines; a beautiful cottage, three gorgeous children, a handsome husband in William and her own flourishing vintage textile business.

But when an interiors magazine sends a good-looking photographer to take pictures of Claire's perfect home, he makes her wonder if the house means more to William than she does.

This is the beautifully observed and poignant love story of a woman who has to find out if home really is where the heart is.

For more information about **Jenny Harper**

and other **Accent Press** titles

please visit

www.accentpress.co.uk

http://www.jennyharperauthor.co.uk